— IN THE —
Shadow
—— OF THE ——
Cathedral

Other books by Christine Schneider:

Hammering at the Doors of Heaven

The Fires of Faith Series

— IN THE —
Shadow
— OF THE —
Cathedral

CHRISTINE SCHNEIDER

kregel
PUBLICATIONS

Grand Rapids, MI 49501

In the Shadow of the Cathedral

Published by Kregel Publications, a division of Kregel, Inc., P.O. Box 2607, Grand Rapids, MI 49501. Kregel Publications provides trusted, biblical publications for Christian growth and service. Your comments and suggestions are valued.

Cover and book design: Nicholas G. Richardson

Library of Congress Cataloging-in-Publication Data
Schneider, Christine C.
    In the shadow of the cathedral / by Christine C. Schneider.
        p.   cm.
        1. Austria—History—to 1273—Fiction. I. Title. II. Series: Schneider, Christine C. Fires of faith series.
PS3569.C52237916   1998   813'.54—dc21   98-44658
                                                      CIP
ISBN 0-8254-3758-x

Printed in the United States of America

1 2 3 / 03 02 01 00 99 98

With love to Floyd,
who always knew that I could tell this story.
Thank you for including me in yours.

ACKNOWLEDGMENTS

his story has been in my heart for over fifteen years. The outline took form as my two sons grew up, and I even laid it aside for three years so that I would have more time for them. I never wanted to think back on their high school years and remember saying, "Don't bother me now. I'm in the middle of a chapter!" Those two boys—young men now—are the only "book" I needed to write.

I did, however, finally finish this one.

I owe the initial ideas to Bernd and Claudia Gruhn. They sparked my curiosity by telling me how things used to be in Austria hundreds of years ago. They also taught me all over again what a joy it is to know what I believe.

I am very grateful to Dee Lopez and her community college writing course. Without her professional support in the beginning stages, this project never would have gone past chapter three. I have kept the kind but honest critiques of my fellow students, and reread them in times of doubt.

The editors at Kregel Publications had unique problems as I disappeared into Russia for a three-month language course. They are efficient and understanding, and they have made my dream come true.

With the book almost finished, David and Renee Sanford's enthusiasm and advice regarding publishing pushed me into that next step. I'm thankful for their prayers and cheerful words as I struggled through rewrites. David also acted as my literary agent, handling the contract and answering questions, while I was learning to write Russian.

I have many friends who, over the years, have tactfully offered to proofread. If I tried to name you all, I fear I might miss one. You know who you are. I wanted this to be a surprise for you.

My mother, Ruth De Haan, deserves thanks too. As soon as I was able to compose stories on Big Chief tablets, she listened to them all. "Write what you know," she told me. So I learned how to do research, and I lived in Austria for fifteen years!

Sisters can be best friends too. As children, Marian and Karolyn applauded my heroes, wept with my heroines, and hissed at my villains. No one could have had a more appreciative fan club.

Husbands and wives always seem to come last in the acknowledgments. I suspect it's because the author wants to leave the reader with the sweet taste of a love that encouraged and sacrificed. My husband, Floyd, is so supportive that I needed these other people to convince me that his love wasn't blind. He believed in me and made time for me to write within a lifestyle that has bridged—so far—twenty-three years, almost all of the European countries, eleven homes, and motherhood. This book is dedicated to him.

INTRODUCTION

hose of us who will usher in a new millennium in the year 2000 may have a difficult time understanding the mind-set of the people of the Middle Ages in A.D. 1000. Decades before the beginning of the year A.D. 1000, the future must have looked very bleak for the simple folk living in western Europe. This Day of Judgment, January 1, hovered over them like a manipulative parent, threatening certain punishment if denied unquestioning obedience. Abbots and monks in the monasteries, bishops and priests from the towns united to encourage or frighten their parishioners into doing—or giving—whatever they deemed necessary to save their cursed souls. Gifts, both voluntary and extorted, poured into the treasuries of the churches and monasteries.

The fateful night of December 31 came. A terrified people flocked to the churches to await certain judgment with tears of repentance streaming down their faces. Vows to God were readily accepted on His behalf by the religious leaders, but the only real hope for common people was that if God did judge the earth that night, their presence in church might convince Him that they were not as guilty as some.

Judgment did not come, and relief must have surged through Europe, lifting much of the oppression that had gone before. With the churches' coffers full at the beginning of the new millennium, it is perhaps no accident that a "cathedral crusade" gripped the continent for the next three centuries. Each city, each bishop, and each noble aimed to surpass the achievements of those who had gone before. Each dreamed of erecting the highest, widest, and most beautiful edifice the world had yet seen, for the "glory" of God.

Their ambition to produce the superlative cathedral drove them to explore new areas of physics, geometry, and algebra. Mathematics had been curtailed by religious taboos, which forbade learning from heathens and heretics (that is, the more advanced Arabs, Persians, and Greeks), so builders were forced to learn by experience. Many of the churches that went up collapsed soon after they were built. Architects of our century are amazed that the people were able to construct any enduring structures given their lack of modern equipment and advanced mathematics.

Nowadays, of course, no one could afford to use the trial-and-error method to erect a skyscraper, nor could any building contractor pay for the astonishing detail work that was once lavished upon each church. Back then, however, manpower was cheap. The guilds—organizations of merchants or craftsmen—were concerned with the quality of workmanship, not the rights of their workers. Workers were a renewable resource, but the work they did would testify to their ability, long after they were dust in the grave.

Freedom and democracy as we know them came from the Greeks and the Romans, but in the Middle Ages, these political ideas had been abandoned for so long that no one except a few monastic readers of Greek knew anything about them. Although modern scholars of the Middle Ages are usually more interested in political situations, throne succession, and territorial expansion, the common people of that time were wrapped up in the real world of climate, shelter, growing seasons, and food provision. It did not matter to them, nor did it much affect them, that there were twelve German duchies, ruled by dukes who had inherited the land from their families. The local lords, who owned the land, were of more interest. In much of medieval Europe, the feudal system had developed, and the common people were relieved to give up their freedom for the security of being able to provide food, clothing, and shelter for their families. They tilled land provided by the landowners, and in return they pledged their loyalty, defended their benefactor, and gave a frighteningly large percentage of their crops as tax. In some instances, they were called into military service and fought in their lord's battles.

It is tempting to envy the simplicity of such a life, but although survival *is* simple, it is also unrelenting. We live in a fast-paced world where almost everything we need and use miraculously appears in the local department store, grocery store, restaurant, or gas station. It's easy to forget that *fast* used to mean by horseback, and it took the entire eighth century for Europe to accept the metal stirrup as a sensible improvement. We measure progress by the month; if they bothered to measure at all, it was by centuries. While our medical ethicists struggle with gene manipulation, they sought healing through supernatural signs revealed to their religious leaders. In a very logical sense, grime and germs did not exist until someone discovered them, so people in the eleventh-century could not be shocked by unsanitary living conditions.

The people of the Middle Ages were an intensely religious people. They sought God's mercy with a passion that residents of our often indifferent society can only imagine. Ever since the Roman emperor Constantine declared Christianity to be the official state religion of the empire in the fourth century, church and state were linked by a mutually self-serving bond. This bond had, over the centuries, been weakened by ambitious kings and corrupt churchmen. Popes, however, still crowned emperors, kings appointed bishops, dukes established monasteries, and priests had to choose between sharing the wealth of the system or serving the people. People who did not or could not become a part of the church lived on the fringes of society or made a living performing jobs forbidden by the new religion. Muslims and Jews were persecuted. Misunderstood Old Testament Scriptures were cited to support the annihilation of infidels. Those groups of people outside the church who revered God's Word and merely wanted to follow the teachings of Jesus Christ had no secure place in the empire. They were known as "sects."

Four centuries before the new millennium, Christianity, in the form of Roman Catholicism, had begun converting illiterate, pagan worshipers of trees and heavenly bodies into faithful followers of a religion based loosely upon a brilliant literary work known as the

Bible. That many were converted at the point of a sword was seen as a necessity; the possibility of attaining eternal life far outweighing the manner of attaining it. The religious leaders soon discovered, however, that although they could force a verbal confession of faith, it was much more difficult to change the religious practices and superstitions. Finally it became necessary to integrate many of the customs of the old religions with the new.

With the conversion of Europe came a degree of literacy through the establishment of monasteries and, much later, cathedral schools. These became the centers of learning for many centuries. Much of the knowledge and literature we have about the ancient world we owe to the faithful scribes and librarians cloistered behind their thick stone walls.

The church taught that God made "some to fight, some to work, some to pray." The political and religious leaders made it very clear to their folk that this enumeration of the classes—nobility, peasant, and clergy—left little room for change. Most of what happened to a person was on account of one's birth or destiny. One of the few vocations of choice was to become a monk, for only in the monasteries were the pauper and the prince supposed to be equal. Usually, the people followed the work of their fathers and their fathers' fathers without giving much thought to choices.

⁓∞⁓ ⁓∞⁓

You will not find Felsenburg as a cathedral city in any atlas. It is a composite of many cities that existed in Europe during the eleventh century. The people and their struggles are also fictional, but you will find similar stories in many art, religion, and history books. If stories of these characters sound familiar, perhaps it is because we are not as different from them as a thousand years of history might make us think.

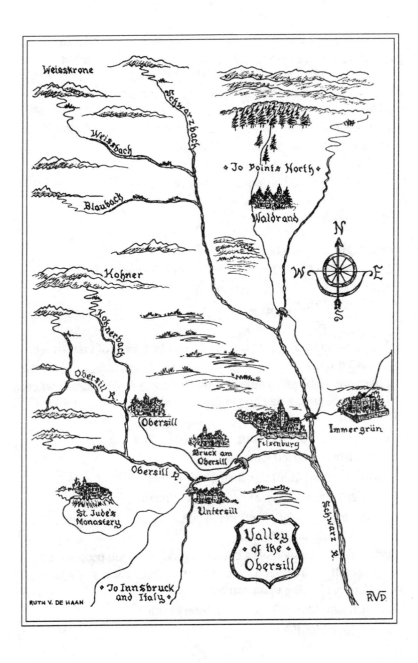

GLOSSARY

ach! (ahck) an exclamation like "oh!"

auf wiedersehen (owf vee'-der-zane) "see you again"

brötchen (broot'-ken) little bread rolls

bürgermeister (boor'-ger-my-ster) mayor of the city; literally, master of the citizens

Bursch (boorsch) slang for "boy"; can be a term of endearment or an insult

Fasching (fah'-shing) the Tuesday before Ash Wednesday when Lent begins; a day and night of revelry before the time of fasting

Felsenburg (fel'-zen-burg) cliff fortress; "city on a cliff"

frau (frow) married woman

fräulein (froy'-line) unmarried young woman

gasthaus (gahst'-house) guesthouse; tavern

gendarme (jen-dar'-may) the local law-and-order keepers, like town policemen

grüss Gott (groos' got) a common greeting when people meet; literally "Greet God," it comes from old customs of wishing God's blessing upon someone

Hauptman (howpt'-mahn) a military rank

Herr (hair) lord; sir

ja (yah) yes

jungfrau (yoong'-frow) virgin

Kohner (ko'-ner) the name of a mountain

Lärchenplatz (lair'-ken-plahtz) literally, "larch place"

lebe wohl (lay'-ba vole) "farewell"; usually forever

liebling (leeb'-ling) "darling"; loved one

mädchen (maid'-ken) girl; unmarried woman

miter or mitre (my'-ter) what a bishop wears while performing
 his official duties

Mutti (moo'-tee) Mommy

nein (nine) no

Onkel (own'-kl) uncle

pfennig (pfen'-nick) penny; at this time, the common currency
 was a silver coin

quatsch (kvatch) "garbage"; usually an exclamation to express
 anger and disgust

schön (schern) beautiful

Tante (tan'-tay) aunt; auntie

Wahrsager (vahr-sah-ger) a fortune teller; literally, "truth teller"

Zur Felder (tsoor fel'-der) literally, "to the fields"; a tavern,
 named in the customary manner of labeling buildings and
 streets according to their physical location

PROLOGUE

ndrew dipped his quill into the ink and copied another word onto the parchment. The perfectly applied strokes dried quickly, and he brushed his slender hand across the smooth manuscript, satisfied with the beauty of his work, done for God. He laid his quill down and read the phrases he had just copied. Hardly daring to believe the words, he reread the original and then stared in astonishment at his copy. Suddenly breathless, he cupped his cold, trembling hands over his flushed cheeks and glanced around to see if anyone had noticed his reaction.

The other copyists and illuminators were still hunched over their work, oblivious to the disturbance pounding in Brother Andrew's brain. He heard the scratching of pens as the young scribes of St. Jude's Benedictine monastery painstakingly copied priceless manuscripts or decorated the magnificent words of God with gold and other bright colors.

The light coming in the round windows had faded, and a monk who sat in a darker corner cleared his table. He walked silently to the fireplace and tossed in his practice parchment. The fire flared suddenly, and Andrew watched the flame with that familiar uneasiness he had grown accustomed to but did not fully understand.

The feeling passed, and Andrew heaved a shaking sigh. He breathed in the familiar scent of ink blended with wood smoke and ventured another look at the manuscript before him. The words were still there. He picked up his pen and scribbled a note on a scrap of rag, then stood and walked slowly to the librarian's table.

He handed the scrap cautiously to the librarian. "Why do you need this?" he asked, barely glancing at the rag. "It's not your work."

Andrew shuffled his feet and wrote another note saying that he wanted to compare the two works.

The monk frowned. "This is not necessary. You are to copy, not read and compare."

Andrew forced a perfunctory smile and bowed his head meekly. He returned to his desk and picked up his pen, but his eyes thirsted to read the sentence. With practiced discipline, he cleaned his pen and dipped it into the ink. He steadied his hand and copied another word, only then permitting himself to read the entire sentence again. Doubts crowded his thoughts as he copied yet another word. He tried not to let his eyes stray to the upcoming section, but he could not stop himself and soon he had unknowingly memorized it. Mechanically, he continued to copy words while his mind wrestled with the wonder of his discovery and the power of his conscience.

ONE

he new millennium came in softly with the feeble pink of dawn. Those who lived in a partially deserted section of the city of Felsenburg had spent the night in the local gasthaus, quenching their fears of the Great Tribulation in bitter brews. They sang and laughed and gossiped, trying to prolong the life of the old age by their own staying power, while their wives and children knelt in the church, praying for mercy. Finally, the longsuffering proprietor of Zur Felder, a tavern with a questionable reputation, escorted his patrons to the door and, with a sigh of relief, locked it behind them.

The revelers tottered home through the biting cold, singing and shouting good wishes until they reached their hovels. With much loud "shushing," they entered their homes and fell into their meager beds. To those saints who might still be awake, they offered prayers that the dawn would come.

When the dawn did come, however, few were conscious of it. The early, rosy light gradually painted the gray and dirty city in flattering hues. It shone first upon the long, crooked rows of rooftops, stretching the length of each alleyway. From a few crumbling chimneys came dark wisps of smoke, evidence of expertly banked fires.

The sunlight crept slowly down the brick and stone walls. What little warmth it offered did nothing to lessen the bitter cold. The shadows retreated slowly to hide between the buildings and in dark alleyways. Where the filth of the streets had not melted or blackened the week-old snow, the sun touched it with mauves and golds, shining in rainbow hues among the icy ruts.

The unrelenting cold lay heavily upon the city. Few ventured out until it was time for Mass because today was a holiday.

In one of the nicer homes—one that had three rooms—fourteen-year-old Martin Steinmetz was up and about. His older brother, Stefan, had dragged him from his sleep, throwing off the blanket to let in the frigid air. Before the boy could protest, Stefan pulled his younger brother to a standing position and wrapped him in his own huge cloak. He shoved the hood over the boy's straight, light brown hair.

"Fetch the midwife and make it fast!" Stefan gasped, as he pushed Martin out the front door. "Klara's in childbirth!"

Martin, at first annoyed, felt the fear rise in his throat until it matched the panic on Stefan's face. He turned and ran.

His cloth shoes slipped as he stumbled along the frozen streets. The ruts, made by carts and the prints of man and beast, were frozen, as if cast in iron, and it was difficult going. Terror made his legs seem heavy.

Warm sewage melted the ice in places, and it ran in steaming rivulets through the streets. Martin preferred to stumble on the ice rather than ruin his shoes in the stinking water.

He staggered into a particularly dreary alley and finally reached the midwife's house. Martin beat upon the door and, receiving no answer, shouted until someone in a neighboring house opened shutters with a bang and swore at him.

Urged by desperation, he tried the door and, finding it unbolted, crept cautiously into the room.

The place was dark, for the midwife had closed the shutters against vandals and the cold—both of which would kill mercilessly. As Martin's eyes adjusted to the gloom, he could see the old woman's shape hidden in a mound of blankets in one corner.

"Frau Grein?" he said softly.

There was no answer, so he called louder and tiptoed toward her. When he stood above her cloaked shape, he gave her a good shake.

She turned over heavily, and the scent of body odor and beer escaped from the warmth of her blankets.

Martin stumbled back as if punched by the foul stench. He approached her again. "Frau Grein, my sister-in-law, Klara, is in childbirth. Stefan says that you must come."

"Go away," she murmured in a gravely voice.

He shook her again, and she turned upon him suddenly and snarled, "I said go away!"

Martin's teeth chattered from the cold. "B-but you told my m-mother that when Klara's t-time came you would help."

"She should not have that baby on the first day of the new millennium. It is a bad omen." With that, she pulled the covers back up over her nose.

Martin growled under his breath. He cast about in his mind for a persuasive means of diffusing her superstition. While he thought, he turned to the fireplace and poked at the ashes until he found a glowing coal. He knelt and, from a ready pile, took a few twigs and laid them upon the embers. He blew carefully until they ignited.

The old lady heard their crackling and poked her greasy, gray head out from the blankets. "What be ya doing?"

"The room is cold. Shall I heat your broth?"

She sighed noisily. "Nein, I'll drink yours. Don't waste my fuel." She sat up and her lips parted into an almost toothless grin. "You be a clever Bursch. Get out of here while I get my clothes on."

He waited in the alley, shivering as he felt the soles of his damp shoes harden in the bitter cold. A few minutes passed, and she emerged, enveloped from the top of her head to her ankles in a huge, red shawl. In one gnarled hand she held a birthing chair—a strange, low-backed stool, with practically no seat, darkly stained from many years of use.

Martin pushed down his revulsion and offered to carry the chair.

"Nein, Bursch, go now and tell the priest. Then come straight home so's I can send you to fetch him at the right time."

Of course! He had forgotten about the priest. Custom required that Father Augustin come at the end of a birth in case a quick baptism was needed, or last rites, or both.

Martin shoved these frightening thoughts from his mind and blinked back the tears that had come so suddenly. He watched Frau Grein waddle toward his home, and he turned toward the church.

The sun, so pretty at dawn, now filtered through dense layers of smoke. It cast no more painted rainbows upon the snow. Martin hurried along, bruising his heels and toes on the ridges of ice.

St. Nathaniel's Cathedral was an unimposing wooden structure, badly in need of repair. Around the tiny windows and above the arched doorway had been carved birds and flowers and various saints. Martin did not pause to gaze at these as he so often did but heaved open the great door and rushed into the atrium, even allowing the door to slam. He reached into the basin of holy water, but he touched ice. His fingers were by this time much too cold to melt even a few drops, so he passed on to the nave, where he bobbed down and up again on one knee and made a hurried sign of the cross.

Not daring to raise his voice, he searched through the various rooms and alcoves until he finally found Father Augustin at breakfast in his warm little apartment behind the church. His housekeeper asked Martin to come in and told him to sit on the hearth.

"But I can't stay," the boy protested. "The midwife told me to come straight back."

The lady smiled. "The first baby always comes slow. You're frozen. I figure you haven't had any breakfast yet."

Father Augustin nodded sagely and sipped from a steaming cup. He was only about the age of Martin's father, but he radiated a venerable dignity that kept him separate from the people in his parish. He seemed somehow untouched by their comparative poverty. Not that he was unkind or even ungenerous. He served them faithfully, but their condition did not seem to follow him home each night.

The housekeeper handed Martin a cup of hot, fragrant broth, which the boy cradled carefully in his numb hands. Each sip seared a path to his empty stomach. She cut him a thick slice of warm bread, and Martin was so grateful he could scarcely stammer out his thanks. He gulped the bread and nearly scalded his tonsils on the hot broth.

Then he stood. "You will be ready when I come for you, Father?" he asked humbly.

Father Augustin nodded and said in a bored tone, "I will be ready."

Martin was further depressed by the priest's apparent apathy. As he ran and slid back home, he prayed to the power he thought could influence the Almighty God the most.

"Beloved Jungfrau Maria," he whispered, "have mercy on Klara.

You, too, gave birth in this cold wintertime, and you know all of the terrible things that could happen. Please, please, please help her, for Stefan does love her so."

"And who might you be talking with?"

Martin stopped, startled by Helmut, the ironmonger, who was walking to Mass with his wife and children. "I . . . I was talking to our Beloved Mother."

"Here in the streets?"

"I was praying. Klara's in childbirth."

"Is she now?" exclaimed the wife. "Well, don't you go praying too much. The salvation of a woman's soul is in the suffering of child-birth." She turned to her husband. "I reckon Frau Grein might use a bit of help. Come, Bursch, lead the way."

Before they reached the house, the ironmonger's wife had per-suaded several other passersby to offer their services to the midwife. Klara's whimperings could be heard from the house before Martin even opened the door.

Inside, Stefan stood, hands folded behind him. He stared into the fire, which burned brightly upon the hearth. The chimney was more like a funnel-shaped roof that hung from the ceiling, and suspended from a bar across the bottom of the chimney was a pot of broth, steaming in the cool room.

"Who are they?" Stefan asked sharply, nodding toward the small throng waiting at the door. "I mean . . . I know who they are. What are they doing here?"

"We be here to see the birthing," explained the ironmonger's wife. The women shooed their husbands away and tried to send Stefan with them, but he resisted. Mumbling about bad luck, the women filed through the room and into the bedroom, which was Stefan and Klara's quarters. Martin heard Frau Grein greet them, and he heard Mama's soft voice ask why they had come.

Stefan turned to Martin with sympathetic eyes. "You couldn't help it. Have some breakfast."

The temptation was great, but Martin knew that if the good Lord provided your meal from one source, you did not eat a second, no matter how hungry and cold you might be. "Father Augustin's house-keeper gave me breakfast."

Stefan nodded and murmured, "He is a good man."

Good. What did it mean? Martin removed his cloak and huddled close to the fire to dry his shoes and warm his feet. He thought of Father Augustin's being good, but Father Augustin lived in a cozy house and had no reason not to be good. God was good, he had been told, but God was allowing his older brother to suffer terrible anxiety.

Stefan paced back and forth, adding a log to the fire from time to time, and Martin's frozen cheeks grew warm and red from the heat. The women talked in loud voices, and at times the two brothers could not hear Klara's moans over the din.

Their waiting turned to hours, and then Mama came from the room, looking tired and worried. "Martin, are you hungry?" She attempted to smile and tousled his brown hair. "You both need to eat something." She moved about the tiny room, dipping a cup of broth for each of them and cutting bread.

Martin was as tall as his mother now. Looking directly into her violet eyes, he would on occasion push the curly, graying hair back from her forehead. He would put his arms around her, and she often said that he was a great comfort to her. Right now, he longed to put his head on her shoulder and sob, but he knew that he had to be strong. He could not expect her to be strong and to be his strength too. He had to find *that* within himself; he was her child. Surely God had given him some of her characteristics besides the violet eyes and the freckles sprinkled across his cheeks.

And then he remembered the verse he had been trying to think of in Frau Grein's house.

"Mama, it's a new year. The Great Tribulation has not come. Remember what Father Augustin said at the Christmas Eve Mass: 'For unto us a child is born; unto us a son is given'? It must be a good omen to give birth on this first day, mustn't it?"

Mama smiled gratefully at Martin and opened her mouth to speak, but at that moment Klara shrieked, and the woman rushed into the bedroom.

After that, there was not much silence in the little house, as Klara lay paying her personal penalty for Adam and Eve's sin. Her tribulation had begun in earnest. She cried and cried, and had it not been for Stefan's pacing, suffering with her, Martin would have clapped his hands over his ears.

Several women rushed in and out of the room, wetting rags from a bucket of snow-water kept near the fire and preparing drinks from some of Frau Grein's secret herbs. After what seemed like an eternity, Frau Grein herself emerged from the bedroom long enough to tell Martin to fetch the priest. Relieved to be leaving, he pulled on his dry shoes and once more fastened Stefan's great cloak around him.

He ran down the street, and even from the corner, he could hear Klara's screams. The fear of Klara's dying without giving a last confession or of the baby's dying without baptism gave his feet wings. He arrived at the church panting.

The housekeeper informed him that Father Augustin had not left yet, and she would send him as soon as she could.

Martin made a detour back through the church to offer a prayer. He touched the still-frozen holy water and crossed himself reverently. Then he walked to a tiny side chapel where a few candles flickered in the half-light and illuminated the Madonna and Child in a carved frame. He wanted to light a candle, but he remembered that they cost a pfennig. It would have been easier to say one prayer and then to let the burning candle continue the prayer until it guttered out, but he would have to do it all himself.

Back home, an eerie calm hung over the house and made his heart thud in his ears. There was no sound from Klara, and Stefan was gone. Mechanically, Martin lay another log on the dying fire and sniffed the broth. He sat once more on the hearth to dry his shoes. He could hear a mumbling coming from the bedroom, but he did not want to guess what the stillness might mean.

Then his ears picked up a squeak, like a crack in the silence. He strained; it sounded like the cry of—a baby! He moved toward Stefan and Klara's door, but he did not dare touch it. He waited, barely breathing, for another cry.

Suddenly the door swung open, and Martin stood inches from his mother's startled face. She grabbed him and hugged him fiercely. The room was breathlessly hot and smelled of sweat and blood.

"Klara?" asked Martin, trying to see further into the room. "Is she—?"

Mama let him go and pushed him toward the bed on which lay an exhausted Klara, her face framed by two limp, blonde braids. Her cheeks were as pale as the smoky sky, and her eyes drooped with weariness. She did not move, but her lips curled into a faint smile. Martin's eyes followed hers' to her arms, in which lay a bundle of blue shawl.

He looked around the room at Frau Grein smugly sipping broth; at the other women smiling, proud of their participation in such a success; and finally at Stefan, kneeling beside the bed. Martin tiptoed to Stefan's side and looked down into the tiniest face he had ever seen. It was red and crumpled, and its mouth was open, but only occasionally did a squeak emerge.

"Well, did you fetch the priest?" Frau Grein's question broke the spell. Mama suddenly remarked that she ought to make some supper.

"I did," said the boy. "He will be here soon."

"No hurry, no hurry," she cackled. But everyone knew that her mirth hid her relief. The priest's speedy arrival was now inconsequential.

TWO

hat same morning, only a day's journey away, Bishop Gernot von Kärnten woke with a start. He was cold to the bone, his knees were sore, and one foot was numb. Raising his head from the warmth of his encircled arms, he looked around. Thin streams of light filtered through the slits in the chapel's thick walls, and he could see his breath steam from his nostrils. He felt a pain in his right fist and opened it tentatively. How long had he been clutching the golden crucifix on the leather cord? An ugly bluish-red imprint of the cross marked his palm. He hung the crucifix around his neck and slowly stood up, feeling the protest in his forty-seven-year-old joints and muscles.

Worse still, his mind protested: to have fallen asleep during meditation and prayer—and on such an important night! He hoped no one had noticed, and he considered kneeling again and kissing his cross, but since no one was watching, he did not. Instead, he hobbled to the great, carved doors of the chapel and pushed them open.

The snow-covered courtyard of the Monastery of St. Jude's blazed with sun in a cloudless sky. Instinctively, he lifted his hand to shade his eyes from the reflected light. He groaned and turned back, grateful for the gloom of the sanctuary.

It was midmorning, he realized, and somehow he had slept not only through his private prayers but through the morning office as

well. He fell to his knees. "Forgive," he murmured automatically.
He had wanted everyone to know of his all-night vigil of prayer,
which would turn the heart of God from certain judgment. Just as
Moses had convinced the Lord to spare the children of Israel from
annihilation, so, too, had Bishop Gernot thought to persuade Him to
postpone the Day of Judgment.

Now, though, in the brightness of the first day of the new millennium, Bishop Gernot felt a sudden embarrassment that he, too, had
succumbed to the panic of the masses. The end of the world had
loomed over every good Christian for so many years that last night
he had felt safer on his knees. Of course he had known that life as he
knew it would not end just because of a date on a calendar—a date
that even the former church fathers disputed. Universal judgment
would not—could not—come; it was not logical. Bishop Gernot's
opinion was that judgment came upon each individual by his or her
own foolish choices. God did not rain fire and brimstone anymore;
He just allowed life to progress, until His glorious kingdom would
arrive in a millennium of peace on earth.

Gernot stood and brushed the dust from his cassock. A bit of penance would calm his own nagging conscience. Perhaps a day of
fasting— Then he remembered that he had accepted an invitation to
eat the midday meal with the Abbot William, the spiritual father of
the monks at St. Jude's. Penance would have to wait; fasting should
be done privately without explanation. He would fast when he had
settled into his comfortable, new residence in Felsenburg. Until then,
the knowledge of his weakness would be his burden.

He went to the doors again and slipped his hood, like those worn
by common monks, over his straight gray hair. Bending humbly to
avoid recognition and to shield his eyes from the glaring sunlight,
he walked across the courtyard.

Rivulets of melting snow muddied the ground, and he stepped
carefully to avoid dampening his leather shoes. He passed several
monks, but as the discipline of the place required, he did not try to
see their faces, nor did they bend to see his.

When he reached the tiny cubicle that was his guest room, he found
it even colder than the chapel. At dawn, warm water had been poured
into a basin for his washing, but now it was icy cold. Perhaps this

was God's penance—meted out for his lack of discipline. But even as the thought fluttered through his mind, he smiled at his own superstition.

As he washed, he opened the small window and looked to the west across the Obersill Valley. In the distance, the Alps, pure white in the morning light, thrust their bright spires into a cobalt sky. His eyes traveled down the slopes of the mighty Kohner to the glacier, which clung to its rocky slopes. Below the glacier, the cliffs dropped abruptly, and snow rarely clung to the pale gray granite. From the glacier flowed the Kohnerbach from a series of icy waterfalls that leveled out into the valley and finally poured their milky-green water into the meandering Obersill River.

The valley was obscured from the bishop's view by a haze of smoke, which ascended like incense from the countless fires within the homes of peasants who lived in the two tiny villages below. In his mind, though, he could see the river, wandering through the snow-covered meadows, then rushing down a series of rapids to meet the equally turbulent Schwarz River. Together, they had carved away a cliff, on which was built the city of Felsenburg. The city had once been a thriving commercial center in more prosperous days when trade had been important. Here the two rivers calmed and became a flowing highway for the few traders still brave enough, or foolhardy enough, to bring their wares from the east and south. Here they were forced to leave their boats and sell them for beasts of burden or for carts to continue their journey over land.

Felsenburg was his city now, and he was their bishop. He thought of the simple people who lived within the walls of the city. They knew that he had made the long trip to St. Jude's for them, but they would never have to know of his lack of diligence. They would be grateful that he had interceded for them and that judgment had not yet come. He shivered and closed the window.

St. Jude's had only two rooms that could truly be called warm: the kitchen and, out of necessity, the scriptorium. The bishop's body ached from his night in the frigid chapel, so he decided to warm himself for the rest of the morning in the scriptorium, watching the scribes and reading from the books of Moses.

The library was dark and cold, for the danger of fire in that priceless collection of books and scrolls was far worse than frostbite. He hurried through it to the scriptorium, where a fire crackled cheerily in the fireplace. From three walls, light flooded in through dozens of round panes of crown glass. Tables lined the walls, and at each a monk, surrounded by the tools of his trade, was bent over his work.

Smoke and dust swirled through the rays of sunlight as the librarian came to greet the bishop politely. "You are well?"

"God be praised, I am," answered the bishop, wondering if perhaps his nap in the chapel was common knowledge. "I would like to read the next scroll of Moses' second book."

The librarian's shoulders sagged as he turned and, with reluctance, shuffled into the freezing library, where the manuscripts were stored. Bishop Gernot paced down a row of copy tables nearest the fire, enjoying its heat on his back. He paused dutifully at the elbow of each monk to admire the intricate designs of the illuminations or to read a few lines that had been copied from older manuscripts.

There was only one copyist who really interested the bishop. His desk was situated farthest from the fire, but the young man was the most talented the bishop had ever seen. He stopped at the copyist's table, just as the young man paused to flex his hand.

"You are weary? You look pale."

The young man looked up at him through a fringe of red hair and shook his head.

"I'm sorry, Brother . . . Andrew, isn't it?" Then the bishop apologized at once. "I had forgotten that you cannot speak."

The young man smiled slightly and returned to his work, but the bishop continued to watch him until the librarian appeared at his side with the requested manuscript. The bishop spent the rest of the morning meditating on the life of Moses.

⌒⌒∾ ⌒⌒∾

The smell of roasted chicken greeted the bishop in the abbot's dining room. The table was already laid with crispy brown breads, soft white cheeses, and a large flask of red wine from the monastery's own vineyards. A young monk brought a steaming bowl of leeks to the table, and another set down a platter heaped with chicken.

William, abbot of St. Jude's, entered the room. Elected by the monastery's monks, he commanded the loyalty and obedience of all who lived there. Although the abbey stood within the bishop's jurisdiction, the abbot had all authority within these walls. He was a slight man of about two-score years. His pointed face was clean-shaven, as were all of the monks'. His dark eyes slanted upward slightly to the edge of his face, and bushy brown eyebrows gave him a mildly sinister look. An apologetic smile played about his lips as he excused himself for being late. He strode to the bishop and took his hand, bowing to kiss the bishop's ring.

The abbot's hands were dry like parchment, and the bishop pulled away and patted him on the shoulder. "My friend, you must not bow to me, for I am no better than you. God's calling may be a higher one for me, but we must each obey His voice. Is that not so?"

William bit his thin bottom lip and did not respond but motioned for the bishop to be seated. His prayer over the food was short and perfunctory. Then he asked the bishop to pray as well.

Bishop Gernot declined. "You see, this is your domain, and I do not want to take the leadership from you."

The abbot's lips curved upward, but the smile did not light his eyes. "You cannot take my leadership, because it was given to me by God. Is that not so?" He poured the wine into two goblets and raised his for a toast. "To God's calling."

"To God's calling," the bishop repeated. As he began to eat, he wondered how the two of them would get along in the same valley. But he realized that they would not have much opportunity to see one another. St. Jude's was a world set apart.

No one alive could remember when the focal point, geographically, of the Obersill Valley had not been the monastery. Two centuries before, it had been planted atop the granite cliff, which jutted out from the wall of mountains surrounding the valley. The summit of the rugged cliff had been smoothed and tamed, its own granite quarried and rearranged to build the monastery walls and buildings. From a distance the abbey was practically invisible.

Its influence upon the people, however, was highly visible, and they would have lived their lives much differently had the monastery chosen another valley as its domain. Their best produce decked the abbot's table, their finest workmanship adorned the chapel, and their ablest young men retreated within its walls to become the most outstanding scholars of their time. The monastery had power, and its abbot oversaw its operation with diligence and discipline. All who came within its gates bore the responsibility to submit to the abbot's dictates.

Bishop Gernot was no exception, and he also recognized that the outside world, including his own bishopric, had very little influence upon St. Jude's. He wondered if he would become well acquainted with the shrewd abbot.

Between mouthfuls, Gernot asked, "How long have you been abbot here?"

"Six months. Konrad died last autumn."

"I knew Konrad from a visit he made to Rome some years ago. He was a good abbot. He put an end to the scandals that had plagued this monastery half a century ago."

"He did indeed, but what is 'good'?" the abbot challenged. "Lack of vice is not always virtue, is that not so?"

The bishop swallowed the tender chicken and fingered his goblet. This was only his second audience with William, but now he was certain that he did not like the abbot. It was pointless to pursue any further attempts at congeniality. He took a long drink of the good wine and came to the point.

"You have here a young man—a copyist—who is very talented," he said lightly. "God has greater uses for him than spending his life in the isolation of these beautiful mountains."

The abbot disagreed. "Many come here to sacrifice 'greater things' and to dedicate their lives to simpler things."

"Brother," the bishop allowed a sharp edge to come into his voice, "there is no need to teach me. Sacrifice and escape are two very different concepts. This should not be a place of escape but of dedication. The young man I am referring to has most certainly come here to escape."

"And who is he?"

"First I will tell you why I need him. As you know, I have given my life to the study of Moses. I have, as well, learned much about this new age. Moses' life is relevant to mine, and an application of his dealings with Israel would do much to heal our great church. There are many factions and sects that would destroy the church, and a knowledge of the things I am studying could bring them back into the fold. My studies may also answer many of the problems that are arising in the eastern areas of the Holy Roman Empire, where the scourge of those Islamic barbarians—the Muselmen—threatens the souls of the faint-hearted." He paused and mopped up the last of the grease on his plate with a chunk of bread.

Abbot William grinned, and this time his eyes smiled too. "And for all of this, you need one of my lowly copyists?"

Bishop Gernot nodded gravely. "I do. For ten years I have been making notes and organizing a modern theology. With the beginning of this new era, I am compelled to proclaim a new message to the only church of our Lord. Your 'lowly copyist' will be the lowly servant of another lowly servant, and together we will heal the land."

"And who is this *blessed* young man?"

The bishop ignored William's sarcasm. "The mute, Andrew." He rushed on without a pause. "Do you understand why I need him? I am certain that God has brought him to my attention for this very purpose."

William pushed his plate away and leaned back. "I do not understand, but I agree."

The bishop could not hide his amazement. "You agree?"

"Did you want to persuade me even more? I agree. Andrew is indeed escaping, although only God—and Abbot Konrad, rest his soul—knows from what." He stood and walked to the fire. "Do you know that there is no medical reason why he should not talk? And yet no one can recall that he has ever spoken a word. He is not good for the community here at St. Jude's. Our disciplines include that of refraining from useless chatter. This requires effort and self-control. This young man cannot talk, and therefore he cannot practice this discipline. It will be good for him to leave and to face whatever it may have been that silenced his voice. I will have him summoned. He will be able to leave with you tomorrow."

The abbot called for one of the monks to fetch Andrew and then paced a few minutes before he said, "You have, of course, recognized Andrew's great talent. But I give him gladly to the man who may be our modern-day Moses."

Bishop Gernot felt his ears burn red. Although he had often considered himself a prophet like Moses, he would never have voiced it. William made it sound absurd. The bishop bowed his head and chose his retort carefully. "Moses was the most humble man on the face of the earth, and I, alas, am not."

⌒◯⌒ ⌒◯⌒

When Brother Erwin informed Andrew of the bishop's request and asked him to come down to the abbot's quarters, Andrew received the news with predictable calm. Walking softly through the cold, dim corridors of the abbey, he wondered briefly why Bishop Gernot von Kärnten would want a mute scribe, but the question was not his to ask. Almost five hundred years earlier, St. Benedict had taught that those who wish to please God have no right to do their own will. Having grown up in a monastery, Andrew had learned that lesson well. When things happen, people have no right to question the reasons.

The abbot's quarters seemed hot, and it smelled of chicken and leeks. When Andrew entered the room, Abbot William and the bishop rose from their chairs, which had been drawn close to the roaring fire.

"Come in, Brother," invited the abbot, shoving another chair toward the fireplace.

Andrew bowed his head in greeting, his thoughts occupied with breathing in the stuffy room.

"This is Bishop Gernot von Kärnten, the new bishop of Felsenburg."

The bishop reached out his hand, and Andrew's rose automatically to be grasped in an uncomfortably strong grip. He drew away and chose a chair at the side of the fireplace, out of the direct heat.

"Ach, ja," said Abbot William, sitting again. "You can put him in the coldest room. He always takes the place furthest from the fire."

The bishop turned his back on Andrew and explained to the abbot, "He doesn't need to stay. I merely wanted to see his reaction to my request."

The abbot's hands slapped the arms of his chair as he clipped his words short: "Then make your request!"

Bishop Gernot shrugged and spoke toward the fire. "Very well. I would like you to come to Felsenburg with me, Brother Andrew. I need your remarkable talents to support the great mission that God has for this new age. I would also like to start a school." He looked at Andrew suddenly. "You do like children, don't you?"

Andrew bit his lip. *I've not had much experience*, he thought.

"Would you like to teach?" the bishop asked, leaning forward as if to show eagerness.

Andrew sensed his insincerity. *Why do you ask? Why do you care?*

Abbot William replied for the young monk. "His destiny is in your hands. You needn't ask. He cannot answer you. Brother Andrew has been trained to do as God wills. You bear the responsibility for deciding God's will for him."

The bishop turned to look at the abbot again. "That does seem very hard," he murmured.

"Bearing responsibility is always hard," Abbot William snapped. "You've been away from school too long."

The bishop, hands on the great, carved arms of the chair, pushed himself slowly to his feet. He turned once more to Andrew. "You are willing to come?"

Willing? Yes. Do I want to? Oh, rebellious thoughts! Don't ask me; tell me.

"He'll come," said Abbot William gently.

Andrew nodded and looked at the rough, wooden floor. Two knot-holes stared up at him like accusing eyes. He felt a twinge behind his ears. *Dear God, I don't need a headache now. Please.* He stood and raised his eyes to Abbot William, silently begging for dismissal.

The abbot smiled kindly. "You may go, Brother Andrew. Bishop Gernot will let you know when he's ready to leave St. Jude's."

Andrew nodded. Without a glance at the bishop, he hurried from the room, quietly closed the door behind him, and took a slow, deep breath.

⤫⤬

Only the bishop knew why he waited another month before leaving St. Jude's, but finally the day Andrew dreaded arrived. Their departure was scheduled for the morning of the Jungfrau Maria's Festival of Lights. The day dawned gray and gloomy. That was a good sign, for on this holiday, if the sun shined and distinct shadows were cast upon the sparkling snow, there would be six more weeks of winter. If no shadow stretched across the open fields, and the snow and sky met in gray monotony, then spring would come soon.

Andrew had awoken early and gone to prayers just as he had for the past fifteen years. It frightened him to contemplate what was to come. Life at the bishop's residence in Felsenburg stretched out before him as a huge unknown. As he knelt to pray, he tried to banish the hollow feeling that disturbed the routine of his prayers. Finally he gave up and returned to his tiny cell to pack his few belongings into a satchel. Impatiently, he shoved his feet into the new leather shoes, which Brother Lukas had made especially for his journey. After fastening the rough, woolen hood over his cleanly shaven head, he swung the satchel over his shoulder and left the cell—forever.

The only home he could remember was St. Jude's. Life here had been secure, sheltered, and predictable. He knew that he had been brought to the monastery as a small child after the death of his parents. He had never learned the particulars, and the abbot, who took him, had died before Andrew was old enough or brave enough to ask. A few times, throughout his years at the monastery, Andrew had tried to discover his past from within himself, but it was as if a heavy door had swung closed upon the memories.

At the monastery gate, Andrew stopped to wait in the frosty courtyard for the bishop to come. As he shuffled his feet and blew on his fingers, it seemed to him that he had been waiting nearly all of his life for something to happen.

When Andrew had first arrived at St. Jude's, some of the monks were totally captivated by the silent, red-haired boy from Britain. Some even dared to express their affection, although many thought that he was an imbecile because he was mute. Brother Viktor, convinced that the child had brains and all the facilities he needed to speak, tried to teach him to talk. As much as Andrew longed to please the older monk, however, when he opened his mouth and tried to make the vibrations in his throat, a sense of helplessness and despair overwhelmed him, and no sound emerged.

By the time Bishop Gernot and the other monks were ready to leave, Andrew was shivering with cold and apprehension. Abbot William pronounced a blessing upon the group and then turned to embrace Andrew. "Lebe wohl. God go with you and bless you," he whispered into the young man's ear. "Live by the rules of our beloved St. Benedict, and you will be safe."

Safe. Andrew returned the embrace and then followed the others out the gate into a world that he knew was filled with unfamiliar dangers.

THREE

artin was balancing on a stool, trying not to bang his head on the low rafters of their house. Dangling around him were strings of onions, sausages, and candles. As he pushed aside their webs, spiders darted away from his long arms. It was smoky, too, and he sneezed, which caused his mother to keep blessing him. His job was to unhook the candles and hand them down to his mother, who laid them carefully on the cloth-covered table.

"Not those, Martin; they're everyday candles. Give me the nicer ones . . . there to your left."

He turned and teetered but successfully removed the candles from their peg. After he had found all of the best ones, he was sent to work, trimming and polishing the dust from them until they glowed in the firelight.

The citizens of Felsenburg loved the many holidays that punctuated the long nights and cold days of this season. They especially looked forward to Jungfrau Maria's Festival of Lights, for it had the possibility of foretelling the end of winter. This year the festival would be even more significant because their new bishop was going to be installed. Their excitement was tempered by the fact that they did not know if he would be benevolent or strict. Bishops held in their hands not only the ultimate destinies of their parishioners; they also shaped the earthly happiness of every follower. The previous bishop, Marcel, had seldom lived in Felsenburg. His lack of involvement had cleared the way for oppression from the less important clergymen. The people were ready for a change, and the more time, energy, and financial resources they invested in the celebration, the more they thought they could please God.

Especially important were the candles. It seemed to Martin that he and Mama and Klara had dipped hundreds of them. The family would not use them until they had chosen the most perfect ones and brought them to the church to be blessed and lit by Father Augustin. Then they would file through the streets to St. Nathaniel's in a bright river of light, singing the haunting melody of "St. Simeon's Song." They would save those candles, which would protect the household from storms and illness and would even relieve the fears and guilt of anyone who lay upon his or her deathbed. Mama provided for these candles each year just as faithfully as she provided for the herbs and vegetables and sausages that fed her family. To her, their spiritual well-being was as important as their physical health.

Tiny, one-month-old Bernhard would also begin his own spiritual life today. Long ago, the tradition had arisen in Felsenburg to baptize first-born sons on this day when the first-born Son of God had been presented in Jerusalem. It was an added expense, of course, as this special ceremony included bringing a sacrifice for the church. The baptism would be held in the late afternoon at the West Church, and then the newly christened babies would be carried in the procession to St. Nathaniel's, where the bishop would be installed.

Mama wanted to make sure that everything ran perfectly. As usual, she began with Papa, who hated holidays because the gasthaus was obliged to be closed. "Do you really think that you should be drinking this early, and this the baby's baptismal day?" Mama asked. "Father Augustin'll be able to smell it."

Martin looked over at Papa, who slouched on a bench set into a nook next to the fire. Through the smoke, which poured into the room, he stared at the opposite wall and raised his tankard to his lips. "Bad weather; the chimney won't draw." Going to church never made Papa happy. He was not drunk, but the bitter ale took the edge off his displeasure.

He was dressed in his Sunday breeches of dark gray wool. Over this he wore a brown, knee-length tunic fastened at the waist with a leather belt. His wool cloak lay in the corner on the narrow cot, which served as Martin's bed.

Wiping his chin with the sleeve of his tunic, he grinned at his wife. "I'll do as I please," he drawled loudly.

Martin looked at Mama for a reaction, but she just bit her lip and finished dressing.

She wore a creamy-colored wool tunic, which fell to her ankles and was sashed in the middle. For luck, she always wore a medallion of her name saint, Ingeborg. Over her hair she draped a long kerchief and wrapped it around her shoulders. Her cloak matched Papa's, but her mood did not.

She wanted to be excited for the holiday, but winters made her sad. Work was plentiful in other seasons, but in the winter, mortar would not set properly, and frozen fingers were not deft enough to maintain the high quality for which Bernhard Steinmetz and his family were well-paid. Although Papa used this time to mend and improve his tools, he bore the comparative idleness poorly. If he stayed home, he was cantankerous or gloomy; if he went out, he got drunk with his employees or relatives. There were even nights when he did not come home at all, and no one ever dared ask him where he had been. Mama had even said once that she did not want to know.

Like most of the folk in the city, this family awaited the coming of spring with impatience. This baptism marked the end of winter; the whole day, there had been no shadows. Soon it would look and feel like spring. The men would return to work, and before long, Papa would be himself again—busy with a purpose.

Martin's mood matched his mother's, but for a different reason. As he pushed his legs into his leather breeches and fastened the closing of his tunic, his heart was heavy with disappointment. This should be a happy day of rejoicing and celebration, but Martin felt that Stefan and Klara were making a big mistake.

They seemed oblivious to it, however. Martin could hear them moving about their room, cooing to the infant—Bernie, they were calling him—who alone seemed to express loudly the fear in Martin's soul. Their door opened, and Martin sighed at the beauty of Stefan's little family. They looked like the Holy Family. Stefan was so proud of that baby and protective of his darling Klara, whose eyes were shining with a mother's secret joy. The baby, though, was not acting like the Christ Child, Martin thought, for who ever saw pictures or icons of Him red-faced with His mouth opened and His eyes scrunched shut in anger?

Martin quickly stuffed his feet into his shoes and went to lift the baby from Klara's arms. At Martin's shushing, the child hiccuped and sobbed, but his squalling ceased.

Klara sighed with relief. "We should have made you his godfather," she said to Martin. "How is it that he obeys you so well?"

Martin did not dare to say that he had spent more time with the baby than anyone else except Klara, so he just smiled and shrugged. He, too, wished that he could have been the godfather. He knew just how he would raise the baby to love God and obey His commandments. He would show the child love, and Bernie's obedience would be in response to that love.

Martin nuzzled the baby's cheek. For godparents, Stefan and Klara had chosen Papa's youngest brother, Hans, and his wife, Maria. It was a nice gesture, but Onkel Hans drank even more than Papa, and everyone in town knew that he was not faithful to poor, plain Tante Maria. Sometimes Martin wished that Father Augustin would stop forgiving his uncle for a while. Maybe living in mortal danger of hellfire would force him to reform his ways.

Martin was the only one, though, who doubted Onkel Hans' ability to represent the holy church and teach his godchild the way to God.

A damp, cold fog had blanketed the city all day, and the ruts were frozen solid. It was only afternoon, but already it grew dark, and Mama gave each of them two candles to carry—an everyday one to light their way and a shiny new one to be blessed by Father Augustin.

West Church was a small stone church, built when there had been a schism a century before. No one could remember what the split had been about, but the thick walls seemed to contain a perpetual cold that people and flickering candlelight could not drive out. Standing in the atrium, the Steinmetz family shifted from foot to foot and tried to keep from shivering. It was the first time in a month that the whole family would be at Mass together. A half dozen other families soon joined them as godparents came, and the people greeted one another. The children who were to be baptized were not yet allowed into the sanctuary, for they were still heathens, and they could not be allowed to defile the holiness of the Lord's temple.

Father Augustin glided into the atrium and each family greeted him reverently. Onkel Hans and Tante Maria had not yet arrived, so Stefan could not introduce them to him.

The baptisms began. Each father proudly bore his offspring to the baptismal font and held the child while the priest asked questions of the godparents. Then Father Augustin took each baby and dribbled water upon his or her head. Dipping his finger into a fragrant oil, he drew a tiny cross on the child's forehead and pronounced him or her as a member of God's family.

Finally only the Steinmetz family remained. Klara's tears were sparkling in the dancing candlelight, and Stefan looked angry. Suddenly, Onkel Hans came puffing into the atrium with Tante Maria shuffling in his shadow. Behind followed their thirteen-year-old daughter, Cecilia.

"So sorry we're late," he said loudly, "We had a sick neighbor. . . ." He let his voice trail off.

Martin glanced at Cecilia, who grimaced and then bowed her head. Martin had no doubt that they had a sick neighbor, but he knew that the neighbor quite likely had nothing to do with their tardiness. Onkel Hans had such a clever way of manipulating words to imply something other than actual circumstances. Those who did not know him well could be easily misled.

The group stepped to the font, and Martin could smell the alcohol blowing from Onkel Hans' lips. He hoped to see disapproval on Father Augustin's face, but the Father looked unconcerned and began questioning the baby.

"How are you called?"

Stefan answered as if he were the baby, "Bernhard, after my grandfather. Johannes, after my great-uncle."

"Bernhard, do you renounce the devil and his angels, his worship and his idols, his thefts and his frauds, his fornications and his drunkenness, and all his evil works?"

At that moment, Martin decided that even if Onkel Hans and Tante

Maria were answering aloud, he, Martin, would answer in his heart. He was sure that God felt the same way as he did about the unsuitability of these godparents, and he knew that with God's help he could do what was best for little Bernie.

Onkel Hans answered for the baby, "I do renounce them."

"Do you believe in God the Father Almighty?"

Martin closed his eyes and thought with all of his heart, *I do believe. He does believe.*

The priest read each part of the Apostles' Creed, about believing in the Virgin Birth, and in the Crucifixion and Resurrection and the Ascension of the Lord Jesus to heaven.

". . . from whence He shall judge the living and the dead. Do you believe?"

I do, Martin thought.

"And do you believe in the Holy Spirit, the holy Catholic church, the remission of all sins, the resurrection of the dead, and life everlasting?"

If only he would not use such big words, thought the young surrogate godfather, *but I do believe, and I shall learn what they all mean in time to teach Bernie. Now they'll have to let me learn to read!* That thought, which he often entertained, cheered the boy considerably.

"Upon confession of your faith, Bernhard Johannes, I do baptize you in the name of the Father, the Son, and the Holy Ghost." As he poured a little of the icy holy water from the baptismal font onto the baby's head, the child started screaming.

His wailing echoed around the atrium and through the rafters high above their heads. It was impossible to hear the rest of the priest's murmured words, but Martin knew that he had welcomed Bernie into the family of God. The priest then repeated the same prayer that he had read for all of the other babies. Martin prayed too.

Then as the whole group moved into the sanctuary for the Mass, young Onkel Martin reached to take the four-week-old, screaming infant from his mother. Securely in Martin's arms, Bernie ceased his crying and hiccuped through his first Mass.

FOUR

artin's cousin, Cecilia, loved babies too, and she could not hold Bernie often enough. Every time Bernie was in her arms, he would look up at her with an expression that melted her heart. He had such a dear little nose and soft, fuzzy hair, and he had even begun to smile at her. When she put her finger against his hand, his tiny fingers would close around it. Martin said that Bernie smelled bad, but she knew that all babies smelled that way—sort of like sour milk. She thought it was a lovely scent.

In the church, she kept leaning forward to see how Bernie was doing in Martin's arms. Judging from how Martin had his face hidden in the folds of the baby's neck, she did not think that he really minded Bernie's smell that much. Mass was very long, for every family must take their candles to Father Augustin to be blessed. Their heels ached from standing, and Bernie grew restless. Martin handed him to Stefan, but the baby began screaming again.

"I'll take him," Cecilia whispered at once. Eventually everyone in the family had held the baby until their arms were numb with fatigue. Only the godparents did not seem to want him.

Finally the last "amen" was said and the parishioners emerged from the church to find that the sun had gone down. An eerie glow lit up Lärchenplatz as hundreds of consecrated candles flickered under the icy wisps of fog. A procession formed and advanced toward St. Nathaniel's. A few voices rose with "St. Simeon's Song," and soon many joined:

> My eyes have seen Thy salvation,
> Which Thou hast prepared
> In the presence of all peoples.

Cecilia shivered and tucked her arm into the crook of her mother's. Just ahead of them trudged Stefan with baby Bernie asleep on his shoulder. Cecilia reached up and pulled his little blanket over his face to protect it from the night chill.

"Isn't he wonderful, Mutti?" sighed Cecilia into her mother's ear.

"Shhh!"

> A light of revelation to the Gentiles,
> And the glory of Thy people Israel.

At St. Nathaniel's church, the procession slowed to gather the monks who had come from St. Jude's. Their voices soared in the damp night air to fill Lärchenplatz with heavenly music. Joined by Bishop Gernot von Kärnten, they led the way into the church, where the religious leaders from all over the bishop's domain waited near the altar. There were so many of them that they spilled out into the partially filled nave. The duke and his family were there, as well as many of the local landowners and their subjects. The church filled rapidly, and most of the city was left to stand outside upon the icy cobblestones of Lärchenplatz.

Cecilia could hear only snatches of the ceremony inside, and she was relieved when Martin's mother suggested that it was foolish to keep the children out in the night air. The men agreed but said that they would stay. For once, Cecilia did not mind being called one of "the children." Martin led the way out of the crowd, and Cecilia stepped carefully with one hand stretched out beyond the candle, so as not to set anyone's clothing on fire. The two families parted where the crowd began to thin.

"We'll see you in a little while?" asked Tante Inge, Martin's mother, with an eager lilt in her voice.

Mutti nodded, but Cecilia could tell by how her mother's shoulders sagged, that she did not want to attend the celebration of Bernie's baptism. Cecilia again took her mother's arm, and they kept one another from slipping and stumbling over the uneven lumps in the road. At home waited the food they had been preparing all morning while Father had been sampling ale at Zur Felder. At this time of year, there was not much food to choose from, but Mutti had been able to make a lovely turnip pie. Cecilia had helped to prepare a gruel of oats and dried plums, which had been cooking since they left the house.

As soon as the two women entered the house, the smell of scorched oats enveloped them. Dropping the basket of consecrated candles, Mutti cried, "It's burnt!" and rushed to where the pot hung over the hearth to poke her huge wooden spoon into the mass.

Cecilia, accustomed to her mother's hysterics, pulled her back from the fire, still holding her own glimmering candle high.

"But it's burnt," she protested again.

"Better it, than you," Cecilia scolded. Hanging on to her mother, she set her candle on the table and then gathered the fullness of the woman's cloak in her arms. "Mutti, you dragged your cloak through the coals. You must be more careful."

Her mother pressed her lips together tightly as she removed her cloak.

She was able to salvage the gruel, but not before she had blamed her husband for the entire episode. "He never learned to bank a fire properly. I told him that he should leave it alone. If Inge notices that the oats are scorched, I shall be so humiliated."

Cecilia snatched up a spoon for a taste. "They are fine. Just don't bring the burnt part."

Mutti's sigh was long and heartbreaking. "Everything I do or want is ruined by that man. What I endure! Saints preserve me from him."

Clenching her teeth together, Cecilia scooped the gruel into a smaller pot and then draped Mutti's cloak back over her shoulders. "Let's go." The words came out as a command, which Cecilia immediately regretted.

For once, her mother did not notice.

Their progress to Bernie's baptismal supper was hindered not only by the ice on the streets but by the many people now celebrating after the installation of the bishop. Arms linked together, Cecilia and her mother slipped and slid and bumped into people—all of whom seemed to be going in the opposite direction.

As they neared the Steinmetz house, Cecilia's thoughts turned from her mother's difficulties to the supper's purpose. "Wasn't Bernie beautiful today, Mutti?"

"Humph."

"I wish we had a baby. They are so dear and—"

"Noisy," Mutti interrupted.

Cecilia pressed on. "Ach, Mutti, they can't be that bad. Why can't you have a baby, so's I can have a little one to take care of?"

Her mother stopped dead and grabbed the girl's arm to stop her. "I'm tired of hearing this," she said, her voice shaking. "You have gone on and on ever since Bernie was born—before he was born. I've heard this enough. I shall never have another baby, and you know that."

The girl knew it, but she did not understand it. "Well, anyway, someday I'm going to have a baby—dozens of them. I'll be so happy and—"

Mutti's hand flashed out and slapped the girl so hard that she staggered backward. "Don't say that ever—ever! It's wicked!"

Tears sprang to Cecilia's eyes, and she reached up to touch her stinging cheek. "Wicked?" she echoed.

Then just as suddenly, Mutti was calm. "You're simply too young." She marched toward the front door.

Cecilia hurried after her, the tears still unspilled. She wanted to ask why she was too young, but she could not force the words from her constricted throat.

Mutti knocked briskly on the door and let herself in. "Grüss Gott. We're here," she said cheerfully.

Cecilia took a deep breath and rubbed away the tears. The dampness on her cheek cooled the spot her mother had slapped, but when Martin came to greet her, he tilted his head and scrutinized her face.

"What—?"

"Mutti," she said simply.

He took the pot of gruel from her and said, "I'm sorry. Please come in."

She laid her scarf and cloak on Martin's mat, which had been tugged nearer the fire for Bernie to lie upon.

The party began without the men. Onkel Bernhard and Stefan arrived with profuse apologies after Bernie had been put to bed.

"We picked up the ale!" they announced with grins designed to smooth over any anger.

"Where's Hans?" asked Tante Inge, trying to sound only mildly interested.

"Zur Felder," Onkel Bernhard retorted, "and so what if he is!"

Cecilia was certain that they would not see her father again that night, but he surprised them all, just as Mutti was handing out turnip pie. Although he reeked of ale, and his red nose and dark eyes glowed, his wife reacted in her usual manner: She relaxed and ignored him. The evening wore on, and all were soon cheered. Martin and Cecilia's parents played games, and the two young people slipped away to sit on Martin's mat next to the hearth.

They sprinkled raisins into the coals and then competed to snatch them out again. While the raisins were still hot—sometimes, too hot—they popped them into their mouths and enjoyed the strong sweetness, which stuck to their teeth. After Cecilia drank a cup of ale, everything Martin said seemed so funny. They burned their fingers and their tongues, and she complained that she always lost the race.

"Well, of course, silly," Martin told her with a saucy cock to his head. "I didn't drink any ale."

"None?"

"You know I hate the stuff."

"It'll make you big and strong," she told him, repeating what her father had told her.

He tugged at one of her braids. "Oh, and you want to be big and strong?"

She laughed again. "Stop it!" she begged. "My cheeks ache!"

"Well, aching or stinging, you've had problems with your cheeks tonight," joked Martin.

Suddenly, nothing seemed funny. "Oh, Martin," she whispered, and misery lodged where mirth had vacated, "Do you know why it's wicked to like babies?" The tears welled up again.

Martin shook his head, obviously bewildered. "I like babies. Who said that?"

"Mutti. That's why . . ." Her voice trailed off and she rubbed her cheek.

Her cousin reached over and gently turned her head so he could see better. The kindness in his touch surprised her, and she pulled away.

"Did I hurt you?" he asked, his hand dropping onto the blanket.

"No, but . . ." She glanced over to where her parents laughed and talked. They had not noticed. "I just don't understand," she murmured, and the tears spilled over.

Martin looked over his shoulder at the adults and then back at her. She knew she was embarrassing him, but she could not stop her silent tears. He flopped down on the cloaks that covered his mat and propped his head with his hand. "Do you remember when we were little, how when we were punished, we'd be sent to your bed or mine without any supper?"

She nodded and a sob escaped her lips.

"Come down here." He pulled her down until they lay looking straight into each others' eyes. The fire was warm on her back. "I never minded. Did you?"

She wiped her eyes and her nose and whispered, "No. I don't want to grow up."

He picked up one of her braids and brushed the end of it across her nose. "Of course you do. You want to have babies."

"Ach, Martin, don't say that!" If they had been alone, it would have been a wail, but she dropped her head down on her arms and sobbed silently. Long ago, they also had consoled one another, and just like long ago, Martin took her hand and rubbed it with his thumb. Back then, he had promised to marry only her, and they would have many babies, but she knew that they could never mention that again. Fresh tears flowed for her lost childhood. She did not understand Mutti's anger, but she did know that growing up meant changes. She moved her hand within Martin's to let him know that she was aware of his comfort. The tears finally stopped, and she fell asleep beside her cousin and best friend on the pile of cloaks.

⁂

It was late when the parents finished their games and their revelry. As they stood to say their good-byes, they noticed Martin and Cecilia lying asleep beside the hearth, facing one another, hands clasped.

Maria frowned and said to Martin's mother, "She's too young for that."

Inge bit her lip and thought for a moment before correcting her. "No," she said with a smile. "They're both too old for that."

FIVE

he luxury of the bishop's residence at Felsenburg stunned Andrew. Life at St. Jude's had not been uncomfortable. Each monk had enjoyed his own bed in his own cell. The food was simple but adequate. And the many disciplines, although almost impossible to fulfill, did contribute to cleanliness and order. The bishop's residence was almost as large as the entire left wing at the monastery. The building was not in the best repair, but renovations were under way, and judging by the furniture and tapestries, no price was too high for the bishop.

Andrew's room was as large as the abbot's quarters at the monastery. He had the use of a table and chair, his own fire (which he could regulate), and the almost unlimited use of the manuscripts in the bishop's library. The food and drink was richer than that to which he was accustomed, but Andrew had the uneasy feeling that life for the ordinary citizens of Felsenburg was poorer even than those who lived in the village below St. Jude's had been. He had as yet, however, been unable to find out.

For the month since he had left the monastery, Andrew had worked like a slave. Between writing letters for the bishop and copying documents, he hoped to snatch a few hours to indulge his curiosity about Felsenburg. Father Augustin eventually provided him the opportunity by inviting the young monk for an afternoon visit. It was shortly before the beginning of the Easter time of fasting, and Andrew accepted gratefully. He planned to leave the residence early to give himself time to walk through the streets.

Anticipating with pleasure the broadening of his experience, Andrew was totally unprepared for his own reaction as he stepped out of the bishop's residence. He faltered and his hand clutched the door as he looked out into the garden, where a carpet of bell-like snowdrops poked up through the mud under the bare fruit trees. Their bright, pure blossoms contrasted with the sudden, dark fright that filled his head. The flower beds had been spaded, but snow still lay in the shady spots, especially against the high, stone wall. His fingers seemed frozen to the door, and his breath came in short little gasps. An image flashed through Andrew's mind: He was twelve and Brother Viktor was lying on his deathbed.

Was that real? he wondered. *Was that really you, Brother Viktor?*

Andrew's body shook as if suddenly waking out of a nightmare. He turned back toward the dusky, paneled entryway of the residence. One bright bar of sunshine streamed through a tiny window above the first floor landing. The monastery had been much more austere, but the cool, dim atmosphere made him suddenly homesick.

"Grüss Gott, Brother." A man's rough voice interrupted Andrew's thoughts. He realized that this old man, kneeling in the dark brown earth, had been watching as Andrew hesitated in the doorway, staring mutely around him. Wrinkled and white-haired, the man had a permanently bowed back from bending over his work.

Andrew smiled and nodded.

"I'm Günther, the gardener," he explained, in an accent that sounded as if he had pebbles in his mouth. He raised one muddy hand apologetically. "I'll not be shaking hands with yoa, if yoa don't mind."

Andrew shook his head.

The man looked uncertain, obviously disconcerted by Andrew's silence. He looked at his knees and poked a few seeds into the soil. Then he looked up at Andrew expectantly. "You one of them that never speaks? I could never be one. I talk too much. I talk to my plants—and I pray, of course. You one of them?"

It would be pointless to explain, for the man probably could not read, and a written explanation was Andrew's only means of communication. The young monk took one more wistful look into the residence and then stepped from the porch, his trepidation diluted by the friendliness of the gardener. He touched the man's fuzzy head, blessed him silently, and then walked down the path and let himself out the huge, iron gate.

Again he stopped as the gate slammed behind him. A woman walked by on the street, carrying a basket. She curtsied and then stared unabashedly at him, even turning around to walk backward until she stubbed her foot on a rock. The frayed edge of her skirt peeked out from under a tattered brown shawl, which she wore pulled tightly over her hair.

Cheeks burning, Andrew looked at his toes and then away from the woman. Coming toward him was a group of children. They chattered like a flock of sparrows and jostled one another. One of them sneezed, and the others all hastily crossed themselves and murmured, "Gott segne dich." When they saw Andrew, they stopped shoving and walked sedately past, the girls bobbing hasty curtsies.

Andrew had not seen the man sitting on the muddy ground across from the bishop's gate, but now the stranger called to him. "Just a pfennig, Brother. Just a pfennig for my daily bread." He tried to grin at Andrew—a hideous, snaggle-toothed grin—and lifted his bony hands in an attitude of prayer. Andrew had no money; he had never needed it. He felt trapped, and his pulse raced in fright and helplessness. *This cannot be happening,* Andrew thought. *I can't just leave him. What can I do?*

He leaned against the gate, trying to think. The beggar, hindered by a deformity of his left foot, did not rise nor approach Andrew, but the monk still felt his grip as surely as if the man held him by his collar. Then he had an idea. He slipped back into the garden and walked around the residence to the separate building behind, which served as the kitchen. The cook, a burly woman with a kind face, was mixing dough. She looked up when Andrew came in and raised one eyebrow. "Ja?"

He looked around. The huge open hearth dominated one end of the kitchen, and a pot of fragrant stew bubbled over the fire. Large, smooth tables took up much of the floor space, and the cook was shaping loaves upon one of them. Shelves lined two sides of the kitchen, and on one shelf sat part of a charred loaf of the rough, peasants' bread, referred to as kuchen—cake. He reached for it.

"What do you think you be doing?"

He sighed. No one had ever asked questions at the monastery; here it seemed that everyone did. He pointed toward the front of the house and imitated the beggar's motions. Then he patted his stomach and pretended to eat.

She understood at once. "You can't be feeding beggars right now," she explained. "We feed 'em on the day before the Sabbath. They're always sitting there, and if we took to feeding them, there'd be no end."

Andrew gritted his teeth in frustration and thought, *Wouldn't it be better to run out of food and know that you at least lessened their suffering?* He smiled at the cook and made pleading motions again— this time toward her.

She smiled and conceded, "Oh, all right, but just this once. Next time, though, you can leave by the back gate. Beggars don't sit there because it's too cold."

He took the bread and smiled his thanks.

The beggar was delighted and began at once to gnaw upon the hard crust. Andrew was certain that he would be back again.

He turned his back on the bishop's residence and headed resolutely toward the center of the city. Already he felt tired. He was not used to coping with such a variety of emotions, and the view of the city ahead of him promised to add even more turmoil to his heart.

The layout of the city looked vaguely like a wagon wheel, with the main market square, Lärchenplatz, in the center and little roads and alleys radiating outward from it.

Andrew's senses were assaulted everywhere he turned. Dust and soot clung to every structure, and the houses on his left were stained dark from it. From some of these dwellings came the sounds of families—children laughing or crying, women talking or shouting in shrill tones. On his right was the tall garden wall of the bishop's residence. It too was grimy, but it did not need as much repair as did so many other buildings in the town.

Men in dirty, graying tunics passed by him, pushing or pulling carts loaded with assorted wares to trade—bits of iron, firewood, piles of woolen yarn. Many of the women had been to the fields to collect bunches of young meadow herbs to cure spring weakness. One woman pushed a cackling cartful of scrawny, red chickens.

Andrew was sure that there was not another place on earth as unlike St. Jude's as Lärchenplatz. It was the main marketplace in the whole region, but he had no way of knowing that it was only a very small marketplace in a city so depleted of population that only half the dwellings were filled.

The center of the platz was cobbled, and here a few farmers and poor craftsmen laid out their wares. They called to the passersby and bargained noisily in competition with one another.

"Fresh grain! Fresh grain! Only five pfennig for a measure."

"Wheat as clean as just harvested! No mold here. Just eight pfennig for two measures!"

At the end of the day, they would pay a percentage of their income to the city magistrates and another percentage to the church for their use of the square.

Andrew, his heart beating with excitement, strolled around the perimeter of the marketplace. He gazed up at the roofs, turning and gaping, until he was dizzy.

St. Nathaniel's Cathedral, humble though it was, dominated the platz and bordered the east end. Next to it was an ancient cemetery, surrounded by a rusty, iron fence. Fresh flowers and candles decorated the graves, demonstrating the love and care lavished upon the beloved relatives who now waited in purgatory for their ultimate release.

Beside the church was a road that curved slightly and then plunged down the steep hill on which the city perched.

The south side of the square was bounded by a semicircular row of one-story hovels, which, even to the stranger, were recognizable as the oldest buildings in town. Their thatch was black with age, and the mud that plastered their fronts was crumbling, revealing the cracked mortar and bricks beneath. Centuries of dust and debris had piled up so that one had to step down to enter these houses. In the spring, nothing could keep the snowmelt from dribbling into them.

In front of Andrew, across the square, lay a road that led between more buildings to the outskirts of the city. At the entrance to that street stood Zur Felder, the tavern, which harbored the town's men folk more often than did St. Nathaniel's. It was a large, blocky building, two stories high, and had obviously received a fresh coat of lime in the recent past. Beside it stood the bakery and another street and then another row of newer houses, the old ones having burned to the ground before anyone could remember. More recently, the population of the city had fallen sharply, as more and more families moved onto the land. If a house burned, one simply moved into another vacant one.

A well stood in this corner, and a young man was drawing the water and filling buckets for those who had come to fetch the day's supply.

Andrew turned to gaze at St. Nathaniel's from across the square. The afternoon sun cast a golden light on the dark brown wooden planks arranged in a zigzag pattern along the sides and front. Above the heavy, double doors hovered clumsily carved angels, saints, and birds in an inept rendering of a story unknown to Andrew. New, honey-colored thatch contrasted with the dark church, giving it an impression of top-heaviness.

His head ached, and Andrew decided that he should hurry on to Father Augustin's. He skirted the marketplace and walked around to the back of the church, where he would find the priest's little house. Behind the church, the evening shadows were already lengthening, and Andrew shivered. Before he reached the door of Father Augustin's, a young woman dressed in black hurried toward him with her hand outstretched. On one arm, she held a baby, and a skinny girl of about three stumbled along beside her, clutching her mother's worn skirt.

"Please, good brother, some pfennig for my children. I am a widow and my children have had nothing to eat today. Could you not spare something for these little ones?"

Andrew's heart twisted at her words. Grimacing at his own inadequacy, he turned his palms upward to show that he had no money, but he was aware of the silent condemnation of his healthy body. Unable to cope with his inadequacy, he simply walked past her and knocked on Father Augustin's door.

The woman followed him, her dashed hopes exposed in the whispered words, "Please, Brother."

Father Augustin's housekeeper answered the door, but before she could speak, the widow called out again, "Oh, good woman, could you not spare a crust of bread for my hungry little ones?"

The little girl gazed dolefully up into the face of the housekeeper, and Andrew hoped that the woman would comply.

"It is so awkward," the housekeeper confided in Andrew, as if the young widow were not even there. "They come every day, all the time. We simply cannot feed them all."

Father Augustin, his guest having been delayed, came to the entrance to find out the cause. "A problem, Frau Busch?"

"Another beggar," she explained with barely concealed disgust.

"Go home to your family," Father Augustin said, not unkindly.

"I have none," she said and bit her lip to stop its trembling.

Suddenly Frau Busch sighed noisily. "Another one?" she questioned, looking over Andrew's shoulder. They all turned to see. Shuffling toward them came the beggar to whom Andrew had given bread outside the bishop's residence. Tucked under his arm was some of the charred kuchen. With great effort he dragged his deformed foot along until he stopped beside the mother and children. He glanced at the priest and his housekeeper and then reached out to pat Andrew shyly on the arm.

"He's God's man, is our young monk," he said to the widow, "but his God gives him no money." He thrust the remainder of the bread into her free hand. "Here. Feed your little ones."

Before she could stammer her thanks, he turned and limped away. The young widow did not waste another look at the priest, but there was the hint of a question in her glance at Andrew.

Father Augustin broke the spell. "Please come in, dear brother," he invited, the incident forgotten.

Andrew took a step toward the door and then turned to watch the woman as she moved away from the church into the golden afternoon sunshine. The little girl hopped along beside her like a little bird, mouth open to receive the morsels her mother offered. The crippled man never looked back, but Andrew sensed an elation in the tilt of his head.

Andrew felt a firm grip on his arm as the priest gently pulled him into the cozy little house. Mimicking the priest, Andrew wiped the mud from his shoes and then allowed himself to be led into the sitting room. It was simply furnished with a table and several chairs, which had been polished to a soft shine. A modest serving of wine, bread, and cheese had been laid out upon a white embroidered cloth. On the hearth a fire crackled and, although the brocade drapes shut out the fading sunlight, carefully trimmed candles beamed a steady glow into every corner of the room.

Father Augustin indicated that Andrew should sit near the fire. "A sad case, that widow," he said. "She ought to look for work." He lowered his rotund body into a chair with padded arms.

The housekeeper poured two cups of wine and rearranged the bread and cheese on the table between the two clerics. "They usually become prostitutes," she spat, disgust in her voice. "They have no pride."

SIX

artin felt as if he could not lift the hoe even one more time. Still, he dragged it toward him, twisted it out of the sticky mortar, and then let it fall with a "thunk" as it hit the bottom of the mortar trough.

Drag . . . twist . . . lift . . . thunk.

His arms and wrists ached, and sharp pains shot through the middle of his back.

Drag . . . twist . . . lift . . . thunk.

Looking at the sun and feeling his empty stomach growl, he instinctively knew that it was nearing midday.

Drag . . . twist . . . lift . . . thunk.

"Martin, Bursch, you can stop." Papa slapped him on the shoulder and took the hoe from him.

Martin straightened up and rubbed his lower back. For a moment he felt dizzy, and he leaned down again until the world stopped spinning.

"You've done a good morning's work, son. We'll quit early today, for tomorrow is Easter. Let's go home; it's time to eat."

One of the men sloshed some water over Martin's arms where he had been splashed by the mixture of sand, lime, and water. He cleaned them carefully so that the lime would not burn him. The water cooled the blisters on his reddened hands.

Other men were climbing down from the scaffolding that

surrounded the first story of the gatehouse. The new construction was for the ruler of the area, Count Robert von Immergrün. They removed their work clothes, locked all of their tools in the shed, and then trudged off in various directions toward their homes scattered around the countryside.

Speaking few words, Martin and his father packed their blankets and cooking utensils and flung them onto their backs. It would feel good to be home. Martin could hardly wait to taste Mama's good cooking after two weeks of living with the masons on the building site. Of course, today they would still eat Lenten food—only grain and herbs—but tomorrow would be their Easter feast!

Tired of the squishy mortar, Martin's bare feet avoided the soft spots in the crude road, still muddy from the frequent spring rains. The road took them through small patches of woods, serene in appearance, where the people had cleared all the fallen timber for firewood. Only a few of the very old trees had foiled the axes of the peasants. These ancient giants towered above the young trees, whose new leaves hung like pale green clouds around their branches.

Where the trees had been cleared entirely, plowed fields spread out in lumpy furrows, not yet planted, for the Frost Men would come once more before the second week in May.

In the pastures, which would later nourish sheep and cows, bright dandelions and forget-me-nots swayed in the breeze, and golden forsythia and pussy willows bordered ravines and brooks. Daffodils and irises bloomed in marshy areas, and a bit back from the road, Martin spied the misty lavender of violets. He left the road and plucked a handful for his mother.

Papa nodded in appreciation. "Your mother would be proud of you. You mix the mortar very well. Wolfgang Mischer commented today on the consistent quality of your mortar."

Martin flushed at the unexpected praise. He hated mixing mortar, but he was still glad that he could do it right.

"I think that it's time to begin your apprenticeship," Papa said. "I'll talk to the other masons about it. You're almost a man!"

Felsenburg had just come into view, perched on the cliff carved by the Schwarz and Obersill rivers. Martin chewed on his bottom lip and concentrated on the view of the city. Arguments and objections rushed through his mind, but each one seemed less valid than the previous one. Finally, he caught at one and blurted out, "I could never be as good a mason as you are!"

"What?"

"Mixing m-mortar is easy, but I could never lay courses like you and Stefan do. I would make you ashamed."

Grabbing Martin by the shoulder, Papa brought both of them to a standstill. "What are you talking about?" he demanded.

"L-laying courses. I . . . don't think I could do it. I . . ." Martin took a deep breath and blurted, "I don't think I want to."

Papa turned abruptly and continued toward home. "There's nothing to discuss. You're the son of a mason—the son of the count's master mason! Of course you can lay courses; it's in the blood."

Martin was not going to let the subject drop. "But Papa I don't want to lay courses; I want to be able to draw the plans and write the instructions." His father was far enough away now that Martin had to shout after him. "I want to learn how to read!" He ran to catch up.

Papa said no more but clenched his mouth shut so tightly that the muscles in his temple bulged. Martin feared that he had said too much. In silence they trudged onward, while ahead, the dark tower of St. Nathaniel's thrust its straw spire, like spun gold, into the blue sky. Clouds fled past it, blown by a brisk wind.

They finally reached the bridge and paid the toll to cross over the Schwarz River, which was swollen with snowmelt. The road up to the city climbed in steep curves to enter the Lärchenplatz from the east end, beside the church.

Lärchenplatz was busier than usual with the extra business of preparing for Easter, and many of the women carried a cloth-covered basket with the Easter roast blessed by Father Augustin. The Lenten fast would be broken the following day, after weeks of fish and grain. Martin knew that Mama would have already been to the priest, and he could hardly wait for Sunday.

As they passed by the hovels, they saw a young girl sitting in a doorway, selling red-dyed eggs. The people who lived in the hovels were the poorest of the poor, and they depended upon the sale of their meager wares to survive. Their rent was low, but the landlord collected it mercilessly, and evictions were common. Those who were forced from these hovels moved to the streets, for there, and there only, was the rent free. These beggars roamed the alleys and marketplace, and often Papa would toss pfennig to the homeless children who played in the dust. Normally Martin tried not to see them, because there was nothing he could do, and the sight of them tore at his heart.

Papa bought two red eggs and handed one to Martin for good luck, the earlier conversation disregarded.

Martin suddenly spied his cousin, Cecilia. She was standing over a gnarled woman who was selling dyed eggs. Cecilia's pink lips were curved downward in contemplation. He stopped and watched her.

She reached up to rub her freckled nose and then closed her eyes. He could see her counting on her long, slender fingers, while trying to juggle the cloth-covered basket that hung upon her arm. Her dress was brown, but the brown of the kerchief that covered her head had turned to a dusty pink with many washings. Tiny blonde hairs had escaped from her braids and peeked from under the kerchief. The sun shone through them, framing her face in a golden halo.

Papa's eyes followed Martin's gaze, and he slapped his son on the back. "Coming, Bursch?"

Martin looked up at Papa sheepishly. "I . . . I haven't seen Cecilia in a long time."

"Go then. I'll tell Mama you'll be late."

"Thank you, Papa."

The old woman was placing eggs in a soft nest of hay in Cecilia's second basket when Martin strode to her side. Although they were the same age, she was slightly taller then he. Her blue eyes, set deeply above her high cheekbones, looked down at him in surprise.

"Why Martin, I haven't seen you since before the fasting time began."

"That wasn't so long ago. But I know that you have been sick. Besides, I've been on a job."

She counted out her pfennig to the woman and picked up the basket with the eggs. Martin took it carefully from her, and they walked toward the bakery.

"Mama just wouldn't let me out—even after I was well," Cecilia lamented. "She's getting odd that way. I don't understand."

Martin was silent.

Cecilia stopped in front of the bakery. "I have to pick up our bread. I'm so glad you're here; could you wait with the baskets?" She handed him her second one with the Easter roast. "And for heaven's sake, don't put this one down in the dirt!"

Before he could answer, she darted into the shop. The people brought their bread here for baking, and the fresh aroma surrounded him, making his stomach gurgle and reminding him of his hunger. His head felt light, and the noises of the market buzzed in his brain. With the handle of a basket hung on each arm, he leaned against the sunny wall of the bakery and stared at the people until they became just colorful, hazy impressions. He even heard singing and thought that he must have drifted to sleep in church.

The singing increased in volume, and gradually he realized that it was coming from the street behind the bakery. He stood up and focused his eyes, turning his head toward the sound. Into the Lärchenplatz came a bedraggled group of men and a few women. Smiles lit their faces, and they were singing, not the bawdy ballads of the public houses, but the pure strains of a Gregorian chant.

Two skinny oxen plodded behind them, pulling a gray, creaking hay cart, upon which sat women with babies and half-a-dozen scraggly children. The children were not singing but looked down instead from their perch in open-mouthed wonder at the busy square with its paltry piles of wares, and the huge, ancient church.

Business in the square ceased, and the townspeople, enchanted by the beautiful music emerging from the lips of such unsightly singers, moved toward the group like iron toward a lodestone. The crowd gathered so quickly that the cart came to a halt in front of the bakery. Customers who emerged from the doorway carrying baskets laden with fragrant breads were trapped behind the cart to be scrutinized by the hungry children.

Martin felt Cecilia's arm bump his own.

"What's going on?" she whispered.

"Don't know."

"They shouldn't sing that song in the market," she said softly. "It's for church."

Martin shrugged.

When the song ended, a tall, slender man climbed up onto the cart. He was dressed in monk's clothing—a long, brown cassock tied with a brown cord. He wore his dark hair longer than most monks did, and he had a short beard.

He raised his hands toward the people and spoke.

"Good people, I am Brother Georg, and we come to you in the midst of our long journey to bring you greetings from God." He spoke the language well, but his pronunciation hinted of another land. "We see that you are drawn to us by the sweetness of our music, which you normally hear only within the walls of your sacred church. What a shame that many do not allow their faith to spill from the doors of that building and to flow through the streets of their fair city, just as we have consecrated your marketplace with the strains of Pope Gregory's songs."

"Whatever is he talking about?" exclaimed a woman beside Cecilia.

The monk turned toward her and smiled. "I am so glad you asked, madam, for I would like to tell you." He turned back toward the larger crowd. "You folks seem so much different than the people in many cities, who are very careful to separate their faith from the shackles of everyday life."

Martin heard the unmistakable sarcasm in the monk's voice and wondered at it.

"Those hypocrites partake of the Mass faithfully, and they hear God's Word. They listen to the teachings of Jesus, but they do not think that He was talking about them." He bent and picked up a little boy of about four years old. "Consequently, little ones like this, whom the Master set upon His knee, must go to sleep every night with their tiny tummies cramped with hunger, shivering from the cold. In some cities, noblemen strut through their streets with their noses in the air, unable and unwilling to see the wretchedness of the beggars who crawl at their feet."

Martin shifted his feet and glanced at Cecilia. Her lovely blue eyes glistened with tears as she watched in rapt attention.

"Good people—and I call you good, for I can see that you are hard workers with generous hearts—I ask you today, on this eve of the Resurrection, to search your hearts and your treasures and to consider what you might give to the poorest of the poor amongst you. And for those of you who on the morrow will have nothing more to eat than you have had during this time of fasting, we invite you to join us here in your lovely Lärchenplatz for a feast that will satisfy your hunger."

"All the poor?" shouted a man from the crowd. "That would take a miracle!"

"So it will," retorted Brother Georg. "But this is the new millennium and God's kingdom is coming. You forget that the Master fed five thousand with five small barley loaves and two pickled fish." He pointed out into the throng. "You are God's miracle. There is enough in this city to feed ten times as many poor as you have." He turned back toward the bakery and pointed at Martin. "You, young man, what do you have in the basket?"

"Easter roast, sir, but—"

"Would you not give a part of it and eat less tomorrow, knowing that you have nourished a little one?"

"It's not mine to give, sir, but—"

Cecilia stepped forward and held up a round of bread. "You may have one of our loaves and half of our eggs. Martin is right; we dare not give the roast."

Brother Georg bent down and rested his hand on her head for a moment. "Bless you, child." He took the eggs and the bread. He broke the bread and handed it out to the children, who devoured it greedily. Then he turned again toward the crowd, which had begun to disperse. "Will no one else give? Will the multitudes be fed on a few colored eggs?"

Gradually, some people did come forward to offer him some of their hard-earned food, and he collected some pfennig too and deposited them in his little pouch. But the majority left, and the pile of food for Brother Georg's feast was pitifully small.

Martin handed Cecilia the basket with the precious roast and stepped to the wagon. "Brother Georg?"

The monk jumped from the cart but still towered over him. "You're the boy who wouldn't give your roast," he said sadly.

"Many others didn't give either."

"So they didn't." He turned to walk away.

"Brother Georg," Martin insisted. "The roast wasn't mine, but I can give you my tunic."

When the monk faced him again, his dark eyes sparkled, and the sternness around his mouth was replaced by a soft smile. He rumpled Martin's hair. "Bless you, my son, but we really need money."

"I have none."

"A big Bursch like you, and you don't work?"

"I do, sir, for my father, but I don't get paid."

"Very well. Your tunic will keep some child warm."

Martin took off his tunic, giving only a fleeting thought to what his mother would say, and handed it to the monk. Although the sun was shining, a slight breeze swirled past his bare skin and raised goose flesh.

"You have another?" asked Brother Georg.

"No, Herr, but it's almost summer. My mother will make me another next winter."

"God bless you both."

Martin returned to the egg basket, suddenly aware of Cecilia and of his own lack of clothing. His cheeks felt warm with embarrassment.

They began walking toward her home, and Cecilia did not seem to notice his discomfort. "You were so noble. Just like your namesake, St. Martin, who gave his cloak to a beggar."

His cheeks burned hotter. "Noble!" He laughed nervously. "You gave me courage."

She sighed. "Papa will be furious, but how could I let those children go hungry?"

"Tonight you could fast and go without your eggs, so that it would be truly your gift."

She liked that idea, and they walked for a few minutes in silence. When they reached her house, she asked, "Are you coming to the bonfire tonight?"

"If Mama's not furious about my tunic." He looked at her for a long moment. "Will you watch the fire with me?"

Cecilia bowed her head and looked at her feet and then back at Martin through the fringe of blonde lashes. "Only if you'll find something to wear." Then she collected the baskets from him and slipped into the house.

SEVEN

hen Martin arrived with his bucket at Lärchenplatz at dusk, he wore one of Stefan's tunics, which fit him better than anyone would have thought.

"You're growing, Bursch," Mama remarked. "You're almost a man."

Almost a man. Papa had said that too. Surely a man could choose his own way in life. He must learn to read.

Lärchenplatz was already full of people dressed in good clothes. They mingled enthusiastically, as if they had not just seen one another that afternoon. Children ran and dodged around the people, screeching with pent-up delight at being allowed to stay up past their bedtime.

In the center of the square, a pile of wood and miscellaneous debris towered above the heads of even the tallest men. Martin stacked his bucket with the others near the woodpile. That afternoon, the fire in almost every hearth in Felsenburg had been extinguished, as tradition required. Before the evening was over, each family would carry home coals from the bonfire to start a new fire for the coming year.

Further back from the pile of rubbish were baskets and carts of every description, filled with refuse and discards from spring cleaning. Lined up near the beggar's hovels were more carts and wagons, which had been pulled into the square by various beasts: good-natured oxen, goats, and even a couple of swaybacked horses.

The wagons groaned with their loads of prunings, foul-smelling floor rushes, roof thatch, hay (which had been used in mattresses for the past year), and bits of clothing too threadbare for even the poor.

In contrast to this disgusting collection of refuse, the homes this time of year had been scrubbed and cleaned and repaired. The men sometimes replaced the old thatch on the roofs with new, honey-colored straw thatch, which suddenly reduced the mouse and rat population in the house. Children pulled the moldy hay from mattresses and stuffed fresh hay back into them. The women washed the wool covers and hung them to dry in the sweet, spring air.

Everyone's clothing was scrubbed as well, and the garments were treated to an extra rinse due to an unexpected rain shower. Furniture was discarded, repaired, and built. Finally, mothers chased everyone out of the house and swept out the previous year's rushes along with the year's accumulation of crumbs, dust, dirt, and numerous varieties of fleas, lice, and spiders. They laid fresh new rushes and replaced the furniture.

The last task was to burn everything at the Easter bonfire. This tradition had originated hundreds of years before with the Norsemen, who burned the refuse to chase out the evil gods of winter. When the first monks arrived in the valley hundreds of years before to convert the people, it seemed advisable to allow the practice to continue. The tradition rid the town of all of its burnable garbage, and, as customs die hard, it was simpler to allow it to exist than to change it. But the evening would always end with a celebration of the Mass.

Martin found Cecilia with her parents. He greeted his aunt and uncle respectfully, and then stood with the family for a few minutes before he whispered to Cecilia, "Let's go stand by the fire."

She nodded, and they slipped quietly away to get as near to the towering pile as they dared. It had just been lit. Tiny red and yellow flames leaped higher and higher through the straw, leaving behind thread-like, white embers that crumbled and fell upon other straws, which in turn flared, glowed, and crumbled. Soon the whole pile of thatch, twigs, and wood was glowing, crackling, and shifting.

Night had settled, and Martin looked around the circle of faces illuminated by the blaze. People talked animatedly or simply stared into the fire. Across from where they were standing, he could see Brother Georg and his wagon filled with followers. They began singing.

Martin's gaze returned to the fire and followed the flames as they climbed higher. Scattered by the evening breeze, orange sparks and glowing embers blew upward to join the stars.

"Isn't it lovely?" sighed Cecilia.

Martin looked at her in surprise. He had almost forgotten that she was there. "The fire?"

"That, too. I meant the singing."

"I thought that it belonged in church," he teased.

"It does, but I feel like I am in a great cathedral. Surely God lives outside of the church too." She reached up and pressed her hands to her cheeks. "It's getting too hot here."

Martin felt a bit scorched, too. He decided that the spot beside Brother Georg's wagon looked cooler. Impulsively, he reached out and took Cecilia's hand in his. He had done it many times before as they had grown up together, but never had the touch of her hand startled him as it did now.

Both of their faces were too red from the fire to show any discomfiture, but when Martin looked at her, she lowered her eyes and would not look up again. Her slender fingers did not, however, move from his grasp, and they walked as one toward the wagon.

Once there, Cecilia pulled her hand from his and clasped it with her other in front of her. Martin took a deep breath and closed his eyes for a moment, fighting off the desire to touch her just once more.

As the men laid more rubbish upon the fire, a mouse ran squealing from a pile of thatch and disappeared into the crowd. The cloud of smoke, blown by the wind, shifted toward them and blew into the faces of those standing near the wagon.

Martin blinked, and his eyes watered.

Cecilia's hands covered her face. "Ooh, I have a cinder in my eye!"

He stepped in front of her and pulled her hands from her eyes. "You mustn't rub it. Just leave it."

She struggled to free her hands. "But it hurts."

The wind was swirling around now, fluttering her cloak and stirring up dust and ashes. People murmured and covered their eyes. Some turned their backs to the fire and looked up into the dark sky, now made darker by sudden storm clouds.

"Come on," said Martin.

He took her wrist and moved upwind, where the flames slanted sharply away from them toward the east. The men who had been piling debris onto the fire now pulled away pieces from the heap.

Cecilia rubbed her eyes again. Martin started to scold her, but then he heard shouting. He turned and saw a little goat, wide-eyed with terror, hitched to a burning cart. The frightened animal was trying to run away from the flames. Martin pulled Cecilia out of the way and tried to remember what he had done with his bucket.

The bleating goat ran among the panicked townsfolk, and the veering cart scattered the burning hay, to be stamped out by those nearby. The poor creature crashed headlong into one of the hovels, and the cart tipped its burning contents underneath a larger wagon, which was still piled high with debris.

Fanned by the strengthening wind, the fire spread rapidly to the wagon and then to the thatch of a nearby roof. The goat's pitiful bleating was drowned out by the noise of the crowd.

Men shouted, trying to organize a bucket brigade from the well on the opposite side of the platz. Women called for their children, who kept darting away and then returning, wanting to experience the sights and sounds but seeking the protection of their parents.

Martin looked at Cecilia, who stood rigid, staring at the spot where the goat had crashed into the wall. Her stricken face was lit by the flames, which now spread eastward toward the next house.

"Celia." He shook her shoulder. "Celia, come. I'll take you to your mother."

Her eyes focused upon him. "That poor little goat."

He felt nothing for the goat. He only wanted to take Cecilia back to her mother so that he could help the men fight the fire. "Cecilia." He grasped her hand once more and pulled her after him. They returned to where his aunt and uncle had been—could it be such a short time ago? But they were gone. Frustrated, Martin looked around.

The fire was spreading rapidly, moving eastward along the row of ancient dwellings. Several groups of men, badly organized, were moving buckets of water toward the fire. From Martin's viewpoint, though, containing the fire looked hopeless. The flames flared high into the night sky, some almost as high as the church. The wind blew harder, and baskets of unburned debris rolled unhindered across Lärchenplatz and bumped up against the church doors.

Martin made his decision. "Come, Celia, your papa will find you easily enough at Zur Felder." Pushing against the wind, they hurried around the north side of the square, skirting the well where the men frantically drew water and passed it man-to-man toward the fire.

The gasthaus was empty and quiet, as every able-bodied man was out fighting the fire. Martin shoved Cecilia into a chair and told her to wait until someone came for her. He could not waste time consoling her.

Outside, he was startled by the force of the wind, which fanned the fire ever eastward. He joined the bucket brigade and watched carefully, timing the swing of the heavy bucket so that he could grasp it or hand it off. Reach—grasp—swing—let go. His arms learned the rhythm, and both arms worked almost independently—full buckets in his right hand, empty in his left.

It seemed like hours; the shouting and the roar of the fire drifted in and out of his consciousness.

And then there was no bucket. He straightened and turned to the man next to him. The man was looking upward to the east, where the fire burned higher than ever.

"Dear Gott," someone murmured before the shouting broke out again. "Our church is on fire. Judgment has come."

EIGHT

ndrew was aware of none of this. He was supposed to be praying, but he could barely endure the throbbing in his head. The temptation to go to the kitchen for a chunk of bread was overwhelming, and he wondered seriously if there was any merit in fasting. He would never express his doubts to anyone else, but the price he paid in unbearable hunger for a four-day fast did not seem to give him in return a quieter conscience or a more peaceful outlook on life. He buried his dizzy, aching head in his hands.

Dear God, he thought, *where is the joy? Where is the fulfillment that should come from assisting such a great man of God as this new bishop? Why must I always ask "Why?" Why can't I stop thinking about food? Think about Easter—glorious, triumphant Easter.*

In his mind he left his dark, curtained chamber and tried to imagine the coming day—the grand Easter procession—as he and the talented young canon, Julian, had planned it. The day would be bright and clear with transparent air that carried the Easter news like a trumpet call. A fragrant breeze would shake the grasses in the meadow outside of the city where the procession would begin. Singers from St. Jude's would stand in a sober circle of black cassocks, while white-clad children would fidget in excitement. Mothers, like gentle Madonnas, would be holding the infants who would have the good fortune to be baptized by the new bishop. The townspeople would carry flowers plucked from the meadow, and each citizen would be dressed in the best clothing.

The altar boys, looking clean and innocent, would lead the procession, followed by the new bishop of Felsenburg, who would wave his hand in a benevolent blessing over those who lined the way. The eight canons from the diocese—men dedicated to caring for the cathedral and managing the finances—would escort him in two dignified columns. As the procession organized, it would move into the streets and shortly arrive in the Lärchenplatz, where it would spread out briefly and then re-form before marching into the cathedral.

Brother Georg, with his ragtag followers, would be silenced by the significance and glory of this day. Even the poor would be scrubbed and smiling as they filed into the ancient building.

Stop! Andrew commanded himself suddenly. *You must stop imagining things. The poor will always be poor; that is their fate, but you cannot expect them to enjoy their life—to be thankful that they are hungry, as you are hungry. Concentrate, you fool,* he told himself. *Why can you not have the faith of other clerics? Think about God's greatness, His loving kindness. His justice.*

Suddenly Andrew knew that he was going to be sick. He rushed to the basin and retched dryly into it. Drenched with sweat, he sank weakly onto the cool floor and lay looking at the ceiling through the gray haze of his pain.

Tears stung his eyes. *God, where are you? I see only the ceiling in my dark room. Give me my voice that I may shout loud enough for you to hear me.*

The noises in the platz were increasing in volume, and the shouts had taken on an urgency that Andrew had not noticed before. He staggered to his feet and went to the window to push aside the draperies.

Fire! Lärchenplatz was as bright as day in the eerie, flickering firelight. He unlatched the window and the wind banged it open. The entire row of hovels on the opposite side of the square formed a wall of flame. Andrew swallowed a sob that came from deep within him. He turned and ran from the room, up a flight of stone steps to the bishop's suite. He knocked on the door and then burst into the room before he heard the bishop admit him.

A lamp glowed upon the table. Rustling and murmuring sounds came from the curtain-shrouded bed. A woman's voice exclaimed and was shushed. "Andrew? Is that you?" the bishop demanded. He moved heavily in his bed.

Shocked by finding the great man of God in a sinful liaison, Andrew stood rooted to the floor, until the bishop poked his head from the curtains around his great bed. "Andrew, what is it?"

Andrew blinked and rushed to the windows to draw aside the heavy draperies. Light from the flames danced upon the knobbed windowpanes.

"Fire?" exclaimed Bishop Gernot.

A frightened gasp came from the bed.

The bishop pushed his bare legs through the curtains and struggled to the floor. He jerked the curtains closed behind him and ordered, "Quickly, my robe, Andrew."

The two men's eyes met for a few seconds. Andrew's initial bewilderment had turned to disappointment and then to rage, which he controlled only by clenching his teeth together. *If only I could speak,* he thought angrily.

"Andrew, my robe." The bishop spit out the words as a challenge, which Andrew chose to ignore. He found the robe and flung it over the bishop's shoulders. Then he went to the windows and wrenched them open. The two men staggered backward in the force of the wind.

From this side of the residence, they could see the church, where tongues of flame danced across the dry roof. Burning debris from the Easter fire blew across the square, igniting the baskets that had piled up against the church. Below, dark figures darted about in irregular patterns, everyone shouting orders and trying to organize the men into fire-fighting units.

A few raindrops splattered the two men's faces, and the bishop announced, "A miracle is what we need. I shall pray for a miracle. For Moses, God gave water from a rock. Water from the clouds should be easy." He turned his back on the scene and looked at the bed. "You are dismissed, Andrew."

Andrew paused a moment longer before he pushed the windows closed. He left the room feeling years older as he plodded down the steps. He was not so sure that the bishop would pray, not so sure that God would hear the bishop's prayers. Where the hallway divided, he turned away from his room and trudged out into the Lärchenplatz.

The wind whipped his cassock around his knees and threw dust and ashes into his face. Shielding his eyes, he made his way to the church and pulled the dry bundles away from the doors, but more blew against them. Some had caught fire already. He had to dodge the burning bits that crackled against the doors. Several men came over to help him, and they finally cleared the archway.

Not realizing the gravity of the situation, Andrew pulled on the doors.

"Of course, the sacred vessels!" cried one of the men.

"We must save the altar!" shouted another.

Together, the three men hauled the doors open, but as they did, the wind rushed into the church, and with a roar the entire roof burst into flames. The men stared upward, open-mouthed, into the church at the underside of the fire. The beams glowed red, and embers floated down through the darkness to the wooden floor. Then larger chunks of burning wood broke off and fell in silent glowing streaks that shattered upon the floor in a shower of red sparks.

"It is the Judgment!" voices cried. "Save us, God. Have mercy upon us, Mother Maria! What shall we do to be saved?"

"The altar! We must save the altar!" urged the devout man.

Andrew looked at him in disbelief.

Almost everyone in the platz stood mesmerized by the ravenous flames that devoured their place of worship. Several of them took up the foolish man's cry: "The altar! Save the altar!"

Andrew grabbed the first man by the shoulders and looked squarely into his face. No! His lips formed the word and he shook his head.

The man shrugged from Andrew's grasp and waved his arm. "Come! Who is brave enough to rescue the altar of our beloved St. Nathaniel from certain destruction? Surely there must be special rewards for those who do this good deed?" He looked hopefully at Andrew, who merely shook his head and looked at the ground.

"A coward. This monk is a coward, but he is not one of us. Father Augustin will bless us. Come, we shall rescue St. Nathaniel's relics."

"Who will join us!" With an unearthly cry, a dozen men and women rushed into the blazing church. The walls had begun to burn, ignited by the kindling blown from the Easter fire. Red coals and golden glowing embers fell from the ceiling like rain—the rain that would not fall from the clouds. The figures in the church darted about in the flickering light and shadows until they reached the altar. With difficulty, they heaved the jewel-encrusted altar onto the shoulders of four men, and retreated to the safety of the platz.

The weakened walls groaned under the weight of the roof and a huge timber broke loose and crashed to the floor beside the four men who bore the altar. Their mouths were moving, but their cries were swallowed by the roar of the fire.

Andrew stood paralyzed at the doorway, unaware of the terrible heat that singed his hair. With a fascination born of horror, he watched the doomed men carry the images from their church, which had become their hell. Their eyes were wide with terror, yet they trudged dutifully toward the door. Fire and brimstone cascaded around them, and coals fell onto the altar and skittered across the golden lid to rest against their cheeks or fall down their collars. Suddenly, with a scream that could be heard above the tumult, one of the men dropped his corner of the altar and bolted toward the door. He tripped and fell flat onto the floor, which had now become a bed of coals. He lay writhing until a beam plunged from above and silenced him.

The other three faltered, adjusted their load, and stepped over him.

Andrew blessed the dead man and prayed for his soul. Does God bless such foolish sincerity?

"Fools," echoed a quiet voice in Andrew's ear. "Hopelessly deluded, stupid, wonderful fools." The speaker took Andrew by the arm and led him away from the church to the middle of the platz, where the townspeople were huddled together, murmuring and weeping.

Andrew looked at the man, who was dressed in a brown cassock. His long, thin face, lit by the flickering firelight, did not seem to reflect the terror of the event. He smiled slightly and introduced himself. "I am Brother Georg and you are, I believe, the bishop's scribe, Andrew."

Andrew nodded and turned to face the church. The crowd had begun to scream and wail. Flames crawled up the walls like giant living things, sucking the strength from the timbers. Then in a final death throe, before the three men, staggering under their load, could reach the door, the remaining roof beams snapped and thundered to the floor. A gust of heat rolled outward from the inferno, and large coals and burning bits of wood were propelled into Lärchenplatz.

Shielding their faces, both Andrew and Brother Georg sketched a cross in the air, their lips moving in rote prayers for the souls of the unwise.

One at a time, the walls fell—the left one onto the cemetery, knocking gravestones askew; the other three rumbled onto the roof and then slid into the street that ran between the church and a row of incinerated hovels.

The fire was quieter now, and Andrew looked around him. Houses still burned down the hill; the fire had not yet reached the river. He could hear shouting, and the smoke blew eastward in a white cloud against the black sky. He felt faintly relieved that it had not rained, although he could not explain why.

"It is God's judgment," said Brother Georg quietly. "It is the fault of every fool, but most of all yours—" Andrew jumped at the accusation, but the monk continued, "—and mine and the bishop's."

Andrew felt his face burn red with the sudden memory of where the bishop had been during the fire.

"And where is our bishop?" asked Georg politely.

Andrew wondered if the man really cared—or already knew. No one must know. He tried to smile, and shrugged, but tears welled up in his eyes, and he turned abruptly to hide them.

Brother Georg gently clasped his shoulder. "It has been a hard night."

Andrew's headache, forgotten in the urgency of the fire, thudded once more behind his eyes. He turned and stumbled back to the bishop's residence.

Once inside, he did not hesitate, but walked deliberately toward the dining room, where he found a piece of stale bread and opened a flask of wine. He sat at the table and slowly ate his first meal in three days. Although he savored each taste of the hard bread and bitter wine, his conscience wrestled with his lack of piety. He ate and prayed, hoping for understanding and mercy—certain of his condemnation.

Dear God, forgive me for my weakness, but I cannot live a life for which I see no purpose. I shall confess—tomorrow or the next day; I shall do penance. He brushed the crumbs onto the fresh rushes that covered the floor. *And God . . . thank you that you have withheld from me the power to speak.*

NINE

athedral. The word contained magic and grandeur.

Martin sat on his doorstep in the afternoon sun and drew squiggly lines in the dust. His mind conjured up pictures of a magnificent edifice. The peace and quiet of the moment calmed him, and the horrifying events of the last twenty-four hours receded to that place in the mind where children can cope.

"A cathedral!" the bishop had exclaimed that morning, trying to encourage his demoralized congregation. There had been no glorious Easter procession. Instead, the townspeople had straggled into Lärchenplatz, heads bowed and hands dangling weakly at their sides. Few spoke or even greeted one another. They stood obediently in a dejected semicircle around the hastily built dais where the bishop stood.

When they dared to look up, they saw before them only the devastation; a quarter of their city in ruins. The hovels were a pile of charred stones and ashes. Blackened chimneys, like the uplifted arms of dark demons begging for mercy, reached toward heaven. Behind them, the vineyards, which had been pruned only the week before, no longer existed. The dead church—for the people could only see it as a slain thing—lay smoldering, tiny wisps of smoke rising straight up in the cool morning air. Heat still radiated from the remains, and the acrid smell filled their nostrils. They dared not look too long, lest they see the charred bodies of their relatives and friends, whose features had been obliterated by the violence of their deaths. For them, the townsfolk wore black.

The bishop dazzled them. Only the hem of his pure white cassock was gray from the puffs of ash stirred up by his fine, leather shoes. He stood before the ruined church like a ministering angel, his arms raised as if to embrace them. They lifted their sullen faces and tried to show their faith by smiling at the bishop.

"A cathedral! God has shown me that we should build a cathedral for His glory. From the ashes of this destruction will rise an edifice so modern and beautiful that people will come from all over the world to behold it. This has been Felsenburg's baptism of fire, which will cleanse this city and make us more worthy to please God. We can learn much from the foolishness of past generations, and this Easter Eve has taught us the truths in the Holy Scriptures.

"Your cathedral was built of wood, hay, and stubble, and it could not stand the test of fire. If it were built of gold, silver, and precious stones, God would be honored and great would be our reward for offering our best to Him.

"As God's chosen people, we must strive to please Him, to bring Him our gold, treasures, and talents to construct a building that will prove to Him that we are unworthy of such judgment." He swept his left arm in a wide arc to indicate the blackened ruins of the hovels, vineyards, and church.

"Search your hearts and see if He will not move you to sacrifice your worldly goods to build Him a house in which He may live."

From somewhere in the crowd, Brother Georg spoke up. "God does not live in temples made by hands."

The bishop pointed to him and chastened him gently, "God commanded Moses to build him a wonderful tent—a tabernacle. In it God lived, and the people came to it to worship Him."

"Moses did not take food from the mouths of children."

The bishop smiled over his flock. "Neither shall I. Give only from your abundance, from your hidden treasure. God will reward you with eternal life."

Martin sat now on the doorstep and thought about abundance and hidden treasure. He had neither and knew he never would. Nor did he ever want to die. He shuddered when he thought about those crushed by the red-hot timbers of the church ceiling.

"Martin, Bursch, what are you thinking about?" Papa did not have much time to spend with him, but Sundays were the best; and this day, Martin sensed a rare gentleness in his father. Papa sat down on the step beside him.

"It has been an awful day."

Papa nodded.

Martin drew another squiggle and then wiped them all out with his hand. "I want to help build the bishop's cathedral."

Papa scrubbed his head with his rough, brown hand. "I think you could. Certainly the master mason will need every able worker to complete such a remarkable task."

Martin looked at his father thoughtfully. "You will be the cathedral's master mason?"

Papa shrugged. "Who else?"

Martin stared at his dusty toes and wiggled them. "Papa, . . . I . . . I want to do more than mix mortar." He paused, trying to lure the thoughts in his head onto his tongue. "Papa, do I have talents?"

His father did not move, did not speak.

"Do I?"

"I don't know if any of us know except Father Augustin. Perhaps you should ask him." He stood and looked down at the tousled hair of his youngest son. "I think it's time to make you a true apprentice. I shall talk to the other masons." He turned and went back into the house.

Martin continued to stare at his toes. Why did Papa have to make it so difficult?

∽∾ ∽∾

Felsenburg wasted little time in self-pity. The town had experienced earthquakes, hurricanes, plagues, Viking raiders, and conflagrations greater than the present one; God rarely left them alone for long. On the surface, the town looked fragile, but underneath was a hard substrata of stamina and determination, which made it possible for the townspeople to turn their backs on the losses without feeling too much pain. In this spirit, they cleared away the ruined part of their town.

Count Robert von Immergrün, although still determined to finish his gatehouse before winter, paid his builders to assist the townspeople. He also sent his fighting men and many of his beasts of burden to expedite the clearing away of the burned debris.

The week following Easter was almost festive, as everyone met in the Lärchenplatz to work. Even a group of silent monks from St. Jude's came to handle the sacred task of removing the remains of the church. The bishop had set a guard out to protect it from looters. Although the priceless goblets, utensils, plates, and even the altars— some of them dating from the earliest church—had been melted down by the intense heat, the bishop planned to hire artisans to reshape them into beautiful things for the glory of God.

Martin's father and his masons had been put to work on the hovels. Little remained to be salvaged, so they knocked down the chimneys and foundations and piled the stones into carts to be removed from the square. Martin glanced over to where the monks worked in eerie stillness. They lifted the giant timbers from the cemetery and carried them into the street. No sooner had they laid them down than men produced saws and, with the Father Augustin's special blessing, sawed the beams into large chunks, which were stacked into tidy piles.

Throughout the morning, people who were not working in the platz came to make their purchases and conduct their business as usual. Martin watched them come and go, and at one point he noticed that the poorer people were carrying away the pieces of the church timbers.

Around noon, there was a shout from someone working at the church. It could have only been one of the monks. People left their work to see what had caused the monk to speak. They rushed to the church, but many withdrew just as quickly, making room for those who were witless enough to take their places.

Martin, too, pushed his way to the front of the crowd but was immediately sorry he had done so. A sickening stench rose from the blackened ruins, and the people shrank back in horror. Martin turned to run away, but it was already too late. He had seen the terrifying figure of death, lying at the feet of a pale, exhausted monk. Martin turned toward the people and looked into their frightened faces. Many of them had covered their mouths and noses in an attempt to filter out the smell of scorched, rotting flesh. But they did not move. A wail rose from one end of the crowd, as a wife or mother recognized her beloved. Frantic hands held her back from hurling herself onto the grisly figure.

Suddenly, Martin saw Cecilia craning her neck to see above the people in front of her. She slipped like a cat between them.

"Cecilia! Stop!" cried Martin, raising his hand to attract her attention.

She looked around and her cousin caught her eye. She changed direction, but kept on coming.

"Cecilia, wait. I'll come and help you." He shoved people aside and finally reached her. "Come." He grabbed her wrist and pulled her back the way she had come.

She struggled in his grasp, but his hands were strong from working the hoe in the mortar day after day. "Martin," she protested, "I wanted to see."

Finally they reached the back of the crowd. He relaxed his grip, and she pulled from him, flouncing back toward the crowd. "Cecilia!" He grabbed her again and shook her. "Don't be foolish," he gasped. "That . . . that man was dead. He smells terrible, and he looks even worse." Martin shuddered and let go of her, his own horror overwhelming him once more. He sank to the ground and buried his face in his hands. They smelled of death; everything smelled of death. He looked at Cecilia, who stood above him looking at him in disbelief. "Can't you smell it?" he whispered.

"I don't smell anything." She turned again to watch the crowd. "They've found something."

Martin's throat tightened in fear.

The murmuring of the crowd grew louder until someone shouted, "It's a miracle."

Cecilia, her eyes bright with joy, stooped to shake Martin's shoulder and to haul him to his feet. "Oh, it's a miracle. Look."

Cautiously, he turned and saw the pale monk holding above his head a small, golden rectangle, about the size of his hand.

"What can it be?" Cecilia pulled Martin toward the people again. "It's a picture. It's—" A slight breeze swirled through the Lärchenplatz. Cecilia gasped and clapped her hands over her mouth. "Oh, Martin, what is that stench?" she mumbled through her fingers.

"Death," he said simply.

It permeated the air now, and the two young people covered their mouths and noses with Cecilia's shawl and sank back into the crowd. The young monk held a small picture, framed in gold. Martin recognized it as the Madonna and Child that had hung over one of the side altars. She was swathed in gold, and all around her bloomed dark roses, outlined in gold.

"It's the Rosen Jungfrau!" exclaimed a woman next to her. "It's a miracle."

The crowd began to spread the word, until they were almost chanting, "It's a miracle." Martin was not sure why the finding of the Rosen Jungfrau was such a miracle, but he kept his thoughts to himself.

Someone had fetched Father Augustin, and the crowd grew still and parted like the waters of the Red Sea, closing behind him until he stood beside the monk. He held a snow-white handkerchief over his nose with one hand. The young man placed the golden picture reverently into the priest's other hand.

"It's a miracle. God has saved the Rosen Jungfrau from the flames," called another woman. Several people murmured assent.

"Yes, of course," agreed Father Augustin in measured tones. "We shall take it to the bishop for safekeeping."

The mother of the deceased suddenly broke away from the crowd and fell in the ashes at the priest's feet. She grabbed his hand and pulled the picture to her lips. Tears streamed down her cheeks as she turned toward the dazed onlookers. A strange smile lit her face. "My Eberhard gave his life to save the Rosen Jungfrau," she cried triumphantly. She pulled the picture from the hand of Father Augustin and held it toward the crowd. Several friends and relatives suddenly clustered around and kissed the picture with a fervor sparked by grief.

Father Augustin stood by helplessly, unsure of his duty.

"Martin, come," said Cecilia, "We must kiss the picture too. It will bring us good luck."

"You can't mean that," he protested. "Celia, that man is dead. The sight of it will frighten you."

Cecilia pulled away from his touch. "Some people," she said coldly, "are just better Christians than others." She stalked toward those waiting their turn to kiss the Rosen Jungfrau, while Martin looked on in bewilderment.

Papa remained within the ruins of the hovels. Even talk of a miracle would not lure him to show his faith publicly. He worked slower than usual, though, glancing from time to time toward the crowd. Martin ambled back to him. He picked up a rock and tossed it into one of the carts. They worked in silence until the crowd dispersed. Finally Papa spoke. "Faith makes fools of us all," he said.

Martin did not know how to answer, and he was saved the trouble by the voice of a man.

"Herr Steinmetz?"

Papa straightened up and looked at the speaker. He was a young man, dressed in poor rags and clutching a tattered cloak around his neck.

"Was this your house?" asked Papa sympathetically.

"No. We . . . my wife and I . . . have always lived against the city wall. But we want to have our own home."

Papa nodded and kicked at a charred timber.

"I . . . we . . . wondered if you were going to rebuild these houses?"

"Probably. Count Robert won't let people spend a winter in the open."

"It . . . it would be nicer if you used new stones for the foundation instead of these."

"The count will not use these," said Papa with the confidence of the count's master mason. "The strength is burned out of them."

"I . . . would you consent to sell the stones here in the cart?"

"They're not mine to sell, but I think that they are to be thrown away."

"May we . . . could we do you the favor of removing them for you?"

Papa looked at Martin and winked. Then he looked around at the other laborers who had returned to their work and were oblivious to the conversation. "You would be doing me a great favor if you did. I was going to dump them beside the eastern wall of the city." He carried another stone to the cart and threw it in. "Just bring the cart back," he said quietly.

"Oh, thank you, sir. I will, sir. God bless you."

Papa turned his back on the young man and gazed at Martin a long time before a slow smile spread across his face.

TEN

ndrew, my brother, is everything organized?" The bishop lowered himself into his richly upholstered chair and picked up his cup of wine.

Andrew nodded. Just after Easter the invitations had been sent to the canons in the bishopric. The canons were secular clergy, and they made up the cathedral chapter, an organization responsible for the construction and upkeep of the cathedral. Although the cathedral was primarily the bishop's building and the focal point of the diocese, the cathedral chapter controlled the money collected from the people of Felsenburg and the surrounding areas. A few of them were also responsible for their own churches, and they knew the region and its people. The men had all accepted promptly and were expected to arrive two days before Pentecost. Andrew had learned from the cook and the housekeeper that the usual rooms had been assigned to the distinguished guests.

"It is a bit premature for this meeting," the bishop admitted, "but one cannot always plan disasters like fires, can one? Surely it was a sign from God that we should proceed."

Andrew, slouched in his chair, smiled slightly, and sipped from his cup.

"I do hope that I can convince them of the wisdom of beginning the rebuilding right away. I should like to contact a certain Titus of Athens—a student of Cleopas—to oversee the construction of the cathedral. Perhaps it's not too late to send a letter to him this summer, and he can plan to arrive next spring. Then we can draw up the plans for my cathedral—"

Andrew's head popped up suddenly. *Your cathedral?* he thought.

"You don't approve?" the bishop asked with a smile. "My apologies. You scribes are such sticklers for semantics. Anyone else would know exactly what I mean, but for you the words have to be exact. All right, then, we will plan *God's* building."

Andrew tore off a piece of bread and dipped it into his wine to soften it.

"Andrew, normally I find your silence refreshing—easy on the ears. But now and then I get the impression that you have a very lot to say and none of it would please me a bit. How loyal are you?"

Andrew set down his food and held both palms open upon the table to indicate his openness. *I am a hypocrite and a coward,* he thought, *but I shall be loyal to you until I have someone else to whom I can turn.*

"Yes, I can see your innocence. Perhaps you mock us both. It might be useful to us if we developed a few hand-signs to facilitate communication between us. For example—" He made a fist and pointed his thumb to the ceiling. "—this could mean that you agree, and this—" He turned his thumb downward. "—that you don't. Which would you use more often, Andrew?"

Andrew shrugged and smiled, hoping that his cynicism did not shine through his eyes. *Communication I do not need. It is very good that I cannot say what I think.*

⌦ ⌦

The canons arrived throughout the afternoon and evening. Weary from their travels, they took supper in their rooms. The following morning, Mass was said at seven in the little chapel adjacent to the bishop's residence, after which they walked back to the chapter house, a sort of dormitory and meeting place for the canons. This was a large utilitarian building stuck off in a corner of the bishop's garden. It had been built according to the specifications of the previous bishop, who had intended for his canons to live in Felsenburg.

As that bishop rarely lived in the city himself, he had been unable to enforce his wishes. Although some canons preferred the dormitory, which distanced them from the people, most chose to live in their parishes, rubbing elbows every day with the people and, in some cases, enjoying their own property.

The bishop ushered the men into the large room built for conferences. It was dominated by a huge, shining oak table with chairs set around it. On one side of the room were tall, narrow windows, but little light came in, as the hedges outside were overgrown. Across from the windows, the bishop's own coat of arms hung on the wall, flanked by two French tapestries depicting the death and resurrection of the Lord. At the end opposite the door, a fire burned brightly in the open fireplace, banishing the bone-chilling cold, which clung to the thick stone walls even in summer. The bishop's chair had been brought from his study and placed at the end of the table nearest the fire.

Andrew's little scribe's table was not far away. He entered the room unobtrusively and slipped onto the stool. The bishop had stressed the import of recording everything that would take place as he talked with the canons.

"Dear brothers," Bishop Gernot began as he stood at the head of the table, "I do appreciate your coming on such short notice. And I do regret that the circumstances behind this meeting are so tragic, but I hope that we may find joy in rebuilding God's house."

Andrew had already written the one word, "Welcome," on the parchment and had been watching the faces of the men throughout the bishop's speech.

The first man to speak was Canon Wilfred from Badenbach. He was a bit more than middle-aged and slightly overweight. His pudgy face crinkled into a pleasant smile. "Excellenz," he began, "I believe that we could have great joy building a cathedral. That we need one is obvious." He leaned forward eagerly, tapping his stubby fingers on the table for emphasis. He expressed his regrets with a touch of hope. "What is not so obvious is the finances."

Bishop Gernot raised his eyebrows and queried, "Finances? The coffers of every other cathedral and church in Europe are full. What happened?"

"I don't wish to speak ill of the dead," Wilfred apologized, "But this bishopric is relatively poor and Bishop Marcel—God rest his soul—did not concern himself with the building. Consequently, there is very little money for that purpose, and the few valuable pieces that we could have used to raise money are now unidentifiable blobs of gold retrieved from the ashes of St. Nathaniel's. Finance is our number one problem."

"Do the rest of you concur?" asked the bishop.

"Concurring is not our prerogative," grumbled Sigismund von Steyer without looking up from the table. "It is Wilfred's job to know. Just as it is Peter Fabian's to oversee this group of men—this chapter. Peter is the dean."

Bishop Gernot sat down abruptly and gripped the carved arms of his chair for control. "I see," he said evenly, "Have I overstepped my boundaries?" He nodded toward his right, where Peter Fabian, the frail overseer of the chapter, sat.

Wilfred looked from Sigismund's scowling face to Peter's, whose pale blue eyes were watering with embarrassment. "Some might think so," Peter admitted with a small smile, "but perhaps this bishopric could use a little more involvement from its bishop than it is accustomed to."

Across from Peter, on the bishop's left, Hugo Aichinger, the former dean and the oldest member of the chapter, cleared his throat and explained, "Bishop Marcel spent his summer months in Felsenburg; otherwise he lived in Vichy."

In the uneasy silence that followed this criticism of the previous bishop, Andrew suddenly remembered that he was supposed to be writing. He dipped his pen and began.

The bishop glanced around the table and let out a dramatic sigh. "Peter Fabian, would you prefer that I allow you to continue?"

Peter rubbed his eyes and wiped the moisture on the front of his cassock. "I did not invite us here, Excellenz," he said in a small apologetic voice, "and I hardly know what your purpose is, so I would prefer that you carry on."

"Any objections?" Bishop Gernot waited for an answer.

Sigismund continued to glare at a spot just behind Wilfred's head. Father Augustin studied his hands, which were folded neatly upon the shiny oak table. Hugo Aichinger silently tried to communicate something to Peter, who studiously kept his eyes fastened on the bishop's Adam's apple. Young Julian, whose cancelled Easter procession would have been so glorious, looked around the table, trying to find a clue to his own convictions. The other men, including Father Augustin, joined with Wilfred in quiet assent.

The bishop looked at Wilfred. "Let's not talk about the money for a moment." He glanced around the table and then said, "I have asked Father Augustin if he would do us the honor of joining us. He is prepared to give up his duties in favor of assisting us in rebuilding St. Nathaniel's."

Most of the men nodded, and Sigismund von Steyer mumbled, "Good decision."

Bishop Gernot cleared his throat and said, "What you may not like as well is that I have a request."

Andrew glanced up to see how these canons would react to Bishop Gernot's "request," which would, in all probability, become compulsory.

The bishop continued. "Building a cathedral is an enormous task. It is our obligation to the people, our duty to God, and the dictates of our church. We cannot complete this responsibility if we are divided."

Peter Fabian was already shaking his head, guessing what was to come.

"It is necessary that the canons of this bishopric unite their wills and their talents under one roof so that the construction can commence as soon as possible."

The men broke out into unanimous, unintelligible protest.

"The dormitory is a disgrace!"

"I cannot leave my parish!"

"I live near enough!"

Pushing himself to his feet, Bishop Gernot held up his hands for silence. "Please let me finish." The objections died down, and the bishop continued, "As you have guessed, I am asking you to move to Felsenburg. You may choose to disregard my request if you like, but in so doing, you will be resigning from the chapter. There are others who can be trained to replace those of you whose duties or loyalties make it impossible for you to make the change."

He paused, and the silence was broken only by the crackle of burning logs in the fireplace. "Shall I go on?" He continued without hesitation, "We will renovate the dormitory for those of you who wish to live there. It is also high time that the bishop of Felsenburg founded a school. One floor of the dormitory will house the deserving students. I do not know you well enough yet, but I am sure that one of you would make an excellent chancellor for the cathedral school. I shall also be appointing an archdeacon to assist me in the many tasks that will be my responsibility. I sense already that wintering in Vichy will be an impossibility."

A few of the canons smiled at his humor. Everyone shifted and seemed to relax.

The bishop sat down again and looked at Wilfred. "As the treasurer, what would be your recommendation for improving the financial predicament this diocese is in?"

"We could go to the people and ask them to give for a glorious new cathedral."

Father Augustin spoke for the first time. "We've already done that. Georg is a problem."

"Georg?" asked Wilfred.

"Oh, forgive me," Father Augustin said patronizingly, "I had forgotten that you don't live here in the city. Georg is a troublemaking renegade monk bent on destroying the church."

"I wouldn't put it quite that way," corrected the bishop. "He simply has a strong sense of social justice and has not been able to understand that each man must fulfill his foreordained destiny."

"I find that a bit difficult myself, now and then," admitted Wilfred.

The bishop considered Wilfred a moment before he asked, "And do you find that your duties as treasurer are in any way hampered?"

"I haven't been put to the test," he answered slowly, "but I expect that I would show mercy to the very poor."

"The poor are the greatest givers," the bishop spoke with gentle admonishment, "and our Lord Himself commended the widow who gave everything she had. Her blessing in heaven was secured."

Wilfred opened his mouth to answer but snapped it shut.

Julian jumped up suddenly and strode to the window. "I have a large estate inherited from my father. I am his only child." He paused and rubbed the side of his large nose thoughtfully. "I will gladly give a portion of it to build a cathedral to our wonderful Savior."

Andrew, surprised by the lack of a reaction among the men, looked up. Each canon seemed to be composing his face into the demeanor he wished the others to see. The bishop, sensing the unwillingness of anyone else to be put on the spot, quickly said, "That would be wonderful, but your offer is a bit premature." Julian's shoulders sagged, and he leaned against the windowsill and folded his arms, tucking his hands into the opposite sleeves of his cassock.

"There's always the Rosen Jungfrau," said Father Augustin helpfully.

Puzzled, several men murmured to one another, but Wilfred understood at once. "Yes, I have heard about it. Please tell us."

Bishop Gernot gestured to Father Augustin, who cleared his throat and rearranged his hands on the shiny table. "When the monks removed the rubble of the church, they also had to move the bodies of the unfortunates who died in the fire. One of the monks found an image of the Rosen Jungfrau, grasped in the hands of one of the dead men. It had been totally preserved from harm."

"You must understand what this meant to the people," explained the bishop. "Every other piece was destroyed, but the picture of the Virgin was miraculously saved."

"Are we sure it was a miracle?" asked Wilfred boldly. "If it was pinned beneath his body, that might make it more of an understandable occurrence."

Father Augustin unfolded his hands and lay his right palm down on the table to demonstrate his patience as he explained. "We couldn't find out the whole story until several hours after the monk had found the picture, but he remembered that it was merely clutched in the man's fingers, totally exposed to the fire. When he tried to pull the picture from his hand, the blackened fingers crumbled into ashes."

Hugo Aichinger covered his face with his hands, and Peter Fabian bit his bottom lip to still the sudden trembling. Julian turned abruptly to look out the window.

"What are you proposing then?" asked Sigismund.

Augustin carefully regarded each man at the table, considering how his words would be taken.

"The people believe that a great miracle took place. If only you could have seen them. Young and old came to pay homage to the dead and to kiss the face of the dear Virgin, who lived through a literal hell."

"News of this miracle must be spread far and wide," said Hugo, who immediately comprehended the significance of Father Augustin's words. "People will come to view her and to pay their last respects to the men who died to save her. Those who come will naturally give, and in giving they will in a sense be saving up for their own eternal life."

"We could collect much money—for the new cathedral, of course—without placing a great burden upon the people in Felsenburg," marveled Wilfred.

The bishop nodded and bestowed a smile upon Father Augustin. "Yes," he said, "The hope of eternal life loosens many purse strings."

ELEVEN

ndrew fidgeted and forced his quill to write in a straight line as the bishop dictated to him. "Please do me the honor of sending me your answer at once with my messenger. Actually, I covet your presence as soon as you can possibly come. With God's blessings, I warmly greet you as Gernot von Kärnten, Bishop of Felsenburg."

The tip of the pen caught on the parchment and snapped off, splattering ink over both the letter and Andrew's chin.

"Dear brother," exclaimed the bishop in disbelief, "I have never seen you make even the tiniest error. And now you have made enough mess for a year."

Andrew's mouth curved into a grim smile.

"I hope you are not ill?"

The young monk shook his head and wiped his chin.

"Now you've made it worse. You look like a chimney sweep." Bishop Gernot signaled for him to leave the room. "Go! Clean yourself up and then come back. I have another task for you."

Andrew restrained the desire to run. He washed in his own room and then stalked back to the bishop's study. The bishop stood before an open window, the spring breeze ruffling the yards of fabric that hung around his body. He was mumbling to himself and stopped at once when he caught sight of Andrew out of the corner of his eye.

"Ja, Andrew. Much better. After you have recopied the letter—" he paused to give his words importance. "—I would like you to deliver it." He paused again for more emphasis. "You are the only one I can trust."

Andrew gulped, swallowing the nausea that swept over him, and lowered himself onto his scribe's stool.

"Are you sure that you are not ill?"

Nodding weakly, Andrew reached for a freshly cut quill. He dipped it into the ink and, in a wobbly script, explained why he could not possibly travel to Milan to deliver a letter.

"Excellenz, I have never traveled anywhere, except from St. Jude's to Felsenburg." He paused and rubbed the feather across his cheek.

Bishop Gernot leaned over him and read the lines. "You are afraid?" he asked with a hint of indifference.

Afraid? *Dear God in heaven, yes I am afraid,* thought Andrew and gripped the quill tighter. "My lack of experience might be a hindrance to the prompt delivery of your missive," he wrote.

The bishop read the line and then scrutinized Andrew for a moment before he asked, "You have so little confidence in your abilities?"

"No experience," he wrote hastily.

"Titus is not difficult to find. Anyone in Milan will tell you where he is."

Anyone? The quill poised above the parchment, Andrew hesitated, uncertain how to continue. Finally he wrote: "I am sure that I could find him. My lack of experience is in travel. Besides, I cannot communicate well with people, and I may need to ask for help."

"You speak—excuse me—understand several languages, and any learned man knows Latin. Andrew, I do not understand. I am giving you a chance to leave Felsenburg, to discover the world. It will be a long winter, and Milan will be warm and balmy." He paused, savoring the sensations in his imagination. "Are you sure that you don't want to go?"

In bold letters he wrote, "I don't wish to go."

Bishop Gernot waved his arms in frustration and paced the length of the room. He returned to the table and bent over Andrew's paper. "Who else can I send?" he demanded of the scribe. "Who else can I trust?"

Questions. Always questions, mused Andrew. He wondered why the bishop had such a sudden need to find someone trustworthy. "One of the count's knights?" he wrote, "Or another of the monks from St. Jude's. Or Father Augustin?"

The bishop's eyes sparkled, and he straightened up with sudden inspiration. "Or Brother Georg! That would accomplish a couple of things."

Andrew bit his lip. He could think of no one who inspired less trust. "He would never leave his group," Andrew scribbled. "Can you trust him?"

"I trust you. He would simply be your guide and spokesman. And if he took his flock with him, that is all the better for us."

Andrew dipped the quill again and underlined, "I don't wish to go."

"And if God wills it?"

There it was: a powerful man invoking God's authority to direct the destiny of the powerless. Andrew laid the pen down and bowed his head. Ever since he could remember, God's will, expressed in this manner, had intruded into every corner of his life. As a child, when Brother Viktor had carved him a horse out of a piece of firewood, the abbot made it very clear that it was not God's will for the boy to wile away the hours in frivolity. Despite the harsh instructions, Andrew still had snatched moments from his solitude to play with the horse, but he enjoyed it less because he feared he would be discovered.

At the monastery, he had learned that it was God's will for some to work, some to fight, and some to pray. That few of them had any choice was also foremost—ordained by the Almighty. He thanked God—or perhaps it was St. Andrew or the Blessed Virgin or someone else with more influence than he—that Abbot Konrad had discovered that the little mute boy, who thirsted for knowledge, could also write a pretty line. Andrew had been content within the confines of the monastery. All he had ever wanted to do was copy and meditate on Scripture.

He could remember a time when he had longed to travel. At that time it was not "God's will," however, and the young man soon resigned himself to the idea of never experiencing the outside world.

Brother Viktor had assured him that it was better that way; too many temptations lurked outside the gates of the abbey, and a young monk's soul was safer inside.

Now Andrew was reminded of the field mouse he had caught for a pet when he was about ten. He had put it in a wooden box and fed it wheat, pilfered from the granary. But the ungrateful creature had spent all of its nocturnal hours gnawing holes in the box. When Andrew finally realized that it was impossible to keep a mouse, he carried the creature's little home to the apple orchard and laid it on its side so that the mouse could climb out. He sat beside that box for over two hours because the stubborn mouse had suddenly developed a fear of the outside world and remained curled up in its nest to sleep. With a heavy heart, Andrew had finally dumped nest and all into a hole at the base of a tree. *It is God's will that you run free*, he had thought. But even then it seemed that God's will was capricious and His victims helpless.

Andrew looked up at the bishop, who was again staring out the window. *I shall go to Milan, but perhaps we will all live to regret it.*

TWELVE

he reason the Johannes Fire was held outside of the city was tradition, not fear of another conflagration. Every year at the summer solstice, the younger citizens of Felsenburg met after dark outside of town and built bonfires. The children of the masons had their own traditional knoll with an excellent view. They would bring sausages and roast them over the coals, after which they would lie in the meadow and watch the stars. They all knew that they were observing an ancient ritual, but none of them really believed in heathen gods. The old celebration had evolved into a sacred holiday to commemorate the conception and birth of John the Baptist, and the old customs had acquired new significance.

Martin was not sure of the significance, but he certainly did not want to call the holiday into question. Every summer since he was old enough to be out on this very special night, he had hauled wood up the knoll with the other boys to build a fire that could be seen from far away. This year as he stacked the branches into a cone-shaped pile, he looked forward to the evening with a strange excitement that he had never felt before. He did not fully understand why until he saw Cecilia come out of the city gate with the other girls.

The sun had gone down, and although the sunset was not colorful, the air had that rare quality that made the coming night seem soft. The clear arc of the heavens changed in a perfect blend from deep blue in the east, through gray, to a band of creamy bright light where the sun had hidden behind the mountains' silhouette. The girls seemed to float up the knoll like pale moths in the dusky light.

Martin ran to meet Cecilia and took her basket from her. She smiled warmly, but when he reached out his free hand for hers, she clasped her hands together and said bluntly, "Mutti told me to be careful."

"Careful?" Martin echoed.

She shook her head and the corners of her mouth turned down in exasperation. "Shhh. I'll try to explain later."

Martin had already spread his cloak on the knoll, facing southeast. The other years, he had not wanted to be seen with his cousin but romped with the other boys, talking about the girls but never with them. Now he was hesitant to ask her: "Do—would you like to sit with me?"

Again she shook her head. "Maybe later," she whispered and returned to her friends.

The young men lit the fire to the appreciative squeals of the young women. When it was burning well, the girls opened their baskets and handed out sausages to be roasted in the flames.

Martin sat on his cloak and chewed on a charred sausage. The dew was settling, and he was glad for the warmth of the fire. In the west, the light had faded, and the stars, especially in the east, shone brightly. He watched Cecilia laughing and talking with her friends and tried to banter with his own friends, but he wished he could be near her. He leaned back and watched the orange sparks rise straight up to where they seemed to join the constellation Cassiopeia, a brilliant zigzag in the darkness.

"Martin?" Cecilia's soft voice was so close to his ear that he could feel the warmth of her breath. He turned to find her kneeling on his cloak.

He sat up. "Please, sit down," he said firmly, suddenly realizing that if he could stop feeling so giddy, he would be able to stop frightening her.

She sat and pulled her knees up to her chin, hiding her feet under her skirt and wrapping her arms around her knees. "Isn't the fire beautiful?"

Martin did not want to talk about the fire. "Tell me what your mother said," he prompted.

She sighed and would not look at Martin as she said, "She told me not to lie beside any of the boys. She wouldn't say why."

Martin searched through the things that he had learned from the other young men and from his brother, and he said, "I think I know why."

She did not inquire. "Mutti said that she did it, and she was sorry."

"I think someone hurt her."

She nodded and murmured, "I think it was my father."

Martin did not know what to say. He did not like his uncle and did not find it difficult to believe that the man would hurt poor Tante Maria.

His silence disturbed her, though, and she started to get up from the ground.

He reached out and pulled her back. "Cecilia, I would never hurt you. You can trust me."

"I know," she said, gently pulling her hand away. "At least, I think I know. But Mutti said you never can tell."

Tante Maria was going to be a problem.

"Oh, Martin, look!" she said, suddenly excited. She pointed straight ahead to where dozens of other bonfires burned upon other hills. "Just think, hundreds of years ago, human sacrifices were made on these hills on this day, and the bonfires burned."

"Cecilia, you're gruesome!"

She laughed. "Don't you come out here to be scared—just a little?"

"I always think of Opa Peter, buried right over there."

Every year, a few days before the summer solstice, Martin and Cecilia's families celebrated the death day of their grandfather Peter, who had died before either of the cousins could remember. After they had paid the priest to say a Mass for Opa, they would go to the graveyard to pray at the grave. He was buried in the cemetery that was located not far from this knoll. In the section of the cemetery that had been set aside for the craftsmen of the city, Martin's mother was determined that Opa's grave would perpetually demonstrate how much they had loved him. She would bring tools and flowers and would set the family to work, pulling weeds and planting primroses around the perimeter of the grave. Papa and Onkel Hans always stood by and watched, but Mama and Tante Maria did most of the work. Martin wondered if Opa really cared. This year, when Stefan and Klara had showed up, lugging Bernie, the family had lit their candles and made their petitions to God on behalf of Opa. Perhaps someday, when Opa was out of purgatory and securely in paradise, he would intercede for them.

In the meantime, it was possible that he haunted the meadows while the young people danced around their bonfire. Martin shivered and tried to see if Cecilia looked frightened.

All of a sudden, she flopped down on her back beside him. "Aren't the stars beautiful?"

He did not want to talk about the stars either.

"Look! A shooting star," she exclaimed. "Maybe it's the end of the world."

"Cecilia."

She turned to look up at him. Her shawl fell from her head, and she did not put it back. The golden firelight behind her played over her face and polished her hair.

"Cecilia, do you ever wonder things?"

"Like what?"

"Like how God talks to the bishop. Or how you can serve God best. Or why you were born into the family you were born into."

"Not those things. Do you get answers?"

"No," Martin had to admit.

"Don't you like your family?"

"Of course I do, silly, but—" Shifting his position, he looked back out toward the dark hills where the bonfires hung like tiny flames in the night.

She reached over and took his hand, and she was his cousin again and not a girl to whom he was wildly attracted. "You can trust me."

"You already know: I don't want to be a mason. But Papa's determined. My initiation is this week, and I really don't want to do it."

"You were born into the family," she said matter-of-factly.

"I know." He lay back on the cloak and pulled her hand onto his chest. "But Sepp Feick is the baker's son," he protested, "and he's going to school this autumn."

She wrinkled her nose. "School?"

"Sepp says the bishop is going to start a school this autumn. It's where great men go to learn to read the Holy Scriptures." He sighed and added, "But Papa doesn't want me to be a great man."

"Maybe something will happen to change your father's mind." She squeezed his hand.

"I don't think that anything will change his mind. I want to learn to read."

"That sounds harder than laying stone."

He said nothing. They lay for several minutes, listening to the movement of the embers as they shifted and settled. Frogs sang. The black dome of sky rose above them, with the countless stars filling it.

Finally Martin asked, "What things do you wonder?"

She shivered.

Martin sat up and pulled her with him. Clumsily he wrapped the cloak around her shoulders while she refastened her shawl.

"I wonder . . . I wonder if God can really see us."

Martin could not understand why she would want to know. "Would it matter?"

She laughed and pulled the cloak tighter around herself. "I don't know. Maybe. If He could see me, He would know everything I did. If I was very good, I wouldn't mind, but if I was bad—" Her voice trailed off, but then she seemed to pull her thoughts together and continued. "There are very bad people in the world. Surely if God could see us, He would do something about that."

Martin shrugged. "If He could."

She exclaimed, "Martin! Of course He *could*." She paused and then said with regret, "I don't think He can see us."

The fire was almost out, and the other young people gathered their belongings. A few had wandered off in pairs, and Martin had an idea where they were going. He could not bear the thought of anyone's being with Cecilia. He pulled her to her feet and found her basket. When he reached for her hand, this time she linked her small, cold fingers with his. Together they walked back into Felsenburg, surrounded by their friends, but alone in their thoughts.

THIRTEEN

ount Robert did not plan to use charred stones for his rebuilding project, but the cathedral chapter did not share the same compunctions. Aware of the excellence of the Steinmetz family's stone masonry, Canon Wilfred commissioned Martin's father to build a temporary shrine to house the Rosen Jungfrau. Although the decision to erect the small building had been delayed by bickering within the cathedral chapter, pressure was now on the builders to begin as soon as possible. The shrine was to be situated on the former site of the eastern-most hovel at the edge of Lärchenplatz and was to be built exclusively of timbers and stones taken from the burned church. Much of this debris still lay in ugly piles in Lärchenplatz.

Papa beamed with pleasure when he came home with the news and a skin of wine.

"We are celebrating. I have finally come to the attention of the bishop. We shall soon be able to afford a nicer home." He sloshed wine into the crude cups of each family member.

"I have even heard that the bishop will be looking for the finest local artisans for his cathedral," said Stefan proudly. "Papa, if you become the bishop's master mason, we will all live securely for many years."

Martin, who had been adding wood to the fire when his father came in, now rose and accepted his cup of wine. Wine he liked because it tasted like fruit, but this was not good wine.

"Martin," Father announced cheerfully, "tomorrow evening we will introduce you to the secrets of the masons. You will have a part in the building of the great cathedral—" He paused to empty his cup. "—beginning, of course, with the shrine."

The boy forced a smile to his lips, hoping that his father would not notice his unhappiness.

Papa strode into his and Mama's room, emerging a minute later with a dark brown, wooden box in his hands.

"What's that?" Klara asked.

"Nothing for you," Papa assured her with a wink. "The secrets of masonry." He set the box carefully on the table and folded his arms. "Tomorrow, Bursch, all will be revealed to you. In the morning," Papa instructed, "you will go to confess your sins to Father Augustin. Your heart must be pure before you can be trusted with secrets."

Martin longed to please his father, and he hoped that, somehow, he might also be allowed to learn to read.

"Where are you going to meet?" Mama asked. "The mason's shed burned with the church."

"Here," stated Papa bluntly. "You and Klara can take the baby to Maria's. We'll have the food and ale brought from the inn."

Mama bit her lip but said nothing. Martin glanced around their comfortable little home and thought of the times he had been forced to clean the mason's shed after a meeting. He did not want his initiation to cause Mama so much work, but he did not dare object.

⚯ ⚯

He had every reason to be concerned. The morning after the mason's meeting, Martin awoke with a terrible taste in his mouth. When he opened his eyes, they felt as if they might pop out of his skull, so he quickly closed them again. Even moving his head caused it to throb. Somewhere on the fuzzy edges of his thoughts hovered something important, which he could not quite recall. With infinite care, he pushed himself up to a sitting position. Shielding his eyes from the brightness of the dim room, he peered around.

Papa, Onkel Hans, and Stefan slept on the floor, their syncopated snores assaulting Martin's ears. Vaguely, Martin could remember when the rest of the men had left, but most of the evening was a dark blur of ale and laughter, firelight and chants. Everyone had been in a bad mood, and Martin had to think a minute to remember why they had been happy at the beginning of the evening.

Initiation. Yesterday morning Martin had gone to confess his sins, but he had not been able to think of any. Of course, he always felt guilty for disobeying Mama and for teasing Klara, but those were not the things that Father Augustin wanted to hear. He finally decided to admit lust toward a woman, for he had heard from some of his friends that those sins were the best. But when Father Augustin asked him which woman, he refused to answer. He would not drag anyone else into his falsehood.

After supper Mama had stoked the fire and then went with Klara to Tante Maria's, carrying Bernie in his basket. The masons kept crowding into the little house until loud, smelly men were sprawled everywhere. Papa and Martin were sitting at the table in front of the fireplace. Before them stood two tankards of the dark, bitter brew that only men drank. Martin grimaced with every swallow but did not complain.

"Martin, Bursch, masonry is not just a job, but it is a sacred trust. Since the days of the early Greeks, the gods have entrusted to a few the ability to understand geometry. It seems to run in the blood, and you possess, no doubt, an understanding that will guide you when my poor words fail."

Martin watched his father's mouth open and close. Rarely had he heard his father deliver such a long speech. The atmosphere was charged with a spookiness that he could not understand and did not like.

Papa looked suddenly at Martin's tankard, which was still almost full. "You don't like it?"

Martin shook his head shyly. "No, Papa."

The men chuckled and Papa said, "No matter. You'll like it someday. It numbs the heart."

Martin wanted to ask why anyone would want such a thing, but Papa was ready to continue.

"Architecture is more than just knowing how to place one stone upon another. There are forces and powers that we must conquer or harness. Remember: wind, rain, cold, heat, and time are our enemies." His words trickled to a halt, and he stared reflectively into the fire. Then he drank deeply from his tankard and smacked his lips. "Fire," he said finally. "Perhaps someday we shall build a building that cannot burn."

He paused again while the others murmured appreciatively. "You will learn many things that you must not tell anyone except your fellow masons. God has made us the sole possessors of all knowledge of geometry and architecture. Guard this knowledge carefully, and it will serve you well. Spread it around to those unworthy of such knowledge, and that which is a golden gift will become soiled."

Martin squirmed uncomfortably. Papa was speaking as if the words were not his. They were infused with a strange power that seemed to have taken control of his father.

"When we return to work, you will no longer mix mortar, but you will watch and learn from us." He waved his tankard around at the other men. "At first we will give you simple jobs to do, but do not underestimate their importance. You must first learn the elementary points of masonry." He stood and stretched. After guzzling his remaining beer, he bent over and tapped Martin's tankard. "Drink up, Bursch, a good mason never leaves a cup undrained, or else the host would be offended."

Martin had obeyed, but now that morning had come, he regretted that he had. His eyes wandered painfully to the table on which sat the wooden box. The lid was askew, and the various instruments were scattered upon the table.

Fighting nausea, Martin struggled to his feet and crept carefully to the table. Sitting on a stool, he held his head in his hands for a while until the dizziness passed, then he picked up the first instrument. It was two thin metal rods, each twice as long as his hand. The rods were heavy and pointed on one end, and the blunt ends were hinged together. He could not remember what it was called, but with it you could make perfect circles in an infinite number of sizes, the largest with a diameter the length of his arm. Onkel Hans had also said that it was useful for dividing angles.

There was another called a square, although it wasn't; it was only two sides of a square. Papa said that it helped to make the buildings square. A tiny image of St. Barbara lay in the box along with several good-luck charms. The plumb line had been returned to the box last night, after Onkel Hans had remarked that he could draw a circle the size of the room if someone stood in the center and held one end of the string. Everyone laughed at him, and his cup was refilled with ale.

In fact, the ale flowed so freely, Papa ran out long before he wanted to. He could not get more because the inn was closed. Christian Mauer had made a loud fuss, and Papa had kicked him out, but not before Christian had been sick all over the rushes. Soon after, the others left, complaining about the smell and the lack of drink. Papa had thrown the filthy rushes out the door after them and then had fallen onto the floor where he now slept.

Martin rested his head upon his arms and listened to the morning noises. A creaking cart passed by the door, then a mother with several noisy children. Stefan stirred in his sleep and turned on his side. Martin idly traced some of the grooves on the table with his fingers, and with a rush he recalled the highlight of the past rowdy evening. Papa had taught him to write the family's mark. *S*. He would write it upon every structure that the Steinmetz men built. *S*. "I can read it," the boy whispered with joy. He had seen the mark many times as he had worked with his father. "I know what it means now. I can read."

∽∾ ∽∾

It was not easy to build the shrine for the Rosen Jungfrau. Papa's excitement had worn off quickly as he hired people to work with the inferior materials. The stonecutter, employed to shape the stones to the specified dimensions, grumbled about the impossibility of getting a clean cut from rock that was riddled with heat fissures. The carpenter, who was to frame the roof, complained of the difficulty of sawing crumbling lumber. At the end of every day, they all gladly escaped the work site, looking more like chimney sweeps than artisans.

When the materials were finally prepared, Martin began learning the real trade of stone masonry. He had been carrying mortar for many years, but now he must learn to determine the consistency of the mortar.

Where the cut stone had not provided a clean surface, they first had to wash off the greasy soot, so that the mortar would stick. Martin learned quickly how to judge the exact amount of mortar for each stone. He would smooth it evenly to the edges of the stone, and then Papa would position the next stone. Martin was fascinated by Papa's ability to smooth the joints so that they were practically invisible.

Stefan, having completed his apprenticeship, worked alone to build the steps to the altar. Onkel Hans was always late to work. Impressed by the sacredness of the task, he appeared before Father Augustin every morning to receive a blessing for his daily work. For once he was not drunk on the job, but his years of drinking had impaired his abilities so much that he was of little help.

In four weeks, though, they were finished. As Martin stood with his family and the other masons on the dedication day, he felt a fierce pride that he had really helped to build the shrine.

It was not an attractive structure. The banks of spring flowers, which the women and children had piled on its two sides, improved the appearance considerably. The entire shrine was black. It was perhaps a little longer and wider than a man is tall, and twice as high. Two pairs of black stone steps led up to the altar, where perhaps four people at a time could kneel and pray. The altar would normally be protected behind a heavy black ornamental gate. For the dedication, the gate had been unlocked and swung open to allow access to the Rosen Jungfrau. Candles in golden holders burned upon the altar, illuminating the glittering, gold filigree frame, which the bishop had commissioned to set off the small, dark portrait from the black interior. Mounted in the two side walls were narrow windows of crown glass to shed light upon the Madonna when the candles were not burning. Over the whole was a gabled roof of charred timbers.

The bishop's dedication concentrated on the miracle of the surviving picture. "It was not because of the goodness of the rescuer that our beloved Jungfrau Maria's image was preserved. Her own goodness radiates from our reminders of her. Before the birth of her Blessed Son, she prophesied, 'From this time on all generations will count me blessed, for the Mighty One has done great things for me.'

God keeps blessing and we become the recipients of that blessing when we revere her. The Scriptures say, 'His mercy is upon generation after generation towards those who fear. He has done mighty deeds with His arm.'"

The bishop paused for effect, and from the crowd, Georg continued the quote. "'He has filled the hungry with good things and sent away the rich empty-handed.'"

Cecilia bent to Martin's ear. "Why does he keep doing that?" she whispered.

"Doing what?"

"Correcting the bishop."

Martin shrugged and turned his attention to the dedication.

Bishop Gernot ignored the interruption and continued, "We are here to dedicate this humble shrine and to pledge to serve God better. We shall build a cathedral in which this tiny miracle will take a place of honor. Do not hesitate to have your part in God's great cathedral. You will be blessed by Him."

After the dedication, everyone who dropped a coin into a box had the opportunity to kneel for a few seconds at the shrine. They whispered quick prayers to the saint whom they believed was nearest to God's heart. When Martin's turn came, he begged the beloved Jungfrau Maria to allow him to learn to read. He even reminded her of the mortar he had mixed to help build her shrine.

FOURTEEN

or some reason, still a mystery to Andrew, Brother Georg agreed to act as spokesman on the journey to Milan. He had chosen a few of his men to accompany him, and their sacrifice was great, for they would be gone almost a whole year. To those men who remained in Felsenburg would fall the responsibility to care for the women and children.

On a warm, dusty summer morning a few days after the dedication of the shrine, the small party gathered in Lärchenplatz. They would soon depart for St. Jude's, the first stop on their long journey to Milan. Andrew and Georg's men carried provisions for a few days upon their backs. Also stashed in various pockets for safekeeping were pieces of gold for purchasing supplies along the way. In addition, Andrew had been given several small but valuable jewels with which to entice Titus.

"—Only if he seems unwilling to come," the bishop had stressed. "The jewels are not his payment, but merely a guarantee that he will be paid. He will be able to trade them for his wages after he has agreed to work for us."

Andrew nodded and wrapped the tiny jeweled box in a grubby rag before he tucked it into his rucksack.

Bishop Gernot smiled his approval. "Good thinking, brother. I have, however, provided for your safety; I'm sending several of my personal armed guard to accompany you."

Andrew was not sure that he wanted the bishop's men with them. Perhaps the best protection against robbers would be the unpromising appearance of their ragtag group of poverty-stricken clergy. But he had given up trying to change the bishop's mind.

The soldiers' horses whinnied and pawed the ground nervously as two of Georg's men picked up the tongue of the little cart that held the supplies. Wives and children kissed their husbands and fathers. The bishop had not risen early to see them off, but Father Augustin was there to bless them and wish them Godspeed. They headed west past the inn, and the crowd gradually thinned, the farewells growing fainter.

The men stayed in two distinct groups—Georg's band, clustered around the cart; the bishop's men, on horseback, keeping watch from behind. The two groups did not know one another, and the awkwardness was evident to all. Andrew walked by himself on the side of the path between them, listening anxiously to the clopping of the huge horses behind him.

Georg chatted with his men, and they sang as they walked. Andrew wondered how Georg would react when he discovered the purpose of the trip. Georg had been told nothing, and Bishop Gernot had insisted that Andrew not reveal the contents of the letter until absolutely necessary.

The meeting between Georg and the bishop had been difficult.

"You want me to accompany your secretary to Milan?" Georg had grinned and leaned back in one of the bishop's large chairs, positioned comfortably near the fire. "Why?"

Bishop Gernot spoke frankly. "It's no secret that Andrew's a mute; I would like a man of the church to travel with him and to act as his voice."

Georg barely glanced at Andrew, who had shoved his chair further back from the glare of the fireplace. "Why me?" Georg asked again.

The bishop pursed his mouth in irritation, but Andrew saw the familiar glint in his eyes as the bishop's mind swiftly searched for the most acceptable answer. "There is no specific reason that I ask you, in particular. I am simply offering you the job."

Andrew stifled a snicker.

Georg was skeptical. "A job? You're going to pay me?"

The bishop nodded, and his smile expressed triumph.

Andrew picked at his fingernails and wondered why Georg was so ready to believe him.

"How much are you paying?" asked Georg, his eagerness barely concealed beneath his businesslike veneer.

Andrew jumped when the bishop snapped sarcastically, "Money does speak to you, doesn't it? You think that you are above avarice—that you are better than I—but your dreams are also realized with the same gold that will realize mine."

He's stalling, thought Andrew bitterly. *He's trying to figure how little he can pay and still get rid of Georg.*

The young monk's expression was unhappy as he studied his fingernails. "Gold can realize dreams," Georg said heatedly, "but it can also hold off nightmares. You go ahead and realize your dreams; I will collect money by any means that I can in order to hold off the nightmare of cold and hunger for my followers. How much will you pay me to leave my people and give voice to your dreams in Milan?"

Andrew heard the icy control as the bishop answered pleasantly, "They are not your people or my people; they are God's people, and in your absence, I will care for them as tenderly as you could. They will be fed and clothed and sheltered, and if it is not too demeaning, those who can will be given work to remove the humiliation of charity."

Georg looked at the bishop in disbelief. "I would have your word that they would be cared for?"

Bishop Gernot slapped the arms of his chair in fury. "Must I swear it? The Holy Father in Rome entrusts me with the spiritual nurturing of the people in Felsenburg, and you are not able to trust me to provide their daily nourishment? You shall also receive a silver piece for each day that you are gone. Or is that still not enough?"

"Your offer is generous," Georg accepted with a smile of triumph. "May I ask the purpose of the trip?"

The bishop stood and paced before the fire. "There are many purposes, some of which you do not need to know. There are, however, many who long to see the blessed Rosen Jungfrau. Andrew and you will take it to Milan. I can imagine that my dear friend, the archbishop, would like to see it before he departs from this earth."

Andrew looked at the bishop in surprise. The archbishop's piety was obviously only an excuse to prevent Georg from discovering Andrew's real mission. The bishop glared at Andrew and continued. "Along your way," he continued, "you will stop in towns and villages, and the people will be given the opportunity to view the miraculous picture. Perhaps some may even be moved to give to the coffers of our parish, that we may rebuild the church."

Cathedral, thought Andrew wearily.

"A cathedral, you mean." Georg echoed Andrew's thoughts. "We ought to feed the poor instead."

"'The poor you have always with you,'" the bishop quoted, "but it is not often that we can show our devotion to God by building Him a beautiful house of worship. Our Lord praised the woman who squandered an expensive gift upon him."

Georg had his own quote ready: "'God does not live in temples built of hands.'"

"Where does He live, then?"

Andrew leaned forward to catch the answer.

Georg sighed, suddenly defeated. "I don't know."

Tears sprang to Andrew's eyes. The fire was still too hot, so he stood and went to the window to look out onto the gardens, which were gradually being tamed by the loving hands of the gardener.

The bishop's voice sounded almost kind. "Will you accompany Andrew?"

"I will."

Andrew felt an overwhelming disappointment. Somehow he had thought that Georg would be above bending to the bishop's will just for money. Once again, his hopes to find someone better than himself were crushed.

⁓⁓   ⁓⁓

For several hours they followed a track along the Obersill River as it rushed past them through the meadows and woods. By noon they had reached Bruck am Obersill, the only bridge across the swollen stream. They ate their lunch in two groups, each band of men mumbling and eyeing the other, each group trading tales and sausages among themselves. After a satisfying drink from the cold glacier water, they paid the bridge toll and resumed their journey.

St. Jude's was barely visible because it blended so well with the cliff on which it was built. As they came nearer, Andrew experienced a strange feeling in his stomach when he thought about spending the night there.

Obviously, Georg's thoughts were similar. He dropped back to Andrew and waved his hand at the monastery. "They tell me you were raised there."

Andrew nodded.

"Were you happy?"

The young monk smiled.

"I'll have to be more clever to carry on a conversation with you," he said with an apologetic grin. "Your parents gave you to the church?"

A shrug.

"I have heard that the abbot is a very difficult man. He and the bishop do not see eye to eye. I find it interesting that he allowed you to leave."

Andrew shrugged again. *The bishop did him a favor,* he thought.

Georg sighed. "I see that my curiosity is not to be satisfied." He slapped Andrew on the shoulder. "All right, then, I'll tell you about myself."

⁓⁓ ⁓⁓

Brother Georg was the youngest son of a local nobleman. His mother promised him to the church if God allowed her to live through childbirth. She did, but she died a year later of a lung infection. Georg was raised by an aunt. She was determined that her sister's promise should be honored, so she indoctrinated the child into the ways of the church. When he came into his adolescence, his one desire was to give his life to God. In the monastery, though, he soon learned that the men there were anything but godly, and he and a few other dissatisfied monks decided to leave and to work in the villages— "in the world," it was called.

Even there, though, he felt that he was not doing enough. While he continued to live on the fortune he had inherited from his uncle, most of his followers were pitifully poor. Driven by his compassion for the poor and by his thirst for justice, he left the valley and became a wandering prophet of poverty. Eloquent and charismatic, he roamed from town to town, preaching the evils of affluence and the virtues of generosity. He collected clothing, food, and money everywhere he went and distributed them to the poor.

"I seem to attract quite an assorted following," he admitted with a chuckle. "Anyone who is unhappy with the church finds a home within our ranks."

Andrew was certain that he would never be attracted to such a group. Why, Brother Georg would be used by the poor and homeless as well as the lazy and criminal! Even heretics would find a platform on which to support their own flimsy doctrines.

Georg seemed to read his thoughts. "Oh, I am forever involved in controversy, but it keeps my mind alive and examining my own beliefs. And in the many years, I have come to a very important discovery." He hesitated and said apologetically, "But I'm boring you. Shall I be quiet?"

Andrew grinned and indicated that he should continue.

"As you wish. My discovery: The church is a political organization in the disguise of a religious organization."

Andrew's face must have betrayed his surprise at the airing of such a controversial opinion.

"Heresy, you say." He shook his head. "Nay, truth. You are young . . . what . . . twenty years?"

Andrew nodded.

"And you grew up at St. Jude's. You will see." They walked a few minutes in the quiet, their thoughts disturbed only by the crunch of the gravel under their shoes. Then Georg said, "Do not think that I have entrusted you with confidential information. You may tell whomever you like, for I do the same. You must never be afraid to express your convictions."

Convictions? thought Andrew with envy. *I wish I had a few.*

Georg continued his story. He told of his sister who had married Count Robert von Immergrün. "My brother-in-law is probably not happy to have me here, but I really do not try to cause him any problems. He is a very good man, and although he will never be a man of the church, he does believe that if the church is going to demand virtue and poverty, then the church should live it!"

Andrew agreed, but he did not think that he agreed with Brother Georg.

"You may have noticed that I have a wife."

Andrew had, and he had been shocked.

"The Holy Scriptures do not forbid marriage for anyone, so I chose to marry. It is a blessed state, and I would encourage any cleric to consider it."

As Georg talked on and on, Andrew became more and more certain that this monk would have a lot of trouble from the bishop.

FIFTEEN

ate in the afternoon, the men drew near Untersill, a fair-sized village at the base of the cliff of St. Jude's. One of the soldiers rode into the village to announce their arrival. About fifteen minutes later, he returned, followed by a few of Georg's men who had arrived the day before and made arrangements for a procession in honor of the Rosen Jungfrau. A small group of monks from the monastery and a few curious children straggled out to join them.

Andrew removed the miraculous picture from the protective chest in which it had been packed. The monks clustered around and murmured in awed whispers.

"Let me see."

"So beautiful!"

"How was the picture preserved?"

The soldiers, until now uninterested in their assignment, were ready to tell and retell and embellish the story as more and more people wandered out from the village to glimpse a preview of the miraculous jungfrau.

Georg, standing faithfully at Andrew's elbow, spoke into the monk's ear. "We had better begin the procession soon or there will be no point. I think that there will be more people in the procession than people to watch."

Andrew nodded and looked at the milling crowd helplessly.

Without speech, he found it difficult to imagine how he could organize things. Georg sensed his feelings of inadequacy and in a very short time, with help from his men, had organized everyone into lines. Andrew was amazed at how eagerly everyone did what Georg requested. He made each group feel that their particular part in the overall effectiveness of the procession was essential.

Meanwhile, Andrew prepared the Rosen Jungfrau. The gold-filigree frame complimented the dark rose and black colors in the picture of the melancholy Madonna. On the back of the frame, the goldsmith had designed a fitting, which Andrew attached to a long pole. Held high above the crowd, the Rosen Jungfrau would be visible to all who wished to worship.

"The altar boys are ready to carry the image of our Virgin," said Georg.

Andrew turned to the boys, who were dressed in colorful, matching robes. They were trying to act dignified, but a girl several years older than they sauntered past, and the oldest boy said something that made them all giggle. Several faces blushed in embarrassment. *I wanted to be an altar boy many years ago,* thought Andrew.

"That was me—many years ago," echoed Georg, watching the boys jostle one another. "My father gave so much money to the church that the old priest was obligated to take me. I was stupid enough to think that he was a fool—my father, I mean. I knew that I wasn't holy enough to be doing a service to God, but my father was blind to my faults."

Perturbed, Andrew waved his hand at Georg to silence him. *Don't speak that way,* he thought. *You will cause us trouble. You are the one who agreed to assist the bishop.*

Georg smiled and shrugged helplessly. "The priest was the greater fool."

Speaking of fools! Andrew thought, and abruptly turned his back on Georg and carried the Rosen Jungfrau on the pole to the group of boys.

The youngsters stopped giggling and the boy with the eye for the girls stepped forward. "I am to carry the blessed Rosen Jungfrau in the procession," he informed Andrew regally. "You will give her to me now."

Andrew was not inclined to obey, and he looked around for Georg, who had heard the boy's claim. Andrew raised his eyebrows to question the wisdom of giving the honor to such an arrogant young man.

"He is the one," Georg assured him. "One of my men arranged it all yesterday."

Reluctantly, Andrew passed the pole to the young man, who smiled smugly. "I am the best boy in the parish," he explained. "Father Sebastian had to choose me."

Suddenly Georg reached out and snatched the pole from the boy's hands. "Father Sebastian may have chosen you, but we don't." Georg looked around the group of boys. "Who among you is the youngest?"

All eyes turned toward a sickly looking child with mousy, brown hair and large brown eyes.

"What is your name, child?"

"That's Karli," offered one of the others. "He's usually too scared to speak to strangers."

"Karli." Georg knelt beside the boy and said gently, "I think that God would like it if you carried the image of the Virgin in the procession." He positioned the pole in the child's hands so that it did not sway too much. "The other boys will help you if you have problems or if it gets too heavy—won't you, boys?"

Glad to be freed from the self-righteousness of their leader, they cheerfully agreed.

"And you—" Georg stood and pulled the oldest boy away from the group. "—so that you won't cause any trouble—ach, ja, I can see trouble in your eyes—you will walk with the monks, where you may begin to recognize your own worthlessness."

That arranged, the procession entered the gates of the village and passed along the one main street. Andrew walked with the monks behind the group of boys. In unison, Georg's men sang praises from the psalms. With cries of joy, the townspeople raised their hands heavenward or fell on their faces in the filthy street to worship.

> I will lift up my eyes to the mountains:
> From whence shall my help come?

Ahead of him, Andrew saw the cliff of St. Jude's and, between the trees, the trail that curved in ever-tighter switchbacks up the mountain to the gates of the monastery.

Am I coming home? he wondered. *Where do I belong?*

His gaze continued upward until it reached the top of the church tower. His glance then leaped into the clouds, which raced across the bright blue sky.

> My help comes from the Lord,
> Who made heaven and earth.

As the street slanted upward, the procession proceeded slowly into the trees on the mountain. When the procession passed, the townspeople joined to follow the Rosen Jungfrau to St. Jude's, where Abbot William would lead a celebration of the Mass.

> He will not allow your foot to slip;
> He who keeps you will not slumber.

The little boy, Karli, stumbled and the Rosen Jungfrau swayed in a wide arc. One of the other boys steadied the pole and murmured in the child's ear. With a look of gratitude, Karli handed the pole to his friend, who looked back to make sure that the switch was approved. Andrew smiled and gave a slight nod, and the boy grinned and turned to do his duty.

> The Lord is your Keeper.
> The Lord is your shade on your right hand.

Before they had reached the monastery, every boy had carried the pole, and every boy had gladly given it up to another when his arms were too weary to hold it any longer. At St. Jude's gate, where the rest of the monks met the procession, the Rosen Jungfrau was returned to Karli, who was able to carry it triumphantly through the courtyard and into the church to the altar.

After the Mass, as each family was leaving the church, they had to pass by a large metal box into which they threw their coins with a satisfying clang—the larger the coin, the louder the clang. Soon the doorway was crowded with curious onlookers, eager to see the givers of the largest amounts. With each gift, Abbot William, who was standing beside the box, would mumble a blessing for the giver.

Later in the afternoon, the crowds thinned as each child left with his family, taking a special gift of flour, oil, and wine from the monastery's private storehouse.

The clerics were shown to their rooms in the guest house, while the soldiers descended the mountain to spend the night in the village, a more stimulating setting than the abbey.

Andrew and Georg and his men enjoyed a modest supper at the abbot's table, the first time Andrew had ever been a guest there. After the meal, Abbot William dismissed Georg's men and invited the two young churchmen to sit nearer the fire. Andrew sat reluctantly, trying not to cringe in the dry heat from the fireplace. One of the monks refilled the goblets and then left quietly.

William spoke to Andrew. "I understand you are traveling to Milan."

Andrew nodded.

"On an errand for the bishop."

Georg answered. "Yes, we carry the Rosen Jungfrau to the archbishop, so that he may worship before he dies."

Abbot William's lips curved into a smile, but his eyes did not follow. "That is all?"

Georg glanced at Andrew and then said resignedly, "Our brother, Andrew, has other errands, but I believe that I will be told them only when the time is right."

William drank from his cup. "I know about you," he said to Georg in a friendlier tone. "You are the champion of the poor, refuge for the downtrodden. Everywhere you go, the sick and unfortunate flock to you like hungry chickens to the farmer's wife."

Georg smiled sadly and with a shrug said, "They are hungry."

"No doubt, but there are also too many of them."

"Too many for whom? For me to feed? For the church to feed?" Georg calmed himself and added, "We ate well enough tonight. What you have in your cellars would feed Untersill for a year."

"I gave them food today—"

"Food that they raised and were required to give to this institution."

"The problem is not feeding them. The problem is—"

"Your pardon for interrupting, Abbot, but I know exactly what the problem is. There is enough food for everyone, but it is not fairly shared. The people who work the hardest to produce the food eat the least. And those who have power over them let them believe that their lives are better so."

William's face had folded into a scowl. "You do not understand the problem at all."

Georg spread his hands, palms up and said softly, "I know what we say—that each human should be satisfied with the lot in life the Lord God has given him."

Abbot William nodded suspiciously.

"I also know how we live—that noblemen and churchmen have an abundance, which they've taken from the tributes of the poor."

William interrupted. "That is not exactly true—"

"Please allow me to finish. I know that we offer the poor the promise of a better afterlife, if they will be satisfied in this life. But we are not satisfied and we abuse our power. We are not even sure of the afterlife, and so we fill this life full of good things—for ourselves. Abbot William, we collected a lot of money for the Rosen Jungfrau today. Are you certain that you had the right to speak for God in blessing those who gave?"

William stood suddenly and threw the rest of his wine into the fire; the hiss reflected William's anger. "You're bordering on heresy, you know. I can only do what I am authorized to do, and I have no right to question that authority."

"It is no secret that you question the authority of Bishop Gernot von Kärnten. Why can you do that?"

William glanced at Andrew and, apparently seeing no threat, exclaimed, "The bishop is a silly fool who thinks that he is the reincarnation of Moses. He is driven only by fame, and he will stop at nothing to achieve that."

"Does that make him fit to dispense God's blessings?"

William clutched his hands behind him, turned his back on Georg, and spoke into the fire. "Our authority comes from the same place. We cannot question it."

"And what if that authority is wrong?"

The question hung in the hot, stuffy room for a full minute before William turned and said, "I am obliged to provide food and shelter for your journeys, but I am not obliged to entertain you. Good night and Godspeed. I shall not see you before you leave in the morning." He turned his back and waited until Georg had left.

The abbot left the fire then and walked to where Andrew sat, slumped in the chair. "It is cold in this corner. Are you ill?"

Andrew sat up and shook his head.

"No, of course not. You've never liked the fire, have you?" He sighed. "You are surrounded by dangerous men, Andrew. You must be careful to choose your own way."

SIXTEEN

ama, how does God talk to the bishop?" Martin had been thinking about this while turning the spit on which their Sunday chicken was roasting.

Mama looked at Martin in surprise and then shrugged.

"I mean, does God have a voice that speaks out of the clouds, or does He speak into the bishop's head?"

"I really don't know, Bursch." She poked the chicken to see if it was done and drops of juice fell into the flames, which momentarily burned brighter. "Turn the spit slower and pay attention to what you're doing."

Martin sighed. "Do women always get sick when they're going to have a baby?"

"Not always. And not for the whole nine months. Klara will be well again—and able to help me again—" She reassured him with a smile, "—in a few weeks."

He turned the spit for a few minutes in silence. "Mama, can God see everyone on earth?"

"Of course."

"Then he can see the poor?"

"Martin, you worry about things that aren't your worry."

"Then you know what I mean: How do you think that God can tell the bishop to build the cathedral, when God knows that there are people who cannot afford to help?"

Mama wrinkled her forehead in dismay. "It does not matter what I think. Our good bishop has the faith to build a cathedral. I shall do all that I can."

"But the farmers have had several bad seasons, and we haven't had enough rain again this year. What if no one has anything to give? How will the workers be paid?"

"I would say that the bishop will have to answer that. Workers who aren't paid usually don't work. He'll find a way. Meanwhile, you can give your hard work. That is all that God expects of you."

Martin felt even more depressed. "That's not enough. I have to think of Bernie."

"And what does Bernie have to do with this?"

"I . . . I made God a promise."

Mama shook her head and did not look hopeful. "Then you'll have to figure out how to keep it."

◆◇◆◇

The following day, the four Steinmetz men packed their things and went back to Immergrün, the site of Count Robert's gatehouse. As Martin walked past the bishop's residence, he thought of the boys his age who this fall would enter the bishop's new school. They would learn to read the language of the educated. They would study the Holy Scriptures. They would—Martin's knowledge and imagination failed, for no one in his acquaintance really knew what a school would be like.

Martin's fate, however, seemed to be bound completely to the rock with which his father was building the count's gatehouse. Day by day, the lovely sandstone gate grew higher and higher inside the framework of scaffolding. It already reached two stories and was only half-finished.

The twenty or so men on the job site worked efficiently and well. Stefan directed the operation from the ground, as he knew just exactly what the masons on the scaffolding needed. He checked the consistency of the mortar before it was raised in a bucket to the top of the gate. He scrutinized the work of the stonecutters and communicated measurements and angles to them. He oversaw the laborers, who were unskilled but necessary for mixing mortar, hoisting buckets, and carrying stones. Martin was glad that he had graduated from those chores.

Small setbacks occurred regularly, but these were the challenges that Martin's father found so fulfilling. As master mason he searched for solutions that kept the workers speaking to one another, and he cleverly invented new devices to solve the technical problems that came up as they built. Papa could do whatever he chose, but he especially took pride in the perfection of the Steinmetz mortar joints and preferred to oversee these himself. He stood on the highest rank of scaffolding and waited for the mortar and cut stone to arrive from below.

Martin's new place was beside his father. He learned to climb the ladders, which were built of straight poles and tied together with rope. The walkways were tightly woven mats of reeds, which were strong enough to support the weight of man and stone. Martin learned very quickly how to estimate the amount of mortar required for each stone. He held the plumb line, watching Papa smooth each joint and trying to act interested. But by midmorning he could no longer stifle his yawns. Martin could not tell if the other masons were content or resigned as they moved predictably through each day. As he chiseled the family *S* onto the end of yet another course, his idle brain, like a pulley with no load, whirled with boredom.

"Martin!" Papa said sharply.

Martin stopped staring at the *S* and looked up.

"Come and lay a stone."

A sudden feeling of rebellion gripped him and he clenched his fists. He took a deep breath and tried to protest. "Papa, I . . ." but he could not find words to express how much he did not want to cooperate, so he just stood up and moved carefully along the narrow scaffold to where the next course would begin.

Martin picked up the plumb line and dangled it down the wall. The stones were lined up exactly. He looked up at his father.

"Go ahead, Bursch," said Papa. "Tell them what you need."

Martin sighed. He looked down at Stefan, who was looking up and grinned at him. "You can do it, little brother. Perfect courses run in our blood."

I know I can do it! the boy thought angrily. "Send up the next four stones and a decent bucket of mortar," he snapped.

Stefan, a bit bewildered by Martin's gruffness, turned to the laborers and gave the orders. The mortar was inspected and then shoveled into a wooden bucket. Stefan hooked the bucket onto a rope and, with the help of a pulley, raised it to Martin's level. There, one of the laborers pulled it onto the scaffold and brought it to Martin.

From the pile of cut sandstone, four more of the laborers each fetched one stone for Stefan to examine. Then they hoisted the stones to their shoulders and climbed the ladders to where Martin and his father waited on the third level. They set their burdens down beside Martin and then climbed down a different ladder in order to avoid those coming up.

Martin unclenched his teeth and tried to relax. He studied all four stones for a minute and then selected one for the corner. From another bucket, he slopped a bit of water onto the finished corner and rubbed it into the stone so that the moisture of the mortar would not soak into the porous sandstone. He did the same to the stone he was about to lay. Then he troweled the proper amount of mortar onto the corner. After distributing the mortar evenly, he set the stone—wet side down—into the mortar, making sure that the vertical joints were not lined up.

Without a word, Papa hung the plumb line for him, and Martin made a few tiny adjustments before he tapped the stone with a mallet to set it. Papa handed him a level. Martin gave the stone a few more taps until the stone lay exactly horizontal in every direction. The boy did not dare to look at his father because he did not want to see the pride in Papa's eyes.

The gray mortar oozed in irregular blobs between the two stones. Martin took the smoothing tool and spread the mortar evenly, flicking the excess crumbs onto the ground two stories below. Dampening his index finger, he gently smoothed the joint until it blended into the stone. He knew he had done a good job, and he felt like a traitor to his own desires. He rinsed his fingers in the bucket of water and chanced a look at Papa.

Papa was smiling. "A little slow, but very good."

"I know," said Martin meekly, "but I still want to read."

It was Papa's turn to sigh. "Lay another stone, Bursch."

He did—quicker this time. The third stone did not fit properly, but Martin didn't discover that until he had tried to level it. He had to remove the stone and send it back to Stefan, who made sure that it was washed thoroughly and recut. The fourth stone fit perfectly.

Papa left Martin and went to the finished corner to begin another course. In this way, the wall went up in stairway fashion. Martin was laying his course one row above and about six stones behind one of the other masons, and now Papa was three stones behind Martin on the course above.

After a lunch, they all returned to their assignments, and it became very clear that Martin would finish his own course. It did cross his mind that if he did a poor job, perhaps he would be relieved of this duty. A return to mixing mortar, however, was worse than setting stones, so he did his best, a tiny bit proud that his best was good enough.

In the late afternoon, Martin finished his course. He met up exactly with a mason named Gerdt, who had laid his course from Martin's first corner, but working around in the opposite direction. Papa was only two stones behind on the course above, but he had taken quite a long break earlier in the afternoon to discuss dimensions with the stonecutters. Martin chiseled the *S* into the end of his course and started walking away.

Papa left his place and took the chisel and mallet from the boy's hand. With great ceremony, Papa tapped out another letter after the *S*.

"That's an *M*," the master mason explained. "Steinmetz, Martin. That is your mark." Papa set the tools down and returned to his stones.

Tears stung Martin's eyes. "I'm sorry, Papa," he murmured. He shuffled back to the starting corner—*I'm sorry that I don't want to do this.* He climbed to the next level—*I'm sorry that I can do it so well.* He ordered more mortar and stone from Stefan and waited dejectedly while the laborers brought them up to him.

Suddenly, there was a tremendous crack and Martin swung his head around to see. One of the horizontal poles that supported the walkway for the adjoining wall had split lengthwise. Under the heavy weight of men, mortar, and stones, the second pole sagged and then broke in half. Stone blocks, buckets, and tools slid and tumbled down the inclined mats. Some landed on the level below; others plunged to the ground. Three masons and two laborers who had been working on that side shouted and screamed, frantically searching for something to grasp on a wall that had been smoothed to perfection.

One of the men was finally pushed off by two of the heavy stones, which tumbled onto him. Another man successfully grabbed one of the vertical poles and tightly wrapped his arms and legs around it.

Martin, safe on his side of the scaffold, stepped cautiously to the edge and extended his hand to the mason nearest him. The man clamored up onto that portion of the scaffolding, nearly pulling Martin off.

Where the stones and mortar met on the third level, the woven mats sagged and tore dangerously.

"Get down!" yelled Stefan to the endangered workers.

Still on his knees, Martin peered over the edge at his brother, who was standing underneath the disintegrating framework, directing the men on the safest way down.

"All of you! Get away! Get down!"

One of the men on the broken scaffolding finally lost his balance and jumped. He landed with a shriek and lay writhing in pain.

Stefan motioned several of the laborers, who had been watching from the ground, to come and stand with him. "Jump!" he shouted to the remaining man. "We'll catch you!" He held up his arms.

The man obeyed at once, but as he pushed off, the third level scaffolding cracked and tipped, dumping its deadly load onto the rescuers below. Horrified, Martin watched as the stones plunged toward Stefan, striking with a sickening thud, breaking bone, crushing lives. Martin put his head on the dusty matting and moaned.

The stones rolled to a stop, and there was silence, broken only by the whimpering of the man who had jumped. As if obeying some inaudible order, all the men on the other section of scaffolding filed wordlessly to the remaining ladder and climbed down. By the time Martin and his father reached Stefan, the laborers had already removed the stones from him and the other two men. Papa bent and brushed mortar from Stefan's still face.

It was at once obvious that the three men were dead. There was little blood, just crushed skulls and chests. Martin felt panic rush through him, so violently he thought his chest would burst. He looked at Papa, but Papa avoided his eyes. Everyone else moved so carefully, so unhurriedly. Could they feel the same despair that threatened to break Martin's heart?

Time lost all meaning. A cart appeared; Stefan, the two laborers, and the two injured men were moved to the count's manor for the night. Three of the laborers were sent back to Felsenburg to break the tragic news to the families. Preparations must be made for a swift burial because of the warm weather.

Martin lay on his mat that night and tried not to relive the terror of those few minutes, which only made the memories flash brighter in his mind. Sometimes he cried, but mostly he lay dry-eyed, wondering if—when he learned to read—he would find answers to Stefan's death in the Holy Scriptures.

SEVENTEEN

ndrew was familiar with the recurring dream. He stood watching the wall of flames, and he cried out, but he was unable to run away. His limbs were weakened by the sluggishness of his horror. He closed his eyes—or he thought he did—and the heat from the flames scorched his eyelids, and he struggled to free himself. A strong arm grabbed his shoulder and shook him.

"Brother!" a hoarse voice rasped in his ear. "Wake up! Get up. Quickly. Quietly. Intruders are coming. You must take the Rosen Jungfrau and hide in the woods."

After a week of travel, Andrew had still not become accustomed to these nocturnal adventures. As he had on other nights, he dragged himself from his fitful sleep while his heart thumped in his ears. The soldier hauled him from the cart where he had been sleeping and pushed the precious box into his arms. Stumbling from the soldier's hard shove, he ran with Georg's men toward the woods, while the guards turned to face the intruders.

Andrew clambered up an embankment, roughly assisted by another soldier. The two of them groped through the pitch-black woods, trying not to impale themselves on the low, dead branches.

Horses galloped nearer and then thundered around the last curve. Several of the horsemen carried torches, and the clearing where the soldiers waited in the darkness was suddenly lit by the flickering, orange light. The riders bore down upon the soldiers until the leader of the riders shouted. Their horses wheeled and skittered to a halt in a shower of gravel. Standing fast, the soldiers drew their swords or fit their arrows to their bows to fight the horsemen.

Crouched behind the tree, Andrew could not hear the soldiers, but it soon became evident that the horsemen were not bent on mischief. He remained hidden, though, clutching the box, which contained hundreds of silver pfennig, collected from the devout parishioners of several towns.

The horsemen dismounted and, through the branches, Andrew could see them waving their arms and talking with the soldiers. Reassured that the men meant no harm, Georg and a few of his men crept to the fringes of the lighted circle to listen. Andrew relaxed and sat down on the ground, setting the chest against the tree. He wished that he could creep closer to hear, but he realized that however honorable the horsemen might be, the sum of money in the chest might strain their honesty. Best to keep his distance.

The horses were tied to the cart, and the men passed around their bottles of ale. Soon the men were laughing and slapping one another on the back. Andrew's eyes grew heavy, and he finally pushed some branches out of the way and made a bed of crisp pine needles.

When Andrew awoke, the sun was already slanting through the trees. Sometime during the night, the visiting horsemen must have left, and his own traveling party was snoring lustily.

He rose to his feet and stretched his arms to the sky. He brushed some pine needles from his robe and went to make breakfast. The two guards on watch took turns helping Andrew prepare the food, and soon the others stirred to the smell of the sausage. Several complained of hangovers, but those who had none told them, in voices none too soft, that they deserved that and more.

After their late breakfast, they resumed their journey to the next town where they would display the Rosen Jungfrau. Reinhold and Sigfried, Georg's messengers, and a middle-aged priest—who paced angrily—awaited them at the gates.

"We simply couldn't wait any longer!" the priest exclaimed cutting the air with his hands. "The people were assembled, and we needed to begin the trial."

Andrew looked at Georg's men for an explanation, but the priest rushed on, punctuating his words with impatient jerks. "We needed to make an example of these troublemakers. You should have come earlier. Now we will have to plan the procession for tomorrow." He spun around in a swirl of robes and stalked through the gate into town.

Hurrying to Georg, their eyes wide with anxiety, Reinhold and Sigfried tried to explain the priest's annoyance.

"You see," Reinhold said, "a wandering clergyman and a small group of followers—much smaller than ours—" he reassured Georg, "—arrived here about a month ago from Basel. They were very kind to the poor, and their leader was a very eloquent speaker—more eloquent than you."

Georg grinned and slapped his man on the shoulder.

"You won't smile when you hear the rest," Sigfried said grimly.

Reinhold continued with a dark look on his face. "Within a day, the poor and many of the not-so-poor were asking the priest—"

"Not this one," interjected Sigfried with a wave toward the cleric ahead of them.

Reinhold shook his head. "The people were asking some difficult questions about the priests' lifestyle and why the poor were dying in the streets when there are many empty houses in town and the storehouses are full of grain."

By now Andrew could barely hear Reinhold's explanation. Georg's men had gathered around to hear better, casting wary glances over their shoulders at the young monk. More explanation was not necessary, though, as they emerged from a narrow street into the town square.

Hundreds of people were gathered around the steps of a well-kept house. The only sound they heard was a baby's fussing from somewhere in the crowd. The prisoner stood to one side of the steps, bound and bruised from beatings.

"They have brought in the local bishop," whispered Reinhold with a nod toward the other man on the steps, "and his soldiers. It will be a death sentence; the pyre is already built."

Andrew couldn't believe what he was hearing. His wide eyes were fixed on the expressionless face of the priest. He turned his gaze to the local bishop to listen to what he was saying. He realized that the cleric was merely defending his own behavior instead of accusing the prisoner.

". . . and I have always been impartial to my parishioners. Only their own transgressions against God and His holy church have kept them from full participation in the sacraments." He raised his chin to project his voice more into the crowd. "My people are happy and content. They have no complaints."

"I wonder if they don't!" hissed Georg.

"Shhh!" His men pushed closer to him and patted his back to calm him.

Georg glanced around at them with appreciation and then looked at Andrew, who stood outside their circle, white-faced and confused.

"Come." Georg mouthed the word and motioned, making a place beside himself for the young monk to stand.

Drawn by the kindness in Georg's eyes, Andrew moved to stand beside him.

Georg leaned toward Andrew's ear and spoke quietly. "You are wondering why the priest has only good words for himself and no accusations for the prisoner?"

Andrew nodded, though his eyes were riveted on the bishop.

"Because the people are sympathetic to the prisoner who is sympathetic to them. The priest must show them that they are wrong and that the consequences for being wrong are too terrible."

But they are so many. Andrew's eyes swept the large crowd and then returned to the awaiting pyre and three lone clergymen next to it who held their attention.

Georg smiled. "I can read your thoughts: Why don't the people speak up and expose the bishop for what he really is—a greedy liar and an immoral sot? Listen, and the sot will tell you why."

The priest's condemnation continued. ". . . and this person . . . this . . . this one-time man of the church has come saying things that are not seemly, spreading discontent. For the Holy Scriptures say that in contentment is great gain. And further that even the great Saint Paul was content in his state of poverty. And what of our Lord, who had nary a place to lay his head while the birds of the air had nests and the foxes their dens?

"What this man has been teaching is heresy, viciously designed to rob his followers of the hope of eternal life. My dear folk, listen not to the wicked, twisted teachings of this man. Save your own souls and return to the safety of our teachings. God has ordained us to watch over your souls. Do not reject us, for in so doing, you will reject our dear Lord God. The consequences, as you can see, are regrettable." He tipped his head slightly to signify that he was finished.

The crowd murmured softly as the bishop stepped forward.

"Anton Felsbacher, what do you have to say in your defense?"

As the prisoner stumbled onto the steps, Andrew was surprised to hear how strong his voice was. "I believe the charge is heresy, but as that is such a broad topic, I shall tell you what I believe. I believe that God is the Creator of the world, that man is His fallen creature in need of redemption, and that Jesus Christ died—"

"That is enough," interrupted the bishop.

At that, the crowd's murmur rose quickly to a shout.

The bishop held up his hands as if in blessing. The crowd was once more quiet. "There is no need for us to hear the whole council of God on which we may agree. I shall ask the prisoner questions that are more to the point." He turned with condescension to the man. "Since Paul the apostle tells us in the Holy Scriptures that it is better to remain unmarried, why do you teach that a clergyman should marry?"

"It is better than living in a sinful union with a woman who is not one's wife. That is forbidden often in the Holy Scriptures. In fact, Paul the apostle writes that the overseer of the church—bishop, if you will—must be the husband of one wife. That seems rather plain to me."

"Are you married?"

"I am."

"Obviously the devil has blinded you to the truth."

"Certainly you have read—"

"What I have read is not in question. Do you or do you not teach that the poor should rebel against the guardians of their souls for a few morsels of bread?"

Georg shifted his feet uncomfortably, glanced at Andrew, and murmured, "I hope you are truly my friends."

Reinhold threw a suspicious glance at Andrew before protesting quietly, "Brother Georg, we love you better than a brother!"

The prisoner was answering. "I teach that it is right for a Christian to care for the more unfortunate around him—to follow the example of the Good Samaritan, who spent his money to help a wounded enemy. If the poor rebel, perhaps it is because they do not have enough morsels to feed their starving children. The church has much wealth; it could do much good with that wealth. Think how many could be fed if we only sold the gold in this church alone!"

The peasants began to look hopeful and to voice their agreement aloud. As if one body, they surged forward.

The bishop also stepped toward them and again held up his hands. "We cannot listen to any more such heresy!" he announced. "Imagine stealing gold from God's house and using it to satisfy our primitive desires! To teach such is the greatest blasphemy. The gold is the Lord God's. Who would steal His treasures?"

The men and women hung their heads that they ever would have considered such a thing!

The bishop continued his sentence. "Blasphemy must be punished—"

"Salvation of your souls cannot be bought with gold!" cried Anton Felsbacher.

"—punished by death. Guards!"

"No!" An anguished cry rose from a back corner of the square. In the sudden silence that followed, Andrew turned with the crowd to see a half dozen men and women being held fast by several guards. One young woman was struggling, her hair disheveled and her dark eyes dilated with terror.

"That's his wife," Andrew overheard a woman say.

Determined to have the last word, the prisoner recovered himself although his voice was thick with emotion. "All of your suffering in this world at the hands of wicked men—be they criminals or clergy—will not guarantee your salvation in the next world."

"Quiet!" ordered the bishop, "Guards!"

Another group of guards had been waiting at a discreet distance, but now they marched through the crowd, which parted in fright.

The prisoner was not finished. "Salvation comes only by faith. No one is good enough!"

Andrew caught his breath. *Say it again, please. Only by faith.*

"Be quiet!" bellowed the bishop.

"No one!" The prisoner repeated. "If you do not repent of your sins, you will meet your bishop and his lecherous priest in hell!"

The bishop was red in the face and screamed, "Shut up!"

The guards pulled the man roughly from the steps, and again the people moved aside to let them pass.

The prisoner's voice was not loud and tears streamed down his face, but the people were hushed so as not to miss a single word. "You cannot silence me. I shall speak so long as I have breath in my body. You cannot take my life; I give it freely to my Savior, who died for my sins. I know that I have eternal life."

The bishop swept through the mass of people at the heels of the guards. "You shall burn in hell!" The throng followed the bishop wordlessly as if their wills were not their own.

"No, I won't," answered Anton firmly.

"How can he be so sure?" whispered Georg.

Andrew was wondering the same thing.

The guards led the man to the stake and tied him to it.

Although formerly at the rear of the crowd, Andrew now found himself, along with Georg and his men, pushed toward the front. He wanted to leave, but the people were packed so tightly there was no way out.

The priest stepped up to Anton Felsbacher to hear his last confession, but the prisoner shook his head vigorously. "'Who will bring a charge against God's chosen people?'" demanded the prisoner boldly. "'God is the one who justifies.'"

"Light the fire!" roared the bishop. "We must silence his heresy."

"'Christ is the one who intercedes for us.'"

Reinhold tapped Georg's shoulder. "He's quoting Scriptures," he said in wonder.

"He is. And in the language of the people."

"But that's . . . that's—"

"Long overdue, I think," Georg said with a slight smile.

The flames licked around the edges of the pyre and tiny twigs quickly turned black and crumbled. Andrew felt faint and clutched the arm nearest him to keep from falling.

Anton Felsbacher's face was wet with tears, but his voice was still strong. "'Who shall separate us from the love of God? Shall tribulation or distress, or persecution or famine—'"

"No!" Again that numbing scream filled the square, and the young wife shoved through the crowd. She stopped and stood in indecision before the flames surrounding her husband.

"Trudi . . . Trudi," the prisoner sobbed.

Andrew could feel the heat of the fire, and the panic of his recurring dreams replaced the initial horror. He looked around wildly for a route of escape.

The bishop's voice was once again calm, just loud enough to be heard above the crackling of the fire. "Anton Felsbacher, you may save yourself. Admit your error, and even now you will be set free."

The man closed his eyes and quoted, "'Just as it is written: 'For your sake we are being put to death all day long.'" He opened his eyes. "Trudi, return to our people; they will care for you."

"Ha! They are cowards!" hissed Reinhold.

Georg shook his head. "It would do no good for all of them to be slaughtered. They are right to be quiet." He looked at Andrew. "You're hurting my arm, you know."

Startled, Andrew looked at his white fingers clamped tightly around Georg's arm. He tried to loosen his grip, but he was too afraid that he would fall.

Georg put his arm around the young monk as support. "You mustn't tip over here; we can't afford to make a scene."

Andrew tried to rein his terror, but the dream was reality, and he felt paralyzed. *How can they just stand here and watch? Are they all as weak as I?*

The prisoner, now surrounded by flames higher than his head, was still able to speak, although his words were punctuated by coughing as the smoke swirled about his face. The fire had burned through his ropes and he raised his hands and announced, "'For I am convinced that neither death nor life nor angels nor principalities—'"

Suddenly, with an unearthly shriek, his wife sprang into the blaze and clambered up the crumbly pile of wood to her husband. By the time she reached him, her hair and skirt were aflame.

Andrew covered his face, but he could still see the scene before him, just as he had seen it as a little boy: his father's arms clasped around his mother as together they had sunk down into the flames, speaking in unison, "'. . . nor height nor depth nor any other created thing . . .'" Their voices had been barely audible above the roar of the fire. "'. . . shall be able to separate us from the love of God . . .'" Andrew was weeping as the little boy had wept—helplessly, hopelessly.

"Andrew. Come." Georg pulled on his arm. "Reinhold, make a path. We must get him out of here."

Andrew felt nothing except the throbbing pain in his head, the suffocating ache in his chest, as he stumbled along supported between Georg and one of his men.

They reached the back edge of the crowd, ignoring the curious looks from the frightened townspeople.

They stopped, and Georg tried once again to pry Andrew's fingers from his arm. "Andrew, you must stop this."

"I cannot," he sobbed, unaware that he had spoken his first words in fifteen years.

Georg raised his eyebrows in surprise. "We have to get him out of here!" he said urgently. "Where are we staying, Reinhold?"

He grasped the situation at once. "The guesthouse on the lake. I'll show you."

Andrew's thoughts were many miles and many years away. They were both dead, and he would have to learn to live without his parents. But he was a big boy. He hated them, but Mama had said that he must not hate them. Someday he would understand why.

Georg hurried Andrew through the streets and alleys of the town and out one of the gates, grateful that all the residents were at the trial. The inn was near.

Once inside, they lay Andrew on a bed in one of the rooms. The innkeeper provided a small glass of something strong, and after a while, Andrew's sobbing quieted. Although the tears continued to flow, he eventually fell asleep.

EIGHTEEN

artin, more ale!" He had been hearing it all afternoon, and it seemed that the thirst of the guests at Stefan's wake would never be quenched. He hitched Bernie more comfortably onto his hip, poured the last of the ale, and went to fetch more.

Mama was serving soup, and her face looked like it was set in stone. Martin was afraid that Mama would never smile again. Tante Maria was angrily tearing chunks of meat off of the boar, which roasted over a fire in the middle of Lärchenplatz. Klara, a widow at nineteen, lay ill in the house. She had not even been able to attend Stefan's funeral that morning. Mama was afraid that Klara would lose the baby, which Stefan had not even known about.

Since Stefan's death, Martin's volunteer role as secret godfather to Bernie had taken on a greater significance. Bernie had become Martin's charge because he was the only person who could keep the one-and-a-half-year-old happy.

Martin was not happy, though. He had been to wakes before, but he had always romped with the other children and eaten until he thought he would burst. For some reason, he had never realized how much the families conducting the wake must have been suffering. He hated the guests for their selfishness.

Tables had been set up in Lärchenplatz, which reverberated with laughter and shouting. The three families of the deceased provided food and drink for all of the people who had honored the dead with their presence at the funeral. To not provide enough food and drink would have been an affront to the deceased, but Martin had been to fairs that had been more restrained. The more ale Martin poured, the more his resentment grew. He clung to Bernie and withdrew into his memories of the funeral that morning.

Lärchenplatz had been a different place then. A dais had been set up at the east end of the platz, near where the doors of the church had been. Stefan and the other two men had been laid out on the dais. Father Augustin had consoled the families and had led in the Holy Sacraments in a way that honored Stefan and the others. All of the masons were there, soberly dressed in their best black. A reverent stillness, punctuated only by the sobs of the bereaved, had settled like an enveloping blanket upon the platz.

Martin's grief found comfort and support in the grief of others. They had prayed to the saints for hours, it seemed, that they would intercede on Stefan's behalf before God. Martin felt certain that God would mercifully honor the agony in his heart. Then they had carried the men out to the cemetery west of town, for the bishop had decreed that the churchyard cemetery not be used anymore. There they prayed again, admitting over and over how defenseless they were in the presence of death. Father Augustin assured them of God's mercy and told them that God honors the prayers of righteous people.

"Martin, more ale!"

Martin looked into the man's red face. His eyes were bleary with drink, and as he stuffed another chunk of meat into his mouth, grease dripped off his chin. Martin was filled with revulsion. He splashed some ale into the man's cup and then fled to where Mama stood over the soup kettle.

He dropped the empty pitcher onto the cobblestones with a clatter. "Mama, I can't do this anymore."

She looked up, not understanding what he meant.

"It's not fair! They have no right!" he cried.

"Shhh, Bursch, they will hear you." Her voice quivered, but she continued. "They will think that we do not love Stefan. Besides, hard work heals the pain."

He took a deep breath and laid his free hand gently on her arm to stop her busyness. "I'm tired of hard work, Mama. I want to pray. I'm going to pray at Stefan's grave," he spoke firmly.

"You'll take Bernie?" she asked and turned back to the soup, the matter settled.

Martin threaded his way through the crowd, ignoring their demands for more ale. Tears blinded his eyes, and he stumbled with the heavy baby and almost knocked over the last table. Someone reached up and caught his arm.

"Martin, where are you going?" Cecilia's kind voice penetrated the noise in the platz.

"Cecilia, I'm sorry. I didn't see you."

"Have you eaten?" She slid over to make a place for him. "Here, sit by me."

Martin glanced around the table, and when his eyes landed on Onkel Hans with a cup of ale, he shook his head. "I'm going to Stefan's grave."

"May I come?" Then she added apologetically, "Perhaps you don't want company?"

"You're always welcome," he said. He adjusted Bernie's weight and turned to stride toward the edge of the square.

Cecilia darted after him. "Did you eat?"

"No. Yes. I mean . . . I wasn't hungry."

She rushed back to the table and wrapped some bread and cheese in her apron before bustling back to walk with her cousin.

When she caught up with him, she opened her apron, and Martin looked at the food. "I'm not hungry, Celia."

She said nothing but hurried along beside him, running a few steps now and then to keep up.

At the edge of the cemetery, Martin stopped abruptly. The late afternoon sun slanted through the trees, casting long shadows across the graves. Three dark gashes had been sliced in the golden autumn meadow where the three men now lay under the heavy earth. Panting after the swift walk, Martin glared at the graves and waited until Cecilia stood beside him.

"I'll watch Bernie while you pray," she offered.

His shoulders sagged. "I don't know how to pray—not the way Father Augustin does." He sat down beside the road and patted a grassy spot next to him for Cecilia. "I just had to get out of Lärchenplatz."

They both listened for a moment. The sounds of the wake were almost drowned out by the soft rushing of the river across the road. Bernie cooed and wiggled in Martin's lap. Cecilia gave him a small piece of bread.

"I'm so sorry about Stefan," she whispered, a tear rolling down her cheek. "I have prayed so much for him."

"I have too. Father Augustin says that God hears the prayers of the righteous." He set the baby down and reached for a piece of bread. Cecilia pressed a chunk of cheese into his hand. He smiled. "I guess I was hungry."

"Are we righteous, Martin?"

Surprised, he stopped chewing. Then he swallowed and said, "You, too? I don't know." He nodded toward town. "They're not," he said bitterly. "I keep thinking about everyone's praying this morning, and I wonder how much God heard. Did we do Stefan any good at all?"

"Oh, Martin, don't say that," she begged.

He brushed off his hands. "Celia," he said sternly, "if God is good and holy and He can see our hearts, how can you think that those people are righteous? They were drunk, and they were telling wicked stories, and . . . and . . ." He groped for the right words. "And they weren't making Mama feel any less grief."

"But how can you be sure?" she asked in a small voice.

"I'm thirsty," he announced. He pulled her to her feet and picked up Bernie. He took her hand and led her to the riverside. They both knelt down and took turns scooping water and holding Bernie. Chins dripping, they sat for a while and watched the water race by.

Martin made up his mind. He set Bernie in her lap and took her two hands in his and said, "I'm going to tell you a secret."

"I can keep a secret," she promised, her cheeks turning pink.

"I'm going to learn how to read."

Her eyes shone with pride. "Oh, Martin, did your papa—"

"No. He didn't. But he said I'm almost a man, and it's my decision if I want to learn to read. Then I will be able to read the Holy Scriptures, and I'll be able to learn all of the answers to our questions."

Bernie fidgeted and whimpered.

"Celia, do you have more bread?" She gave Bernie a small piece, and the baby gnawed contentedly on it.

"When I can read," he continued, "I will know who is righteous, and I will be able to care for Bernie and pray for Stefan."

"But if your papa—"

"Celia! Don't make it impossible for me. I will leave Felsenburg. There are other schools besides the bishop's."

She pulled her hands away and hugged Bernie. "But then I won't ever see you," she whispered.

Martin moved closer to her. Her stray curls brushed his face. "Celia, I'll come back."

She turned and looked at him with a joy that constricted his throat. He touched her face and bent to brush his lips across her cheek. His heart was pounding loudly, and he wanted to kiss her again. She closed her eyes and leaned toward him, so he pressed his lips to hers. Strange and wonderful feelings surged through his body, and he reached up to touch the back of her neck and lingered on yet another kiss—harder this time.

Suddenly she pushed Bernie into Martin's lap and scrambled to her feet. "Stop, please," she breathed. "I . . . we shouldn't."

"Probably not," he admitted, getting up. "But I'd never hurt you. I wouldn't do anything wrong."

"No, you wouldn't," she agreed.

"I think we'd better go back," he decided. "Mama might need me."

The setting sun was still warm and cast long, thin shadows before them all the way back to town. Martin tried to concentrate on holding Bernie, but when he licked his lips, he could still taste hers. He tried to think of something to say. "It was kind of you to bring the bread and cheese. Danke schön."

"Bitte schön," she answered shyly.

Too soon, they entered Lärchenplatz once more. The revelry had died down somewhat, as many of the women had taken the younger children home to bed. But two of the tables had been moved together near the fire, and a large group of men sat there. Martin knew that they would be there long after dark.

"Good night, Martin," Cecilia said softly.

"Good night, Celia. Thanks for going with me."

She smiled, bowed her head, and walked away.

Avoiding the tables, Martin circled the perimeter of the square and turned down his street to take Bernie home. Just before he reached the front door, he paused and closed his eyes, remembering Cecilia's kiss. A smile came across his face as he remembered her soft lips. Still smiling, he went in.

Mama was just sitting, staring into the fire.

Martin handed her Bernie. "He was very good."

"He's always good," she said in her grandmother's voice.

"I'm glad that today is over, Mama. I'll never act the way those people did at anyone's wake."

"You're a good boy, too, Martin. Did you eat?"

"I did," he said, glad that the dusk hid the flush in his cheeks.

"Did your papa find you? He wants to talk to you."

"No. Where is he?"

She jerked her chin toward the front door. "With the other men in the platz."

"I'll talk with him tomorrow," Martin said flatly. "I'm very tired."

NINETEEN

ndrew slept the whole night through and then spent most of the next day alone while Georg and the local priest organized the procession for the Rosen Jungfrau. The visions in his mind drove his thoughts into forbidden places. Never could he have imagined a past as bizarre as the one from which he seemed to have come. Awake, anger toward such cruelty fought with self-pity for the little boy, who was cruelty's victim. Asleep, the visions tormented him, until he awoke again, glad for the day. He was very relieved when the men finally returned to the inn in the late afternoon, astonished by the huge sum of money they had collected.

"The people were ripe for the picking," Georg lamented to Andrew. "They were frightened by yesterday's ordeal, and they were eager to prove how far away they were from the heretic's point of view." He closed the door and handed Andrew a cup of broth, which the innkeeper had sent up to him.

Andrew nodded his thanks and took a sip of the hot broth.

"Oh, no you don't," Georg scolded. "No more of this silence. What happened to you yesterday?"

The young monk leaned back against his pillow and breathed a quivering sigh. "I . . ." He hesitated, surprised by how loud his voice sounded. "I remembered." The words, so clear in his head were difficult to form with his inexperienced lips and tongue.

"Yes?"

"My parents. They were burned . . . as those two were." He swallowed and fought for control. "I had . . . mercifully . . . forgotten."

"I am sorry. You were a child?"

"Perhaps five or six years old. I feel . . . robbed." He closed his eyes, and hot tears spilled from them.

"They were heretics?"

"They told me not to hate the people who killed them."

Georg nodded in agreement. "Our Lord did the same. Were they devout followers of our beloved church?"

Andrew opened his eyes and sat up. "Are you?" He wiped the tears with the heel of his hand. "Sometimes I wonder."

Georg grinned. "You should see the treasures we have picked up today—all for our beloved bishop's grand cathedral."

Andrew grew suspicious of Georg's grin. "Is that all you have picked up?"

"Well," Georg drawled, "Anton Felsbacher's followers don't want to stay here anymore, but it would have been unsafe for them to travel without a guard. We have invited the heretic's followers to join us on our trip to Milan. Their women can do the cooking, and I think they just might share many of my well-thought-out convictions."

"You force us all to walk a very narrow path."

Georg shrugged. "I enjoy my life, and I am controversial, but I am also a man of honor. I will do what I said I would. You will be delivered safely to Milan and then brought back to Felsenburg with all of the treasure that we have collected. If I can ever figure out how to relieve the bishop of the money for my followers, I will do it. But I would never steal from you; you are too honest."

They headed south that day. Georg had given the authorities in town a vague explanation of what had caused Andrew to behave so strangely at an execution. "I think I told them that something you ate didn't agree with you. Meat or berries. I can't remember."

⚮ ⚮

The high passes through the Alps were still spotted with snow although it was the end of summer. Andrew inhaled the scents of fresh pine and cool tundra and felt revived. Milky streams, fed by melting glaciers, cascaded down ravines strewn with gray boulders. Eventually these streams emptied into the Inn River. As they climbed higher along the river, patches of old snow made puddles in the path. Sometimes the men would reach what they thought was a summit, only to gaze at a panorama of jagged mountains separated by glaciers and split by an even higher pass ahead. At the summit of Julier Pass perched the mysterious, blue-green glacier. It fed the Inn River and was inaccessible to any living creature except the birds.

The group spent their nights in mountain huts, lulled to sleep by the clanging of cowbells. Cattle grazed on the sweet, alpine grasses. In the spring, they had been brought there by local farmers, who were hospitable but poor. The milk and cheeses were delicious, but the travelers very often shared their own provisions with the farmers— and charitably paid money besides for space to sleep.

Finally, Maloja Pass was behind them, and they began the welcome descent toward Chiavenna, Lake Como, and finally Milan. Each day the air became warmer and the accommodations more comfortable. There were villagers who once again clamored to see the Rosen Jungfrau, and the treasury box gained weight.

Their first sight of Milan, one of the largest cities in the world, was on an early evening in late August. From a hill, Andrew and his companions stopped to gaze across colorful fields, which spread to the walls of the huge city. The buildings, with numerous church spires as their crown, were glowing with the golden light of sunset.

"It's breathtaking," murmured Andrew, a child of the monastery. "I've never seen anything like it."

Georg shook his head. "There are prettier—and bigger—cities."

"I found Felsenburg bustled to exhaustion!"

"You won't like Milan," Georg warned.

⁂

The next morning two men were sent to search for rooms among the wretched collection of dilapidated guest houses that ringed Milan outside the city walls. Their group was much larger because Georg had picked up quite an assortment of discontents along the way.

Periodic arguments between Georg's original followers and the "heretics" marked the hours until a place to lodge was found. The main point of conflict seemed to stem from the unwillingness of the heretics to get involved in the overthrow of oppressors.

One of Georg's more outspoken followers was trying to explain his position. "We will someday be numerous enough that we will be able to take the treasure from the wealthy church leaders and distribute it to the poor."

All eyes turned to Josef Radl, the soft-spoken, new leader of the sect, but all he said was the obvious: "They won't let you."

The entire group roared with laughter, and Reinhold said, "Of course they won't, but if they try to stop us, we are prepared to use force."

"You will be slaughtered. If you threaten their livelihood, they will utterly destroy you."

"Don't you even care that the poor go hungry and that the church leaders are the ones who make sure they go hungry?" Sigfried broke in.

"Of course I care," Josef blurted, "but if our kingdom is in heaven, what point is there in hurling ourselves onto their earthly swords?"

"Your leader and his wife seemed willing enough to climb onto the execution pyre," Reinhold remarked. "You'd accomplish more if you'd fight back."

Josef shook his head. "They were not fighting for bread; the bishop asked them to give up their faith. There is a big difference."

"But our faith is the same, is it not?"

Josef leaned back and smiled. "Is it?"

Sigfried returned to the subject. "Our Lord Jesus fed the poor, and He defied the religious authorities of His day every time He got the chance."

Josef nodded. "But Jesus never attacked them with swords."

Sigfried ignored that. "They will destroy us one way or another— swiftly by sword or slowly by starvation. We must destroy them first."

"But that won't do *you* any good."

"I don't understand," Reinhold said, raking his fingers through his scraggly hair. "You defy the church authorities. Your friends were even burned at the stake. Yet you seem to be defending the church."

"I'm not. They are our enemies—but only because they have declared themselves to be our enemies. I would not kill them though; I pity them. And I pray that they will repent before it is too late."

"Repent? A bishop? That *is* blasphemy," Reinhold murmured. "You must be crazy."

"No," Josef responded slowly, "but you have a problem."

Reinhold smiled. "Which is . . . ?"

"I don't know if you can bear it," Josef answered, returning the smile, "for it is a very harsh truth."

Reinhold was offended and sputtered, "There is nothing—nothing—that you could say that I can't bear."

"Very well; I did warn you." Josef looked slowly around the circle of men and then said, "I am quoting the words of our Lord Jesus from the gospel of St. John: 'An hour is coming for everyone who kills you to think that he is offering a service to God. And these things they will do, because they have not known the Father, or Me.'"

Everyone sat in stunned silence for a moment, and then one of Georg's men blurted out, "Liar!"

Andrew had heard enough. He had been listening halfheartedly, but he could not bear the loud argument that now broke out. He had other things to worry about.

While wandering through deserted mountain passes, Andrew had assumed that it would be fairly easy to find Titus of Athens: simply inquire after him at the inn in Milan, find him, and convince him to come to Felsenburg with them. Now that he had seen Milan—and only from a distance—he realized that there were probably dozens of inns, and too many streets in which to search. The task was impossible.

Although Andrew knew that the bishop would have advised against it, he decided to take Georg, at least partially, into his confidence. The monk had not been present during the discussion between his men and Josef Radl's. He was repairing the wheel on one of the carts in a tumbled-down shed when Andrew asked him if he had any idea how to find someone in Milan.

"Who?"

Andrew was unnerved by Georg's intense reaction but told him anyway. "Titus of Athens?" he shouted, dropping his tools with a clatter. "Of course I've heard of him! Why do you ask?"

"I . . . I need to find him."

"You need to—!" Georg rolled his eyes heavenward and leaned heavily against the wall, realization sweeping over him. "Dear God in heaven, do you mean to tell me that you were sent here by our benevolent bishop to find—I mean, hire—Titus?"

Andrew gulped and nodded, steadying himself against the cart. *What could be so wrong?*

Georg closed the space between them in two angry strides. "Don't retreat into silence! Speak, man, for you are a part of this!"

Andrew shrank back from Georg's rage. "Speaking is . . . so difficult." He took a breath and chose the simplest words he could think of. "I . . . I know nothing about the man," he answered quietly.

"The man's a heretic!" Georg roared.

Andrew shoved past Georg and escaped to the other side of the cart. "You've sur—surrrounded yourself with heretics," he said evenly, surprised at his own boldness. "Why should you care?"

Georg shook his clerical finger at the young monk and lowered his voice. "That's where you're wrong. I surround myself with the discontented. There is a difference."

It was Andrew's turn to roll his eyes. The emotion allowed the words to form more quickly in his mouth. "The results are the same. Confusion. Unhap . . . unhappiness. They could even be burned at the stake. And for what? Do they even know what they believe in? Do you know what you believe in?"

Georg pursed his mouth for a moment and then threw the question back. "Do you?"

Something deep within Andrew gave a slow sigh. "Titus," he said, coming back to the original problem. "How do I find him?"

Georg's agitation returned. "You can't be serious. Why couldn't he find an architect in Prag or Aachen? Surely there are good ones there."

Andrew turned and started to leave the shed. "I'll ask someone else."

"Why don't you tell the bishop that you couldn't find him?" Georg grinned.

"Do you know how to find him or not?"

"The man's a heretic," Georg repeated.

"What kind?"

"He studied architecture in Egypt."

"That doesn't make him dangerous."

"He's a Greek who converted to Islam. He's a Muselman now."

Andrew's heart sank. "So what am I supposed to do?"

"You tell me."

"I'm supposed to find Titus, give him jewels as a . . . a . . ."

"Bribe?"

"Whatever. And to invite him to come to Fels—to come and build the bishop's cathedral."

"Shouldn't that be God's cathedral?" Georg asked in amusement.

Andrew answered hotly, "I'm telling you what I was told. Now can you help me find him?"

Georg nodded unhappily. "The last I heard, he was living at the archbishop's palace." He paused and cocked his head to one side. "Didn't Bishop Gernot say that his 'dear friend' the archbishop would surely like to see the Rosen Jungfrau before his death?"

Andrew's mouth tipped into a faint smile. "I really know nothing about that, although I heard him say it, as well. Just help me find Titus."

"Everyone is going to regret this."

"Probably." Andrew started to leave the barn but paused a moment. *It was so much easier to live in the monastery and not be able to speak.*

TWENTY

eorg was right, of course. Andrew hated Milan. He had expected the activity and noise as people went about their business through the narrow streets; he was more surprised by their rudeness. Too preoccupied to notice, they bumped into one another, and walking through the streets, one had to be ever alert to carts and wagons that rumbled by. The innumerable marketplaces were disorderly and gaudy.

Andrew felt like he was suffocating in the humid heat. He now understood why Josef Radl's heretics had decided to spend the time until next spring in one of the cool, fertile valleys north of Milan. The buildings that lined the streets of the city were three and four stories high. They blocked out the light, and the stench of the sewers was trapped between them in the motionless air. The canal, which ringed the city, was unspeakably foul. When the sun shone on it, the odor was revolting. In fact, Andrew thought that the entire city—streets, river, buildings, people—was dirtier than anywhere he had ever been.

"You might be correct," agreed Georg, "but then you haven't been to any other city." Once more, Andrew was silenced by Georg's unusual viewpoint.

All of the inns were built outside the walls as close as possible to the city. The landlords had to accept responsibility for every paying guest, and if the inns had been within the city, perhaps an unscrupulous guest might have opened the gates at night to enemies.

They chose an inn as far away from the canal as possible, but the odor still hung in the air. On the first evening, they were treated to an almost decent stew of meat and garlic. The innkeeper was a dark, enthusiastic man who spoke only a local dialect. In spite of this disadvantage, he seemed friendly enough, and they were able to communicate most of their desires by smiles and gestures. After three days, Andrew's party had decided that this might be the place to spend the winter. At breakfast the next morning, Georg asked one of the other guests of the inn the way to the archbishop's palace.

Andrew and Georg were completely unprepared for their reaction to his request. Those who heard his question simply lowered their heads and resumed eating. One of them, however, spit a large mouthful of ale into Georg's face. The innkeeper, after a loud, unintelligible exchange with the guests, marched over to Georg and Andrew and snatched the food away from them, all the while shouting at them and waving his free hand in their faces.

For the first time since Andrew had met Georg, his friend looked confused. "I'm sorry," he said contritely, wiping his face on his sleeve, "Did I say something wrong?"

The innkeeper finished his tirade and stormed back into the kitchen.

The guests roared in laughter, and one who spoke a German dialect they could understand snorted, "Anyone who has business with the archbishop is an enemy of the people!"

Andrew's heart was pounding, and he wondered what would happen if he tried to leave the room. The rest of Georg's men had not come down yet, and he felt danger.

Georg spoke calmly. "I don't know the archbishop. Could you tell me, please, what is wrong?"

The man leaned forward and shook his hand at Georg. "How is it that you can afford to stay at an inn? Why don't you go to your own kind at the abbey? You would be safer there," he finished threateningly.

Georg stood slowly and stepped over the bench. "Thank you for your advice." He pulled Andrew to his feet, but, before they could return to their quarters, the innkeeper stepped into the room, blocking their exit. Behind him stood his son, whose arms were full of Georg's and Andrew's few possessions. He pushed past the two bewildered men, opened the front door, and threw their belongings into the street. The treasure box and the Rosen Jungfrau, which had been brought in under cover of night, were not among them. Georg glanced around at the angry faces and then left the inn, with Andrew close behind. The innkeeper slammed the door.

The two men gathered their things and stuffed them into their satchels. Then Georg flopped onto the bench beside the door.

"The Rosen Jungfrau?" asked Andrew, feeling panic rise as he thought of the consequences of losing her.

Georg shrugged. "We'll wait till the others wake up and send them back in for her and the treasure box. Don't worry; no one can find them."

It worked just as he said, even though the rest of their party were also obliged to find new quarters.

The search for new lodging used up the morning, and before long they were both drenched in sweat, suffering in their long, woolen cassocks. During their search, however, they met several priests who were able to give them directions to the archbishop's palace. One of them, Father Tasso, was even able to explain the animosity of the innkeeper and his guests.

"It is very difficult for the merchants to make a living. The more successful they are, the more they are taxed because the poor cannot be taxed. Most of the merchants' taxes find their way into the coffers of the archbishop or the duke. They cannot tax the poor." He waved his arm in a wide semicircle, indicating the many beggars who lined the streets with their hands raised to every passerby. "But the merchants are taxed so heavily that they have little left for even basic charity." He sighed. "There is trouble coming."

Georg laughed. "Milan is not alone. I can hardly believe that I was accused of friendship with an archbishop. Usually I have the bishops threatening *me*!"

"You need a place to stay?"

Georg nodded. "For eight men. The bishop's guards who journeyed with us will fend for themselves for the winter."

Father Tasso said, "I know of a hostel not far from my church. I live in the glassmakers' quarter."

They entered the city and threaded their way through alleys. The hostel Father Tasso spoke of had once been the refectory for the church, which Father Tasso had converted into a refuge for beggars. Its one large room was cluttered with shreds of cloth and thin blankets, which were probably the only coverings the people owned.

"The people are called 'ragpickers,'" the priest explained. "They collect things in order to survive."

Meals were cooked out back in the courtyard, Father Tasso explained, and if Andrew, Georg , and his men were not on time, there would be nothing left over. At this time of day, the building was fairly empty. A few old women, seeking shelter from the heat, gossiped in one corner. Georg and his party were assigned another corner and then were told the price for the food and shelter.

"If you can afford an inn," Father Tasso said with a grin, "then you can afford this place."

Georg shrugged good-naturedly. "Bishop Gernot's paying."

Andrew and the other men deposited their satchels in their corner while Georg held a whispered conversation with Father Tasso concerning the Rosen Jungfrau. They decided to store the picture and the treasure in the church vaults where they would be safe from taxes and beggars.

Andrew and Georg thanked the priest and left the rest of the men to settle in at the hostel. They followed the directions to the archbishop's palace. They were jostled and shoved by crowds nearly the whole route. The beggars seemed so different from the intense but taciturn Germans who lived north of the Alps. Andrew remembered the quiet misery of the hungry, young widow outside Father Augustin's house. These Milanese beggars expressed their unhappiness loudly and insistently, and there were so many of them. Andrew doubted that they could ever all be fed.

The palace came into view, and they were questioned extensively at its entrance before the archbishop's guards would let them past the gate into the cool, green courtyard. The palace was grander than anything Andrew had ever seen. He and Georg agreed that its opulence was grossly indecent when compared to the rest of the city.

The two men were led down several cool, dark corridors. They passed carved wooden doors, but none had been left ajar to satisfy the curiosity of the two men. Several brightly colored tapestries hung opposite the few windows that lit the dim passageways. "I do not understand how the archbishop can ignore the poverty of his people," Andrew murmured. "A man who represents God—"

"—who *claims* to represent God," Georg corrected in a whisper. "Do you really believe that a true man of God could close his eyes to such inequities?"

In his surprise at Georg's heresy, Andrew stumbled over the corner of one of the sandstone paving tiles, rounded after decades of footsteps. "Are you saying that these men are not God's representatives?"

Georg narrowed his eyes. "What kind of a God do you have?"

"I—" Andrew began but was silenced as their guide stopped abruptly and banged a knocker on an oversized bronze door cast with figures of flowers and animals.

The door was opened, and they entered past a bowing servant and were led into a breezy sitting room, where the open windows admitted the fragrance of the flowers and trees from the courtyard below. Two maids entered almost at once, bringing silver trays of pastries, bowls of peaches and plums, and a sweet, red wine in crystal goblets.

After the girls left, Georg raised his goblet. "Nice place," he said with a grin.

Andrew sighed. "My life was much too sheltered. I can't believe that someone would live like this. I've always assumed that the things taught us at the monastery were eternal principles, lived out by all of God's people."

"Mmmm," Georg agreed, "Loving your neighbor as yourself, doing unto others, giving up your second cloak. It doesn't happen much out here."

"What about loving God with all of your heart and mind and soul? How can anyone do that and then ignore—rob, even—the poor?"

"You're looking at it the wrong way. I asked you what kind of a God you have. He's not bad, but neither is He involved. Perhaps He just gave the universe a spin and now we have to fend for ourselves."

Andrew frowned. "You don't really believe that."

Georg shrugged. "I'm going to make my world better. Not—" he assured, "—that I want to live like this. What I really want is to leave everyone I meet better off—happier, better fed, and feeling like life has finally treated them fairly. It can be done. All I need are people willing to pay the price to accomplish this." He cut a peach in half and tossed the stone out the window. "You're welcome to join me."

Andrew could only stare at Georg as he groped for a fitting reply. His confusion was interrupted as Titus of Athens strode into the room. Both clergymen jumped to their feet. Titus greeted them formally in Latin, the language they had in common. "My apologies for being late. The archbishop wanted to see the plans for his new summer residence. He finds the heat here unbearable."

"He is well?" Georg asked smoothly.

"Alas, no, and he suffers so with the heat and the stench from the streets." Titus sniffed and rubbed his nose with a scented handkerchief.

Georg's teeth snapped violently into the peach half.

Andrew drew a deep breath. "We bring you greetings from Gernot von Kärnten, now Bishop of Felsenburg."

"I was told that he had sent you. How is he?" The tone of his voice conveyed no trace of interest.

"Quite well, thank you," said Andrew, trying to say the acceptable thing. "He'll be glad you asked."

"Really." The boredom in his voice was deliberate.

Andrew pressed on. "He . . . um . . . sent us here to make you an offer. It's a bit awkward, for I'm sure you're quite content here in Milan."

Titus poured himself a glass of wine and bowed slightly to Georg and Andrew, a faint smile touching his lips before he drank.

Andrew looked at Georg, his eyes begging for help, but Georg turned away. Andrew continued. "The . . . the cathedral—well, it wasn't a cathedral really, just a church—in Felsenburg burned to the ground. The bishop feels that this would be a good time to build something really striking." Andrew gave up trying to be tactful and blurted out, "The bishop wants you to come to Felsenburg to build him—I mean, God—a cathedral."

Titus set his goblet down, the smile gone, surprise evident. "You're serious," he stated flatly.

Andrew nodded silently, his face unhappy.

George intervened. "My young friend here is just learning the fine art of diplomacy. We do hope that we haven't offended you in any way. Our intention was to make you a very generous offer on behalf of the bishop. If it is impudent of us, or if you find it distasteful, please forgive us, and we will leave at once."

Titus indicated the comfortable seats. "Please won't you sit down," he said kindly. "I will spare your young friend any further agony. I would be delighted to come." He raised his hand before they could say anything. "But this must remain between us until I find the right moment to make the decision public."

"But—" protested Andrew.

"Just like that," said Georg dryly.

Andrew persisted. "Don't you even want—"

"I'm sorry," said Titus, "Did you bring me a . . . a—"

Andrew held out the tiny leather pouch of jewels.

"A bribe." Georg intercepted the pouch, amusement dancing in his eyes. "I don't think you need one. Why are you so willing to come?"

"I want to finally build something. I came to Milan and became the archbishop's architect because I thought I would be able to build wonderful things. Well, the archbishop enjoys the planning, but he spends his money on other pleasures. Before I knew better, I did some of my best work for him, and now the plans lie in his treasury."

"So there is no summer residence?" Georg asked slyly.

"No. Nor will there ever be one."

"Will he let you go?"

"He will have no choice."

"You seem very confident," Georg remarked. "Suppose that he chooses to retain you?"

"Leave that to me." He munched on a plum for a moment and then suddenly asked, "So. To which god will we build a church?"

Andrew choked on his wine and looked at Georg. "To which—" he stammered. "But we only have one God."

"Ah, yes," Titus scoffed, "The Father, the Son, the Holy Spirit, St. Maria, many saints. You worship them all, do you not?"

"I . . . we—" The young monk was stunned by the blasphemy.

"Well?"

Andrew pulled himself together, having observed the smirk on Georg's face. "We honor them," he said haughtily.

"You bow down to them," said Titus with finality. "It's the same thing."

"Brother Georg has told me of your unorthodox views. Wouldn't you find it difficult to build a church that represents that which you do not believe?"

"Not at all! No more than you have trouble building a church when you do not even know what you believe."

"I do."

"You do not! You say you worship one God when, in fact, you bow down to many. You don't even know your own Ten Commandments."

"I do."

Georg interrupted. "This is getting nowhere. Do you intend to stir up a hornet's nest in Felsenburg?"

"The bishop knows exactly where I stand," Titus assured them. He stood and paced back and forth between the window and Andrew's chair. "He wants me, for I am the best architect on this side of the Danube. We will build a cathedral like no one has ever seen before—higher, wider, more beautiful. It will be a monument—almost everlasting—to the achievements of men, who are given unlimited abilities by their Creator." He stopped and shook his finger at Andrew. "By their one Creator, young Andrew. Do not quote me the Ten Commandments; read them. You shall see that I am right."

Andrew looked at his hands in his lap and vowed to do that very thing. An infidel should not be building a cathedral. He was glad when Georg announced that it was time for them to leave.

Andrew stood and finished his assignment. "Bishop Gernot would like you to plan on leaving Milan as soon as the passes are clear in the spring. Then there will be time to finalize plans and begin digging the foundation."

"Excavating," Titus corrected. He clapped Andrew on the shoulder. "Tell him I will come. And don't worry; I won't stir up any hornet's nests." He turned to Georg. "You weren't planning to leave the bishop's 'bribe' with me, were you?"

"I hardly think you need it. There are others who need it desperately," Georg said, pulling the leather pouch from the folds of his cassock. "Many of them live in this wretched city, not a stone's throw from this palace. I trust you notice these people and feel some pity for them."

"I'm glad *you* do. Keep it. Bishop Gernot needn't find out."

TWENTY-ONE

t was a dismal victory. Martin's desire to read faltered at the gate to the bishop's residence, and he felt as if he had lost instead of won. He had wanted to read so badly that he had never bothered to ask what the cost of his rebellion might be. That's how Papa saw it, though. Learning to read came at the expense of Stefan's life; the two were inseparable.

"I simply can't take the risk," Papa had said in a rare talkative moment. "I thought that God gave a mason sons so that those sons could be masons, too. That is the law of things. And if I would have had many sons—I would have given one to the church—" he paused and then added bitterly, "but your mother couldn't have any more children."

Martin felt that Papa expected him to say something, but there seemed nothing fitting to say.

"The risk is too great," his father said again. "God has taken my oldest son. I never asked Stefan if he wanted to be a mason; no one ever asked me. Somehow your prayers were heard, and God has told me—through Stefan—that you must do what your heart desires."

Martin could not understand how Papa could remain dry-eyed, for his own throat ached with suppressed emotion. It horrified him to think that his resistance may have somehow turned God against Stefan. He still could not speak, and he tried to swallow the lump in his throat.

"After the first frost, you will go to the bishop's school, and I will apprentice one of the Mischer boys. Wolfgang Mischer cannot train all of his sons anyway. Perhaps someday," Papa added dejectedly, "little Bernhard will follow in my footsteps."

That thought jerked Martin back to the present. He grabbed the latch on the bishop's gate and wrenched it open. "Bernhard," he whispered fiercely, "is my whole reason for learning to read. How will he ever learn to please God with a drunken godfather?" He marched to the side entrance where several other boys already waited.

He was older and a bit taller than most of them, but they were better dressed. They were the sons of merchants and landowners and had been sent to the big city for a necessary education. A few of them had been to school elsewhere and now had returned home to learn at the new cathedral school. These stood on the top-most step at the side entrance and tried to look distinguished.

"What are you doing here?" whispered a voice behind him.

He turned to see Sepp Feick, the baker's youngest son. "I'm going to learn to read!"

"Some of us get to choose," Sepp said enviously. Everyone in the city knew that there was nothing for the baker to do with his seventh son but to give him to the church.

In the next few weeks, Martin and Sepp stepped over the boundaries usually observed between mason's son and baker's son and became friends. Most of the boys in the cathedral school boarded in the quarters over the bishop's kitchen, and those who did not were often viewed with disfavor, a situation that Martin and Sepp did not understand.

Going to school meant learning more than just reading. The instructors, most of whom came from St. Jude's, began by speaking the local dialect to the new pupils, but the more advanced boys were taught almost exclusively in Latin. The chancellor of the cathedral school, Canon Wilfred, trained the boys in memory skills, which they practiced by memorizing the Psalms both in Latin and in Greek. Computing the seasons was considered to be very important to the children of landowners, and that was taught along with classes on the stars, the zodiac, and heavenly signs and their interpretations. Martin's favorite class was writing, which was the careful copying of figures from one manuscript to the other. One did not need to know how to read to be able to write neatly. The boys learned reading by deciphering the scraps of manuscripts copied painstakingly during writing class.

The main purpose of the school was to provide the cathedral with choirboys. The soft-spoken Canon Julian introduced the pupils to the Gregorian chants and taught them to sing. As Martin learned more and more Latin, the chants evolved from a jumble of hypnotizing sounds into intelligible praises to God.

Winter blew in at the end of October, and, just as the Wahrsager had predicted, it was the coldest winter anyone could remember. That first morning of the storm, Martin lay on his cot, curled in a tiny ball, listening to the wind howl around the chimney. He dreaded the moment when he would finally have to jump from his bed and pull on all of the clothes he owned, trying to control the chattering of his teeth. When he was dressed, he arranged sticks and wood over the coals and stirred them gently, blowing until they caught fire. The pot of broth was frozen, and he moved it over the fire for the family's breakfast before he threw on his cloak and ventured out into Lärchenplatz. The snow was already heaped in drifts.

The blowing snowflakes stung his face, and by the time he reached the bishop's gate, he was panting from the difficult walk through hardened drifts. He leaned all of his weight against the gate, and it pushed the snow aside enough for him to slip through into the garden, where eerie, white shapes had replaced the trees and shrubs of yesterday. The steps at the side entrance of the bishop's residence had been cleared, and Martin was glad when he could close the great door and leave the snowstorm outside.

A huge fire crackled in the dining room fireplace, and most of the boys had already shed their cloaks. Martin went to thaw by the fire before joining the others at the breakfast table. The hot milk from the bishop's cows and the hearty bread soon warmed him, and he forgot the cold in his dedication to his lessons.

The storm raged for two weeks, and the boys grew restless. Then one day Martin and Sepp were just finishing their midday meal in the bishop's dining room when one of the other boys said much too loudly, "Listen!"

They listened and heard nothing.

"No wind," someone whispered.

They scrambled from their benches and ran to fling open the doors to the garden. It was still very cold, but the white sun in the blue sky scattered sparkles on the smooth drifts of snow. Chancellor Wilfred ordered the doors closed, but the boys were already energized by the beauty of the day. During the afternoon's lessons, they had such trouble concentrating that finally the chancellor, in a rare display of consideration, sent them out into the garden to play.

They had not been out more than ten minutes, however, when Father Augustin came to the doors and called them in.

"But Chancellor Wilfred told us we could," protested one of the more vocal boys.

"Chancellor Wilfred had no right," Father Augustin said softly. "The gardener has informed me that if you trample the snow, then in the spring, the grass and flowers will not grow where you have run."

The boys hung their heads and returned to their studies.

The next day another blizzard swooped down from the north. It deposited a layer of snow over the first one. After that, one storm upon another crippled the city of Felsenburg, and the cold, gloomy winter stretched out ahead. They were cut off from one another, and there was no escape from the harsh cold. Caring for their personal needs was difficult, and it was impossible to hold a market in the platz. The egg woman had nothing but eggs (if her chickens did not freeze), and the miller had only grains—and maybe no fire over which to bake bread. Those who had firewood were warm, but they could not eat firewood, and soon they were leaving the safety of their homes to trade fuel for food.

Martin ate his meals at the cathedral school. His cheeks grew rosy, but it pained him to see how cold and hungry the members of his family were becoming. When the guilt became too great, he would put his bread allotment from the school's table into his pocket for Bernie and Klara. In the evenings, the little boy would devour the bread as if he had not eaten all day. Klara, pale and sad in her second pregnancy (which had begun just a few weeks before Stefan's accident), always had to be coaxed by Mama, but she would finally eat it just so it would not go to waste. Mama admitted that Martin's being at the school was a blessing, for God was providing not only the bread, but Martin's meals as well.

Mama's viewpoint gave her son a feeling of purpose, which inspired him. He threw himself more completely into his studies. He began to grasp the principles of reading, and his ability with a pen was envied by many of the other boys. The fulfillment he had been seeking all his life hovered within reach now. Through the long, tedious months when the winter seemed eternal, he basked in his successes, but his self-satisfaction came crashing down on the day that Theo Rube's father was arrested for poaching.

The boys were in the middle of reciting a lengthy passage from the Latin Psalms when Theo's older brother, Willi, barged into the classroom and ordered Theo to come with him.

Theo, being only ten years old, was pinned to his chair by his fear of the chancellor. Willi grabbed the boy and pulled him to his feet.

Chancellor Wilfred rose slowly from his place beside the fire. "That will be enough, Wilhelm," he admonished. "Would you please tell me what the problem is?"

Willi focused a contemptuous look on the chancellor. "It wouldn't matter to you. It never matters to people like you!" He suddenly sobbed and bent to whisper in Theo's ear.

Theo shook his brother's hands off and remembered his position in the school. "Please, Herr," he asked politely, "May I go home?"

Willi, calmed by Theo's poise, added, "My mother needs us, Herr."

The other boys gasped, wondering what calamity would bring forth such a careful choice of words. They were not enlightened, however, and Chancellor Wilfred, without further conversation, allowed the boy to go.

The next day, Theo was back in class, uncommunicative and unable to tell the boys much more than the fact that his father had been arrested and was in a cell below the bishop's residence. He did not know why.

That day, the pauses between teachers were times of solemn reflection as each boy tried to imagine what might have happened to result in imprisonment in the cells below their feet. Other men and women had been there before, but usually the charges were severe. Comforting Theo was a task too large for them, so they avoided him.

Their midday meal was interrupted by Father Augustin, who solved the mystery. He stood beside Theo, who fixed his eyes on the opposite wall, ashamed and frightened.

"I know that you young men have by now heard that Günther Rube has been imprisoned for theft."

The boys, of course, had not heard, and they stifled their gasps and darted sympathetic looks toward Theo.

Father Augustin pressed on, "Stealing is wrong, and God is angered when we take things that do not belong to us. When we do this, we must confess to avoid punishment. There are, however, degrees of guilt, and Theobald Rube's father has crossed that boundary." He paused and glanced around the room.

Martin felt his gaze heavily and lowered his eyes to his bowl. The soup had stopped steaming.

"Herr Rube took the liberty of hunting on the bishop's game preserve and killed one of the bishop's stags. It was while he was dragging it home that his transgression was discovered. He said that he needed the meat for his family, but you boys must never make the mistake of assuming that you may take something that you need." Augustin pointed out the window, where fat snowflakes whirled against the knobby glass. "That stag did not belong to Herr Rube, but it also did not belong to His Excellenz. The preserve was a gift to the church many years ago, and the land, and everything on it, belongs to our dear Lord God." He patted Theo on the shoulder and asked, "You boys would never steal from God would you?"

They shook their heads in unison—all except Theo, who continued to sit as if frozen. Martin shoved his hands into his pockets, and his knuckles scraped unexpectedly against the edges of the bread crusts. A sickening lump crept into his stomach and his face grew warm, but he kept his eyes riveted to the table. He had not thought that he was stealing—especially from God.

Father Augustin was speaking again. "Always remember: That which is God's is sacred. In the Holy Scriptures, God struck dead a man and woman who stole from Him. But God blesses those who reverence Him." He turned abruptly and glided from the room.

In the silence that followed, Theo suddenly spoke. "Dead? What will happen to my father?"

Chancellor Wilfred bit his lip and then said, "I . . . I'm not sure. He will not die. Perhaps he will have to pay a fine."

"But we have no money," the boy protested.

"Then I fear he may have to remain imprisoned until the debt is paid." He turned to the other boys and explained, "It's a serious thing to rob God."

No one had an appetite to finish the cold soup. The bowls were cleared, and the pupils returned to their classrooms.

The bread weighed heavily in Martin's mind, although he did not think that it was visible to others. Feeling a need to cleanse his own conscience, he came up alongside Theo and tried to think of a few comforting words to say. "Perhaps it won't be as Chancellor Wilfred said," he offered.

Theo shook his head. "My family has nothing to eat," he murmured sadly. "Papa was just trying to feed them. Why does God need the stag?" Suddenly Theo pulled several pieces of bread from his pocket. "I take these home to my little sisters every evening."

Martin gulped and looked around at the other boys. He did not know what to say but pushed the bread back toward Theo's pocket.

His reaction disturbed Theo, who asked cautiously, "You won't tell, will you?"

Vigorously Martin shook his head, but he couldn't look the boy in the eyes.

"God doesn't want my little sisters to starve to death," Theo announced firmly.

Martin was spared answering because the teacher entered the room, and the boys scurried to their places. He had difficulty concentrating on his lessons, and finally he made a desperate vow to God that he would never again steal from the cathedral school.

At the end of classes, Chancellor Wilfred came to give the evening benediction, after which he announced, "For those of you who live at home, you will find bread and meat in the hallway. Take them home for your families, and remember the goodness of God."

As Martin waited in line to collect his share, he leaned over and whispered into Theo's ear, "You see, God *does* take care of us."

Ten-year-old Theo, matured by hardship, turned a look of pity and disdain upon Martin, but Martin was not able to interpret it.

"Well, look." Martin tried again, pointing to the piles of bread with a smile. "How happy our families will be!"

One of the monks handed Theo his loaf of bread and packet of meat, wrapped in a cloth. The boy considered the bloody packet for a moment before saying to Martin, "How stupid can you be?"

Martin pondered the problem as he fought his way home through the snowdrifts. Finally it occurred to him that the meat was probably stag meat. He thought of the bread in his pockets and realized that after today, he would have to face Bernie's hungry eyes every evening, and there was nothing he could do about it for he had made a vow to God.

TWENTY-TWO

here was plenty of food in Milan that winter. But Father Tasso's hostel could afford to feed and shelter the poorest in Milan only through the benevolence of the artisans and merchants who lived in the area. They were not by nature merciful, nor were they particularly wealthy, but the priest had convinced them that beggars with food in their stomachs and a place to sleep were less likely to rob others.

Andrew, Georg, and Georg's men could not return to Felsenburg until the passes were clear in the early summer. Although grateful to have a roof over their heads within Milan's city walls, they had to share their room with an ever increasing collection of hungry, homeless, and bad-smelling ragpickers. Georg seemed to thrive on the noise and activity. Andrew, accustomed to solitude and an organized schedule, escaped each day to wander the turbulent streets of the city, wondering how he could endure the noise, filth, and boredom until spring.

Then one day Father Tasso asked him to write a letter for a young man whose wealthy father had died. The young man was the estranged son of the deceased landowner, and he wanted to present his case to the duke to claim his inheritance. The claim was successful, and the young man—until then, permanently homeless—was able to make a generous donation to Father Tasso's hostel before moving to his new home. After that, Andrew began to write letters and documents for many of the poor, who could neither read nor write and who had no money to pay a scribe. At first he was glad to be busy, but news of his ability with a pen and words spread, and there came a time when he longed for the former quiet days of boredom.

Brother Georg also found meaningful things to do, for Milan was a city in upheaval, and Georg's clever wit and logic contributed support to those who fought for change.

And change was long overdue, as the crowded conditions at Father Tasso's hostel demonstrated. Normally as the Christmas season ended, the residents of Milan would look forward to carnival, the weeks of festival and celebration preceding Lent. The merchants generally increased their giving to the hostel in order to cover their own spiritual indiscretions, and the poor could enjoy the results. That was their hope.

This year the duke of Milan raised the price of flour.

"Actually," Brother Georg sputtered when he heard of it, "he raised the *tax* on the milling of the flour. But I hardly think that those who live here will appreciate the distinction."

Higher prices meant fewer donations to the hostel, and the meals—never fancy—became more sparse. Anxiety crept into the lives of those whose survival depended upon the mercy of others. Andrew and Father Tasso spent long hours calming frayed tempers, while Georg and some of his men contributed to that fraying by arguing that only a confrontation would solve the problem.

The merchants and artisans, who felt the taxes most directly, did not keep their unhappiness to themselves. They met at the local guild house and decided to compensate by increasing their own prices. Though a bit inflated, life could continue as it had. They assumed that the duke would not notice as long as he received his money. Their assumption was incorrect. He dispatched an emissary to remind them that prices were fixed—which, of course, they had not forgotten—and that raising prices without the duke's approval was forbidden.

Against his will, Father Tasso saw his hostel evolve into a gathering place for dissidents. Brother Georg's wit and charisma became the hub around which every legitimate complaint revolved. Merchants and artisans dropped by to discuss their difficulties, and the Bavarian monk was invariably able to turn each difficulty into further proof of the unsuitability of those who ruled.

Andrew felt that Georg enjoyed too much the arguments and discussions of those who had a stake in the dispute and feared that his popularity would give his fanaticism courage. Given enough time, the merchants were apt to reach the inevitable solution: Seize the granary.

No one could remember afterward who first dared to say it aloud, but once the suggestion was made, it flew around the crowded room like a bird set free. The merchants laughed and tolerated the undesired familiarity of the ragpickers, who slapped their new friends on the back. Georg's dark eyes glittered in anticipation. Father Tasso's objections dropped unheard into the excitement, for the idea had a life of its own, and the merchants heard only what they wanted to hear. Plans were made, assignments given, a date set, vows of silence taken. The merchants rushed home to their families, lighthearted for the first time in months.

Before they went to bed that night, Andrew confronted Brother Georg on the wisdom of seizing the duke's granary.

"You're condemning many of them to death," Andrew protested, "and you know it."

"Don't be ridiculous," Georg explained, as if Andrew were a fool. "We are going unarmed to insist that the duke give the people what is by rights theirs. There are too many of us. We'll simply overwhelm them."

Andrew shook his head. "I think you are mistaken. They are prepared to take the grain, and what will they do when they are met by the duke's armed men?"

"We will ask to see the duke, and we will take what is ours."

Andrew found it difficult to understand why Georg, usually logical and compassionate, would overlook the obvious outcome. He tried to reason with him again. "These are not your people. You need to let them fight their own battles."

"You're afraid to die," Georg said mockingly.

Andrew opened his mouth but closed it again quickly. He did not know what to say.

"And besides," Georg added, "there are some things worth dying for."

It did not seem right. "But for grain?"

"Don't you see? They are not seizing grain; they are seizing control of their own lives."

"Do they know that?"

Georg shrugged. "The merchants are not as stupid as you suppose."

Andrew doubted that the ragpickers were sophisticated enough to fight for ideals. "They are hungry. They will confront the duke's soldiers for a sack full of grain. Georg, you have control of this situation," he pleaded. "Stop this before it goes too far!"

"Brother Andrew, I asked you some months ago if you wish to join us in our struggle to provide basic food and shelter for the poor of this world. Surely you can't be saying that you prefer for the poor to starve."

"They're not starving," Andrew told him bluntly.

Georg's frustration with the younger man was evident. "I have a chance to right a wrong, but I cannot do it alone. If you are afraid, you don't need to come; others will take your place. But it is clear that your cowardice is greater than your compassion."

The insult cut deeply. Andrew was afraid, but not only for his own life. It had been a long time since he'd had a friend, and he now realized that he liked Georg. This was not the time to say so.

Georg lay down on his mat and arranged his cloak under his head. "No one's going to die," he said with finality.

~∞ ∞~

The day of the festival of St. Timothy and St. Titus had been chosen for their confiscation of the granary. The late January morning was drizzly and cold, but the crowd of three hundred men and boys did not allow the weather to discourage them as they met in the glassblowers' market. Standing apart from the group, Andrew and Father Tasso watched from the steps of the church, arms folded to ward off the chill that not only swirled around their heads but penetrated their hearts. Andrew still felt Georg's challenge keenly, but even the mocking of his friend could not convince him that this cause was worth dying for. Yes, he was afraid to die, and until he conquered that, no risk was worth taking.

The mood was festive and undisciplined, but the ragpickers and the merchants still formed two distinct groups. When it seemed that everyone had arrived, the horde surged toward the northern city wall with the ragpickers in the lead. They swept through the streets like a flood, picking up the debris of jobless ragpickers, homeless beggars, and idle boys along the way. Before they arrived at the granaries, talk of free grain had ripped through their ranks and had kindled a mood of aggression, which gave them their initial victory.

᷒᷒ ᷒᷒

"It happened as I thought it would," Georg gloated later that afternoon as he related the events to Father Tasso while Andrew listened in the background. "We frightened the guards—there were only about ten of them—and our noise was truly awesome. They had no communications with their superiors. We simply surrounded them and took their weapons from them. None of them had keys, but some of the rabble that we had picked up had axes. I had been worried about that," Georg gave a glance over to Andrew, "but no one was hurt. We used the axes to hack at the gates until the wood gave way. Then they chopped holes in the storage houses and filled their containers with wheat, barley, and rye. We left about twenty of the ragpickers with the soldiers' weapons and axes to guard the granary."

Father Tasso and Andrew had not accompanied the mob on their expedition, and they did not share Brother Georg's exhilaration. "So you stole the grain?" Father Tasso asked.

"Stole? No! Many of these people sweat in the fields to grow the grain. It doesn't belong to the duke." Sarcasm crept into Georg's voice. "Then the duke generously offers to store it for them and allows them to buy their grain back."

Father Tasso sighed. "The fields belong to the duke and the bishop. You don't know these men. It's not over."

The following morning passed very quietly, the participants of the riot keeping out of sight. Around noon, however, two carts drawn by horses and driven by the duke's soldiers pulled into the glassblowers' market. In the first cart, a messenger stood to announce: "The duke has taken his granary back, and those criminals have been punished. The wounded are being held prisoner in the palace. The price of grain must be raised to pay for the damage inflicted upon the granary and to increase the guard. A monetary reward is being offered for information on the perpetrators of this insurrection."

Before he could say more, curious onlookers discovered with cries of horror the lifeless bodies of six of their friends and acquaintances in the second cart. These had been a part of the contingent left to guard the conquered granary. A crowd gathered quickly, and the messenger, fearing for his life, threw a parchment scroll into the crowd and ordered his cart to go. Two soldiers in the second cart lifted the bodies and tossed them into the mud before their cart also departed behind the trotting horses.

Georg came from the church, his face white from the news. Father Tasso prayed over each of the deceased, while Georg wept and wiped mud from their expressionless faces, unaware of the mood of those who stood around watching.

Father Tasso insisted that Georg and his men leave the city at once. "The scroll is a promise of reward. They search for the ringleader, and you, as a foreigner, will be blamed. Loylaties to family run deep. You must leave so that everyone can blame you without having your blood upon their conscience."

Taking the priest's advice, Andrew retrieved the Rosen Jungfrau and the treasury box, and by midafternoon, their party left through the northern gate and began a muddy walk into the hills. Georg did not protest, following where they led. He contributed nothing toward the decisions that had to be made, however, and the others were insecure without his leadership. They did know that it was still much too early to return to Felsenburg, for the passes would not be open for at least four more months.

⁂

As they headed north, they discussed their options, now and then casting glances backward toward Georg, who straggled behind. He seemed to be wrapped up in his own world of grief until they decided that the best place to spend the rest of the winter would be the abbey on the shores of Lake Como. It lay only two days away.

"No!" Georg said suddenly, hurrying to catch up with them. "We can't stay there."

"Why not?" asked Reinhold, surprised at the sudden interest.

"None of us wants to be locked up in a monastery for four months—especially during Lent."

Andrew was shocked. "If we participated in the fasting there, then we would not have to contend with the temptations in the world."

"Temptations! There are temptations everywhere. Surely we are all disciplined enough to fast without someone's telling us what and when we may or may not eat."

Sigfried agreed. "We could stay at the inn where we left the heretics."

Georg shook his head. "We'll find something else, but Lake Como is not an option."

Andrew suddenly realized that he no longer trusted Georg's instincts to lead him. With no apologies for how badly things had gone in Milan, he was once more telling others what was best for their lives. How did he know? Andrew's throat ached with the desire to say what he had been thinking, but all he finally said was: "I'm going to winter at the abbey. You can pick me up in the spring."

All seven men gaped, and Reinhold stammered, "With . . . without us?"

Taking a deep breath, Andrew settled it. "There is work for me there, and I prefer to fast there, for I have no discipline."

TWENTY-THREE

n truth, Andrew possessed a large portion of discipline. What he lacked was the opportunity to prove it to himself. His four months at the abbey crept by slowly, their monotony broken only by the joy to be copying manuscripts again. The isolation of the monastery seemed unnatural now. Worse, just as Abbot William had said long ago, Andrew had never learned the discipline of silence. He learned it that winter, but he was glad that he would soon return to the real world where people talked and laughed. He looked forward to spring, not just because the monastery was so cold, but because he longed to see Brother Georg again. As provoking as the man was at times, he was honest and said what he thought.

It was Pentecost again before news came that the passes were open. Georg and his men arrived a few days later. His group had grown to include many people whom Andrew thought did not look altogether reliable.

"Nonsense!" Georg exclaimed, surveying the scroungy collection of beggars, renegade monks, and pilgrims, traveling to religious shrines north of the Alps. "What reason could they have to trust us? Certainly we don't look very trustworthy either."

Andrew had to admit it was true, but he felt uncomfortable surrounded by so many strangers. He was relieved when the heretics found them again and asked if they could travel together back across the Alps. It seemed that they were not welcome anywhere they stopped. Georg, so adamant on many subjects, seemed incapable of refusing anyone.

Before Andrew left Como, they displayed the Rosen Jungfrau and began once more to collect offerings for the cathedral. After such a long time away, Andrew found it difficult to fit back into the patterns that had been established while they were traveling to Milan. Gradually, though, everyone fell into a routine. Or almost everyone did. After about a week, Andrew was certain that someone was stealing money from the treasury box.

One evening, while the men were sitting around the fire swapping stories, Andrew told Georg his suspicions.

"How do you know?" Georg objected. "You sleep with the box."

"I've suspected ever since the third day out of Como, but during the past two days I've been watching how much people put in; then I've begun counting it before I add it to the box." He raised his eyebrows. "Big difference."

"It's not my men."

Andrew sighed. "Which ones are your men?"

Georg grinned, conceding the distinction. "The ones who came from Felsenburg with us."

"It's also probably not the bishop's guards," Andrew said.

"And it's not the horses."

"So it's either the heretics, or it's one or many of the scoundrels you've picked up along the way."

Georg rubbed his beard and mumbled, "Scoundrels?"

"What do you know about them? We're probably fortunate that they haven't murdered us in our sleep."

"All right. I'll take care of it." He patted Andrew's shoulder and said condescendingly, "My men and I will keep your bishop's treasure safe."

"Stop it!" Andrew shouted, shoving Georg's hand away.

Georg stepped backward at the intensity of Andrew's anger, and the men around the fire stopped talking and looked in their direction.

"It's nothing," Andrew said to them. They went back to their stories. He turned on Georg in quiet fury. "You are patronizing me, and there is no need for it. You do not like the bishop; I do not like the bishop. But I am assigned to do the bishop's bidding. That does not mean that I do it gladly. It simply means that . . . that I don't know what to do."

Georg raised his hands in defense. "Andrew, I did not mean—"

"Ach, ja, you did!" Andrew interrupted. "If you like, I will say it: I am weak, without conviction, the bishop's puppet; I do not know what I believe anymore."

"But none of us—" he protested.

"The heretics know what they believe," Andrew said grimly and glanced toward the fire. "But let me finish. The money we are collecting is not the bishop's money. It is God's money. It was given by simple, well-meaning folk who truly believe that they are pleasing God with their tiny gifts. They are sacrificing—giving up coins that might be better used for bread and seed. And I want to believe that God is pleased."

"Of course He is, but the bishop—"

Andrew lowered his voice. "You see, it doesn't matter what the bishop does with the money. I think the good deeds have already been done and noticed by all the holy saints and angels. What the bishop does with the money cannot undo all of that good."

Georg took a couple of steps to close the distance between them. "I think that you do indeed know what you believe, my friend."

Andrew shook his head sadly. "No, I only hope that God is pleased. If He's not, then I truly do not understand Him."

"And in your theology, does it matter how the bishop uses the money? Do you have a God who is just?"

Andrew thought of the ragpickers' children he had seen in Milan. He remembered the widow at the door of Father Augustin's. And he remembered his parents. *If God is not just,* he thought, *then I do not want Him.* He stood for a moment, watching and listening to the men at the fire; then he said good night to Georg and went to his bed in the cart.

❧❧   ❧❧

The next morning dawned cool and damp. It was once more spring in the foothills, and as they began the climb up the river valley, the temperatures became cooler, the air less dusty. Andrew enjoyed the cheerful splashing of the river and delighted in the birds that flitted over the water, scooping up insects. The band of travelers was spread out along the trail, and Andrew walked alone near the cart in the center of the group. Some of the heretics' women and children rode in the cart with the treasure box. Ahead, out of sight around a bend, were three of the bishop's guards on horseback, Georg's original band of men, and many of the "scoundrels." Straggling behind him were the heretics and the rest of the guard. Their party numbered about thirty now, and several had expressed that the large number gave them safety.

When the ambush came, they were just climbing out of a narrow ravine. The bandits had been waiting above them on the rocks and jumped onto the guards' horses. One of the guards was stabbed to death and the others thrown off their horses.

Andrew was first aware of the attack when Georg came charging back down the steep path, cassock flying, stumbling over rocks. "Run!" he screamed. "Robbers!" As Georg raced through each group, they scattered like chickens, some up the hills and into the trees and others down the embankment toward the river.

Andrew, never far from the cart, lifted several screeching children down and then scrambled into it, handing the treasure box down to Georg. It was so heavy, now, that one person could no longer carry it. Together, they struggled down the steep embankment toward the river.

Georg was mumbling, "Stupid . . . dumb . . . too heavy . . ." as he puffed along.

In their haste, they bruised their feet and knees on the rocks. They finally reached the river and looked for a safe hiding place. A large boulder blocked their progress downstream, so they waded into the cold river, lugging the box with them. As Andrew stepped onto a slippery rock, it tipped and fell onto his other foot. He lost his balance and sat down, pulling the box onto his lap.

The water closed over his head. The river swirled and bubbled in his ears as he shoved at the box. His lungs were burning, and he flailed with his arms, trying to get a gulp of air. Then the box tipped off his legs, and Georg's hand grasped his arm and pulled him to his feet. He coughed and sputtered, at first unaware that Georg was shouting. "Come on! Get behind the rock."

Andrew shook his head and then took a breath before plunging beneath the water again, this time to free his foot. He tore his fingernails and bruised his fingers pulling at the rock until it shifted, and he could draw his foot out of the hole. He surfaced, gulped air, and, with Georg's assistance, hauled himself onto the bank behind the boulder, where they both lay gasping.

When the blood stopped roaring in Andrew's ears, he could hear the cries of the people above them. He opened his eyes. Georg was peering over the rock to the trail above.

"We should help the women and children," whispered Andrew.

"I don't know what we could do."

"How many were there?"

"I don't know."

"Ten? A hundred?"

"Five maybe."

Andrew looked over the boulder in disbelief. "Five bandits . . . can attack . . . all of us?"

"Surprise. Besides, some of the men from Milan probably arranged it."

Disgusted, Andrew snorted, "Your scoundrels! Well, I'm going up to help. I can't just sit here and guard gold."

Georg pulled Andrew down. "I'll go." He pointed at the monk's ankle. "You're not going anywhere."

Andrew looked. The cold water had dulled the pain, but his ankle was bleeding, and when he moved it, the ache shot all the way up his leg. He nodded.

Georg stepped down into the water and then disappeared around the boulder. In a minute, Andrew could see him as he struggled back up the embankment, dragging his water-logged cassock with each step. There was less noise up there now, and one of Georg's men righted the cart, which had been turned over.

Andrew put his head down and tried to relax. His cassock was soaked through, and he began to shiver in spite of the sunshine.

Suddenly, Georg yelled, "You, there! Andrew, watch out!"

Andrew popped his head up and saw a shadow moving across the bank. He turned around quickly. About twenty paces away—moving rapidly toward him—was a huge man with a grimy face. The sun glinted on the blade of his drawn dagger. Andrew sat up and shrank against the boulder. There was nowhere to go.

"Would you risk hellfire?" Georg bellowed at him.

The man hesitated and looked at Georg.

"Strike a man of God and you will rot in eternal hell!" Georg roared.

Andrew hid his face in terror. "Dear God, please help me," he croaked. He heard the man's approach across the river and buried his head in his arms, waiting for the fatal blow, wondering how badly he would suffer and hoping that God would take him in. Then the man was upon Andrew, grasping him at the throat and shaking him like an old garment.

"Where's the money?" he demanded, waving his dagger close to Andrew's face.

With trembling fingers, Andrew pointed to the spot in the river where the box had fallen.

The bandit shoved Andrew away roughly and slid into the water. He had no trouble finding the treasure box, and he hauled it out. Muscles bulging, he heaved it onto his right shoulder and without a glance at Andrew trudged down the river where his associates probably waited.

Andrew leaned back against the boulder and watched him go. He was trembling from cold and fear, his ankle throbbed, and his torn fingernails burned. Tears of relief and gratefulness stung his eyes. "Thank you, God," he whispered, very sure that God had personally intervened.

Because Andrew's ankle was swollen and useless, Georg and two other men half-carried, half-dragged him back up the embankment. They loaded him into the cart beside the slain soldier and one of the heretics, who had been killed trying to save his child. The child had survived.

The group—smaller now, as some of them had indeed been bandits—proceeded once more up the trail. They had to continue until they found a place suitable to bury the dead.

The ride in the cart was bumpy and painful, but Andrew was also mindful of his duty to the deceased. He prayed aloud for the guard, and then turned to the other man.

"Don't touch him!" warned a soft, stern voice beside the cart. She was about twenty with dark, disheveled hair. She rested one hand on the cart as it bumped along. The other held tightly to the hand of a little boy. Tears streaked her face, but a slight smile danced on her lips. "He doesn't need your prayers."

Andrew groped for words. "But . . . but his soul. When we come to a village with a priest, I shall have him give your husband's soul absolution."

"He doesn't need it," she said softly.

"Actually," corrected the man who walked up beside her, "he already has it."

"Someone else prayed?" Andrew asked, trying to remember who this man was.

"He did," said the man, nodding at the dead man. "Many years ago. He's in heaven right now with his Savior."

Andrew looked down at the lifeless body beside him. "How can you know?"

"Read your Scriptures, young man, and pray for your own soul," he chided. He turned to the woman. "Come walk with us, Birgit." He pried her hand from the cart and led her and the child back to their group.

Andrew lay back and closed his eyes. His leg ached dreadfully, and the simple statements of the woman gnawed at his mind. He could understand neither where she got her assurance nor how she could be so contented and so deceived.

Several people walked a while beside the cart and tried to console Andrew for the loss of the treasure. He appreciated their sympathy, but he felt curiously ambiguous that the treasure box was gone—sad that the gifts of well-meaning peasants could not be used for a noble cause but relieved that he was no longer responsible for the care of those gifts. It was all so unimportant.

His relief, though, did not last long. Around midday, the group finally came out of the valley into a large open meadow. Although it was too early to stop, Georg decided that they were all tired enough to deserve a rest. The men set up camp and the women built fires and prepared food. Andrew hobbled to a sheltered, sunny spot where his blanket had been spread out. He felt very useless as preparations were made to bury the two men.

When food was prepared, Georg brought Andrew his portion.

"The money's gone," Andrew told Georg.

Georg nodded gravely.

"It doesn't really matter, you know."

Georg smiled. "I'm glad to hear you say that. But I need to show you something." He pulled a cloth pouch from his cassock and opened it.

Andrew reached his fingers into the pouch and felt coins. "What? I don't understand."

"I told you I'd take care of the bishop's money," he said softly. "It's all hidden among my men—the men from Felsenburg, that is."

Bewildered, Andrew thought back through the morning to the time of the ambush when he had handed the box off the cart to Georg. "You mean—"

"I mean the bandits stole a box of rocks!" Georg said merrily. "With enough coins to keep them happy." With that statement, he dismissed all of the danger Andrew had experienced for the sake of the money. "We'll keep it this way. It's safer." Andrew understood even more why Georg's men respected him so much.

∽✕∾ ∽✕∾

The two men were buried in two very different ceremonies in the late afternoon. The larger group gathered around the grave and stared at the lifeless body of the guard who had died so swiftly. A priest from a tiny village was found, and he led the ritual very capably. The other guards had a few kind words to say about their colleague, and then the rocky earth was thrown in on his body. They chanted their prayers to the saints.

No one really mourned the death of the guard, for no one knew him. His death was merely a horrible reminder of human mortality. Andrew knew that the heretics across the field must be mourning the death of a man who was a husband, father, and friend. They stood around his grave, yet in spite of bowed heads and heaving shoulders, they were quiet. He could detect none of the hopeless wailing that normally accompanied the death of a loved one.

From memory, Andrew chanted with the group around him while he watched the little group of heretics across the field lay their friend's body tenderly in his grave. The wife stood bravely by, supported by the strong arms of friends. Someone else held the child.

Andrew's eyes filled with tears, and the words to the chant stuck in his throat. Even from this distance, he had the feeling of being in the presence of something very holy. The heretics began to sing.

The group around the guard ceased chanting and stood breathlessly, listening to the unfamiliar song. From that distance, the words were not distinguishable, but the joy with which they sang was unmistakable. They finished one song and began a second. One of the guards near Andrew cursed, someone else laughed, and the group dispersed.

"Don't look too rapt, my friend," murmured Georg into Andrew's ear. "They are not angels, and their heresies could be a great stumbling block to many."

Andrew wiped tears away with the back of his hand. "Who are they?"

"I don't know. But I think I am going to regret bringing them with us. The devil and his demons can wear some strange disguises."

"They're not from the devil," said Andrew, and he knew he was right.

TWENTY-FOUR

or the schoolboys in Felsenburg, the winter did not finish as difficult as it had begun, for the incident with Theo Rube's father had reached Bishop Gernot's ears. The bishop allowed himself to be persuaded to provide minimal aid to the families of the schoolboys. To take home each day, they were given a loaf of bread or a measure of barley or wheat and, once a week, a portion of meat. Martin learned very quickly that God honors those who keep their vows to Him.

The seasons meant less to Martin now. Blizzards continued to batter Felsenburg while he sat beside the bishop's fire and memorized Latin verbs. While the burghers rejoiced that no snow fell on the day of Maria's Festival of Lights, Martin laboriously copied a psalm onto a mediocre piece of parchment. A few weeks later, the stockpiles of snow began melting, and Martin would hop over puddles, while he hummed the chants of Gregory. By the time the winter wheat was ready for harvest, it was no longer necessary to build a fire anywhere in the bishop's residence. Then many of the boys went home for the summer. Martin returned to mixing mortar—admittedly a boring task, but one he now viewed with tolerance, knowing that it was temporary. The life of a stonemason seemed a long way from the world that Martin had chosen.

Women did not choose their world, and Cecilia felt hers closing in on her. Mutti rarely asked her to run errands, and even when she offered, her mother usually had good reasons why it was not necessary for her to leave the house.

"You're almost finished sewing that tunic, liebling," she would tell Cecilia with the transparent smile of a martyr, allowing inconvenience to shine through solicitude. "I'll go to the market, and you finish up before I get back."

Cecilia would stay, tears of frustration sometimes dripping onto the rough, homespun fabrics. She would blink them away and try to see her needle through the blur. She felt like a prisoner. She had only been out to Mass each week, and always with Mutti. Only at church could she see any of her friends—or Martin.

One of those bright, sunny Lord's Days, Mutti had been sick and stayed home, so Cecilia and Martin went for a walk after Mass. They left by the west gate and strolled down the hill and along the Obersill. It had been nine months since Stefan's death, and they had hardly spoken since then. She had the impression that the more he learned, the less he had to say to her. Their conversation on this day was sparse but comfortable as they commented on the flowers and the swollen river, on the heavy heads of winter wheat and the greedy crows. When they reached the spot near the river where they had kissed, however, neither of them said anything. Cecilia tucked her hands primly beneath her apron, and Martin tried to whistle. Once they left the river, they skirted the city wall and went in at the western gate. Martin took her home and squeezed her hand in farewell. It had been a pleasant afternoon.

An unexpected storm broke over her the moment she entered her home.

"*Where* have you been?" her mother cried, sitting up on her mat, where she had been lying.

"Walking." Simple answers were best, but she wished that her hands would not shake so.

"Alone?"

Cecilia pulled her scarf from her head. "No. With Martin."

"Is that all you were doing?"

"Of course."

Her mother gave her a look of complete distrust. "You were gone a long time." She paused and added, "A very long time. Isn't there something you should tell me?"

The girl felt her face grow warm, and she reached up to cover her cheeks with hands that were suddenly icy.

"Ach! I knew it!" the older woman exclaimed.

"Mutti, I have done nothing wrong."

"How do you know?"

"Because I hear things—things that you won't tell me. I know what's right and wrong. I have not ever lain with a man, nor do I intend to do so until I marry."

"Wicked girl!" Her mother sobbed and put her face in her hands.

There it was again. "Why is it wicked to marry and have children?"

"It's unnecessary," Mutti countered, suddenly calm again. "Oh, Cecilia," she coaxed, "Come to me." She patted a spot on the mat.

Cecilia went curiously. Things had been easier between them before Cecilia became a woman. She leaned back in her mother's arms, secure for the moment to enjoy true compassion.

"Cecilia, you don't know what you're saying. I had so hoped that you would come to these conclusions yourself."

"What conclusions?"

"Give your life to God, Liebling. You can enter a convent—maybe someday take your vows. That was my heart's yearning. And you need never suffer what most women suffer."

"Suffer? But there is joy at the end of childbirth!"

"Joy is short-lived. Children die. But even worse; to have a child, you must first suffer at the hands of ... of ..." Mutti paused, and around her lips a hard, white line formed. "... of a man," she finished with disgust.

Cecilia gulped. Was Papa so terrible? She had known that he was drunk most of the time and that he rarely came home. She had heard the rumors about his escapades with other women, but she had never thought about Mutti's suffering because of "things" that he did to her. She turned and hugged her mother. "I'm so sorry, Mutti."

They sat for awhile in silence, each listening to the breathing of the other, Mutti stroking her hair. Cecilia wished that these moments happened more frequently, but she had to set things right. She took a deep breath and said boldly, "Martin would never hurt me."

Mutti pushed her daughter away. "Martin!"

"It's always been Martin, Mutti. It's the most natural thing in the world."

"But . . . but he's never spoken to me or to your father about you," she protested, genuinely bewildered.

Cecilia bowed her head and sighed. "I know."

"Does he want to marry you?"

Cecilia remembered his gentle kisses and said, "I think he would."

"Well, then," Mutti announced with finality, "We shall just have to talk to him."

That startled her. "Is that . . . ? Would that be . . . ? Are you sure?"

Her mother shrugged. "What other choice do we have?"

Cecilia hugged her mother. "I could never enter a convent," she assured her.

"It would have been better."

Cecilia pushed herself to her feet. "Martin is a good man. And besides, I want to sew pretty clothes for noblewomen!"

"You will be sorry," her mother moaned, and she flopped back down on her mat, the conversation over.

⌖ ⌖

Klara's second child had been born in the middle of May. Named Stefanie after her dear, departed Papa, her name day fell in the middle of August. The day honored her saint and Papa's. Klara and Cecilia's families were invited to take part in the rituals at the grave and then to come home for a meal afterward. Bernie sat on a mat beside the hearth, stacking towers from blocks of wood sanded smooth by his young uncle. Tiny Stefanie lay in her basket and waved her fingers in the air.

Cecilia's father, slightly intoxicated from an early morning visit to Zur Felder, arrived late, bearing a skin of good, red wine to toast the baby's health. Then he poured another round and raised his cup to Martin. "To our son-in-law."

Cecilia's face flushed with embarrassment, and Martin almost dropped his cup. The young man looked over at Cecilia mouthing, "What?" and she gave one shoulder a slight shrug, ashamed of her part in another of her father's blunders.

"I beg your pardon, Herr," said Martin, "What does this mean?"

"'I beg your pardon, Herr!'" mimicked her father. "That school has made you a fine lord." He shook his partially emptied cup at Martin and proclaimed happily, "This means that you will be marrying my daughter, and—"

Martin was grateful when his own father interrupted, "This was not the way we wanted to discuss this, Hans."

Hans ignored his brother. "Drink up, drink up, Bursch! The maiden is yours."

"Mine?" echoed Martin. He tried to chuckle.

Cecilia's glance traveled around the table and came back to rest on Martin, who suddenly grinned at her across the potful of lentils. She shook her head and peered into the wine cup, searching for her reflection.

Martin spoke. "Papa, do you know anything about this?"

"I know that you two have always been good friends," he said reasonably, "and cousins make excellent companions. You can't have much to say against the arrangement."

"But I didn't make an arrangement. There is no reason for Cecilia and I to marry."

"None?"

"None."

All eyes swiveled to Cecilia, who looked up in the silence.

Martin's father looked on her with pity as he said, "No reason?"

She shook her head.

He grabbed Cecilia's father by the arm and dragged him from his seat. The corner of the room was meant to ensure a private conversation, but emotions were too high to ensure whispers. "You told me that my son *had* to marry Cecilia," he hissed.

Cecilia's heart seemed to skip a beat, and she tried to search her mother's face, but her mother avoided her eyes.

"Wha-at!" Martin croaked, jumping to his feet.

Stefanie, startled by the noise, wailed, and Klara went to pick her up from the basket.

Martin's father put his hand back to ward off his shocked son. "Let me take care of this, Bursch."

Cecilia's father was too full of ale and good, red wine to be anything but amused. "She loves him," he drawled, "and I've seen how he looks at her."

Cecilia wished that she could run from the house, but it seemed to be her destiny to sit frozen to her stool until the end of the world.

"You're a much bigger fool than I thought," Martin's father shouted, all attempts at privacy abandoned. "Just because you took your wife before the wedding night and you had to marry her—"

Martin's mother gasped, "Bernhard, that is too much!" She pulled her sister-in-law's head into her protective embrace.

Obediently, he snapped his mouth shut and looked over at Maria. "I'm sorry," he said more calmly, "but what have you two done?"

Martin spoke again. "We are talking about my cousin's honor and purity—about my honor."

"*Your* honor?" Cecilia's father sneered. "Since when do the young men have honor? The only honorable thing to do is to marry her."

Suddenly Cecilia knew what was going to happen. Martin did not want to marry her, and he would say so. Her hands were cold and trembling, and she tried to warm them by wrapping them in her skirt. As she knew it would, the terrible conversation unfolded.

"I never did or said anything that would have made it necessary for me to marry her," Martin stated, avoiding her eyes.

"Nothing?"

He smiled a tender smile of remembrance. "Well, not since we were children."

Tears that had been collecting in her eyes spilled down her cheeks. She wanted to go home.

Seeing this, Cecilia's mother pushed Martin's mother away and asked the dreadful question: "Martin, do you want to marry Cecilia?"

In the silence that followed, Martin's gaze fixed upon Cecilia's. She knew that he was trying to find the courage, and she loved him more, but she knew that in a moment her hopes would be gone. He spoke very softly. "I can't."

Cecilia bowed her head and threaded her fingers together, in and out.

His father sounded startled. "Can't?"

"Don't make me say more," Martin begged.

"What's wrong with my daughter?" demanded Hans.

"Nothing. It's me." He looked at his father and then said, "I want to continue studying. And maybe someday I'll enter the service of the church. A wife would keep me from that."

Martin's father turned his anger onto his son. "You want to—! What sort of foolishness do they put into your head? A son's place is beside his father!"

"Papa," Martin told him calmly, "this is not the time."

The two of them looked over at Cecilia.

With great effort, Martin's father controlled himself. "Hans, please take your wife home," he ordered.

His will weakened by the wine, Hans obediently went to Cecilia's mother, pulled her to her feet, and together they left the house without saying good-bye.

Martin's father held out his hand to his wife. "Inge, Klara, let's take the children for a walk."

Cecilia knew that this time she was not one of the children. They left, and she and Martin were alone. For now, her tears had stopped.

Wisely, Martin did not allow the silence between them to grow long. "I'll walk you home," he said simply.

She followed him out the door, but when he reached for her hand, she pulled away.

"Cecilia, I'm so sorry. I . . . I never meant to hurt you."

She cleared her throat and said, "It's my fault." She was glad that he did not pursue her statement further. They walked in silence to Cecilia's door, and without looking at Martin, she opened the door, went in, and pushed it closed behind her.

TWENTY-FIVE

artin stopped growing that summer, and he became strong and grew ruddy in the sunshine. He mixed mortar and waited impatiently for school to begin after the autumn harvest, and when it did, he felt as if he had come home.

The new writing teacher was a young, red-haired monk, Brother Andrew, who was nearer to Martin's age than any other teacher. The boys enjoyed the delicious mystery of Andrew's person; rumors said that he had once been mute but had been healed by a miracle. At the beginning of school, Brother Andrew had limped around the class-room, using a cane to favor a very swollen ankle. Some of the pupils had heard that Brother Andrew had marvelously escaped a bloody death on his trip back from Milan—a story that became embellished with each telling. Even the trip to Milan was food for speculation, as no one really knew why he had gone. They only knew that he had returned carrying a very large sum of money with which to begin work on the cathedral.

One afternoon in late September, Brother Andrew surprised the boys with a trip to the bishop's library. Martin was thrilled with the sight of so many manuscripts safely secured behind locked, glass doors. The polished edges of the dark, wooden shelves reflected the light from the tall windows. Andrew unlocked one cabinet, and each boy was allowed to choose a manuscript and to carry it reverently to the table where he might admire the beautifully formed letters. Martin could read a little now, and his heart beat faster as he picked out words that he had learned.

"You all hold in your hands portions of the Holy Scriptures," Brother Andrew told them. "These are not the original manuscripts, but they have been carefully copied by dedicated scribes over the many centuries. As you learn to write, you must never, never give in to the temptation to change anything that you copy. God's Word is sacred, and damnation awaits anyone who would dare to alter any of it for any reason."

The boys nodded solemnly, and some of them removed their hands from the precious documents. Martin gazed at his manuscript—the bold black strokes ending in slender curves, the occasional decorations like bright-colored jewels at the beginnings of certain sections. The idea that these black figures on buff-colored parchment were God's words filled him with an eager curiosity that made his hands tremble. Only his awe of Brother Andrew helped him control his urge to demand immediate understanding.

Brother Andrew continued, "These parchments remain locked in these cabinets to protect them. Those of you who go on to enter the church will be educated in the proper interpretation of the Holy Scriptures. Then you will be allowed to study them."

Sepp Feick was more bold. "What is this one, please, Teacher?" he asked, his gentlemanly manners excusing his lack of restraint.

Brother Andrew did not seem to mind. He came around the table and looked over the boy's shoulder. "It's the portion of the Old Testament that contains the Ten Commandments—in Greek, of course."

Sepp nodded gravely.

"Do you know them?" asked their teacher, ever mindful of an opportunity for learning.

Sepp grinned up at him. "Not in Greek."

Brother Andrew bowed his head to concede. "All right, then: in German." He looked at Eberhard, the young son of the bürgermeister— the mayor. "You first."

The boy blushed vividly and stammered, "'You . . . you shall have no other gods before me.'"

"That's correct, but don't forget the first part: 'I am the LORD your God.'"

"Please read it in Greek, Teacher," requested Sepp.

Martin saw a look of admiration pass between Brother Andrew and Sepp, and he wished that he had had the courage to ask. The teacher read the passage in a gentle voice. Martin thought that the words sounded so much more holy in the foreign language, and he wondered how long it would be before Greek would roll off his tongue with such ease.

"Steinmetz?"

Martin realized that Brother Andrew had been speaking to him.

"I'm sorry, Teacher, I . . . I wasn't listening." In some of the other classes, this would have been grounds for punishment, but Brother Andrew, though firm, usually excused their lapses of attention with an admonitory glance.

"The second commandment, if you please."

Martin cleared his throat and said, "'You shall not take the name of the LORD your God in vain.'"

Brother Andrew nodded and then read again from the manuscript. He only read a few words, though, before he faltered and stopped, confusion spreading across his face. He looked around at the boys and then said apologetically, "I'm sorry; it reads differently here. Perhaps we should return to the classroom."

The boys, of course, had not noticed the difference, and some of them were still so ignorant of the mechanics of language and translation that Brother Andrew's confusion held no significance other then a premature end to the lessons.

Martin, however, having already caught the passion of preserving the purity of God's Word, found the teacher's statement incompatible with his previous cautions. He took a deep breath and broke the uneasy silence. "How can it be different, Teacher? It's God's Word."

Brother Andrew turned toward him and said haltingly, "I . . . it's very difficult to explain."

Sepp picked up on the possibility of learning more. "Could you read it to us and tell us how it is different, Teacher?"

Their teacher glanced uncertainly at the manuscript and then around the table before saying lightly, "Teachers don't know everything, and sometimes we must be careful not to teach the wrong things. I will explain in your next lesson. Put your manuscripts away where you found them, and then you are dismissed."

Reluctantly, they obeyed, disappointed that the mystery was so quickly at an end. Martin was certain that the next lesson would contain a very short, unsatisfactory explanation, and he decided to press the teacher after the others left.

Obviously, Sepp had the same idea. The two of them dawdled until the others had left and then Sepp carried the manuscript to Brother Andrew and asked charmingly, "Would you not translate for us, Teacher? We are able to understand."

Their teacher smiled and took the manuscript. "You must realize that in Greek, the words are in different order than we would speak them. Here is what it says—approximately: 'Not make to yourselves idols or any likeness—whatever things in the heaven above, whatever things in the earth below, whatever things in the waters under the earth. Not bowing down to them and in no way serving them. For I am LORD the God your God, a jealous one.'"

"It is quite a bit different," observed Martin. "Isn't the commandment about taking the name of the LORD God in vain even there?"

The teacher studied for a moment and then nodded, "It seems to be the third."

"So there are eleven commandments?" exclaimed Sepp with sudden perception.

Brother Andrew smiled. "I think not. You must be careful not to come to hasty conclusions. Wait for all of the evidence before making changes. That is why I said that I would explain in the next lesson. I, too, continue to learn." He carefully rolled the parchment and tied it with the cord that had been dangling from Sepp's hand. He looked up from his neat knot. "You're dismissed."

Outside, the remaining autumn sunshine kept the cold from entirely taking over the valley.

"Odd, isn't it?" said Sepp, once outside.

Martin nodded. "Confusing, I'd say. I wish I could understand it all now. Learning takes so much time."

The two boys walked through the marketplace to the bakery, where Sepp's father gave both boys a small brötchen from the pile of fragrant baked goods in a large basket. They wandered back out into Lärchenplatz.

"Just imagine," muttered Sepp through his bread, "if there should be eleven commandments! And our own Brother Andrew discovered it."

"I could never believe that. There have to be ten; otherwise it would be impossible to have five on each tablet."

Sepp laughed. "Who says that there are five on each tablet?"

"Don't you remember the picture on the wall in St. Nathaniel's before it burned?" Martin protested.

"All that proves is that someone thought that there were five on each tablet," Sepp retorted.

Martin was growing impatient with Sepp's obtuseness. "Father—I mean, Canon— Augustin told us during classes," he said slowly, "that the painted pictures were of stories in the Holy Scriptures. The reason for the pictures was because most people can't read. Those pictures are the Holy Scriptures for most people. Would you tell Canon Augustin that the picture of Moses with the Ten Commandments was wrong?"

Sepp had stopped suddenly and was staring off into the distance. "What is it?"

He blinked and looked at his friend with a grin. "You're very clever, you know."

They began to walk again. "What are you talking about?"

"You've solved two problems. First, of course there have to be Ten Commandments. Canon Augustin would never tell an untruth, nor would the other bishop . . . what was his name?"

Martin shrugged.

Sepp thought a moment and then continued. "Anyway, he would not have allowed someone to put something in our church that wasn't in the Holy Scriptures."

"You're right," Martin conceded, glad that the tension between them had only been temporary. "What was the second problem?"

"The commandment itself: not to make any images or pictures," he announced triumphantly.

"So?"

"Well, we need the pictures and images because so few people can read. Pictures are a great idea, and Moses didn't know it."

Martin clapped Sepp on the shoulder. "We think very well together. We ought to use this in Brother Karolus' rhetoric class. I think we're learning something."

TWENTY-SIX

ell, Brother Andrew, I suppose I shouldn't be surprised," Bishop Gernot muttered, sarcasm slipping through his words, "You spent twenty years in silence; I guess you're entitled to blurt out foolishness now and then."

Andrew stood in the bishop's study, the wide, shiny table bridging a distance that their words could not. He, too, longed for his old excuse of silence.

The bishop had not been pleased when Andrew had returned from Milan in August with his tongue loosened and his thoughts tumbling out.

"Of course, it does facilitate our communication," Bishop Gernot had conceded then, "but the airing of every thought is certainly not necessary and definitely overrated."

Andrew had said nothing. *If he only knew how little I say about what I truly think.*

"So tell me: What miracle caused the tongue of the dumb to speak?"

"It was no miracle," Andrew had answered quickly. "I . . . I merely remembered something that happened to me . . . in my childhood." The memories were too personal, too new and raw, too sacred. The last person on earth he wanted to tell was this pompous, manipulative fraud.

"And that memory was . . . ?" the bishop had prodded.

Andrew shook his head. "Too painful," he had murmured.

"Ahh." He had nodded sympathetically. "Perhaps another time, then."

Now, Andrew's memories were pierced by the annoyed voice of the bishop, intent upon dealing out a scolding.

"Silence, eh? Try the silence on the boys. You'll teach them fewer falsehoods."

Andrew continued to stare at the reflections on the table and gathered his thoughts. "I really am sorry if I confused them. The boys discovered that the manuscript was different from the Ten Commandments that we all learn."

"You told them. They can't read Greek," he reminded.

"They can't read much at all," Andrew agreed quietly.

The bishop raised his admonitory forefinger in artificial amusement. "Always plan ahead. Never let them ask you a question that you don't already know the answer to."

The young monk looked up suddenly and caught the bishop's eye. "So, please tell me why the third commandment in the Holy Scriptures is the second one in our catechism."

"You don't even teach catechism," the bishop snapped. "Stick to handwriting."

Andrew caught his breath in anger and leaned forward on the table. "There has to be an answer . . . for me. I just gave them a lecture on the holiness of the Scriptures—on the danger of ever changing one tiny word or letter. I wanted them to recognize that to alter God's Word in any way is a terrible sin, and that God will be angry."

The bishop was nodding. "But what can He do?"

Andrew flinched as if he had been slapped. "What?"

Bishop Gernot did not repeat himself and said soothingly, "Greater men than you and I have grappled with these issues for many centuries. I think they have solved most of the problems. Just teach what you are supposed to and leave the things you do not know to those who do."

Andrew straightened and chewed on his bottom lip. He still wanted an explanation. "I did tell the boys that I would explain the contradiction to them in the next lesson."

The bishop slapped the table and said sharply, "Your mouth just keeps talking. Abbot William was right: You never learned the discipline of silence." He stood. "You will tell them . . . tell them, that . . . that the great fathers of our holy church studied for many years and that it is they who decided which commandments would be in our catechism."

Andrew was not satisfied, "But what—"

"That is all you will say, and if they argue, then perhaps you do not have that class under control. They must learn discipline . . . and so must you."

He opened his mouth to speak, but Bishop Gernot stopped him. "Outside the classroom you will maintain silence for one month. One month." The forefinger rose again. "You are to speak to no one. There is nothing so urgent, nothing so important, that it will not keep. One month. It is God's will."

Andrew whirled on his heels and strode from the room. With great self-control, he closed the door quietly behind him. Out in the hallway, he took a deep breath. His hands were shaking. He felt light-headed. At the end of the hallway, the great door stood open to the garden, and the autumn sunshine beckoned. He abandoned his plans for the afternoon and left the residence.

Lärchenplatz on Saturday afternoon was fairly quiet, the market having ended at midday. The square was now twice its original size, since the ruined church and hovels had been removed, and the tiniest sound echoed across the cobblestones. Andrew headed quickly for the fields west of the city, his legs pumping the wrath from him. Soon he was breathing hard, and he slowed to a more human pace.

The autumn sunshine was barely warm even in the open, and the occasional shadow chilled the sweat that clung to his head and back. A slight breeze stirred the dust from the stubble left in the harvested barley fields. A few crows hopped about, searching for fallen kernels, and chased the smaller birds, which had paused for dinner on their journey south.

His feet carried him across one of the fields to the bank of the Obersill River. He sat down on a warm, buff-colored rock that was sheltered from the wind. Part of the river to his left was hidden from him by thick bushes, which were covered with crackling, brown leaves and red berries. He reached out and crushed some of the leaves in his hand, sprinkling the pieces on the rock beside him.

The river made a wonderful, loud noise that seemed to wash away his feelings of frustration. The greenish-brown water swirled in eddies and whirlpools, and occasionally sticks and leaves rushed past. His eyes followed the river upstream, until it vanished from his sight. Up in the hills, lost in the haze, life at St. Jude's continued as it always had. Andrew was glad that he was no longer there.

A murmuring noise, more irregular than the cheerful rushing of the river, intruded into his drowsy thoughts. By shifting his position on the rock, he could see a small procession of men, women, and children walking across the field toward the river. He recognized many of them as members of the heretics, and he shrank back into the bushes to see what they were going to do.

The procession seemed to be led by a young man, about Andrew's own age. He carried himself with a confidence that Andrew could only imagine, and his mouth was curved into a mysterious smile that lit his eyes.

Spontaneously, the group broke into one of their haunting songs as they arrived at the river. They descended the bank on the other side of the bushes that shielded Andrew from their sight. Andrew moved slightly so that he could see through the branches.

As the song came to an end, the people formed a semicircle around the young man, and one of the older men, clothed in a ragged, brown tunic, opened a scroll and began reading.

"'Jesus the Nazarene performed many signs and wonders and miracles, but He was delivered up to His people and was nailed to a cross by the hands of godless men.' We would have been guilty, had we been there. God raised Him up again, putting an end to the agony of death."

"We praise God for this," said another, "and we are here to rejoice that Dietmar has given his life to his Savior."

Andrew realized suddenly that he was about to witness one of their secret rituals, and he looked around for a way to escape without being seen.

"'When the people of Jerusalem heard that they had crucified their

Messiah, they were pierced to the heart and cried out to Peter, "Brethren, what shall we do?"'"

The young man looked as if he would gladly answer the question, but the reader continued. "'Peter answered, "Repent, and let each of you be baptized in the name of Jesus Christ for the forgiveness of your sins; and you shall receive the gift of the Holy Ghost."'"

Andrew closed his eyes and covered his ears, but in the dark silence, his duty to the church and his curiosity fought for the right to assert themselves. Georg had said that these people were dangerous. Everyone called them the heretics, but surely they did not identify themselves by such an uncomplimentary label. They thought they were right. Andrew wondered what it must feel like to know that you are right—to have the certainty that what you have done is what you were supposed to have done.

He opened his eyes a crack and uncovered his ears. The bushes grew out from the bank, and the water downstream of them was more still. One of the older men was already standing waist-deep in the pool, and the young man, his eyes wide with the shock of the cold, walked toward him, his hand outstretched.

"We have seen the changes in the life of our dear Dietmar, and he has chosen this day to testify of his faith. Tell me," he addressed the young man, "Do you believe in Jesus Christ as your only Savior, Redeemer, and Intercessor?"

His voice rang above the bubbling water. "I do."

"And do you admit that by grace you have been saved by faith and that not of yourself, it is the gift of God—"

Andrew put his fingers into his ears, but the words had been said, and the rest followed in his mind, just as he had memorized them so long ago in the scriptorium at St. Jude's: "—*not of works, lest any man should boast.*" He continued to watch as the man pulled Dietmar deeper into the water. Someone handed the older man a pitcher. He scooped it into the cold greenness and poured it over the head of Dietmar, who waited with his eyes closed. Twice more he poured water over the young man's head, his lips moving silently, as Andrew kept his fingers tightly in his own ears.

The water flowed down off Dietmar's clothing and dripped from his hair. A smile lit his face. Many hands reached down to assist him up the bank, and someone threw a blanket around him and around the older man. For a split second, as Dietmar turned to one of the women, Andrew thought that his eye had caught his own. Andrew looked quickly toward St. Jude's and did not turn around again until he was sure they were gone.

Cautiously, he pulled his fingers from his ears and glanced around. Perhaps it had been a dream. No one was in sight, but as he stood to leave, he could see the imprints of their shoes in the soft mud along the bank.

"Dear God, can it be true? I must find out."

TWENTY-SEVEN

hat following Monday, Andrew obediently related the bishop's rationalizations to the boys in a dry monotone. He quelled further questions by pointing out that the bishop was God's representative in Felsenburg. Andrew was alarmed to see how easy it was to silence opposition if it was linked to a fall from God's favor. Although he had ignored his own conscience many times before, he felt much more guilty for having encouraged the students to ignore theirs. The boys had no more objections.

Andrew continued to enjoy the teaching, but he avoided any controversial topics and concentrated on the mechanics of penmanship. It was a difficult way to live, but Andrew was convinced that nothing was to be gained by subjecting the boys to the confused musings of a guilt-ridden monk.

A week before All Saints' Day, the cathedral chapter gathered for their autumn meeting. Temporarily relieved of his teaching duties, Andrew occupied his accustomed place near the window, surrounded by enough pens, parchment, and ink to take prolific notes. So much had happened since the last meeting, and he was surprised to see that the canons looked much the same.

There were changes, though. Peter Fabian had taken it upon himself to call the meeting, and he seemed to radiate a confidence in his role as the new dean that he had lacked the year before. The former dean, Hugo Aichinger, looked decidedly more frail, although the other canons refrained from mentioning the fact. Wilfred von Badenbach, chancellor of the cathedral school, waddled into the room, smiling as usual. Quiet Julian still moved uncertainly, looking for a key to his own convictions. Father Augustin had earlier been made an official canon so he might be chosen by the bishop to serve as archdeacon, a type of assistant bishop. And of course Sigismund von Steyer was there to liberally scatter his gloom and lessons on protocol into their midst.

The bishop chose a place on the side of the table so that Peter Fabian could lead the meeting from the head. One of the purposes of this particular gathering was to figure out what to do about the annual Advent festivities, usually attended not only by the folk from Felsenburg but by people from the surrounding areas as well. The previous year had revealed the necessity for a declaration of some sort.

"Since we no longer have a church big enough for everyone, I suggest that we each hold our own service in our own area," said Peter, ready to move on to the next subject.

"Some of the people won't understand," warned Sigismund darkly.

Wilfred tapped his pudgy fingers on the table and asked, "What can't they understand? There's no church."

Sigismund sat up straighter as if to deliver a lesson to a difficult schoolboy. "Many of the women travel the long distance, even in the cold and snow, because they long to reap the blessings for undertaking such a difficult journey at their age. Many are very old and do not have much time left to store up treasures for heaven."

Andrew happened to catch Gallus' eye, and Gallus turned his palms to the ceiling questioningly.

Augustin said helpfully, "Perhaps an alternative?"

Peter Fabian had been staring at Sigismund but now his eyes fell on the new archdeacon. "What . . . alternative?" he stammered in disbelief.

"What do you propose?" said Hugo Aichinger in his rough, elderly voice, which had so often diffused a confrontation.

Peter Fabian glanced at him gratefully and said more carefully, "Yes, what?"

"We can meet in Lärchenplatz as we did last year," said Sigismund bluntly. "It's large enough—"

"—and cold enough and wet enough," interrupted Gallus, who had already heard enough. "What kind of men are we—are you? I'm sorry," he said, glancing at Peter Fabian, "this is only my third year at St. Maria's, but I can no longer suggest to my elderly parishioners that there is any good to come of a December journey to Felsenburg. They did it last year, and many of them died of exposure."

"It pleases God," Archdeacon Augustin stated bluntly.

Andrew's hand jerked and his pen tip broke, making a splotch on the parchment. He flexed his hand to relax it and dipped another pen into the ink.

"It would kill them," said Julian softly to no one in particular.

"They want to come," insisted Sigismund. "It is a way for them to show their devotion to God. He must reward them. Besides, Bishop Marcel always held a regional Mass."

Gallus appealed to Wilfred. "Brother Wilfred, surely you have never encouraged such foolishness."

Andrew looked up to see how Sigismund and Augustin enjoyed being called fools. They were both glaring at Wilfred.

Suddenly the bishop spoke up. "I will conduct no Mass on Heilige Abend this year. I am tired of hearing what Bishop Marcel used to do. I tend to agree that the elderly should not make such an arduous journey at that time. I also realize, however, that many of them wish to. Perhaps next year we will have a temporary shelter for the purpose. In the meantime, I shall hold a service the day after All Saints' Day. It is called All Souls' Day, and I shall teach the people wonderful new rituals that will add to their blessings in the next life."

The tension was eased a bit, and the men mumbled to one another for about thirty seconds before Peter Fabian held up his hand for silence. "We do have one more thing we must discuss—with our Bishop Gernot," he announced, turning toward the bishop.

Andrew glanced up and saw several of the men bow their heads and look at the table. Only Sigismund and Julian looked puzzled.

Peter Fabian nodded to Hugo Aichinger, who spoke in his querulous voice. "You do not know us very well, and we do not know you. But there are certain things that you must know concerning your service in the bishopric of Felsenburg—or a bishopric anywhere, for that matter."

Bishop Gernot nodded politely. Andrew wondered if the bishop was as puzzled as he about the upcoming topic.

Hugo Aichinger continued. "The men in this room form the cathedral chapter. It is our duty to oversee the maintenance and building of the cathedral. While it is certainly a welcome change to have the bishop actually living in his bishopric, we would like to request that the bishop recognize that his duties do not include the building and maintenance of the cathedral. We do that for you."

A smile danced around the corners of the bishop's mouth, but he conquered it and said, "I see."

Andrew saw too. Titus had leaked out.

Peter Fabian continued. "It has come to our attention that you thought it was your responsibility to find a suitable architect to be the master builder for the new cathedral. While your support is appreciated, your choice is—"

"Dear brothers," Bishop Gernot interrupted, "you seem to think that I am in the dark concerning my duties—and yours." He paused and glanced around the table. "I'm not. Since the news of my great coup has somehow leaked out—" he paused again and turned a piercing look on Andrew, who returned it coldly, "—let me officially tell you whom I was able to obtain," he finished cheerfully.

"It's not your prerogative," Sigismund told him.

"We already know," Peter Fabian informed him.

"Titus of Athens!" announced someone.

"An infidel."

"To build a cathedral!"

The bewilderment spread around the table until suddenly Andrew realized that he had not been writing for quite some time. He bent his head and tried to concentrate.

When the initial shock had subsided, the bishop used the opportunity to speak again. "I can imagine how you found out. My scribe looks sufficiently innocent, so I know that it wasn't from him." Andrew struggled to keep his eyes on the parchment. The bishop continued, "You fail to realize that we have hired the best architect in the world. Titus has studied in cities where they construct buildings that we can only dream about. Our St. Nathaniel's Cathedral will be the biggest, tallest, most beautiful building in existence." His excitement colored his words. "People will come from all over the Christian world to see it!"

"A cathedral built by an infidel," Gallus muttered dryly.

"His religious beliefs have nothing to do with his talents," protested the bishop, allowing himself to be drawn into a defensive position.

"Excuse me," asked Julian the Quiet, "but who is this Titus of Athens?"

"He is an infidel Muselman!" barked Gallus.

Wilfred, who had been silent until now, corrected him gently. "He is also a gifted architect who would certainly build a cathedral unlike anything that has ever been seen."

"It is *our* responsibility to hire the master builder," Sigismund announced suddenly from the depths of his thoughts.

Peter Fabian grabbed the opportunity to return the conversation to his main point. "Excellenz, we would like to request that you allow us to carry out our responsibilities."

Bishop Gernot shrugged. "It is too late. He's here."

"He's here?" demanded Sigismund.

"Have you paid him?" asked Wilfred.

"He's here," the bishop repeated firmly, "and I intend to pay him. There really is nothing to talk about."

"Where do you plan to get the money?" asked Wilfred, the treasurer.

"Do you remember the Rosen Jungfrau?" he reminded them.

"But that money was to be given to the chapter," growled Sigismund.

"The Rosen Jungfrau belongs to Felsenburg, and the money is here."

Every eye turned to Augustin, who suddenly smiled. "If we want a cathedral, why do we care from where the money comes?"

Hugo Aichinger gave Augustin a puzzled look and then said to the bishop, "It is not fitting for the chapter to sit by while you meddle in our affairs."

"If you're going to handle the finances," added Wilfred, "then we hardly need a treasurer."

"You could have at least asked!" protested Gallus, more to the point.

Andrew happened to look up in the pause and caught the bishop's eyes. "Are you getting all of this?" he asked his young secretary in amusement.

Embarrassed, Andrew ducked his head.

"We don't need him either," said Gallus angrily, waving his hand at Andrew.

"Either?" asked His Excellency. "I don't need any of you. Bishops have built their own cathedrals before—appointed their own canons—collected their own money. You need me, for you cannot get rid of me. The king has appointed me, and here I stay. This is where God wants me."

"There is no need for ultimatums or threats," said Wilfred in an attempt to calm the hurt feelings. "I really do think that there must be a compromise."

"Certainly," replied the bishop brightly. "I have hired the best architect in the world, but there is still much to be done. You shall meet Titus, and then following his recommendations, you shall hire the rest of the artisans."

"We have no money," murmured Wilfred doubtfully.

"You wanted a compromise!" Sigismund reminded him grimly.

"Excuse me," Julian asked meekly, "but is this about money or about Titus?"

Andrew looked up and saw his own admiration mirrored on the faces of Gallus, Wilfred, and Peter Fabian. "Your impudence—" began Sigismund severely.

"No," said Peter Fabian, "our quiet brother, Julian, is right. We are arguing from injured feelings, and that keeps us from knowing what we are arguing about."

"So what are we arguing about?" asked Eduard.

Hugo Aichinger raised his hand and spoke slowly. "The chapter has no money. When the bishop's church burned, the only thing saved was the Rosen Jungfrau, which has brought in quite a lot of money, according to, . . ." he paused and considered before saying lamely, "according to my sources. Bishop Gernot would like to hire Titus of Athens, but there is no money for such a prestigious master builder unless we can use the money from the Rosen Jungfrau. Archdeacon Augustin is willing to allow that. If we have done things a bit backward, well, they will still get done."

"In fact," conceded Bishop Gernot, "I shall turn over the offerings to the Rosen Jungfrau to you—to Canon Wilfred. You shall then be able to pay Titus, as well as many other workmen. The sum is indeed staggering."

"Are we happy with Titus?" said Sigismund.

They all looked around the table, until finally Wilfred said wearily, "I don't think our happiness is to be considered."

"Can he build a cathedral that doesn't look like a Muselman's church?" demanded Gallus.

"Mosque," corrected Julian quietly.

"I'm not a fool!" retorted the bishop. "Titus will do as I say."

Right, thought Andrew suddenly, remembering Titus's complete lack of reverence for the archbishop of Milan, *exactly the way Titus did what the archbishop wanted—not at all.*

The canons nodded in agreement, and the meeting was brought to a close.

TWENTY-EIGHT

week later, the precipitation that had failed to fall for so many months now covered the city with a foot of heavy snow. The November storm buffeted the houses, and the people, surprised by the sudden cold, had not gathered enough fuel. No one had expected another winter like the last one.

Even with school each day, Martin felt cooped up at home, and he now understood why his father spent most of his waking hours at the inn. "I would too, but I still hate ale!" he exclaimed in a rare show of anger.

His mother looked at him sadly and pushed more evergreen branches toward him to weave into wreathes for the All Souls' Day service the next day. Mama and Klara were dipping candles to be lit on the graves of the relatives in the family. Martin was looking forward to the new holiday, but he tried very hard not to think about Stefan's lying under so much snow. More than a year had passed, but the pain did not seem to ease.

"You mustn't be too hard on your father," Mama said, "but neither should you follow his example."

Martin shoved a branch too hard and pricked his fingers on the needles. "I'm learning to read, Mama," he retorted.

She bit her lip and hung two more candles on a peg on the wall. "You've gotten your way, Bursch. Don't expect him to be happy about it."

Martin bent his head to his work. No one ever asked him about his classes. He loved the learning, but when he came home, he was not welcome to express his joy. Papa drank too much ale and complained about the weather, but he did not want to hear his weather predictions. Mama cooked and cleaned and prayed, but she was not interested in Martin's own prayers. And Klara still cried a great deal over the loss of Stefan, but when Martin pointed out that Stefan, in heaven, could take better care of her than Stefan, on earth, ever could have, she only howled louder. Martin tried to think of something that they would want to hear about.

He finished one wreath and began another. The branches were fresh and the scent of pine filled the little house with a pleasant fragrance. The holiday was a new one, the bishop having learned of it during his time of study at the Abbey of Cluny. The bishop had stressed the importance of this holiday for those who had died. They would pray for mercy from the saints, both for themselves and for those who had already died and were waiting for deliverance from purgatory. Laying the wreaths would demonstrate their continued affection for their loved ones, and the candles would assist them in their prayers.

The wind whistled around the smoke-hole in the ceiling, and Martin saw Mama make a sign of the cross in case an evil spirit had come in with the wind. It was so cold outside; Martin did not look forward to going to the cemetery the next day.

Then he remembered. "Mama, Klara, I have some really good news. I know that Papa will be happy about this. The bishop has finally hired a master builder for the new cathedral."

"Has he?" She sounded weary.

"I heard it from some of the boys who live in the residence. They hear things . . ." He hesitated, unsure of his sources, but then added quickly, "well, maybe they shouldn't listen, but it can't hurt to know that; everyone will know soon!"

Mama scraped the last of the cooling wax into a glob that fit into her hand. She wrapped it around a piece of wick and set it to cool, pressing on it until it stood straight. "So who did he hire?"

"A man named Titus of Athens."

"A foreigner!"

Martin's heart sank. "Is that bad?"

Klara wiped her hands and bent to pull Bernie to his feet. She rarely spoke, but she always seemed to understand things. "He ought to hire the craftsmen from town," she said firmly. "A foreigner doesn't know our ways." She led Bernie by the hand into her room and closed the door.

Mama nodded, and Martin decided not to say any more. He still had three more wreaths to make; he would just endure the silence.

⚬⚬⚬ ⚬⚬⚬

The next morning was gray and gloomy. The wind had calmed, but it still blew in fitful gusts that pushed and swirled the snow from one place and drifted it to another. Martin and his parents dressed warmly in preparation for the hours to be spent out in the elements. In spite of Klara's protestations, Mama decided that Klara would stay home with Bernie and baby Stefanie.

"You would put Stefan's children in danger to pray for their father? No. Stefan would want his babies to stay home. We will pray in your place."

Martin thought that it was one of the smartest things that his mother had said.

The townspeople gathered near the bishop's residence and huddled against the wall to seek refuge from the capricious wind. By the time the bishop, dressed in a great wool cloak, emerged from his garden, big, fat clumps of snowflakes were dancing around them.

Silently, the crowd followed him as he led the way to his chapel. Not everyone could fit inside, so they stood outside and listened as the service was read. One of the deacons came out to distribute the bread, which had become the blessed body of the Savior. Martin was very cold and was glad when that part was over. After giving some instructions, Bishop Gernot plodded solemnly down the aisle and pushed his way through the shivering group of people huddled near the doorway. He turned and went to his residence.

Augustin, now the bishop's archdeacon, led the people across the blank whiteness of Lärchenplatz to the small cemetery that lay to the north of the burned-out church. Most of them carried lit tapers, which flickered and sometimes had to be relighted from a neighbor's flame. The archdeacon stood before them and led them in prayers to each individual saint. He would pray, and then they would repeat in a sing-song monotone that Martin found haunting in its sameness and yet comforting in its thoroughness. He was sure that without Archdeacon Augustin's reading from his manuscript, they would have omitted some of the saints, and that would have been a terrible loss. Each one had his or her significance.

After that, Augustin, too, went home, and the family members took their wreaths and candles and walked back across Lärchenplatz past Zur Felder to the newer cemetery, where most of the more recent burials had taken place. Papa did not actually participate in the rituals. He stood back with his arms folded under his cloak and looked on—not really detached, but not willing to display any vulnerability. In this ceremony, they would strive for strengthening the ties between those who had died and those who remained alive.

Mama knelt in the snow at each of the family graves and laid a wreath carefully on it. On most of the older graves, hardy shrubs of holly or ivy or juniper flourished. Even in the coldest winter, no one could doubt that the Steinmetz family still loved and cared for its departed members. Mama took good care of them.

After she laid the wreath, she lit a candle with Martin's taper and set the candle in the center of the wreath where it was a bit sheltered from the wind. She prayed, asking God to shorten the suffering of each of their dear ones and promising to give to the church in their name. Tradition held that as long as the candle burned, her prayers would continue to rise to God and the saints. Sometimes she would pull Martin down beside her, light a candle for him, and mouth her prayers into his ear. Martin wanted to pray too, but all he could think of was, *Dear God, I don't want to die—to lie here under the snow.*

Onkel Hans and Tante Maria joined them at the graves of the grandparents. Cecilia was with them as well, but she avoided Martin's eyes.

Stefan's grave was last. Even Papa fell to his knees, and everyone was sobbing. Martin was sure that his heart would burst—it hurt so much. The wind had come up again, and the candles would not stay burning; Martin lit them three or four times.

Finally, he felt snow melting down his back, and he realized how cold he was. Mama was bowed over and trembling. He stood up suddenly and pulled her to her feet.

Her lips were blue. She brushed the tears from her face and tried to push him away, but he was stronger.

"Come, Mama, it's cold. We have to go home now."

She nodded and looked back at the grave where Papa still knelt. The candles had blown out again. "Th . . . the candles."

"Just one time more," Martin said. He pushed the candles further into the wreath and lit them again. When he turned, Mama was on the ground in a heap. "Mama!" He looked at Papa, but his father was staring at the flickering flames, unaware of the snow and cold. Martin went to his mother and picked her up, suddenly overcome by her frailty and humanness. How small and light she was!

He carried her home to the warm fire where Klara dressed her in dry clothes and Martin fed her some warm broth. By the time Papa came in, stomping the snow from his shoes, it was obvious that Mama was very ill.

TWENTY-NINE

teinmetz, is there any way I can help you?" Andrew had been watching young Martin in the classroom all afternoon, ever since the boy had burst into tears after spilling his ink onto his parchment. Now the other boys were gone, and the December dusk filled the room with chill shadows. And still Martin sat.

"Are you ill?" Andrew prodded.

Martin turned his reddened eyes to his teacher and shook his head. "I think not," he whispered.

Andrew sat down on the bench beside him. "Well?"

Martin sighed. "I did want to talk to you . . . to ask you something . . . but I hardly dare."

"Am I so frightening?"

The boy gave a wry smile and shook his head again.

"Are things not well at home?"

"Mama's so sick!" he blurted out. "She's been this way so long."

Andrew nodded slowly, his face sad. "Since All Souls'," he stated knowingly. "Everyone has . . . even the bishop."

The bishop did not matter. "The . . . the doctors came to see Mama and did what they could, but we can't keep paying them. Papa has no work in the winter."

"Ach, ja, he's the mason, isn't he?"

"And I pray and pray, but she doesn't get well. Isn't there some way that I can . . . can . . ." Martin trailed off.

Andrew understood. " . . . force God to give you what you want? I don't think so." The monk contemplated Martin's dejected countenance, longing to comfort the boy. *Dear God,* he thought, *if I could force you to hear me, I should be grateful.*

Martin sat up abruptly and said, "But that's not my problem. At least not directly. It's Cecilia."

It was Andrew's turn to smile. "Cecilia?"

"She's my cousin," he explained, a tinge of pink rising into his cheeks, "and her Mama died of the same sickness just a few days ago that my Mama has. We really ought to take her in because Onkel Hans is . . . isn't . . . well, he can't care for her right."

Andrew groped to discern Martin's meaning. "It would be nice to have your cousin living with you?" he asked, his lack of experience making him feel foolish.

Martin looked surprised. "Well, I guess so." Then: "Yes! But Papa said that she must earn a living, and Mama—even though she's sick— told me to ask you."

Andrew stood up and paced a few steps and tried to figure out what he was supposed to do. Baffled, he finally turned and asked, "Why?"

"She . . . she said that a bishop's residence would be a proper place for a young girl to work," he blurted out.

"I see. So you're asking me to inquire if there is anything that she could do here?"

Martin nodded, obviously relieved to have it behind him.

Andrew still felt like he knew nothing about the subject, but he decided to help Martin. "I'll see what I can do," and when Martin looked too excited, Andrew added, "I won't promise anything, though."

Martin stood up and bowed to Andrew politely. "Thank you, Teacher. Thank you so much." He walked to the schoolroom door and opened it. Just before he went out, he turned and asked, "Do you think that God would make Mama sick to punish me?"

"Have you sinned?"

"I didn't think I had, but maybe I did."

Andrew identified with the feelings of unexplainable guilt. He knew how deeply the soul must be searched before that tiny wicked deed is found. To reveal his own struggles to the boy seemed so pointless. Even when the sin had been dug out, the crushing guilt would creep back.

When Andrew did not answer, Martin continued. "Papa says that Stefan died because I wanted to go to school too badly."

Andrew's heart cringed at the cruelty of that statement, yet he was not sure that he should meddle in the affairs of the family. "You will make your Papa proud, someday, I'm sure."

Martin nodded slowly. "I want to learn about God so that I can be a good godfather to Bernie—he's my nephew. But now Mama's sick. I hope it's not because of me."

"It's because of the cold and snow," Andrew said with finality, but he thought: *It's also because of a holy day that should never have been scheduled on such a miserable day. Did God make the holy days for the people or the people for the holy days?*

Satisfied, Martin said, "Oh. Well, thank you again for helping Cecilia," and then he was gone.

⁕

The bishop's housekeeper admitted that she always needed extra help during the Christmas season of Advent, so she was glad to take Cecilia in. When Andrew met the girl, she embarrassed him at once by seizing his hand and kissing it.

Martin pulled her back in surprise. "Celia, that's not necessary."

Andrew agreed, having been startled by the softness of her touch. "The only person in this house who receives that treatment is the bishop, and I don't think that you will see him often, if at all."

She smiled and curtsied in apology. "Thank you for helping me, Herr."

"Brother Andrew will do," he told her. "There is one thing you must know. The housekeeper, Frau Schmidt, would like you to live in the servant's quarters, at least through Advent."

The corners of Cecilia's mouth drooped a little, but she answered bravely, "Th-that would be all right, I guess."

"Your pay will be the same whether you live here or at home," Andrew explained. "Here you get your food and a room. But I should take you to meet Frau Schmidt. She'll tell you what to expect." He turned and led the two cousins through a labyrinth of hallways to the little room on the second floor where the housekeeper organized her day.

At the door he turned to Cecilia. "Today is your saint's day, is it not?"

"And my birthday," she confided shyly.

"Congratulations. Did you pray to St. Cecilia this morning?"

She nodded. "I usually don't forget, but I felt that I needed extra courage today."

"Frau Schmidt is strict but not unkind. I think if you try to please her that you will do fine."

Andrew knocked and opened the door. The girl curtsied to him again and then entered Frau Schmidt's room with a solemn face.

"This is the girl I told you about," Andrew introduced.

Frau Schmidt smiled and nodded. "Thank you, Brother Andrew, that will be all."

Andrew closed the door, and he and Martin stood a moment looking at it. "She'll be all right," Andrew told Martin.

Martin nodded as they turned down a long corridor. "She's much braver than I am."

"Is she?" Andrew tried to imagine what it must be like to have a cousin. "She's pretty, don't you think?"

"Most people think so," Martin said calmly.

Andrew did not know what else to say, so they walked to the classroom in silence.

∝∾ ∝∾

Apparently Cecilia learned quickly, for it was shortly before Christmas that she began appearing at mealtimes, submissively carrying a bowl of vegetables or a board with sliced bread. When her eyes were not properly riveted on the floor, Cecilia would cast Andrew a friendly glance. Toward everyone else, she seemed wary. Obviously, Frau Schmidt had been able to teach her correct behavior.

The girl never dropped things, and she was a pleasant, although peripheral, addition to the dining atmosphere.

It was not until the midnight supper on Holy Night before Christmas Day that Andrew began to fear for Cecilia. Earlier in the evening, the bishop, who was somewhat recovered from his recent illness, had conducted a midnight Mass in his own chapel on the grounds of the residence. Andrew had been asked to organize things, in spite of the bishop's previous promise that he would not hold the Christmas Eucharist.

"We have not invited the whole area, and no one is going to freeze to death on a walk across town," Bishop Gernot had protested dryly. "The people need these ceremonies; the rituals keep their faith strong. We really need to begin the cathedral."

So the townspeople had dressed in their best clothes and had crowded into the chapel on Christmas Eve with their candles burning to ward off the spirits of darkness. The Mass had been said, and all of the children had filed past the beautiful, two-hundred-year-old krippe, the manger scene, where they were allowed to kiss the tiny Christkindl—the Christ Child. Afterward, they went home to their simple suppers.

The bishop's residence was the scene of a bountiful table with several large carp as the splendid main course. The guest list included Archdeacon Augustin, the bürgermeister and his wife, some visiting family members, the schoolteachers, and Titus of Athens. All of the servants were needed to keep such an event running smoothly, and Cecilia was in her usual place, fetching bowls from the kitchen as they were needed.

At one point during the meal, the teachers were talking at their end of the table while the bishop was listening to Titus on the subject of supporting columns. Andrew caught a movement at the corner of his eye. He looked up and noticed the bishop's countenance soften and his eyes turn slowly across the room. Andrew followed his gaze and was unnerved to see that the bishop's attentions were focused upon Cecilia.

Andrew had never before been responsible for the well-being of someone else, and he felt an unfamiliar protectiveness stirring within him. During his two and a half years living under the bishop's roof, he had chosen to ignore the bishop's affairs. He still remembered his shock and revulsion at finding the bishop in bed with someone while the church was burning. Andrew despised the bishop's loose morals, but then, Andrew despised so many things about the bishop, so he tried to organize his own life to avoid confrontations.

Now, however, he watched that despicable, selfish old man lusting after a girl thirty years his junior—a girl that he, Andrew, was responsible for bringing into this house. *Lusting.* Andrew was startled that this word came to his mind. The word was usually thrown about by the clergy to explain the escapades of the uneducated masses.

"So, are the teachers enjoying the carp?" The bishop's loud, cheerful voice interrupted Andrew's brooding, but their eyes met in a defiant challenge.

"Very nice," they all murmured, amazed at the sudden attention.

Bishop Gernot nodded, self-satisfied, and turned back to Titus. Andrew vowed to keep a closer watch on the girl.

A week later was Silvester—New Year's Eve. The town was caught up in the revelry that always accompanied this holiday, and it was intensified by the realization that God's final judgment had again not come during the past year. Some sort of a reprieve had been granted, so they assumed that God would close His eyes to the sowing of a few wild oats. Even past midnight, there was still a lot of shouting and singing in Lärchenplatz as the people staggered home in the crisp, cold night.

As usual, Andrew's headache had made its appearance after midnight and a tankard of ale. He had been celebrating with the teachers, so after wishing them a "lucky slide" into the new year, he had shuffled back toward his room to nurse his pounding head. As he passed the bishop's quarters, he heard a little scream.

Those sorts of noises were not uncommon, coming from the bishop's room, but because of the bishop's challenge at supper a week before, Andrew stopped and listened. He could not make out what the bishop was saying, but the female protests were fairly clear. When he heard a pitiful, "Please, Excellenz, not again," he hesitated no longer. He pounded on the door and tried the latch; it was locked.

He knocked again but did not call, as he refused to speak to the bishop, even though the month of enforced silence was long past. There was a shuffle and then the sound of the key grating in the lock.

Bishop Gernot stood before him in his robe. "What is it?" he hissed.

Andrew elbowed past him into the room. As he had feared, Cecilia stood in the center of the dim room, eyes wide with confusion. Her curly, blond hair was tumbled about her shoulders and she clutched her shawl tightly around herself.

"Get out of here!" Bishop Gernot ordered. "This is none of your business."

Andrew ignored him and went to Cecilia. "Shall I take you home?"

Mutely she nodded. When Andrew drew closer to her and saw the tears upon her face, his throat tightened in compassion.

The bishop came nearer and tried to force Andrew out of the way. Andrew spun around and thrust the groping hands away. "Do not touch me!" were the first words that he had spoken to this man for four months. He grabbed Cecilia's wrist and shoved past the angry man and into the hallway. From his doorway, the bishop menaced, "If either of you tell anyone, I will have you both excommunicated!"

Andrew checked his progress down the corridor and turned to retort, "I could never let words vile enough escape from my lips! I'd rather be dumb again."

The bishop slammed his door, and Andrew led Cecilia to the great front door and then stopped with his hand on the latch.

"What is it?" she whispered, her eyes wide with fear.

The throbbing in his head threatened to overpower clear thoughts. He led her into the library and locked the door. "I must think," he murmured.

She seemed to understand and slowly moved to the windows overlooking Lärchenplatz. Andrew leaned against the locked door and closed his eyes. He could not take her home, for she would relate what had happened, and he had no doubt that the bishop would ruin the lives of anyone who challenged his right to do as he pleased. *Is there no one to whom I can take her? No one who would not be surprised and who will protect her and her family?*

His tortured mind groped through the pitifully short list of his acquaintances and finally settled on Georg, whom he had not seen since summer. Georg already had a low opinion of the bishop, but he also recognized that the clergyman's power was nothing to be underestimated. Andrew hoped Georg would help, for he did not have the energy to think of anyone else.

He walked to the window and looked out at the merrymaking still taking place in the platz. "Fräulein Cecilia, we must go, but I cannot take you home."

She turned questioning eyes upon him.

"Your aunt and uncle—probably your cousin—would be so upset, that they might do something rash. You heard the bishop. You must believe that he would do what he said. I will take you away from here to friends who will understand and who will protect both you and your family."

"But what shall I tell my family?"

Andrew felt so ill that he could think of nothing. "I don't know. Perhaps Brother Georg will have an idea. Here," he said grasping her shawl and putting it over her head. "Bundle up. It's cold outside."

They left the library and the residence and hurried across Lärchenplatz and down the hill toward the bridge. Georg and his followers lived by the river in a row of old houses that they had made habitable. At an hour past midnight, this quarter of the city was obviously asleep. Andrew had never before visited Georg, so he had to awaken one irritated household to apologetically ask for directions to his friend's house.

Georg answered Andrew's knock in his nightshirt. His initial grogginess turned to amazement when he saw who stood on his doorstep.

"Come in, come in," he whispered, looking at the sleeping forms of other family members on their mats. "You are welcome—but at such an hour!"

Andrew pulled Cecilia in after him and closed the door. She stood so close to him that he could feel her shivering.

The room was very dark, but with a bit of bumping and a curse, Georg managed to light a candle from the embers in the banked fire. He set it on the table and then stirred up the coals and laid a few small pieces of wood upon it.

"Sit down," he urged, pulling stools nearer the fire. He pushed Cecilia onto one of them and remarked, "You're freezing. Move closer. I'm sorry I have nothing warm to offer you."

Andrew fought the nausea that so often accompanied the head-aches and watched the wood flicker and catch fire.

"Andrew," Georg prompted, "it's late. What can I do for you?"

"May she stay here for a couple of days?"

Georg looked at the girl and then back to Andrew. "Of course, but tell me why."

Andrew sighed. "She will tell you." He turned to her. "Fräulein Cecilia, you must tell Brother Georg and his wife everything."

Her thin shoulders sagged with shame.

"Everything," he insisted. "You can trust them, as . . . as you trust me. They will believe your innocence." He turned back to Georg. "It's the bishop. I . . . I cannot speak of it now. I'm ill. I must sleep." He stood and reached out to touch Cecilia's head to bless her. The shawl had slipped, and his hand rested for a second on her silky hair before he snatched his hand away.

Georg's wife had arisen, and she now draped a blanket around Cecilia, rubbing the girl's arms to stimulate warmth.

Andrew stepped to the door. "Thank you, my friend," he said wearily. "I didn't know who else to ask."

"You did the right thing," Georg assured him.

Andrew shook his head doubtfully and left the house. Just before Georg closed the door, Andrew turned and, feeling a profound despair, said, "I don't know how much more I can endure."

On the walk back up the hill, he found that tears had frozen on his cheeks.

THIRTY

ama was still alive. She spent most of the winter on her pallet beside the fire, which Martin made sure burned continually. Every morning before school, he would pile enough wood for the day right outside the front door so that Klara did not need to do any heavy lifting. Klara, who even a year later was still weak from the birth of little Stefanie, cooked Mama fragrant meat broths and hearty lentil soups to strengthen her. Little Bernie, who was talking now, provided laughter and unconditional love for his grandmother. Papa spent the larger part of each day at the inn, drowning his boredom in countless tankards of ale.

One evening near the beginning of Lent, Papa slammed into the house earlier than usual. He knelt on the hearth beside Mama and murmured to her until he could no longer contain his wrath in whispers.

"I gave my life to masonry!" he exclaimed. "And they chose a foreigner—a lousy Gaul!"

"Shhh," soothed Mama, taking his big hands in her frail, almost transparent ones. "Your hands are cold. Klara, some lentils for your Papa. Now, tell me what's wrong."

Anger struggled with coherency. "The master builder—that—French mason. The—the cathedral," he finished desperately.

Martin still did not understand, but he sat quietly in his corner, carving the handle for a hammer and hoping that an explanation would come.

Klara brought the lentils, and Papa took the cup in his trembling hands and tipped some into his mouth. He chewed and swallowed and then tried again. "That Greek architect that the bishop hired has been drawing up plans the whole winter long. He also has been looking for the best craftsmen that money can buy."

"But Papa, that's you!" Martin blurted out.

His father turned and glared at him. "Tell the bishop! That proud little Greek can't imagine that a suitable mason can be found right here in Felsenburg. He has sent to France for someone he knows—a student of someone I never heard of."

Mama patted Papa's hand while he drank his broth. Then he continued, more subdued. "All I ever wanted to be was a mason. I believed that I could be the best one in the valley. And I am the best." He bowed his head over Mama, and for a long time there was no sound in the room except for the quiet crackling of the fire. Then he drew a huge, quivering breath and let it out in a blast. "I am the best. Everyone knows it. Everyone except that Greek b—" Mama clapped her hand over his mouth and looked at Martin over Papa's shoulder.

"Ha!" Papa mocked. "He's heard worse in His Excellency's residence." He turned to Martin and said firmly, "We were born to work."

Martin looked at his carving and dug the knife into the soft wood. *And what if I want to pray or fight? Why should I suffer what you're suffering?* he thought bitterly.

"I need you, Bursch," Papa's voice was suddenly softer. "You can't imagine what it's like to have no son to follow in my footsteps. You can read now, can't you?"

Martin nodded, unhappy at the unexpected turn the conversation was taking.

"In a few more months they'll begin to dig the foundation, and next spring the bishop will need more masons than he can imagine to lay the foundation. You'll be out of school then, won't you?"

"Ja, Papa."

"There's no reason for you to return to school. Masonry is a good occupation."

Suddenly, Martin wished that Papa would go back to Zur Felder and get drunk. *I can't give up school now!* he thought violently. *There is so much to learn. I want to learn it all—to teach it, like Brother Andrew.* But Martin held his tongue, and Papa turned back to Mama, satisfied that Martin was under control.

⟨∽⟩ ⟨∽⟩

Fasching, the night before Ash Wednesday in February, was a time of celebration and dancing—a dispensation to allow transgression before the period of fasting and self-denial began. Since Canon Augustin had accepted his new position as archdeacon, there was a new priest, Father Nikolaus. Normally, the priests were very tolerant when they heard confessions the week after Fasching. They knew that the six weeks of Lent was a long time to abstain from the simple pleasures of life. Everyone hoped that Father Nikolaus would understand.

The masons held their Fasching's festival in their new workshop, which had been rebuilt at the southern edge of Lärchenplatz. It was much larger than the old one, and it smelled of new wood instead of sweat and ale and other things that Martin did not like to think about. Mama was still not well enough to attend, and Klara wanted to stay home with her babies, but most of the masons' families arrived in their festival clothes, prepared to celebrate for the whole night. There were plenty of girls to dance with.

Martin was sorry that Cecilia was absent. She had been working at Count Robert's manor at Immergrün since after New Year's, and he had only seen her once since then. That meeting had been very strange, for she had never told him why she had left the bishop's residence, although he had asked several times. She had seemed content, though, so he had let her keep her secret.

The merrymakers danced to the music of pipes, played by three of the local men. Martin danced with several girls with whom he and Cecilia had grown up. Later in the evening, he danced with some girls who came whom he did not know. They were dressed finer than many of the masons' wives and daughters, and their manners were much more bold.

A very pretty girl with smooth, brown hair and dark, liquid eyes attracted his attention because every time he danced past her in the lines, she would smile or speak to him. Occasionally their hands would touch as they whirled and stomped through the complicated figures, and he began to notice her hands. They were soft and warm, not at all like Mama's or Klara's hands.

When the musicians took a break, she sought Martin out and he took her to the table, which was laden with all sorts of pastries and honey confections. They were thirsty and drank a spiced, fermented apple drink. It was hot, and Martin burned his tongue.

"Oooh!" exclaimed the girl when he winced. "Did you hurt yourself?"

He nodded sheepishly.

Her eyes were bright with fun when she retorted, "Perhaps someone ought to kiss it for you."

Her impertinence shocked him, and he looked around uncertainly. The room seemed suddenly very warm, and he set the cup down and said, "I . . . I think I'll go get a drink of water. Excuse me."

He rushed for the door, which was on the other side of the room, but when he got there, she was there with her cloak. Polite and inexperienced, he helped her with her cloak and together they left the festival.

Outside was misty and cold, and frost clung to every surface. Martin shuddered as the cold hit his sweaty body. "Water," he said for lack of something more inspiring. "It's over here." He headed quickly toward the well, slipping and sliding on the icy cobblestones. He had already dropped the bucket into the well when she caught up with him.

"I'm freezing," she pouted, moving close to him and slipping her arm through his.

He pulled the bucket up with difficulty and set it on the wall. Dipping the ladle into the water, she drank from it and then held it to his lips. The water was so cold that it felt like it was burning his throat as he gulped it down. They were both shivering and water dribbled down his chin and spilled onto his shirt. He took the ladle from her and poured what they had not drunk onto the ground.

"Come," he said, his teeth chattering uncontrollably. "Let's get back." He started pushing her around the side of the well and toward the mason's workshop. As he touched her, though, she slid close to him and slipped her arms around his neck. She pushed her face into the crook of his neck, and when he looked down at her, she kissed him.

He found he wanted to kiss her back, but as he did, he thought of how different her kiss was from Cecilia's. He lifted his face and tried to extricate himself from her embrace.

"I don't even know you," he protested.

"Anni," she quipped and kissed him again.

He hated himself—that he could enjoy her kisses and think of Cecilia. A part of him found her sweet and fun, and he wanted to stay in her embrace forever. Another part of him was revolted by his own body's betrayal to his dreams. That part finally triumphed, and he pushed her away gently. "Go back to the party, Fräulein Anni. I'm going home."

"But why? Don't you like me? You could come home with me."

Why was she doing this? He uttered the first excuse he could think of. "I'm studying to become a priest or a . . . a monk." Why did he feel so confused?

Her laughter rang like bells across Lärchenplatz. "Don't you think that priests have fun?"

Her question sent an enormous shudder through him. She took his reticence as an invitation, and she moved to him again, arranging his arms around her waist underneath the cloak.

He could hardly catch his breath. "Fräulein Anni, I . . . I don't think this is right." With great effort, he drew away from the warmth inside of her cloak. "I . . . I hate going to confession, don't you?"

"What do you know of confession?" she said, and the sadness in her voice made Martin almost pity her. "You're just a boy."

Martin could not understand her sudden change, so he answered naively, "Father Augustin—he's the archdeacon now—taught us all to confess our sins, and then he would give us something to do to pay for them."

She laughed again, banishing the sadness. "Father Augustin! And who does he confess to?"

Martin was confused. "Father Augustin? Why would he need to confess? He's a priest."

She threw her arms around his neck and said knowingly, "Priests are men too."

He shook his head in disbelief.

With a little sigh, she whispered, "Come, Master Martin, give us another little kiss."

He obeyed as if he had no will but hers.

"Come home with me?" she begged.

He breathed the fragrance of her hair one last time and then the words, "I can't!" burst from his lips.

Now she shoved him away. "Oh," she said in a tone much different than before, "you're just a boy!"

He felt the insult deeply, but he knew that he had offended her as well. He offered to take her back to the workshop.

"I can find my own way, thanks," she said primly.

He watched her flounce away, but then her feet slipped out from under her and she landed with a squeal of protest. Before he could go to her, two monks who were crossing Lärchenplatz rushed to her side. It was too dark to see who they were, but Martin was fairly certain that the only monks in the city were the teachers at the cathedral school. He could hear Anni's bright voice, laughing sweetly in the crisp night air. They stood talking for a minute or two; then, with Anni between them, they left the square.

Dismayed, Martin watched them go. He wandered back to the workshop to retrieve his cloak, carefully reviewing each moment with her to impress them onto his memory. He found that if he tried very hard, he could even recapture the feeling of her lips upon his. When he entered the workshop, however, he felt very embarrassed. But no one seemed to have noticed the inexperienced boy come or go.

He walked home slowly, but the enjoyable feelings became more difficult to summon, and in their place came disgust at his own stupidity and at her brazen behavior. He was glad that Mama and Klara were sleeping when he got home. He slipped into his bed and lay awake, remembering what it was like to be kissed by Anni. Finally he slept, exhausted by the evening's intense emotions.

Sometime during the night, he dreamed of Anni and awoke with a jerk. As he lay there, listening to his heart beating, he realized that he would have to go to confession in the morning. His guilt at having yielded to Anni and his indignation at her having tempted him kept him awake for several hours. He rehearsed how he would phrase his confession, giving the most blame where it was due. Somehow it did not seem important whether Father Nikolas or anyone else was qualified to listen to confessions or not; Martin just needed relief from his own guilt, and he didn't care who gave it.

THIRTY-ONE

f Andrew had possessed any money, or if he had been related to anyone in the whole world, he would have left the bishop's residence that terrible New Year's Eve. As it was, he had absolutely nowhere to go, and life at the monastery had taught him one absolute truth: Where you are is where God wants you until He moves you.

During the next few months, Andrew's few encounters with the bishop were uncomfortable, but the bishop's hostility declined with each meeting as he realized that Andrew had no intention of ever mentioning Cecilia. Andrew could not understand why the bishop continued to want him around. Had the situation been reversed, Andrew knew that he would have immediately thrown out the insubordinate scribe. He could only believe that the bishop was so jaded by his wickedness that he did not really acknowledge his foremost accuser.

Either that, or Bishop Gernot was so distracted by the management of the cathedral plans that he had no time to worry about antagonists. He spent most of the late winter huddled with Titus of Athens and Canons Wilfred and Peter Fabian, watching his dream develop in black lines on creamy parchment.

Using the Old Testament tabernacle as a very rough model, the men had achieved a plan that promised a building unsurpassed by any in the empire. Bishop Gernot's biblical knowledge—at least in the particulars concerning Israel's Tent of Meeting—provided Titus with original ideas. Titus's strength was his education and his ambition to build something stunning. And Canon Wilfred took his responsibilities very seriously. His wise management of the treasury cleared the way for the bishop's vision and Titus' creativity.

Quiet as he was, Peter Fabian knew the diocese and was able to locate the workmen and the materials suitable for such an undertaking. Plans were made for housing and feeding the workmen, who, at each phase of the construction process, would number around two hundred. Fortunately, many buildings in Felsenburg were still empty, although more and more people moved from the countryside every year. A minimal renovation of the houses required very little of the precious funds.

Even before the last frosts, carpenters traveled to the foothills of the Blue Alps to bring back timber for scaffolding, workshops, tools, and supporting frames. They were able to float the logs back to Felsenburg on the Schwarz River, where they were then sawed into lumber. Soon Lärchenplatz was alive once more, not only with the life that spring ushers in, but with the noise and chaos of craftsmen building their workshops.

To save money, Wilfred decided to use the local granite near St. Jude's for the foundation. Although hard to cut, it would be strong and resistant to water. A new quarry was opened above Obersill, which provided jobs for the men in that tiny town. The stone was cut to approximate dimensions and shipped on rafts down the Obersill River to Felsenburg, where it was carefully piled along the banks until it would be required. It had not yet been agreed on what stone to use for the cathedral itself.

Andrew continued to attend these meetings, recording each day's events even as Titus sketched and scribbled. Ever aware of the mark he would make on history, Bishop Gernot insisted that a detailed journal be kept for posterity. Andrew spent many hours each day recopying his notes after the bishop had edited them to his advantage.

This left little time for teaching, and Andrew sorely missed the stimulation of passing on knowledge to young, fertile minds. He, himself, learned much by listening to Titus, but he disliked the bishop so much that sitting in the same room with him became a torture. Andrew longed to escape, but until God provided an alternative, he believed that he should persevere in his present position.

One afternoon, however, the subject of finances came up once more. Wilfred assured the men that there were enough funds for the foundation, but, beyond that, they would have to raise more money or the work would stop.

"Is there no way that we can cut corners?" asked Peter Fabian.

Titus shook his head at such ignorance. "If we do not use the best materials and the best workmen, the cathedral will not stand. I have seen the results of inferior workmanship. It is a greater waste of money than doing it right the first time." He looked around the table. "I will show you."

He stood and gathered the four cups out of which they had been drinking. "The foundation is laid," he said setting the first cup down with a firm clunk. "An unskilled laborer begins to build upon the foundation." He placed the second cup slightly askew upon the first. "Perhaps by that time more money has come in, and we can again afford more competent workmen." The next cup was positioned exactly upon the second. "And the last. Then we wish to build a roof over it." He looked around and motioned for Canon Wilfred to pass him the carved wooden tray, which he then tried to balance upon the cups. The wobbly structure tipped over and the tray thudded to the floor. "We have so little margin for error. If the first few courses are so much as a finger's width out of line, the entire building will be many feet out of line by the time we want to add the roof."

"No cutting corners," the bishop agreed. "We must raise more money."

Andrew returned to his writing; he was so tired of this subject.

"But how?" asked Peter Fabian.

The bishop was ready with an answer. "In the second book of Moses, as God gives the prophet His plans for a glorious tabernacle, He also suggests a way in which it may be paid for. Every adult twenty years and older was to pay a silver coin to atone for his sins. The rich were not to pay more and the poor were not to pay less."

"Coins to atone for sins?" Gallus asked. "And these silver coins paid for the building materials and workers?"

Andrew watched the bishop's face as he said guardedly, "More or less."

He's lying, Andrew thought in horror. *He's going to tax the people based upon their fear of punishment for sins. He knows the Scriptures, and he has twisted them to his own benefit.*

"That is in your Holy Scriptures?" asked Titus in amazement.

Bishop Gernot nodded, pleased. "It is. The Israelites also gave building materials, and they gave freely of their labor, but we can hardly expect the people to work for nothing."

Peter Fabian turned to Canon Wilfred. "How much silver could we collect?"

"I will find out. We would need to take a census. But are we sure that everyone would be able to pay?"

"They would have to if they wanted to have the forgiveness of sins," said the bishop matter-of-factly.

Before Andrew could stop himself, the words burst from his own lips, "But what if they don't want your forgiveness?"

All four men turned slowly toward him with looks of disapproval.

Andrew quickly apologized. "Forgive me. The words were involuntary. I'm . . ." He was not sorry; he groped for another word. "I . . . I spoke out of turn."

The men relaxed, and Peter Fabian said, "I should say so. But youth is impetuous."

"Absolutely," the bishop allowed, "but I cannot permit it to go unchecked within my house. Brother Andrew, you shall report to me when we are finished."

Andrew bowed his head to his writing, rebellion racing through his mind and heart. *You can no longer force your will upon me!* he raged inwardly.

"So," continued Titus, willing to ignore Andrew's outburst but now aware of a problem, "What can we do if the people do not care to give their silver coins?"

"They will give," Bishop Gernot said scornfully.

The two canons nodded sagely, and Wilfred said, "I will issue an edict to each of the parishes. They will take a census first and then will collect silver coins from each adult twenty years and over. Is that satisfactory?"

"They must be offered forgiveness for certain sins," the bishop added. "I shall make up a list. Those who cannot or will not pay will have thirty days to change their minds."

They talked of other things, then, until it was time for the late afternoon meal. Before Andrew could be cornered by the bishop, the young monk escaped to his room and then hurried down the back stairs and out through the courtyard. He strode quickly across Lärchenplatz, where the cathedral's future foundation was marked out with stakes and where workmen had begun to excavate. The afternoon's conversations had finally pushed him into implementing a decision for which he formerly would not have had the courage.

First he needed to talk with Georg, who was just sitting down to a watery stew when Andrew knocked upon his door.

"You do choose the most unusual times to come calling, my friend," Georg accused with good humor. A stool was found for Andrew, who protested that he had no intention of eating with them.

"Nonsense! With your headaches? My Gerti has enough for you." The family made room at their table, and Andrew ate gratefully.

When they were finished, the children went outside, and Andrew told him, "There is to be a tax for the cathedral."

"Of course there is. How much?"

"One silver coin for every adult twenty years of age and older."

"That is much." Georg sat and rubbed the ancient grooves in the table with his forefinger. "And if we cannot pay?"

"You'll have thirty days to change your mind. After that, a punishment, which has not yet been decided. His Excellenz needs the approval and support of the bürgermeister to decree a penalty."

"Any incentives? There have to be incentives."

Andrew was surprised. "How did you know?"

"The promise of eternal life is a powerful motivation."

"In this case, forgiveness for a selection of sins."

"But why tell me?" asked Georg. "You sound very cynical!"

"I can no longer be a part of this. The man supports his decrees with lies. I don't even know what the lies are, but I can tell when he is lying. Does he really have the right to forgive sins?"

"I think," Georg said thoughtfully, "he would say that he has the right to tell people which sins God will forgive."

"It's the same thing. God can't possibly be talking with Bishop Gernot von Kärnten. The man's making it up!"

"So what will you do?"

Andrew took a deep, calming breath. "Well, I came to warn you about the tax. Then I would like to warn the group that we call the heretics." He paused and cocked his head to one side. "What do they call themselves?"

"Christians," Georg told him with a delighted smile.

"But we are all Christians."

"Are we?"

Andrew stood and offered his hand to Georg. "They live on the count's grounds at Immergrün, don't they?"

Georg nodded reluctantly. "You need to be careful. Not everyone who opposes the bishop is right."

"I don't need to embrace their religion to warn them of the tax. I can't sit by and let people be punished for being poor."

"Do you know the way?" Before Andrew could answer, Georg said, "Of course you don't. I'll go with you. We can be there in an hour, but we will not be able to return until tomorrow."

"I no longer care what the bishop says or does," Andrew boasted. "He cannot hurt me more than he has."

Georg snorted. "Oh, yes he can. You would do well to care, for his power is great."

The hour to Immergrün passed quickly, for Andrew and Georg talked of many things that had happened in the past months. Most puzzling to Andrew was why the count allowed the Christians to live on his property.

Georg was not sure of the details, but he said, "I do know that there was a dispute between the count's father and the former bishop, Marcel. It had to do with a daughter, and you can probably guess the rest. The count keeps his own priest for his chapel, and he insists upon the most devout behavior among those who claim to be clergy."

"Count Robert is your brother-in-law, is he not? Why does he shelter this group we brought with us from Milan?"

"Back in the autumn, they held one of their secret ceremonies— a baptism of an adult. Our new archdeacon, Augustin, found out about it and arrested the leaders. When this news reached the count, he

offered to let them live at Immergrün, where they would be safe from
the bishop's jurisdiction."

"And the leaders?"

"Count Robert paid the ransom."

"But why?"

"He really despises most clergymen."

"I can sympathize."

"I hope not," warned Georg. "The Christians are balancing on the
edge of a very sharp sword. It is one thing to feud with a bishop;
quite another to feud with God."

"Does the count believe as the sect believes?"

"No. But they live very moral lives, and he respects their religion
because of that. This is why," he added, "I was able to find a position for Fräulein Cecilia there. The count was ready to believe the
worst about Bishop Gernot, and he was eager to rescue her from the
terrible situation in Felsenburg."

⟨⟨∘⟩ ⟨∘⟩⟩

When they arrived, the count's guards admitted them through the
enormous gatehouse. Georg seemed to know the way and led Andrew behind the palace and into a woods, where stood a collection
of huts. Many of the servants lived here. Georg asked a workman
for directions, and the man waved his arm toward the largest hut.
Even before they knocked, they knew they had found the right place,
for that haunting singing drifted out to mingle with the whispering
of the breeze in the spring leaves.

Georg and Andrew were warmly welcomed by about thirty members of the sect, who were tightly packed into the sparsely furnished
room. Andrew recognized some of them from the journey the previous summer, but there were new faces as well. The two travelers sat
on stools, and the women provided a little refreshment for them while
Georg performed the introductions.

Josef Radl, the leader of the group, remembered Andrew from the
trip to Milan. He was about ten years older than Andrew and wore a
scraggly blond beard. His eyes were steady and peaceful. "You are
the young monk whose tongue was loosed at Anton's execution."

Shocked and frightened by the memory, Andrew nodded. His mouth turned unaccountably dry, but he answered as well as he could. "I am. It was a terrible thing. I am sorry for your friends."

"They are in heaven with their Savior," he said gently. "Death makes us feel sorry for for ourselves, for we no longer enjoy their company."

Andrew tried to swallow the lump in his throat and choked. Josef Radl motioned for one of the women to give the monk more to drink. It was Cecilia who came forward and poured water into his cup. He gulped it and muttered his thanks.

"So what brings you to us, young Andrew?" Josef asked.

He felt foolish and ignorant. Unexpectedly, his mission had lost its importance when he realized that life carried on in other places, untouched by his own crises. He reined in his insecurity and said softly, "Bishop Gernot has authorized a tax for the new cathedral, and a census is to be taken. Everyone twenty years of age and older will be required to pay one silver coin to atone for his sins."

Before Josef could answer, Georg exclaimed, "Badly done!"

Josef patted Georg's shoulder to calm him and turned to Andrew. "So have you come as the bishop's emissary?"

Andrew covered his face with his hands and groaned. "No. I have indeed done this badly." He raised his face and said plainly, "I came to warn you, for there will be a penalty for those who do not pay."

"I see."

Andrew looked around the room and was surprised to see every eye resting expectantly upon Josef, but Josef was looking at Andrew.

"It took great courage to come here," Josef said. "We thank you."

Andrew shook his head, his confidence returning, "I came because I was—am—angry. And because I felt pity for those who could not or would not pay."

"We appreciate your kindness, but you don't need to pity us. Our sins have already been atoned for."

"How . . . ? I don't understand," Andrew stammered, his heart hammering with the hope of finally learning more.

Georg stood abruptly. "We really need to get back before dark," he said with a frown.

Andrew was surprised. "But you said we would leave in the morn—"

"I know what I said. But it is best that we leave now," he said severely. "Come, Andrew, let's be off."

Andrew had no desire to argue with Georg before so many strangers, but he had the feeling that he was near to finding out the answers to so many questions. Wishing for the courage that Josef had attributed to him, Andrew whispered, "I can't go now."

Georg shook his head sadly, "Oh, Andrew," he groaned, "may you not spend the rest of your life regretting this." He walked to the door and then turned to say, "I will visit my sister. We can leave in the morning."

THIRTY-TWO

hen Georg and Andrew had first come into the room, they had interrupted a meeting. Now that Georg was gone, Josef asked Andrew's permission to finish. He explained that they were learning from the Epistle of St. Paul to the Galatians, and then he read from a small parchment, first in Greek and then translating flawlessly into the local German.

Andrew had never heard the portion, and he found it very confusing. He recognized that Josef was teaching with authority, but the subject was so unfamiliar and expressed in such nontheological terms, that Andrew did not recognize it at all. The teacher referred frequently to the Scripture in his hand. Several times Josef said, "Well, let's see what Paul said," and then he would read. Andrew had never heard the Holy Scriptures handled in such a way. He sat quietly beside Josef, astounded at the strength and peace that seemed to flow from this man.

Finally, Josef dismissed them with a prayer that seemed to come from the bottom of his heart. Andrew watched him as he smiled and gestured to God. He spoke as if God were his friend and were in that very room with him. After a chorus of amens, several men came to thank Josef and to say good-bye to Andrew.

Andrew felt very uncomfortable and did not know what was expected of him. He stood also and looked around uncertainly.

"Brother Andrew?" Cecilia stood before him, looking more beautiful than he had remembered. She curtsied and her loose-fitting dress swept the dusty floor. "I wanted to thank you for helping me."

Andrew smiled slightly, uncomfortable in her praise but strangely glad that she had spoken to him. "Are you happy here?" he asked.

She nodded enthusiastically. "They are very kind to me."

"What is your work?"

"I am learning how to sew beautiful dresses for Count Robert's wife."

Just then Josef broke in. "You did a very heroic thing by taking Fräulein Cecilia from the bishop. We are all grateful."

Andrew was embarrassed by the use of the word *heroic*.

"Fräulein Cecilia," said Josef, as if he had been her father, "We have things to discuss now."

"Oh, of course!" Cheerfully, she curtsied again and hurried from the room.

Josef pointed at the stool. "I believe you have questions?"

Andrew sat down and looked around the small circle of four men who had remained behind. Josef introduced them.

Herbert was a big, burly man with a charming smile. He jumped up and grabbed Andrew's hand, shaking his whole arm. "We're glad you've come!" his voice boomed. The other two men, Markus and Wolfgang, merely nodded politely.

Josef smiled at Andrew's silence and prompted, "So tell us again about the decree regarding the silver for the cathedral."

Andrew was glad for his confused thoughts to be given a direction. "Everyone twenty years or older, whether rich or poor, will be required to pay one silver coin."

"And what is the purpose of the silver coin?" said Josef.

"To pay for the cathedral."

Josef waved his hand impatiently, "Yes, yes, but why would the people want to give this silver coin?"

"The bishop says that it is a coin of atonement, to pay for their sins."

Josef winced. "And which sins?"

Andrew shrugged. "The bishop is making up a list."

"I see." He thought for a moment and then said, "And if the people cannot or will not pay?"

"They'll be given thirty days to change their minds. After that, they'll be punished. The punishment has also not been decided."

"Does this not all seem very ironic to you?"

"Very."

"Tell me how you see it."

Andrew blurted out at once, "I don't understand how the people can be forced to pay for their sins, or punished if they don't want to do it in that way!"

"Surely, though, it is a good thing for people to pay for their sins," Josef remarked wryly.

Andrew started to say that it was, when he detected a movement to his right and looked over just in time to see Markus and Herbert exchange a confidential glance. Josef saw it too and said apologetically, "Please excuse our evasive manner. We are naturally cautious when someone of your . . . your persuasion unexpectedly shows interest in our unimportant little group."

Andrew suddenly realized how threatening his visit must seem. He raised his hand in a reassuring gesture and said firmly, "I mean you no harm, and I suspect that I would be the one in danger if I were found out."

Wolfgang spoke for the first time. "Maybe," he said, "But Anton and his wife were killed by your kind."

Andrew's head snapped back as if he had been hit. Scenes of fire and pain flashed behind his eyes and sent a chill through him. These men had every reason to hate him, but if they blamed him for the death of their friends, was he then also responsible for the death of his own parents?

He propped his elbows on his knees and dropped his face into his hands. *Do I deserve such condemnation? What is my kind? I was so sure that these people would give me answers, but they don't trust me. Dear God, is there no hope?* He was tired of tears, and he dashed them away as he raised his head to face his accusers.

He did not, however, see accusation in any of their faces; they looked at him instead with—*Could it be?*—pity. Startled by their lack of malice, Andrew was no longer afraid to reveal his confusion to them. "I . . . I am so sorry about what has been done to you. I don't know how to convince you that I would never hurt you. Perhaps . . ."

he hesitated and then tried again. "I don't like 'my kind' . . . I don't even know what I believe . . . but—" Did he dare tell them?

"You have nothing to fear from us," Josef reassured him.

Andrew nodded and made his decision. "I know. And you have nothing to fear from me, for my . . . my father and mother were killed by . . . in the same way as your friends."

Josef sighed, and Wolfgang shook his head slowly. "That must be very hard."

Andrew was not used to having compassion directed at him. He forced a small smile onto his lips. "It was harder not to know . . . harder to keep the knowledge from myself."

"Well," said Markus to the others after a long pause, "I think God has sent him to us. God will protect us."

They nodded, and Josef said to Andrew, "We can probably answer many questions that you have, but you must ask them. There's no point in giving you answers to questions that you do not yet have."

Andrew was ready. "You just told Brother Georg and me that you don't need to worry about the atonement money because your sins have already been atoned for. How is that possible?"

"We base our faith upon the Holy Scriptures. Any time you are taught about God, make sure that what you are taught is supported by God's Word."

Andrew agreed. "That's what the church says as well."

"Is it?" Josef did not let Andrew answer, but continued, "Never mind that. The answer to your question can be found in St. Peter's first epistle. Have you ever read it?"

Andrew chewed on his lip, trying to remember. He had not read much of the Holy Scriptures, and what he had read, he had not understood.

"Unfortunately," Herbert interjected, "We do not have access to many pages of Scripture."

Josef ignored that. "Peter says that our motivation for good works is not so that we can purchase our redemption—atonement, salvation—but so that we are grateful that we have already been redeemed. He specifically mentions gold and silver."

In his excitement, Herbert interrupted. "Those who believe in traditions that say we can purchase favor with God are stuck in an aimless quest. I used to always feel that if I could do one more good thing, then I would feel better. I didn't."

"There isn't enough gold and silver in the whole world to please God for even one of us!" exclaimed Markus.

Andrew understood the words, but he could not believe that there was nothing one could do to earn God's approval. He murmured, "But—" and stopped.

Josef continued. "The only thing that can save us from our sins and from the guilt is 'the precious blood of Christ, as of a lamb without blemish and without spot.' I'm quoting."

The verses that Andrew had memorized so long ago at St. Jude's popped into his head and he quoted it aloud, "'For by grace you have been saved through faith and that not of yourselves; it is the gift of God not of works, lest anyone should boast.'"

Josef nodded, pleased. "Ephesians."

"Is that true? What I just said?" said Andrew, not yet sure he could believe such a wonderful thing.

"It is true."

"But if forgiveness of sins is free, what keeps people from living evil lives?"

Markus reached out and touched Josef's arm. "Allow me?"

Josef smiled.

"I have a son, who is almost grown," said Markus. "You don't know my son, but if you did, I am sure that you would love him. Suppose one day you were on the road and robbers attacked you. My son, whom you don't know, rushed in and saved your life, but he was killed. Would you offer me money in payment?"

"I think that would dishonor your son."

Wolfgang continued, "Now assuming that there was an inheritance—" He broke off to allow the men to laugh at the impossibility, "—an inheritance, and I offered it to you. How would you respond?"

Andrew looked around the circle and then tried to say the correct answer: "To honor your son, I would be obligated to accept."

"Obligated?" asked Josef in surprise. "How do you think that Wolfgang would feel to discover that you only took the inheritance because you felt obligated?"

The young monk squirmed and searched for another word. "I suppose I should be . . . grateful?"

"Better," said Josef.

Herbert burst in again, "And would you squander the inheritance on ale and prostitutes?"

"No," said Andrew with conviction.

"Do you doubt that humans are sinners?"

"No," he said again, not sure of the connection.

"The penalty for sin is death. But God allowed His Son to die in your place . . . in my place. Do you still want to pay for your own sins?"

Gradually, things were becoming clearer. Andrew said slowly, "No, that would dishonor the Son."

"And if you decided to accept the inheritance—in this case, eternal life—would you live an evil life to show your contempt for the gift?"

"I understand," Andrew exclaimed. "The good works are to show gratefulness, but we cannot purchase the salvation." He thought for a moment and then asked, "But don't we still have to keep the Ten Commandments?"

"What for?" Herbert demanded.

Andrew was not sure. "Well . . . in order to please God."

"Why?"

The monk suddenly realized that Herbert had set a verbal trap, which was unavoidable because he did not know the answer to the question. "I assume," he said warily, "that the reason is *not* so that God won't allow me to go to hell."

Josef smiled and admitted, "You are very clever. What is the first commandment?"

"To have no other Gods before Him."

"And the second?"

"That's my question," Andrew remembered unhappily. "I had a terrible argument with the bishop about that. He told me that I have no right to question the traditions of the church."

"If you don't question them, you will never know the truth," Markus assured him.

"So what is the second commandment?" said Andrew.

"To not make any carved images or pictures to bow down to and worship. But don't believe me; read it yourself."

"I did," Andrew said, his voice low and flat. "So why are we taught otherwise?"

Herbert opened his mouth to answer, but Josef halted him and said, "You'll have to ask the people who taught you. Do you have access to the Holy Scriptures?"

"I do."

"You must be careful not to believe what people say about God's Word—even what we say. People will try to mislead you. Read it yourself and make your own decisions."

"Where shall I begin?"

"What portions do you have?" asked Wolfgang.

"Hundreds," answered Andrew.

"If the bishop will allow you, then read the whole New Testament."

"You have the whole New Testament?" gasped Herbert.

"Probably," said Andrew, almost embarrassed.

Markus nodded. "That would be a good place to begin."

"I'll start tomorrow," the monk said eagerly. Satisfied that he had indeed found people to answer his doubts, he asked his next question, "Why do you baptize adults?"

Josef stood and stretched. "Another time, young Andrew. You've learned much this evening, and it is late. You should rise early and return to the city before you are missed. It would be better if you don't tell the bishop about our conversations. We have nothing to hide, but we fear for your safety."

Before Andrew knew what was happening, Josef had enveloped Andrew in a powerful hug. Gripping Andrew by the shoulders, he said, "If you search for the truth, you will find it. Just make sure that you really want it."

The men said good night, and Josef led Andrew to a corner of the room where some blankets were piled on a mat. He lay awake for a long time thinking about how simple life would be if all that they had said was true. For the first time in many months, his heart did not feel so heavy, and he fell asleep, thanking God for the possibility of real joy.

THIRTY-THREE

rnst Blumental knew numbers. He had an uncanny ability in mathematics that most people in Felsenburg considered almost magical. He worked for himself, and people hired him for their most difficult figuring. When the bishop started looking around for someone to conduct a census, he asked the advice of the canons and several prominent citizens, including the bürgermeister. What he needed was a man capable in figuring, unquestioningly loyal, and indifferent to criticism. The name suggested most often was Ernst Blumental.

Nothing about the man's appearance gave a clue to his granite core. When Bishop Gernot greeted him for the first time, he wondered if this tall, round-faced man with the bright blue eyes would really be able to collect taxes from reluctant parishioners. He did not wonder long.

After the preliminary civilities, Blumental actually steered the conversation to its purpose. "I understand that you are looking for a man to collect the taxes for the cathedral."

"We don't like to call them taxes," said the bishop wearily. "I realize that this rumor has spread throughout the town and even the diocese, but it is not a tax, for a tax benefits only the ones who collect it."

"I see." It was obvious that the man saw very well. The blue eyes glinted like ice. "So what will we be calling it?" he asked wryly.

"It is atonement silver, straight out of commandments that God gave Moses. And it is completely fair, for no one pays more or less than one silver coin—all of which will be used for the cathedral."

"How do you intend to pay me? I usually get a percentage of the coins that I collect."

The bishop thought for a moment and then said, "Every single one of the coins must be used for the building. I could, however, pay your fee out of the cathedral treasury. Would that suffice?"

Blumental tipped his head to one side and smiled. "That would be one way to handle it."

Their conversation was long and dealt with many particulars, including how to warn and punish those who would not pay. The bishop promised to send two of his personal armed guards to accompany Blumental as he traveled around the diocese. In each town, the local priest would also be on hand to dispense the papers certifying atonement from certain sins for a specified length of time. With these four men appearing on each doorstep, the bishop doubted that anyone could refuse to pay. Blumental was not quite so optimistic, but he estimated that he could cover Felsenburg before autumn and finish the entire area before construction resumed the next spring.

For two months, Blumental knocked on every door in the city. He collected coins and recorded names onto sheets of parchment, which he had cleverly stacked into a pile and sewn together along one side to bind the sheets together.

The wealthier burghers had no objection to paying such a small sum for the avoidance of confession. Even the innkeepers, the baker, and others of the tradesmen only grumbled that they ought to receive more for their money. The laborers, who had been hired to dig the foundation holes, were also able to pay, and many seemed glad for the special dispensation for their nightly carousing. On market days, Blumental easily collected coins from the farmers' wives, while their husbands, who were disinclined even to attend church, labored doggedly in the fields. A few of the poorest were given their thirty days to beg, borrow, or steal the necessary coins, but the presence of the guards enforced the edict without emotional threats.

The problem came when Blumental knocked upon the door of the first little house built alongside the river. Archdeacon Augustin was along that day, and he warned Blumental about the dissident Georg.

Brother Georg came to the door with a scowl firmly imbedded into his forehead. "Ja?"

Blumental plunged in. "How many persons twenty years and older live within this house?"

"Why?" Georg, of course, knew, but he intended to make it as difficult as possible.

Augustin, who usually did not take part in the interviews, decided to make an exception. "Brother Georg," he uttered the name as if it were a blasphemy, "there is no need to be difficult. You know perfectly well why we are collecting these coins; you are the one who started all of the rumors."

"Truth. I spread truth," he said, his manner uncowed. He looked at Blumental. "So you're the one who takes money from the poor to give to the rich."

The mathematician ignored him and asked again, "How many persons twenty years and older live in this house?"

Their eyes met and neither saw a hint of surrender. "One hundred and forty-three," snapped Georg mockingly.

Blumental scowled and flipped his pages closed. "I am sorry that you cannot pay. You will have thirty days to find the money for your atonement silver. At the end of that time, you will be imprisoned for thirty days." He stepped away from the door and started toward the next hovel.

"If you knock on one more door along this row," Georg called after him, "I can promise you will regret it."

The guards looked at Archdeacon Augustin for permission to intervene. The priest made a motion with his head, and the four men turned and trudged back through the city gate and up the hill.

The third week in August the townspeople gathered for their annual celebration to honor St. Nathaniel. After a service of dedication for the deep trenches that would eventually become the cathedral's foundation, tables were set up once more in Lärchenplatz. The women prepared a sumptuous dinner, and, since the town's two-year-old grapevines were still not producing well, wine was brought in from the count's vineyards. The inns were full, for this was a holiday for the entire diocese.

At the bishop's request, Ernst Blumental sat at a table near the well, settling the accounts of cheerful givers who did not want to wait to obtain their atonement. The canons seemed relieved that major dissension had not erupted, and the bishop was delighted to have found such a painless way to raise money.

Blumental was busily adding figures when he looked up to see Georg and several other men, equally unkempt, ranged around his table. He jumped to his feet in alarm.

"We are not here to hurt you," Georg informed him coldly. "We wish to give you silver coins."

One of the bishop's guards had paced quickly to the table to give support to the surprised collector.

Blumental eased back onto his stool. "How many in your household—"

"I'm not paying for myself!" Georg told him impatiently. "Here . . ." Before Blumental could stop him, Georg grabbed the ledger and ran his finger down the first page. He stopped about halfway down. "Lorenz Altmann. Has he paid you yet?"

Blumental looked. "He's imprisoned at the moment."

Georg reached into the folds of his cassock and pulled out a black pouch. He fished a coin out and banged it onto the table. "How much does Lorenz owe?"

"Two coins."

Georg gave him another. "You!" He waved at the guard. "Go release Lorenz Altmann."

The guard looked uncertainly at Blumental, who nodded his permission. The guard strode off in the direction of the cells.

"How many are in prison?" asked Georg with feigned civility.

Blumental leafed through his ledger, counting silently. "Ten."

"And how much do they owe?"

Blumental tried to pierce Georg's composure with an icy stare, but the monk merely smiled and stared back. Blumental ducked his head and paged through the ledger a second time. "Twenty-nine."

"Twenty-nine," Georg said evenly, "Not thirty? How fitting it would be if the folk were betrayed for thirty pieces of silver. Are you sure it's not thirty?"

Blumental did not blink nor did he recount. "Twenty-nine."

Georg and his men counted out the coins and piled them painstakingly upon the table. The guard returned with the man who must have been Lorenz Altmann, for he rushed to Georg and fell on his knees, seizing his hand to kiss it.

"Nonsense, man!" The monk pulled his hand away and rested it upon the man's head. "It is God you must thank, and God bless you." The man hurried away to find his family in the milling throng of St. Nathaniel's Day merrymakers.

Georg spun around to the guard, who had been in a whispered conversation with Blumental. "Back to the cell!" he commanded. "Set them all free. And don't bring them back here; send them home to their families."

Blumental nodded, and the guard trudged back toward the residence.

"So," said Blumental civilly, "Now you can pay for your own households."

Georg shook his head. "I still have fifteen days of freedom, but then you'll have to lock me up."

"And the rest of us," growled Reinhold, who was still one of Georg's most faithful followers.

"But you have the money," protested Blumental, at once sorry that he had allowed himself to be goaded into a begging position.

Georg waved in the direction in which Lorenz had gone. A small crowd was gathering to see the men who had paid Lorenz Altmann's atonement silver. "I would rather buy food and shelter for the likes of them than to have my silver squandered on a stone edifice built to the glory of our infamous bishop."

"The edifice will stand forever, and the silver benefits every person as it pays for the atonement of their sins."

Georg chuckled. "I had forgotten that part."

Blumental allowed himself to feel relief too soon.

"So who gets the atonement for the thirty-one pieces of silver?" Georg asked Reinhold.

Reinhold shrugged.

Blumental saw the problem. "I think that I shall have to ask the bishop," he muttered, eyeing the increasing number of people around his table. "By rights, the atonement should belong to those who paid, but each person was only supposed to pay one coin." He sat for a moment looking at his ledger.

"The man's a fool!" exclaimed Georg to the sky.

Blumental jumped up and rushed around the table to confront Georg, who was at once protected by his four men. "No one calls me a fool," Blumental said through clenched teeth, controlling his desire to strike the nearest man. "I am doing the bishop's bidding, and God is on our side."

"I doubt that!" Georg pushed forward and waved his finger in Blumental's face. "If you harass any of my people," he said softly, "you will have to contend with me. You would be better off to defy the bishop than to cross me. You may do as you like to me, but do not even go for a walk along the river on the east side of town." Georg and his men spun around and pushed their way through the townsfolk. The crowd mumbled their disappointment; they had wanted to see a fight.

Of course, the guard reported to the bishop. Blumental, however, was embarrassed that he could not get the better of Brother Georg, so he related only the essentials. The bishop was preoccupied planning a bedroom tryst with one of the women in town, so Blumental's quest for admiration was left unfulfilled. He wandered out to the festival and stuffed himself with chicken and wild boar, washing them down with many cups of wine and ale.

∞   ∞

Around midnight, it rained, cutting the celebration short. Everyone grabbed whatever food or drink they could and moved the revelry into the various houses and inns.

Martin and Sepp had been invited to spend a raucous evening with the other young men in the school dormitory above the bishop's kitchen. It was an eye-opening experience. In spite of his father's winters spent at the inn, Martin's mother had tried to keep a household where God was honored. At the dormitory, the students seemed to revel in obscenity, and they ate and drank ale until they were sick. Martin and Sepp were shocked. Had they not been together, they might have joined in, but their friendship to each other strengthened their resolve to remain aloof. Finally, after midnight, they decided to escape to their homes.

Sepp and Martin slipped out and ran down the steps and out into the rain. There they stood, letting the fresh, earthy scent fill their lungs. After a short conversation, they parted, Sepp to run through the back of the bishop's garden, and Martin to cross Lärchenplatz.

The square was very dark; dim light from a few small windows reflected upon the wet cobblestones. Martin knew that the cathedral excavation presented a hazard in the dark. If he should fall in, it was now too deep to climb out without a ladder. He estimated where the holes were and gave them a wide berth.

Unexpectedly, out of the darkness loomed a tall man. He was murmuring incoherently and staggering dangerously close to the excavation. The boy cried out a warning, but at that moment the man vanished. Martin's heart jumped to his throat as he thought of ghosts and demons who wander about freely, looking for victims. Then below him, he heard a thud and a groan. He dropped to his knees and reached out. A chill went through him as he almost pitched into a deep, black hole. He struggled to regain his balance, and then he drew carefully back from the edge, wondering if there was a trench behind him as well.

When he had caught his breath, he finally dared to call, "Hallo, is anybody there?"

He listened, but all he could hear was the patter of rain on the stones and the musical sound it made in puddles.

"I know it's a ghost," he announced. "I am not afraid, for St. Martin is with me!"

There was no more movement. Martin turned and looked across the platz. Surely there were no more excavations in the way. Just to be certain, he crept on his hands and knees until he was almost to the houses on the other side. Then he stood up and ran home as fast as he could.

THIRTY-FOUR

t school the next day, Martin dashed into class to find that most of his classmates were pale and ill from the effects of the revelry. He could hardly wait to tell Sepp about the ghost, but Sepp did not arrive until halfway through his second class. The two boys had no opportunity to communicate until the midday meal. They sat on the steps of the kitchen and both tried to talk at the same time. Finally Martin allowed Sepp to begin.

"Ernst Blumental's dead!" he blurted out. Blumental had been boarding in a room above Sepp's father's bakery.

"How did it happen?"

"No one knows. They found him in one of the excavations."

Martin's heart jumped once more, and he said, "Oh." He sat thinking for some time before Sepp prodded, "What do you mean, 'Oh'? I thought you'd be excited."

Martin gathered his thoughts and said, "I am, only different than you'd think." He paused this time for effect and then said, "I thought I saw a ghost last night."

Sepp was exasperated. "Oh, don't be silly. This is real. The gendarme thinks that he may have been murdered!"

"He wasn't," said Martin softly. "I saw him fall."

"Did you really!"

"I almost fell in myself! I didn't know who it was. This man suddenly came out of the darkness and then disappeared. I thought it was a ghost. But I heard him land in the excavation, only he wouldn't answer when I called."

"He must have drowned in the mud," Sepp whispered, his eyes growing wide at the thought.

"Don't say that!" pleaded Martin.

"We need to tell someone."

"Who? Why?"

"I heard that the bishop is going to arrest Brother Georg."

"That's ridiculous!" Martin exclaimed. "Why?"

"Didn't you see them yesterday afternoon at the festival? Brother Georg refused to pay the money for the cathedral even though he has bags and bags of silver. The bishop says that Brother Georg threatened to kill Herr Blumental."

"I don't think he really would."

"Well, he's going to be arrested."

Martin shot to his feet. "I think I'd better tell someone."

"That's what I said. Who shall we tell?"

"Brother Andrew!" they shouted in unison.

They dashed into the classroom and poured out their story in wide-eyed confusion. Despite his lack of understanding, Brother Andrew felt that if they knew anything that might help Brother Georg, they should not hide it. It was decided that only Martin should go. "You'll have to speak to His Excellenz. Does that frighten you?" asked Brother Andrew.

Martin, heart pounding, shook his head.

The audience was scheduled for late afternoon, so there was plenty of time for Martin to develop an acute nervous stomach. Andrew accompanied him only to the door and pushed him through.

The bishop sat in a large, wooden chair near the window, which looked out onto the gardens. Martin tiptoed across the soft carpets and bent to grasp the bishop's hand and raise it to his lips.

"Sit down, my child." He indicated another large, wooden chair.

Martin sat on the edge and clasped his hands in his lap.

"Martin Steinmetz, isn't it?"

"Ja, Excellenz." He felt so clumsy, and yet he really wanted to please this important man.

"Your father built the shrine for the lovely Rosen Jungfrau."

Martin nodded.

"I have heard that you are a very good student."

"I like to learn, Herr," he said brightly.

"In what subjects do you excel?"

"In Latin and handwriting, Excellenz."

"You could have a great future in the church. There are never enough scribes to copy all of the important manuscripts for the generations to come. Is that what you would like?"

The boy nodded again, but his eyes clouded, and he bit his lip.

"You don't need to be afraid of me. Tell me about it."

"Papa—" his voice cracked with a screech, and he cleared his throat and began again. "My father would like me to become a master mason someday."

"Of course. Is that what you would like?"

"Well, God made some to fight and some to pray and some to work. Papa says that we were made to work."

"That is generally true," agreed the bishop, "but you must follow your calling."

"I . . ." Martin paused and then decided to impress the bishop in a small way. "I would like to be like Brother Andrew."

The bishop frowned slightly and said, "I see. Is he a good teacher?"

Martin nodded his head vigorously. "We all think so."

"And what is it that makes him so desirable?"

"He listens to us, and he values our opinions. He encourages us to think for ourselves. But some of the other teachers—" Martin broke off, flustered, suddenly realizing that he was criticizing the bishop's choice of teachers. "I . . . I'm sorry, Excellenz, I spoke out of turn. I really do like all of the teachers—just some more than others. Some of the boys," he added cleverly, "don't care for Brother Andrew!"

Bishop Gernot smiled. "It's natural that each boy would have his favorite teacher. Tell me, do you think that you would enjoy me as a teacher?"

Martin knew that the answer must be positive. To say "no" would have been a danger to his education. "Oh, yes, Excellenz!"

"Well, perhaps it's time that I got a bit more involved in the education of my boys. How does a class in church history sound?"

"Wonderful, Herr."

"Good. Now. Brother Andrew tells me that you know something about the death of Ernst Blumental."

"Ja, Excellenz."

"So tell me what you know."

Martin explained to the best of his ability the events of the previous night, omitting his reason for leaving the dormitory party.

When he finished, Bishop Gernot asked, "Did you know Ernst Blumental?"

"He came to our house to collect the atonement silver."

"You saw him?"

"Ja, Herr."

"Now you said that it was very dark last night in Lärchenplatz. Did you know that the man in the darkness was, in fact, Herr Blumental? Did you recognize him?"

Martin saw the problem, and he wondered if he was mistaken or if this was a trap. "I . . . no, I . . . thought he was a ghost. I . . . I guess if I had known that he was a man, I would have gotten help."

"Of course you would have," the bishop assured him. "Do you know many tall men?"

"A few, Excellenz."

"Maybe one of them fell into the excavation as well."

"But did they find two men this morning?"

The bishop raised his eyebrows. "He might have climbed out."

Martin was very doubtful. "I don't know—" He stopped when he saw a look of disapproval cross the bishop's face.

"He might have climbed out," the bishop insisted forcefully.

Martin nodded.

The bishop stood. "Well, perhaps it would help if you would show me which trench your 'ghost' disappeared into."

Martin jumped to his feet and followed the bishop out of the chamber and down the hall, where he motioned to one of the guards to accompany them. Out in the garden, the sun was hot, and the plants smelled especially fragrant after last night's rain. They walked across the road and into Lärchenplatz. People stopped to bow and stare, for the bishop rarely appeared in public without previous notice.

At the building site, all work came to an abrupt halt as every laborer tried to get a glimpse of the important personage. The bishop graciously raised his hands and uttered a loud blessing in Latin, most of which Martin now understood. Then the bishop turned to Martin and said, "So, where did your 'ghost' fall?"

Martin looked around, unsure and embarrassed. Lärchenplatz had appeared so differently last night. He could not even be sure that he was facing in the same direction. In daylight, it was obvious where the excavations lay, and it would be easy to skirt them. Last night, he had been so confident that he would avoid them, but he had, in fact, nearly walked into one himself.

Martin randomly pointed at one of the trenches. "It could have been that one, Excellenz."

"But you're not sure?"

Martin tried another approach. "Where did they find Herr Blumental?"

The bishop smiled and shook his finger. "Very clever, but you must tell me."

Martin sighed and looked at his feet. "I am sorry, but I don't know, Herr. Everything looks so different this afternoon."

"It is better to be honest and say so," Bishop Gernot said in a mild voice and patted Martin on the shoulder.

"But Brother Georg could not have killed anyone!" Martin protested, forgetting with whom he spoke.

"Brother Georg," the bishop instructed, "threatened Herr Blumental twice. That is better evidence than your 'ghost.'" They started back toward the residence. "You must be careful how you express yourself, Steinmetz. Some would say that you should not disagree with a church official."

Martin bowed his head, "I am sorry, Excellenz. I just wouldn't want Brother Georg to be imprisoned unjustly."

"I can assure you, he will not be. You just leave this to me. There really is no reason why you need to worry yourself about this again." They strolled through the warm garden and entered the chilly halls of the residence. "You may have a great future ahead of you, Martin Steinmetz. Would you like for me to talk with your father about allowing you to enter the church?"

Martin thought for a moment. "Perhaps when my education here is finished. Papa needs a long time to change his mind. I'll mention it a few times first, but I thank you, Excellenz."

"You're a good boy, Steinmetz." He rested his hand on the boy's head. "God bless you."

Martin bowed over the offered hand and kissed it. Then he hurried toward the classroom. Just before he slipped through the door the bishop called.

"Oh, Steinmetz?"

Martin whirled around.

"Ghosts flee when we stand up to them."

Martin nodded and slipped into the room.

THIRTY-FIVE

he bishop was prevented from executing Georg. Most people had forgotten that Count Robert was Georg's brother-in-law. Too many people had heard of young Martin Steinmetz's encounter with the "ghost" for the account to be ignored. The boy ended up testifying before the town magistrates, although he was vague about the identity of his midnight apparition and noncommittal about which trench the apparition had fallen into. Georg was released because of pressure from the count.

Against Georg's wishes, the count also paid the atonement silver for Georg's band of dissidents, as well as for the Christians who were under his guardianship. Although the bishop would have preferred a confrontation that would have eliminated opposition, he got his silver, which would continue the construction for a little longer.

Throughout the summer, Andrew made the long trip several times a week to Immergrün. He listened in on the regular meetings of the Christians, and Josef and several other men were always available to give him answers to his searching questions. At first, Cecilia attended every meeting, with her sewing in her lap. Sometimes she would meet him at the gatehouse with a group of children, and they would conduct him to the little houses nestled between huge oak trees at the back of the property. She was maturing into a serene young woman, and Andrew's attraction to her was adding a tremendous weight of guilt upon his conscience. She seemed not to notice and talked easily with him in the short times they had. He could not understand why his cassock and his shaved head did not discourage her friendliness.

But he had many problems and many sources of guilt, and he tried to deal with them in order of importance. Then he did not see her anymore, and although he missed her, he was too timid to ask anyone where she was.

Other things troubled him as well. Since the trip from Milan, he had often thought about the assurance of the young widow whose husband was killed in the ambush. He asked Josef why she had not wanted Andrew's blessing and prayer.

"Her exact words were, 'He doesn't need your prayers.'" Andrew quoted. "Don't we all need the prayers of others to shorten our suffering before we reach heaven?"

"That is what the church teaches," admitted Josef, "but you will look in vain for any mention of it in the Holy Scriptures."

"That's why one of your followers said to me, 'Read your Scriptures, and pray for your own soul.'"

Josef nodded. "I said that."

"That was you?" asked Andrew in surprise.

"That was me. Actually," Josef added thoughtfully, "I probably should warn you that reading God's Word can be dangerous."

"Dangerous? How?"

"Well, some people are burned at the stake for it."

Andrew remembered that scene, but he shook his head. "I think that they were executed because they were spreading a blasphemous interpretation of God's Word."

"Do you?" Josef asked dryly. He folded and unfolded his hands several times and then changed the subject. "What was your question about Birgit?"

Andrew organized his thoughts. "How could she be so certain that her husband was not suffering after death?"

"I'm certain," Josef informed him, "and I'm also certain that I have eternal life."

Andrew wanted to accuse Josef of arrogance, but he knew him too well. He said instead, "'Certain' sounds like you have no doubt."

"I usually don't."

"Do you never sin?"

"What do you think?"

Andrew grinned and shrugged. "We are all sinners."

"Who, then, should be allowed to enter heaven?"

"Only those who have done enough good works to outweigh their sins," Andrew answered. He felt like a schoolboy who had given the wrong answer but does not know the correct one.

"How many sins are allowed?"

Andrew bit his lip and struggled with the implications of naming a number. Would God forbid someone to enter heaven because of one sin too many?

Josef said it. "Many good works cannot wipe out even one little sin."

"Then who can go to heaven?"

"No one—" Josef let Andrew think about that for a moment before he coaxed, "—unless—"

"Unless?" Andrew asked, feeling hope rise within him.

"Let me give you an example. Why was Brother Georg released? Did he do something to convince the bishop of his good will?"

Andrew laughed aloud. "Georg would rather die!"

"Then what saved him?"

"His relationship with Count Robert," Andrew said slowly. "Are you saying—?" but he was not sure what Josef was saying.

Josef understood Andrew's bewilderment, and his answer was deliberate. "I know God." He waved his hand around to indicate those who were not in the room at the moment. "We know God."

"Like you know the count?" Andrew asked, skeptical once more.

"I *do* know the count. Do you?" Josef threw back.

"No. But it sounds so arrogant to say you know God."

"Unless it's true. Look what Brother Georg's connection with the count got him!"

"No charges held against him," Andrew said in wonder. "And you know that you are going to heaven?"

Josef nodded. "I am assured of eternal life."

"Do you have Scripture that you can show me?"

"Good question." Josef shook his head sadly. "Show you—no. Tell you—yes. You know, I have never seen them, but I have heard that besides his gospel, the apostle John wrote three small letters. In them are many assurances that we can know that we have eternal life. I want to read them someday."

Andrew wanted to as well.

A few days later Andrew had the opportunity to be alone in the bishop's library. He unlocked each cabinet and searched through manuscript after manuscript, marveling once again that there were so many and that they were never used. He was beginning to doubt that the bishop owned St. John's letters when he finally found them, rolled together into one bundle. He relocked the cabinet and sat down to read. After the first paragraph, he had to lean back from the table so that his tears would not drip onto the parchment. Joy. These things were written so that joy might be full. Andrew desired joy so deeply, yet it eluded him.

Someone was outside the library door. Quietly and with no hesitation, Andrew rolled the manuscripts and pushed them hastily into his wide sleeves. He heard the footsteps fade away down the hallway, but the decision had been made. He slipped from the library and went to his room to read. Over the months he had been stealing moments to read, he gradually understood more and more.

The next afternoon, as soon as classes were dismissed, he gathered the manuscripts and hurried to the manor. As usual, the Christians greeted him warmly, but Andrew's excitement made him feel giddy, and he impatiently waited until he and Josef could be alone in their usual discussion corner.

"I've brought you something!" Andrew pulled the manuscripts from his sleeve and triumphantly placed them into Josef's hands.

Josef, wearing a puzzled expression, glanced at Andrew, then untied the band and unrolled the parchment. He read for a moment and then looked up, eyes glistening with gladness. "So they exist." He sat for a moment wearing a look of affection and admiration, studying Andrew's face. "You are a fine friend." Then he took a deep breath and stood, setting the parchments reverently on the table. "I'll return in a few minutes."

Andrew's heart felt tight with a pleasure that he had never felt before. He watched Josef leave the room and then pulled the first page closer to read it again. This time he was impressed by the author's tenderness toward the recipients of the letters. Before he could read very far, Josef returned with two smiling men, whom Andrew knew as the brothers, Michael and Erich. In the opposite corner of the room, they rummaged through a cabinet and then hurried to the table, bearing parchment, ink, knives, and pens.

Josef explained. "You have brought us a wonderful gift. Erich and Michael will copy as much as they can during your visit; then we can study them anytime we like."

Andrew scrutinized the two men with a sudden feeling of apprehension. Did they have the right to make copies of the Holy Scriptures? Were they skilled enough to accurately commit to parchment the Words of God? He did not realize that his thoughts were being read, until Josef said, "Should the bishop be the only one to possess a copy of God's Word?"

"I . . . I hadn't thought about it."

The two men had been standing quietly, their eyes riveted by longing upon the bishop's parchments. Finally, Erich spoke. "These are the very words of God, given through the apostle John. When John wrote them, he was telling of the things that he had seen and heard and touched. Others, who had experienced them right along with the disciples, could have refuted anything that John wrote, but they refuted none of it. For a thousand years these words have been faithfully copied by talented scribes, but at the start, they were written by a fisherman and copied by his friends and converts."

His brother pleaded, "Allow us to copy the two smaller letters. If you're not satisfied, we will burn them."

Andrew handed them the manuscripts. At the end of the afternoon, they returned the parchments, having only reproduced one. In his room that night, Andrew carefully compared the original manuscript with their copy. The brothers' script was not well executed—merely legible and functional, but every word and every line had been faithfully duplicated.

Throughout September, Andrew smuggled parchments to the manor every time he visited. When the children saw him coming, they would scatter to tell the others. By the time Andrew arrived at Josef's door, he would be surrounded by jumping, chattering children, and Erich or Michael would be eagerly waiting to copy that week's manuscript. He was amazed at the priority this work took in their everyday lives—and at the sacrifices the others made so that someone would be free to copy the Word of God. Their joy was contagious, and Andrew pursued it tirelessly. He began to read the parchments on his own, and when the deep winter snow made further trips to the manor impossible, Andrew continued sneaking manuscripts from St. Nathaniel's library to his room, without a thought to the dangers that such deep knowledge could bring.

∞ ∞

The joy came slowly. When the winter had begun, Andrew had feared loneliness, and he missed his new-found friends, but he filled the time with reading the parchments. And joy crept in. Each longing in his soul was met with texts that satisfied. He no longer feared that his questions had no answers; he dared to ask them all, and he learned from experience that if he read God's Word long enough, he would find a way to deal with every problem.

The danger came slowly also. It began when the peace and joy that he had admired in Josef's eyes began to shine from his own. People at the bishop's residence saw it and did not understand.

Then Andrew got the idea to make his own copies. After all, he had been the best scribe at St. Jude's. His copies would be beautiful, and he would make a present of them to Josef's people in the spring. It was difficult to collect the materials, for he had no money. He could reuse the classroom parchments by scraping off a thin layer, which would remove the ink. The bishop kept him supplied with pens and ink, and if he was thrifty, perhaps the bishop would not notice how much more he was using. He never really examined his behavior, but he seemed instinctively to know that the church would not approve of his unauthorized duplication of the bishop's library.

THIRTY-SIX

 artin spent his winter honing his memorization skills. He learned Latin verbs and wrote speeches, which he delivered in schoolboy Latin. He felt an exhilaration as he discovered more and more things to learn, but he never felt satisfied. True to his word, Bishop Gernot taught a class on church history. He filled every lesson with praise for the great saints of the past few centuries who had transmitted the doctrines of the church to the masses. Martin's language skills were good enough to understand the writings of these people as the bishop read from the different works. He yearned for the day when he could study them in depth.

Just before Martin's eighteenth birthday, the bishop suggested that it was time for Martin to begin making his own decisions. Martin felt that he could hardly correct the bishop by pointing out that going to school had been his own idea, so he said nothing.

"You are very bright, Steinmetz, and you would have much to offer the church. I would like you to talk to your father about allowing you to go to St. Jude's."

They were sitting in the bishop's cozy sitting room, and the housekeeper had brought in steaming cups of cider. Martin sipped his and watched the snowflakes swoop and dance outside the tall, crown-glass windows. For all of his lessons in communication, he found it difficult to choose a place to begin. Finally he simply said, "I have."

"Good. And what did he say?"

"I am Papa's only son. It's very difficult for him to give up his dream of training me to follow in his footsteps."

"It is not always easy to follow God's will," the bishop said evenly.

"You . . they . . . that master builder did not hire my papa as his master mason and—"

"The cathedral chapter hires whom they will," Bishop Gernot broke in. He paused to catch his breath and then said, "Forgive me for saying so, but perhaps your papa was not the best."

"He is the best!" Martin retorted. He felt as if the bishop's gaze pierced his soul and he added softly, "but he cannot read. One of the other masons told Papa that they were hiring as overseers only those who can."

"A cathedral is much more complicated than a shrine or a gatehouse. I'm sure that they will hire your papa to work, for he is a very talented mason."

"He's the best, Excellenz," Martin repeated, afraid to belabor the point but needing to make sure that the bishop understood.

"But you are one of our best students, and we would not want to waste your talents either."

"It is enough for me that Papa wants me to continue to study. He believes that it will make me a better mason. Papa needs time. I will give him that time."

"I can recommend you to St. Jude's. You've been here . . . what, two years?"

Martin nodded unhappily.

"That's probably enough for a mason. If you want to continue your education, you must decide soon. Don't wait too long. Someday it will be too late."

Their conversation ended, and Martin left, unaccountably depressed by the bishop's pressure. The boy had no way of knowing what the bishop had suspected for several months now. Ever since Christmas, the bishop had felt his life's strength slipping from his body, and he found it difficult to breathe. When he lay down to sleep, coughing racked his lungs, and so he sat up and slept poorly. When he was able to sleep, he dreamed of a cathedral that could not rise out of the deep trenches, and he would awake coughing again. He paced and schemed, for he wanted the cathedral to bear his imprint, but he feared that if he left too soon, the vision would die. If he could just instill loyalty into a few talented people, then perhaps they would carry his plan to its end.

Finally the long winter seemed to be over, and one March morning the bishop called for Titus and Andrew. As usual, the two men arrived in two very dissimilar moods. Andrew's cheerfulness of late had perplexed the bishop and irritated everyone else around. The young man was changing, and Bishop Gernot was quite sure that he did not like the confidence that lit Andrew's eyes. Yet he could not find its source.

Titus, having lived most of his life in the balmy south, was thoroughly sick of the cold gray weather, and he made sure that everyone knew it. He was fairly certain that it was too early to begin construction, but his ignorance of northern weather prohibited him from voicing too adamant an opinion.

"I really believe that it is too early to lay the foundation. We don't want the mortar to freeze. I heard the women at the market talking about the Frost Men. They will come again after the first part of May."

"The Frost Men!" Bishop Gernot scoffed, stifling a cough. "Old wives' tales."

Titus demurred. "I have also talked to Viktor Bauer. He never begins to lay courses until the spring melt is finished. Surely the master mason knows what he's talking about."

The bishop never asked Andrew what he thought. The monk was merely present to write any necessary letters or notices. In the end, it was decided to write a letter to Viktor Bauer, asking him to arrive before Easter so that the foundation stone could be laid at a festive ceremony on the Monday following that holiday.

∞ ∞

Easter Saturday arrived bright and sunny, and the inns were full to bursting. There was little to remind the citizens that three years before, St. Nathaniel's Church had burned to the ground. For this reason, Archdeacon Augustin had insisted that every Easter bonfire begin with a Mass for the dead, complete with prayers and honor for those who had died trying to save St. Nathaniel's relics.

Although still horrified by the memories, Martin thought it was a good idea that the city never forget, and he participated wholeheartedly. The cemetery was banked with spring field-flowers, the graves had been weeded and were decorated with loving care. A procession, led by an altar boy bearing the Rosen Jungfrau, crept from Lärchenplatz, past Zur Felder, and out to where the graves lay in gaudy rows, awaiting the somber blessings of young Father Nikolaus.

Martin prayed too. He had learned "Our Father" and praises to the Jungfrau Maria and the saints, and it pleased him that he also understood them. One of the monks at the school had suggested an easy way to keep track of prayers: Keep a pocketful of pebbles. As he knelt to pray in the soft earth, he transferred the pebbles from one pocket to the other, and by the end of the day, he knew just how many times he had prayed.

There had been no more disastrous Easter bonfires, and the weather remained nice through Easter Sunday morning. As was the custom, Martin and his family took a long walk after their Easter dinner. Mama carried little Stefanie. Bernie babbled constantly as he tripped along beside his young Onkel Martin, but Martin was only vaguely aware of his chatter. While the sun was shining and Papa's stomach was satisfied with Mama's good roast, Martin wanted to ask if he might continue to study.

They walked along the swollen Obersill River, which rushed in muddy swirls through the meadows west of the city. The water table was quite high, and some of the fields were flooded. Bernie was drawn to every puddle in the road, and Mama kept reminding Martin that if Bernie got his feet wet, he would catch cold. Finally, Martin lifted the child to his shoulders and strode nearer to Papa. Martin hardly knew how to begin.

Suddenly Papa turned to him and said, "Tomorrow we begin the foundation."

"I know, Papa."

"The master mason needs his best masons on the foundation."

Martin remained silent. He was so tired of hearing how talented the Steinmetz masons were—how privileged they were to be chosen to lay the foundation. Papa was like two people. One of them boasted about his expertise, as if he could work anywhere and demand any wage. The other side of Papa groveled and whined to be included in a project that could not be completed without him. Martin decided to abandon tact.

"Papa, I'm not going to be a mason."

"Well, not until school is finished," he agreed.

Why was he so obtuse? "No, I mean I am going to stay in school. I want to be a scribe and maybe a teacher, like Brother Andrew. I'm going to enter the church."

His father stopped abruptly. His gaze was fixed on the distant mountains, and the muscle in his temple throbbed with tension. "You are throwing away your talents," he announced.

"The bishop says that I have other talents. I am very good at languages. He says that there are many monasteries that need my abilities. I could become a great theologian."

"Quatsch!" he spat out in anger, still refusing to look at his son. "You could build a great cathedral, which will still be standing after the languages you learn are long forgotten." He stalked away to join his wife. "I tried to train him," he protested to her loudly. "I wanted to give him a profession that he could be proud of. That bishop has cluttered my son's head with useless ideas. I blame myself for allowing him to begin the school. No one expects me to give my only son to the church. Why can't he be reasonable?"

Reasonable. Martin could think of nothing more reasonable than studying the Scriptures and guiding others in their journey to eternal life. Troweling mortar onto stones was so mind-deadening. His time for escape had come.

∞ ∞

Easter Monday was another fine day. The cool, sunny air was fragrant with the scents of damp earth and fresh foliage. Many of the merchants set up their tables to take advantage of the visitors from other towns. By midmorning, crowds were milling around Lärchenplatz, trying to get a glimpse into the deep trenches that would contain the foundation. The excavations were five times deeper than a man is tall, and fences had been erected to prevent people from falling in. To keep the banks from crumbling during the snowy winter, carpenters had constructed elaborate supports attached to the scaffolding.

On occasion, Martin and some of his friends had slipped through the barriers to watch the progress. He knew that at the bottom, a generous layer of pebbles and small stones had been spread as a moisture barrier between the sticky soil and the foundation.

Just before noon, the bishop emerged from his residence, resplendent in his robes and miter. Titus of Athens and the canons of the cathedral chapter followed him. The crowds moved aside to allow their bishop to move slowly past them to the building site. Lined up along the excavation, waiting humbly for their blessing, were the master craftsmen—the quarry man, the stonecutter, the mortar maker, the carpenter, the blacksmith, and Viktor Bauer, the master mason. Some of the masters had not yet been hired because it would be many years before they would be needed.

Martin stood behind about six people, and although he was tall and he knew that most of the assistants were ranked behind the masters, he could not see Papa and Onkel Hans. He could see the cornerstone, which was tied with a rope and dangling from a pulley above the excavation. The bishop came to stand beside it. He blessed it, and then one of the men lowered it into the foundation trench while the master stonecutter supervised.

The crowd strained forward as the perfectly rectangular stone disappeared below ground. Martin knew that it would be positioned at the southeastern corner. The master mortar maker handed one of his assistants a container of mortar, which had been perfectly mixed. The assistant climbed carefully down the ladder onto the scaffolding and vanished from sight. Down below, two masons would begin the process of laying the walls at right angles to each other.

Suddenly a cheer spread from the canons and the assistants out into the crowd. The people pushed forward to see the small stone, planted so deep beneath them, from which would rise a mighty cathedral. They ducked under the barriers and teetered precariously at the edge of the excavation. They were prevented from falling by the frantic hands of those behind, who also wanted a glimpse.

Perhaps it was too early to lay the foundation. Perhaps the soil was still too saturated with the spring thaw. Blame would be laid at many doors, but no one could blame the enthusiasm of the folk. The ground, softened by the spring rains and weakened by the removal of so much soil, began to move. Right in front of Martin, a crack formed and widened rapidly. Hastened by the weight of the people, the earth broke away and slowly slid into the deep trench, bearing with it a dozen screaming, flailing onlookers.

Martin pressed backward from the ever widening gap, as the horrified faces of the workers below were buried under mud and rock. The scaffolding, which had already been constructed within the excavation, prevented the spectators from falling to the bottom.

A short silence was broken by a quick-thinking carpenter, who ordered, "Don't move. We'll get you!" The people froze in awkward positions, afraid that the least movement would send them plunging into the abyss. Several ladders were fetched from another part of the scaffolding, and the carpenters let them down to the victims, who, one by one, clambered onto them and were pulled to safety by cautious, willing hands.

The workers in the trench were not so fortunate. Several had been buried underneath so much earth that there was little chance for their survival. Their colleagues began digging for them as soon as possible, but there were no spades immediately available, and all they had were a few mortar trowels and their hands.

The crowd was pushed back, and the workers scrambled to find ways into the excavation so that they could dig out the unfortunates. Very few noticed when the bishop, his canons, and the monks returned to the residence. As the area around the excavation cleared out, Martin realized that Papa was still standing there, hands on his head, while rescuers rushed back and forth around him.

Martin walked over, afraid, but not sure of what. Tears glistened in Papa's eyes, and he dropped his hands to let them dangle helplessly at his sides. He turned a look of despair onto his son and said hopelessly, "Hans is down there."

Martin's heart sank. He said nothing, but he gathered his stricken father in his arms, while his mind screamed out to a God who seemed to delight in taking everyone they loved.

Papa did not stay long within Martin's embrace. He pushed the boy away and walked to the edge of the trench, where the laborers dug frantically to free their friends. When Martin came to stand beside him, he said, "It would take a miracle."

There were not many miracles that day. Papa and Martin carried Onkel Hans home and washed the mud from him. His face seemed eternally frozen in a look of unhappiness. Word came that the bishop would personally oversee the burial the following day, as these men had given their lives for the holy task of erecting a cathedral.

That brought a bitter laugh to Papa's lips. "Hans was drunk. I was so angry that Viktor Bauer chose him to help lay the foundation stone. It should have been me."

Later in the afternoon, Martin wandered over to the bishop's chapel. Many others had the same idea, and the sound of murmured prayers filled the small room with a sound like mournful breezes. To keep his mind occupied, Martin shifted his prayer pebbles back and forth from one pocket to the other, until he had lost track of how many times he had prayed for Onkel Hans.

"Steinmetz?" It was Brother Andrew who knelt beside him. "I heard about your uncle."

Martin nodded, his throat too tight to speak.

"Do you want to talk?"

Through the haze of his grief, Martin realized that this teacher was offering him a strength that few could offer. The boy nodded again. Together they stood and left the chapel to wander through the bishop's garden. Martin's thoughts roamed over Onkel Hans' uselessness and over Martin's own betrayal of his father's dreams, to rest finally upon his selfishness in wanting to be a teacher.

Finally he blurted out, "I wanted to be like you!"

Brother Andrew's reaction was unexpected: "What a terrible thing to want."

"But you are my model," Martin protested. "You have the tools to please God. I think that becoming a monk would be the noblest profession."

His teacher shook his head. "You are wrong. Kind, but wrong. I have spent my life trying to find God."

"But you were raised in a monastery, surrounded by God's people. It must have been like being in . . . in heaven."

"It wasn't. God wasn't there."

Martin had the sudden, sickening feeling that he had made a terrible error in judgment. Perhaps he had confided in the wrong person. Warily, he asked, "Where is He?"

Martin could see Brother Andrew pause to evaluate before he answered, "God lives only in hearts."

Heresy, thought Martin with instant dismay.

Brother Andrew seemed to read his thoughts. "You mustn't believe me. You must seek God yourself. You will find Him."

Martin relaxed a little. "That's why I wanted to become a monk. The bishop even said that he will help me." He hesitated and then contradicted himself. "But I think that I had better be a mason. Papa's had too many disappointments." It broke his heart to say it.

Brother Andrew said, "I think that you have made a wise decision."

"How would you know?" Martin snapped, his sadness shortening his temper.

"Because I never had a family, and I wish I had."

"You mean, you want to get married?" the boy exclaimed.

The monk gave a gentle smile. "Not quite. I meant that I never knew my mother and father. Family is very important."

Martin agreed, but still had doubts. "I am so afraid of what the bishop will say, and I'm so afraid that Papa will say, 'There, I won!' I'm so afraid that I'll regret my decision someday."

"You don't need to live your life in fear. It doesn't matter what the bishop says. Let your love for your papa bear the humility of his victory. You will have no regrets if you do what is right."

osef Radl and his people were completely overwhelmed by Andrew's gift. Even Andrew was unprepared for the emotion that was shown when he presented them with a complete collection of the apostle John's writings. Men and women alike wept, and they hardly dared to touch the parchments until their damp tears had dried.

"It's so beautiful!" Wolfgang exclaimed, fingering the manuscripts reverently.

The others scolded Wolfgang for the inadequacy of his words. Andrew, motivated by his gratitude toward these people, had done his finest work. The parchments were all trimmed to the same size, so that any page could be rolled up with any other page for study. Andrew's ability with a pen was obviously unsurpassed, and every letter was uniform, every line perfectly straight. Each book began with a pen-and-ink illumination, a large letter surrounded by birds and flowers.

"I had no colors," Andrew murmured apologetically.

That day, those who had duties to perform for the count did them, but every moment they had free, they were drawn back to Josef's hut by the beautiful parchments. Then they would beg Andrew to read to them, and because he was free until the evening, he did gladly. He read with relish, and translated everything easily into the local tongue, adding explanations and ideas that left Josef shaking his head in wonder.

"So when will you leave the church?" Josef asked after he had listened for a while.

Andrew flinched. "What?"

Josef smiled gently, "Surely it's crossed your mind."

Andrew was loathe to admit it. "Ye-ess. But perhaps I should help those who are in the church."

"Help them?"

"I have learned so much this past winter. I did not just copy those words," Andrew said, indicating the pages lying on the table. "I read them, and God wrote joy on my heart. I am not the same person I once was."

"So how do you plan to help others?"

"The same way you helped me—by convincing them to read God's Holy Scriptures."

Josef disagreed. "But we are not in the church. You came to us because we were different."

Andrew had not thought of it that way.

"What makes you think that Augustin or the bishop or even your friend, Brother Georg, would ever listen to you?" challenged Josef.

Andrew shrugged.

"I don't think that you should leave the church," Josef said unexpectedly. "I'm sorry that I mentioned it. Finding God can be a very dangerous and difficult thing."

Andrew laughed. "I'm not complaining. I feel like my soul has finally found a home. No one could do anything to me that would take that away."

Josef grinned and said in wonder, "This is one of the most amazing days in my life!"

Toward evening, they were surprised by a knock on the door. In came Cecilia, looking pale and weary. Andrew had not seen her for a long time, and he stood to greet her. His pleasure was arrested by the entrance of young Martin Steinmetz right behind her. He wore an expression of wary confidence, and his protective attitude surrounded the girl.

Andrew was dismayed that the unexpected appearance of young

Steinmetz should cause his heart to flop over in fear, yet he was glad to see Cecilia after so many months. Martin's countenance betrayed how stunned he was to find his teacher chatting comfortably in the home of one of the heretics.

Collecting his thoughts, Andrew made the introductions. "Josef Radl, this is one of my students, Martin Steinmetz."

The two greeted one another formally, coolly distant.

"Martin's my cousin," Cecilia told Josef, unaware of the awkward undercurrents. She had been to Felsenburg the day before for her father's funeral, she explained to Andrew, her face drooping in sadness. "Cousin Martin was kind enough to accompany me back to Immergrün," she said. "I wanted him to meet the people who have been so good to me." She was as surprised to see Brother Andrew as he was to see Cecilia and Martin.

Martin glanced around the room with disdainful curiosity, his eyes finally coming to rest on the parchments scattered upon the table. "What's this?" He picked up one of the pages.

"It's Scripture," Josef answered simply.

Martin looked to Andrew for an explanation. "I thought only men of the church had access to the Holy Scriptures."

Andrew opened his mouth to answer, but Josef was quicker, "God's Word is for every man."

Cecilia's love for the Holy Scriptures brought a light to her weary eyes. Innocently, she broke in. "Where did we get them? Did you bring them?" she accused Andrew sweetly, with an affectionate dip in her voice that caused his cheeks to burn.

Martin contemplated Andrew in surprise. Andrew returned the look and then glanced from Josef to Cecilia before taking a deep breath. "Yes," he admitted, "I brought them."

Indignantly, Martin exclaimed, "The bishop's manuscripts?"

"No," said Josef, "They're ours."

"More precisely," corrected Andrew, "they are copies of the bishop's manuscripts. I made them this winter. They're a gift to my friends here." He felt better for having said it all, but he was glad that no one could see how his hands were shaking inside the folds of his cassock.

Martin was at a loss for words, and he tried to gather the fragments of his bewildered thoughts. "What are you . . . ? I don't understand why you . . . ? I always thought that . . ."

"I'm sorry that I have disappointed you," Andrew said. He felt sympathy for Martin's dismay and confusion. "I am not who you thought I was, but neither am I who you now think I am."

Tears dribbled down Martin's face.

It was very still in the room, and Andrew thought it was so strange that he should suddenly notice Cecilia's tiny blond curls, peeking out from under her shawl.

Josef broke the silence. "Won't you sit down, Martin Steinmetz? Perhaps we can explain—"

"No!" he cried, shaking off Josef's friendly touch. He glared at Andrew and whirled to where Cecilia stood, her eyes wide with unhappiness. "This is no place for you, Celia. Please come home with me. Papa will help you find another place to sew." He dashed away the tears angrily and grabbed her wrist.

Shaking her head, she wrenched her hand from his grasp. Tears welled up in her eyes, but she refused to let them spill over. "I can't," she whispered. "These are my only friends."

Andrew took a step toward her, but Martin blocked him.

"They're heretics!" Martin shouted at her. "Don't you realize that your soul is in danger of hellfire? And him—!" He pointed an accusing finger at Andrew. "He is the worst of them all—abandoning his faith to join in their ignorance of what the church expects of us all. Bringing them parchments to encourage their rebellion toward the bishop!" He leaned over the table and brushed the manuscripts onto the floor.

With a little "ach, nein!" Cecilia knelt to retrieve them.

"These are worthless, Cecilia," he said more quietly, "without the church's interpretation. My favorite teacher taught me that." He glared again at Andrew.

"I was wrong," said the monk. "I'm sorry."

Martin ignored him. "Cecilia, come home with me," he begged again. "No one here loves you like we do. They are intentionally deceiving you, and if you believe them, you will spend many eternities in hellfire."

Cecilia stood and placed the parchments on the table. "Martin, I know that I have eternal life."

"You can't know that!" he cried. "Are you so stupid that you cannot see that they have bewitched you?"

Andrew longed to protect her from her cousin's anger, but Josef intervened first. "That's enough, Steinmetz," he said firmly. "You may stay or go, but you can't force Cecilia to go with you. That's her decision."

Martin's eyes snapped with anger, even as the tears continued their courses down his cheeks. "She is incapable of making a decision, for you have stolen her will."

"That's not true," she protested. "I have chosen to give my life to God, who has forgiven all of my sins."

"Celia!" Martin exclaimed in frustration. "I, too, want to give my life to God. We cannot both be right. Come with me, and I will ask the bishop to send you to a convent. There you may serve God with no danger of stumbling into heresy."

"The bishop!" she cried with a shudder. "There is no danger here," she countered. "And I certainly can't be a nun!"

"Can't? You mock," Martin said bitterly, "but your condemnation is certain." He walked to the door. "Are you coming or not?"

"'There is no condemnation to those who are in Christ Jesus,'" she quoted softly, her eyes glittering with tears.

Martin wrenched the door open. "Farewell, Cecilia," he cried as he bolted through the door.

Cecilia watched him go. Her tears finally flowed to make dark little spots upon her shawl. Feeling powerless to lessen her grief, Andrew watched her turn her stricken face to Josef, who went to her and put his arm around her. Holding Cecilia tightly, Josef walked to where Andrew stood and pushed her into Andrew's embrace.

As if they had a will of their own, Andrew's arms enfolded the sobbing girl. She looked up into his eyes, and then burrowed her face into his cassock. The shawl slipped from her head, and Andrew bent to rest his cheek upon her silky hair. He never even noticed when Josef slipped from the room, and he could only marvel how, in the midst of so much tragedy, his heart could be singing.

THIRTY-EIGHT

ndrew's conscience penetrated the mists of happiness that had enveloped him. Cecilia had ceased her wild sobbing, and he wiped her tears away with the sleeve of his cassock. She smiled up at him, but he held her gently away from him.

"This is not right," he whispered.

She gasped and contradicted him. "It can't be wrong. Josef would never encourage me to do something wrong."

Andrew shook his head and dropped his hands to hold hers. He had never felt anything so soft and alive. The urge to raise them to his lips almost overwhelmed him, but he was well-practiced in resisting temptation. He dropped her hands and crossed his arms, shoving his own hands into the sleeves of his robe. "I made vows to the church," he moaned. "They cannot be undone without harm to my soul."

Blinking in disbelief, she retorted, "Neither of us knows God's Word well enough to know what is right!" She turned her back on Andrew and looked at the manuscripts on the table.

"We can sort them," Andrew suggested, hoping to dilute her disappointment.

Andrew read and sorted and handed the pages to Cecilia, carefully avoiding even a brush with her hands. He watched her fingers as she lovingly tied the cords around each complete manuscript. After they were finished, she agreed to sit at Josef's table, and they talked, while Josef's wife discreetly prepared supper around them.

Josef came back, carrying a parchment, with a baby in his arms. He handed the child to Cecilia and pressed her shoulder as a father would do. "Are you all right?" he asked, lowering himself onto a stool.

Cecilia nodded but asked, "Something has changed Martin. He was never cruel."

"Fear makes him cruel," Josef explained.

"But what is he afraid of?"

"Have you forgotten so quickly what it is like to be held in chains of tradition and dogma?"

She nodded slowly. The baby grabbed Cecilia's finger and stuffed it into her mouth.

"Your cousin is afraid of being wrong. He is doesn't want to be responsible for your fate, which he fears will be opposed to the things he is learning in the bishop's school."

Andrew had been studying her pretty face as she struggled with Josef's ideas. She suddenly turned to him and asked, "Is the bishop's school really so . . . so—"

They were all at a loss of words, and Andrew answered simply, "He doesn't want to see you go to hell, and he doesn't want to see you condemned with the others."

Josef added, "He also doesn't want to lose the position he has before the bishop. Obviously, he regards the opinion of the bishop very highly."

The baby became restless, and Cecilia stood to walk with it around the room. Andrew watched her, until he became aware of Josef's scrutiny of him. Embarrassed, Andrew turned his attention to the parchments on the table.

Josef gave them a push toward Andrew. "Read," he urged.

Andrew read and then looked up at Josef in awe. "How did you know? Does this mean what I think it means?"

"Could it have any other interpretation?"

"I don't see how."

Cecilia interrupted. "What does it say?" The baby squirmed and whimpered.

"You tell her," murmured Andrew, his face warm with emotion.

Josef translated slowly, "'The Holy Spirit says that some people will fall away from the faith . . . and will even be so deceitful . . . as to forbid marriage. . . .' Do you need more?"

Two pink spots appeared on Cecilia's cheeks, and she shook her head as a tiny smile crept onto her lips. "I must go now. Good night."

Andrew had the feeling that she was speaking only to him, and he tried to understand the sadness in her farewell.

Josef's wife set a large loaf of peasant's bread down in the middle of the table. "You're embarrassing them," she informed her husband after Cecilia had gone.

Josef's eyes grew wide in mock innocence. "Am I wrong?" he asked Andrew.

"No," Andrew confessed. "I just didn't think that anyone could see how I feel about her."

"We see."

After the blessing, Josef said, "There is something that you should know."

Andrew waited, unsure of himself.

"The child is hers."

Andrew's heart thudded in his ears, and he wondered if it would stop beating from the shock. Dear, sweet Cecilia? He picked his bread to pieces on the table and finally stammered, "How—? Why—? I don't understand."

Josef's wife said simply. "The bishop."

Horror swept over Andrew in waves as he remembered that Silvester night so long ago. He groaned and put his face in his hands. "I didn't know," he managed to choke out. "How could I? I . . ." *What a poor, stupid fool you are,* he told himself.

"It was not her fault," Josef reassured him. "And she is a new person now, her sins forgiven forever. We will raise Cecilia's daughter to love God, and maybe the child will never have to know who sired her."

⸎   ⸎

Toward evening, Andrew left the haven of the Radl home to return to Felsenburg. With increasing anxiety, he climbed the hill to the city, knowing that Martin Steinmetz had surely reported every-thing to the bishop. Andrew tried to relive his moments with Cecilia, but every time he did, he could only think of the terrible thing that the bishop had done to that young girl. His revulsion at the thought of ever having to see the bishop again even overcame his fear of a confrontation about the manuscripts. But his initial joy of discover-ing the rightness of his love for a woman was lost in the terrible thoughts tearing through his mind.

He slipped quietly into the residence and tiptoed to his room. The night grew darker, and Andrew prepared for bed. He prayed as Josef had taught, speaking to God as a friend and ally. As he prayed, he promised himself that Cecilia's secret would never cross his lips. Finally, he fell into a light sleep.

It was not until three days later that he was summoned to stand at the foot of the bishop's bed. Bishop Gernot was too weak to leave his room, but his anger had given him the strength to sit up without the support of his pillows.

"Is it true?" the bishop demanded with no preliminaries.

Andrew almost said yes, but thought better of it. "Is what true?"

"Don't play games! Are you guilty or innocent?"

The young monk was surprised to find a great calm enveloping him, and the words came clearly to him. "I think it would be wise to hear the charges before I admit my guilt—or protest my innocence."

Provoked, Bishop Gernot snapped, "Have you been traveling to Immergrün to visit with the group called the heretics?"

"I have."

"And have you been taking the manuscripts that are under my protection and making unauthorized copies to give away?"

Andrew dissected the question. "I borrowed the manuscripts from the library, and I made copies, which I gave to the Christians living under the count's protection."

The bishop shifted and sat straighter. "You think you're so clever at choosing your words. Picking at jots and tittles will not absolve you of your great wrongs."

"I've always chosen my words carefully—even before I could speak. And I was not aware that it was wrong to make copies. Am I not, in fact, the best scribe in the valley? Isn't that why you brought me here?"

"Not to give precious manuscripts to unworthy radicals!" he exclaimed in a voice that attempted to display more control. "Are you so lacking in understanding that you cannot see how those people will misuse God's Holy Word? They will twist the words so that they contradict the holy doctrines of our church. The fate of anyone who follows them will lead straight to the fires of hades."

Andrew objected. "I've been reading the manuscripts. Everything that I read, the people at Immergrün teach and believe and live."

"How would you know? You're a scribe, not a theologian."

"I'm a cleric, as you are, and we clerics are the only ones who have the authority to interpret the Holy Scriptures," he said slyly. "Yet I read them now with new eyes—a new heart—and for the first time I understand that I have been taught wrongly for many, many years."

"You are wrong now."

Andrew began to realize that this bishop was so twisted that whatever he thought was wrong was probably, in fact, right. If Andrew disagreed with the bishop, that was good. "If I read the Scriptures and they contradict our church doctrines, whom do I believe?"

"That's impossible!"

"But it's true. For example, it states in the Scriptures that our salvation comes by faith alone. Works don't help."

"Obviously, you've misunderstood."

Andrew clenched his fists in frustration. "Have you even read those parts that seem to indicate what I say?"

"I don't have to read them to know that you're wrong."

"How can you be sure? On what do you base your assurance?"

"I am the bishop. That is enough."

"Not for me." Shocked by the arrogance of that statement, Andrew whirled and headed for the door.

The bishop's voice was softer now. "Dear Brother, it breaks my heart to see you so."

Andrew turned around politely just in time to see the bishop sag theatrically back into his pillows. "You have been deceived," he continued. "I blame myself, for I am the one who exposed you to Brother Georg and the perils of that long journey to Milan. I think you are ill."

Andrew laughed. "It might surprise you to know that you and Brother Georg share the same opinions on that!"

The older man waved his hand halfheartedly. "It doesn't matter. What you need is peace and quiet—a time for your bruised soul to find healing. Perhaps a few months at St. Jude's."

"I don't need it. My soul has never been better."

The bishop ignored his flippancy and said regretfully, "It is God's will. You will leave at the end of the week."

For the first time in his life, Andrew felt free from the will of powerful men who used God's name to manipulate others. "I'm not going."

This was new to the bishop, and he sat up again. "What?"

"I said that I'm not going. I have other duties and other relationships. I can't go."

"Do you mean that you can no longer submit to my authority?"

"People who do, do so at their own peril."

"Then I have no choice but to turn you over to the Devil, whom you obviously serve so well!"

"Actually, I am serving God for the first time in my life!" Without another word, Andrew left the room.

He had never owned many things, and so his departure from the bishop's residence was a simple one. He gathered the few manuscripts that he considered his own, his writing tools (which he had brought from St. Jude's), and the wooden horse that Brother Viktor had carved for him nearly two decades before. He stuffed them into a bag and slipped out the side door into the street.

Lärchenplatz, on that sunny June day, was a very ugly spot. In spite of the flowers blooming cheerfully from so many windows, and the children romping in the sunshine, the square seemed to him a very dismal place. Half of it was cluttered with the muddy debris from the excavation, and a dozen men were hauling away dirt. The sounds of hammering and sawing accompanied the carpenters as they replaced and strengthened the scaffolding and supports in the trenches. In a separate section, the masons were laying the foundation.

As Andrew walked past, looking into the grim, grubby faces of the laborers, an unexpected hatred for the cathedral came over him.

He suddenly had a vision of how many lives would be affected or ruined by it. The sunshine that now poured uninhibited across Lärchenplatz would one day be completely blocked by the bishop's dream, and all of the people in Felsenburg would live in the shadow of the cathedral. It would drain them of their wealth, their time, their children, their lives. People would be born, grow up, marry, give birth, and die, but the cathedral would live on, exhausting every resource. Andrew wondered how many centuries it would take before these people realized that they were slaves to stone—that they had not been served by the cathedral, but that they had instead served it.

He left the city and knocked at Georg's door. Georg threw open the door and grabbed Andrew in a crushing hug.

"Come in, come in! Are you well?"

"I've never been better."

Georg looked pointedly at Andrew's meager satchel. "Are you going on a journey?"

Andrew shook his head. "Not really. I've . . . I've left the residence."

Georg frowned. "I see." He cleared off a stool. "Please sit down. Gerti'll bring us something to drink."

"Thank you, but I really don't have time. I need to get to Immergrün before dark."

"Immergrün." The statement bristled with disapproval.

"I only came to—" Andrew's courage suddenly failed him and he abruptly sat on the stool and said softly, "This is very difficult. It's one thing to sever a relationship with the bishop. But you—you taught me to think for myself."

"I didn't teach you to reject the sacred teachings of our church. I thought you would join us to reform it, improve it, change it. The doctrines must stand, for they are infallible; it is the hypocrisy we must stop."

Andrew shook his head vigorously, wondering if Georg had changed so much in the past few months. He did not wish to argue with Georg, but he could not leave him with the wrong impression. "We cannot change how we live if the doctrines are false. Read the Scriptures, Georg. You will see."

"There is too much to do. I must help while I can."

"How can you help, when you don't even know what you believe?"

"I seem to recall that you have the same problem."

"Not anymore. I believe every word that is written in God's Holy Scriptures, and I refuse to believe anyone who tells me anything that contradicts."

"You've lost all respect for the traditions and doctrines that we have served for so many centuries," Georg lamented, hoping to show Andrew how alone he was in his rebellious ideas. To Georg's discomfort, Andrew agreed. Georg, stunned by Andrew's rejection of everything that he should have held dear, tried another approach. "You know that the bishop will make an example of you."

"I will stay out of his way."

"Your parents would not want you to throw your life away."

"My parents," Andrew shot back heatedly, "died for the things that I now believe."

"You don't know that."

Andrew felt very tired. Leaving was the only way to avoid a major confrontation. He was almost afraid to state his purpose for the visit. "I didn't come to persuade you; I only came to ask you if you have any clothes."

"Clothes?" Georg asked as if he had never heard of them.

"A tunic, a cloak. I don't even know what I need."

Georg's bewilderment continued. "For you?"

Andrew smiled and said stoutly, "I am leaving the church. I need clothes."

Wordlessly, Georg walked to the corner and opened a trunk. He pulled out a few tattered garments and handed them to Andrew. "Keep the cassock; it's warm," he said tersely.

Andrew thanked him and stuffed the clothing into his satchel.

Georg tried again. "My friend, when I met you, I never dreamed that someday we would stand on opposite sides. Our ideals were kindred, our hatreds were mutual. Nothing would be so distasteful to me as to stand with the bishop against you."

"That will be your choice, Georg—not mine and not the bishop's. You must do what you think is right, if you have the courage."

"You are the one who will need courage."

"There you are wrong. If the time comes for me to stand as my parents did and watch the flames roar around me, you will need more courage to watch than I will to stand, for God will stand with me."

"Stop! That is enough!" Georg cried.

Andrew stood. "Read the Holy Scriptures, Georg," he pleaded. "They will lead you to what is right."

Georg was calmer now. "I don't have time, for there are far more important things to do." They shook hands. "Lebe wohl, Andrew. I wish that you were on our side."

"If I must choose, I'd rather be on God's side. My prayer is that you, too, will one day make that choice." Andrew left the little hovel, regretting that their friendship was so fragile. When Andrew turned to take one last glimpse of Felsenburg before rounding a bend, Georg was still standing in the doorway.

THIRTY-NINE

he silence at St. Jude's was a physical presence that hovered over each man and monitored his piety. The silence of the monk's cell was broken only by the involuntary sounds of heart and lungs. The silence of the dining room was not silence at all, as utensils clacked against wooden bowls, but speech was kept to a minimum. Words startled. Each day, the noisy tasks (like gardening and cooking and building repairs) were also punctuated by silence. The stillest time was prayers, a silence accented by the whispers of cassocks in movement.

In the two weeks since Martin's arrival, he had reveled in the many silences, and because he knew no one, it was not difficult to keep his thoughts to himself. The strict disciplines represented the long-awaited fulfillment of his dreams, and he was once more grateful that the bishop had helped him to resist his own foolish impulses.

A bell rang, and Martin left his tiny cubicle and went down to the chapel for evening prayers. He transferred all of the pebbles to one pocket and knelt shoulder to shoulder with other men—men about whom he would probably never know much. The pebbles facilitated his devotion to the prayers, but his thoughts still wandered.

He missed home. He missed Mama's good cooking and her gentle mannerisms. He missed the reliable gruffness of Papa and the comfort of his presence at night. Although he enjoyed the many silences of the monastery, he longed for Bernie's laughter, and he regretted the many times when he had shoved the little boy aside for "more important things."

Tears prickled behind his tightly closed eyelids, but he sternly reminded himself that sacrifice would mean nothing if it did not bring pain. Only the pain would finally bring an end to the guilt that he felt at having escaped the hardships with which his family must deal. Only his devotion and mediation on their behalf would shelter them from further misfortunes.

Pray! he told himself, and for a while he would transfer pebbles back and forth, soundlessly murmuring the prayers that he now knew well enough to recite without thinking about them.

Papa had never known how close he had come to getting his son back. Martin had left the bishop's chapel on the day that Onkel Hans had been killed, planning to go straight home and tell Papa that he would, after all, learn the family's trade. Brother Andrew had been a strange comfort to him with his unexpected phrases designed to provoke thought. As Martin had watched his teacher enter the residence, though, one sentence from their final conversation came back to him in distracting clarity: "It doesn't matter what the bishop says."

Martin had stood rooted to the spot until he decided that it did indeed matter very much. After the wake, he would seek an audience with the bishop. Perhaps that great man could once for all shed a defining light on all of Martin's confusion.

The bishop had been kind but firm: "Serving God is the greatest thing that a man can do. Giving your life to the church shows your dedication to God."

Back then, Martin had not been so sure. Onkel Hans had been buried only a week, and Martin was fairly certain that his place was at Papa's side. "Can't I serve God by helping to build the cathedral?"

"Mmmm, you could," Bishop Gernot admitted slowly, "but the sacrifice of monastery life would more surely secure your rewards in the next life."

"I am . . ." Martin hesitated. It was only a little lie, and it was mostly true: "I am little Bernie's godfather. How can I fulfill my duty to him if I live so far away?"

"Prayer and sacrifice. God will take care of Bernie for your sake, if you choose to serve His church. If, however, you miss this opportunity, there is no way of knowing what sort of trials will come upon those you love. God only gives us one chance."

In the end, Martin chose—not because of the bishop's veiled threats but because of his own aspirations—St. Jude's. Perched high atop its granite mountain, it simply seemed closer to heaven.

At times, however, his conscience rose up to accuse him. When he had walked into the bleak hovel at Immergrün, he was glad he had already made the decision to go to St. Jude's. The decision had given him certainty and courage to confront the frightful heresies contaminating that place. He was sorry for Cecilia, but loyalty to the church and to the bishop meant loyalty to God, and if he must someday turn Cecilia's soul over to the Devil, God would understand.

Bishop Gernot had been very interested when Martin informed him of the whereabouts of his talented scribe. "Immergrün, you say? I always knew Brother Andrew did not have the heart for the holy church. It is a dangerous thing to turn away from God."

"But he thinks he has finally found God," Martin explained.

"And what do you think, Martin Steinmetz?"

Martin had searched for the proper answer. "I believe Brother Andrew has been misled by his own dissatisfaction."

"Dissatisfaction?"

"He told me once that God could not be found in the monastery; he said God lives only in hearts."

The bishop smiled. "Ja, well, we can certainly understand how someone like that could be misled, can't we? Thank you for bringing this to my attention. We will deal with Brother Andrew in such a way that this sort of thing never happens again."

Martin said nothing.

Bishop Gernot continued. "Are you ready to go to St. Jude's?"

"I am."

"It will be a big step to give up the world for the disciplines and piety in the monastery."

"That doesn't matter, Excellenz. I'm tired of the turmoils."

"I'll make arrangements for you to go to St. Jude's as soon as you are ready."

The young man could not suppress the grin that spread across his face. "I'm ready, now, Excellenz."

"Good, then you can leave at the end of the week."

The bell rang, interrupting Martin's memories. Prayers were ended, and Martin walked slowly back to his cubicle, eyes cast humbly downward. Outside his window, the sun was setting, tinting the snow at the top of the kohner a pale pink. Martin opened the window and let the pine-scented air fill his room. He leaned on the sill and let his gaze sweep down the rocky precipice to the spires of the fir trees far below. Mama would like this.

Mama, who had never been further from Felsenburg than the cemetery, had valiantly blinked away tears when Martin had made his announcement about going to St. Jude's.

"It's not very far, Mama. I'm sure that I can come back for a visit. Perhaps you can even come visit me." Of course, Martin had since learned that his assurances were false, but Mama did not know that, and besides, she would probably never try to come.

He sucked the spicy air into his lungs. The last rays of sunlight, like a candle extinguished, left the Kohner.

Papa had expected Martin to leave. He had not even argued. "You must do what you must do," he had growled. "Don't give another thought to the Steinmetz masons. We—I—" he corrected, "I will manage." It would have been more difficult to leave if Papa had not begun to pity himself. Right then, Martin decided that "the Steinmetz Masons" would never have amounted to much.

"Families are blessed who give their sons to the church," Martin quoted the bishop. Papa looked skeptical, but when Martin's departure time came, Papa's hug was strong and sincere. "Perhaps we shall meet again," he murmured, but Martin detected doubt.

Here in the mountains, the air was cooler, and Martin shivered and closed the window. He had a candle, but it could only be lit by another flame, brought by one of the authorized monks. Martin knelt to pray for his family and then crawled into bed.

Pretty little Anni was haunting his dreams when he was awakened about an hour later by a knock on his door. Reluctantly, he dragged himself from a deep sleep and opened the door a crack. Outside, Brother Lukas waited with a flickering candle to say, "The abbot would like for you to partake of supper with him tomorrow after evening prayer." Martin nodded and Brother Lukas turned and glided silently down the hallway. Martin was too tired to worry, but as he went back to sleep, he wondered what to expect.

The next evening Abbot William greeted Martin cordially, and they sat down to a luxurious meal of lamb, turnips, bread, and fruit. About halfway through the meal, the abbot spoke, "You are fond of lamb?"

"Ja, Herr." He wiped his lips with the cloth provided for such purposes.

"I am told that you are very good in Greek and Latin."

Martin did not know how to answer.

"Have I embarrassed you? Let's put it another way: Your ability in the languages could be a great asset to the Christian world."

"I love the languages, Herr. I hope that I may serve God with my ability." He put a piece of lamb into his mouth to bring the subject to a close.

"Well answered, son. Although sometimes we are not allowed to serve God as we have imagined."

Martin stopped chewing and looked up in dismay.

"Your devotion is not measured by what you do but by how you do it."

Martin had to swallow twice before the lump of meat would go down. "I . . . I don't understand, Herr. The bishop said that some service is more worthy than others."

The abbot rubbed his cheek for a moment before asking, "You admire the bishop?"

"Of course! He is the reason I am here," Martin declared.

"Really?" the abbot questioned doubtfully.

"Well . . . ," Martin faltered. What was the truth? "Actually, it was one of my teachers—Brother Andrew."

Abbot William smiled. "I know him. A very talented scribe. Bishop Gernot took our best man, but God is pleased when we give our best." He paused, but when Martin did not continue, he prodded, "So you were sorry to leave Brother Andrew?"

"No! I had to leave!"

"So emphatic! You ran away?"

"The bishop thought it best for me to leave."

"Why was that?"

Martin studied the abbot for a quarter of a minute before he decided to answer, "Brother Andrew has left the church. There is a group of heretics who somehow influenced him—and others."

The abbot wiped his fingers on his cloth and said solemnly, "I did not know. The bishop told me nothing in the letter he sent with you." His lips tipped upward into a smile that did not reach his eyes. "Perhaps Bishop Gernot viewed Brother Andrew's defection as a personal failure."

Martin remained silent, puzzled by the abbot's conclusions.

Abbot William sighed. "Well, it is a great loss to the church, but I can do nothing from here. Actually, the reason I called you here was to tell you of a change."

"A change?" Martin repeated.

Abbot William nodded. "The cathedral chapter has requested that we send some men to work on the cathedral. The weather is favorable, and the work will progress much faster with the additional laborers."

Martin looked once more at his plate, but he was no longer hungry. "So the bishop wants me to come back?" he asked, disappointment destroying his appetite.

"No, I am sending you. They need masons, and you know that trade, I assume. You will teach the others who go with you."

"But I know very little about masonry," the young man protested. "I want to take my vows!"

The older man raised a calming hand. "There will be time for that when it is too cold to lay stone. You will return to St. Jude's after the first frost."

"I didn't really ever serve my apprenticeship," Martin warned. "I've been in school these past three years."

The abbot stood, the conversation almost at an end. "I assume that you know where you can learn more?"

Dejectedly, Martin nodded. How Papa would exult in the curious turn that fate had taken!

"You have things that you need to face before you take any vows. This house is not a haven from which to escape your problems. Brother Andrew had to learn that. Deal with the problems and then return to serve God unencumbered."

Martin pushed back his chair and said regretfully, "When I first longed to come here, I had no problems."

"The price of sacrifice is high." The abbot led the young novice to the door. "God will show you what is right, if you truly seek Him. You will leave next week. God bless your sleep, my son."

Martin did not sleep much that night, but he could not dislike Abbot William. Somehow he felt that even the abbot was caught up in an uncontrollable destiny.

FORTY

he icy water ran over Andrew's head. He remembered the last time that he had heard water bubbling in his ears. That time, beneath the waters of a frigid mountain stream, he had only hoped that God would take him in. Now he shared the confidence that Josef and his followers had demonstrated ever since the former monk had known them. He closed his eyes and listened to Josef.

"—and in the name of the Son," Josef continued, as he poured a second pitcherful over Andrew's head, "—and in the name of the Holy Spirit."

For a few seconds, it seemed as if no one existed except Andrew and God. How safe and certain he felt! Then Josef's strong arms propelled him toward the bank. Andrew gasped and wiped his eyes.

On the bank of the count's fishing pond, every one of the Christians from Immergrün watched him with smiles of joy and encouragement. Several men reached their hands out to help him slosh from the squishy sediment. Cecilia tossed a blanket around his shoulders. Someone began singing one of the psalms that still seemed so foreign to Andrew. On the fringes of their group stood Count Robert, curious, observant, but supportive.

Josef waded from the murky pond and gave Andrew a soggy hug. "You are now truly our brother," he exulted.

Andrew's life was full of happiness now, and he would have found it difficult to name which day was the happiest. He had been given a tiny room facing south high up in the count's home. There were plenty of crown-glass windows to facilitate his writing, and Count Robert was enjoying the fact that the scribe who had once served the bishop now served him instead. For the first time, Andrew was actually earning a few small coins, and he felt wealthy and independent. He worked hard for his money, but even the long hours left him with a sense of fulfillment he had never had before.

The count was a puzzle to Andrew, and one time after dinner he asked Josef why Count Robert seemed so sympathetic to their cause.

"Those are not the words I would use," Josef answered. "We don't want people merely sympathetic. A person believes or doesn't. And our 'cause' is not really 'ours,' nor can a person merely become a member. You, yourself, know that the cost is too high for a quick decision. Count Robert is a very good person, and I have no doubt that he would go to great lengths to protect us. As for his faith . . . we think he is very near."

"What makes us want to be good," said Andrew, "even though we don't know God? I was a good person, too, but I could never manage to be good enough to keep the guilt away. I am so glad that pleasing God is as easy as believing."

"Easy?"

"Well . . ." Andrew immediately regretted his glib choice of words. "Easy it's not. I guess I just meant that letting God pay for my sins and guilt is much more simple—and certain—than trying to do it myself."

Josef nodded in approval. "You still have a lot to learn."

"And unlearn," Andrew added, his tone dry.

Andrew used much of his free time to study God's Word, but he still had time to sit in Josef's kitchen and visit with Cecilia while she sewed. Her daughter, Susanna, was ten months old—a cheerful child, who giggled easily and seemed to take a special liking to Andrew. Andrew was not sure where the thought came from, but he had come to disagree with the traditional viewpoint of that time: that a child born out of wedlock was somehow responsible for the inconvenience.

By the end of the summer, Andrew asked Josef to speak to Cecilia about marriage. Their mentor was all too glad to do so, and the couple were to be married a week before Susanna's first birthday.

It would be the first wedding at Immergrün since the group had moved there, and Count Robert offered his best scribe the use of his chapel for the occasion. Andrew and Cecilia were delighted, until they saw it.

For almost two years, the Christians had been reading the Holy Scriptures and singing and worshiping in the Radl home. Their worship had been uncomplicated, personal, and unfettered by all of the traditions and trappings with which they had grown up. When the betrothed couple walked into the cold, dark little chapel, their hearts sank.

Cecilia pressed close to Andrew and whispered, "We can't."

Andrew agreed, but he put his finger to his lips.

Politely, they followed Count Robert's caretaker around the inside of the chapel as he pointed out the worthy objects throughout the building. Here was the sarcophagus of Grandfather Xavier von Immergrün. There was the Madonna that Emperor Karl the Great had given Grandfather Xavier's grandfather. The chapel simply contained too many paintings and stone coffins, and it smelled damp and unused, although Mass was said here daily. Thick dust covered everything, but the aide assured them that the place would sparkle for the wedding. Cecilia's fingers, held fast in Andrew's hand, trembled and grew cold.

Andrew had to be the one to tell the count that they did not want to use the chapel.

"You have been very kind to make us the offer, Herr, but we are not used to worshiping with saints and icons looking over our shoulders. I'm afraid that we must seem ungrateful, but we are not."

The count was not a terribly practical man, but he followed things to their logical conclusions. "Perhaps we could remove the icons?" he suggested hopefully.

Andrew smiled. "I suspect that your priest might object."

"Ach, ja, that he might." He thought for a moment and then said reasonably, "He also would want to perform the rites, and that—" He paused to allow Andrew to shake his head. "—would be unacceptable as well."

Andrew tried to lessen the man's disappointment. "We really prefer to have our wedding in the place where we always worship, Herr. I know it's not elaborate, but we would be very honored if you would come." Andrew regretted his boldness at once. To imagine that a count would humble himself to attend the wedding of a renegade monk!

But Count Robert seemed touched. "Thank you, Andrew. I'm not quite ready for that yet, but you must let me do something for you."

In the end, Count Robert gave Andrew and Cecilia each a set of new clothes and offered to provide the wedding supper. After a simple ceremony in which Andrew and Cecilia agreed to follow God's plan for marriage as given in St. Paul's letter to the Ephesians, the people at Immergrün gathered in the count's garden for roasted pig and other delicacies. The evening bore little resemblance to the drunken affairs usually associated with weddings. The group had abandoned many superstitious practices, and one of the hallmarks of their faith was self-control, so the bridal pair was permitted to enjoy their friends and each other without fear of any unexpected or obscene pranks.

Even before dark, torches were lit in the garden. There was music and dancing, which Andrew and Cecilia only watched, for Andrew did not know any of the intricate steps. Susanna sat on Andrew's lap and played with his beard, which was beginning to grow. He also had hair on the top of his head, which felt warmer.

Shortly after Josef's wife put Susanna to bed, there was a commotion at the other end of the garden. A large horse galloped into the courtyard and was reined in by a finely dressed man, who leaped to the ground before the horse had come to a full stop.

"I have a message for Steinmetz, Cecilia!" he announced, holding a sealed scroll above his head.

Cecilia, her face white with concern, jumped up from the table, pulling Andrew with her. Before she could reach the messenger, however, Count Robert emerged from an alcove, where he had been eating with his family. He strode toward the man, and Cecilia sank into a deep curtsy, while the others backed away to make a path for their benefactor. The garden grew quiet as the count snatched the scroll from the messenger's hand.

"I come from the bishop," the man announced indignantly.

"You might be trespassing," Count Robert informed him softly. He broke the seal and unrolled the parchment.

Andrew slipped his arm around his new wife. When she looked sideways at him, he could see fear in her eyes.

Count Robert looked around at his laborers, each frozen in expectation. He waved the scroll at them and smiled. "Go back to your supper. It's just a family message."

Wanting to believe him, most of them turned and resumed their various activities. Josef walked to Cecilia's other side.

"What is the message, Herr?" Andrew asked.

Count Robert looked at him in surprise. "What right do you have—? Oh, of course, the bridegroom."

"I . . ." He stopped, feeling awkward and unsure. He had forgotten that the easiness in their private conversations should never be used in public. Once, he would have had the right to speak to a count as he liked, but the count now did not need to answer to him as in days past. Andrew bowed his head and meekly took a step backward.

"Frau Cecilia, your message." Count Robert handed it to her with almost a flourish.

Cecilia shook her head. "I can't read it," she murmured, handing it back.

The count nodded and read the message aloud: "'Cecilia, I am back in the city, and I urgently need to talk with you. The bearer of this message will escort you. You can stay with Mama and Papa. Steinmetz, Martin.' He is your . . . brother?"

"My cousin, Herr," she answered, relief evident.

"Will you go?"

She looked first at Josef and then at Andrew. "I . . ."

"You wish to discuss it with your family first, I see. Would you like the messenger to wait?"

Her answer was immediate: "No, Herr. Please tell him I will come, but not . . . not . . ."

The count turned to the bishop's emissary. "You heard her. If you'd like to eat before you return, please be my guest."

The messenger turned to the food, and Count Robert went back to his family. Cecilia asked Josef, "Do I have to go back with the bishop's man?"

Andrew answered quickly, "Of course not. I will take you." He glanced over at Josef whose eyes were lit with pleasure. "That is, unless—"

"Naturally you shall accompany her!" exclaimed Josef. "She is your responsibility now."

Andrew accepted it gladly.

The evening was still young when Andrew and Cecilia decided to leave the supper. In a shower of flower petals and good wishes, they left the garden and walked arm in arm toward the little hut that had been prepared for them. Halfway there, they veered toward Count Robert's fishing pond and ended up sitting on the bank in the moonlight.

Andrew bent to kiss her, savoring the taste of her lips.

But Cecilia's mind was not completely on her husband's caresses. "I don't know why Martin sent a message instead of coming."

"You knew he was coming?" Andrew asked in surprise. "I thought he was at St. Jude's."

"I had hoped my family—Martin's family—would come. I invited them. I don't understand why they didn't come."

Andrew understood perfectly. "They're afraid of us."

Cecilia turned expectant eyes upon Andrew. "Us?"

His heart warmed and he held her near to him, saying, "Not you and me. I mean all of us here at Immergrün. Martin's afraid that he will be tainted. More than that, he's afraid that he will lose you. Cecilia, he loves you, and he truly believes that your soul is in danger."

She shook her head and the new shawl slipped from her shiny hair. "He doesn't love me. I thought he did once, and I . . ."

Andrew watched her hands as she fidgeted with them in her lap. Then he reached over and laid his hand on top of hers. She turned one over and threaded her fingers through his before she confessed. "Once I let him kiss me because I thought that he really loved me."

Andrew looked down on her flushed cheeks and trembling lips, and he appreciated why Martin would succumb to the temptation. He kissed her cheek, cleared his throat, and said calmly, "He does love you, as a cousin should. Maybe there was even a time when he thought he loved you as a man should, but you made that impossible for him."

She nodded.

"You made a decision that he could not live with. Your new faith is intolerable to him. Are you sorry?"

"No." She sighed contentedly and her fingers moved within his grasp.

He raised those dear fingers to his lips and planted a kiss on each fingertip. "Cecilia, do you love Martin?"

She nodded. "As a cousin should. I am sorry that I let him kiss me. And . . ." She hesitated.

"Ja, liebling?" he encouraged.

Suddenly her shoulders were shaking, and he realized that she was weeping. "What is it? Why do you cry?" For one horrible moment, he thought that maybe she did, indeed, love Martin, but he discarded the idea immediately. He knew she was too honest for that.

He soothed her, until she could speak. "I . . . I'm sorry that Susanna was born." The tears broke out again.

Unexpectedly, Andrew's anger toward the bishop flared up after so many months of dormancy. Would there ever come a time when the bishop could no longer stir up unhappiness in Andrew's life?

Keeping his voice steady, he asked, "Cecilia, do you believe what I say?"

She nodded.

"Then listen to this and know that every word is true. I love you, and I will never mention the bishop again if you won't. I love Susanna, and she is going to be my child—our child. If possible, I never want her to know about the bishop. I'd rather that she think she was a product of our sin—yours and mine—before we married. At least then she will never doubt the love we have for her. Do you understand what I'm saying? Do you trust me?"

She did not hesitate but turned her tear-streaked face up into the moonlight. "Ja, Herr," she said softly.

He was suddenly overwhelmed with her preciousness. He closed his eyes to stop his dizziness. *Dear God, she is such a gift. Do I love her too much? I want to love You more.* He had prayed about her before, but before he had not realized what an enormous decision this was. Her "Ja, Herr," conveyed in just two words her willingness and her commitment to him. Somehow those words meant more than the ones they had exchanged a few hours before. He opened his eyes and met hers, which were studying his face.

"And I trust you, now and always," he said, "but we must seal it with a kiss."

She nodded and wiped away the tears.

"May I kiss you? You must decide."

She laughed then and asked, "Why do you wait?"

He laughed too, and pulled her into his embrace. Looking down at her, he could see her love for him shining out. He pressed his lips to hers.

When the promise was adequately sealed, Cecilia drew back and exclaimed happily, "I married a monk!"

Still laughing, they stood and walked to their little house.

FORTY-ONE

 osef had a serious warning for Andrew and Cecilia before they left for Felsenburg a week later. "You must avoid the bishop. I am probably a fool for letting you go at all. You must realize that you are in danger. Please don't forget Anton Felsbacher and his wife."

Andrew would never forget the brave couple who had died for their faith in southern Bavaria. "Although I would be willing to die for my faith, I have no desire to do so," he told Josef.

Josef nodded. "There is nothing to be gained by seeking martyrdom. Take care of yourself, my friend. May God go with you."

The walk to Felsenburg was a time of revelation to Andrew and Cecilia. They talked of many things, making plans for their future life together. Sometimes, however, they would lapse into a comfortable silence, shared only by those who want to understand each another.

Andrew grew even quieter as they drew near the city. The last time he had rushed through its streets, he had been wearing a cassock, and the bishop had just promised him punishment for associating with the people at Immergrün. He hoped that his new clothing and scraggly beard would provide adequate anonymity for them.

When they got to the city, Cecilia headed straight to her aunt and uncle's house. As they walked through Lärchenplatz, Andrew noticed several dozen monks who were carrying stone blocks and buckets of mortar. In the six months since he had been at Immergrün, the foundation had risen out of the trenches until most of it was level with the ground. Soon it would be winter and the construction would stop, but next year, they would begin again in earnest.

Martin's mother was pleased to see her niece but not so pleased to see Andrew, who showed no inclination to go somewhere else. The couple had agreed that they would not speak of their marriage unless someone else brought it up.

"Is Martin here?" the girl wanted to know.

"He lives at the bishop's residence now," Inge Steinmetz told them proudly.

"Why did he leave St. Jude's?"

"The bishop needed monks to help with the foundation."

Andrew knew how that came about. The bishop's will had been twisted to become the indisputable will of God. He wondered how young Martin was coping with the disappointment.

Cecilia was saying, "Well, Martin sent me a note—that he needed me to come urgently. Do you know why?"

Martin's mother did not. "He's probably at the cathedral site right now. You wouldn't be allowed to go near it."

They sat at the rough-hewn table, and the older woman gave them cups of some weak wine. Cecilia drank a little and then said, "Perhaps I could send a message."

Since the initial introductions, Andrew had not spoken, but now he pointed out, "Who will deliver it?"

Martin's mother was shocked. "And what's wrong with your legs, young man?"

Cecilia grasped the problem but only to a point. "He can't go, Tante, because—" She stopped, flustered, obviously sorry that she had said anything.

Inge Steinmetz looked alarmed and said, "You're not the one who started that group of heretics at Immergrün, are you?"

Andrew smiled. "I'm not."

The lady was not reassured. "But you are one of them, aren't you?"

Before Andrew could answer, Cecilia soothed, "Tante Inge, I'm one of them. Andrew is my husband. You don't need to worry, though. We won't be staying long."

Tante Inge glared. "The monk!" she cried, "And sitting at my table. What'll my friends say?"

Suddenly it swept over Andrew that this whole trip was too risky—for Cecilia as well as for him. Controlling his agitation, he stood and said kindly, "Frau Steinmetz, you are, of course, right. Cecilia and I are certainly capable of leaving a message at the bishop's residence without troubling you further."

Cecilia, questions in her eyes, nonetheless followed her husband's lead. "Ja, Tante, and thank you for your hospitality." She kissed her aunt and the couple left the humble house.

When they were away, Cecilia asked, "What's wrong?"

He grasped her hand and hurried her past the shrine to the Rosen Jungfrau and around the south edge of Lärchenplatz. "It's dangerous. I don't know why your cousin would ask you here, but if his mother doesn't know, then something's wrong."

She stopped walking, and her eyes grew round. "Are you saying that Martin wants to hurt me?"

"Not directly, but he's so positive that he knows what is best for you, that if he hurts you in the process, then so be it. He thinks he is saving your soul."

"How do you know?"

He rolled his eyes. "Cecilia, I was one of them. I know what they think, what they believe, what they teach." He paused and then added miserably, "I taught him, and he was learning so well." The tears in her eyes broke his heart, and he wanted to take her into his arms, but he felt the threat even more keenly. "Come, liebling," he said, "we must get back to Immergrün."

She followed willingly, but they were stopped at the gate by one of the bürgermeister's guards, who grasped Andrew by the arms and steered him to their superior.

"You are Brother Andrew?"

"I was."

"Bishop Gernot von Kärnten has requested that you appear before him."

Andrew's heart was pounding, and he found it difficult to organize his thoughts, but one thought stood out: Cecilia must be allowed to return to Immergrün. He nodded and told them, "I will come. Please let Fräulein Steinmetz through."

Her face mirrored the fear in his heart, as she murmured, "I don't want to see the bishop." Andrew hoped that he did not look as scared as she did.

The guard had his orders. "The Fräulein should come with us."

Andrew shook off the guards' hands and moved to Cecilia. Grasping her hand, he declared, "Very well, let's go."

They tramped back up the hill, two guards in front, two flanking the couple, and four behind. By the time they entered Lärchenplatz, they had gathered a large group of onlookers. The monks even paused in their work on the cathedral foundation, and one young man, not yet a monk, but clothed in a cassock, climbed out of a trench and approached the guards. Young Martin Steinmetz had changed. He swung into step beside Cecilia.

"I see the bishop finally caught up with you," he said to Andrew.

Cecilia piped up, "Martin, what is this about? Did you want to see me?"

"I always enjoy seeing you, Celia," he said looking deliberately at their clasped hands.

"What did you want to see her about?" Andrew demanded.

"What did I . . . ? I don't understand."

If it were possible, Andrew's fright multiplied. "Didn't you send her a message, asking her to come?"

Martin's bewilderment was evident.

Andrew stopped walking and pulled Cecilia to stand close beside him. One of the guards ran into them and gave them a shove, which sent Cecilia sprawling to her knees. Martin rushed to grasp her other hand and pull her to her feet.

"Martin!" Andrew exclaimed. "Ask the guards to wait."

The guards jostled and pushed them, and people in the crowd offered advice, oblivious to the problem.

When Martin showed no sign of complying, Andrew grabbed him by the arm and said into his ear, "Martin, the bishop has tricked us into coming to Felsenburg. He wrote Cecilia a message in your name. You must take her back to Immergrün."

Martin pulled from Andrew's grasp and spoke to the Hauptman, who reluctantly told the guards to wait a moment. Then he said, "Bishop Gernot doesn't want to hurt either of you."

Again Cecilia said in a small, frightened voice, "I don't want to see the bishop."

"You've nothing to fear," Martin assured her.

"Nothing to fear!" Andrew cried. "What do you know about this? What have you done?"

Martin shook his head. "I just told him that I was concerned for Cecilia, and he offered to help."

"Help?" Andrew echoed in disbelief.

"To get her away from all of you who are misleading her."

Cecilia opened her mouth to protest, but Andrew silenced her. "She's not a fool. The decision was hers. There are plenty of people at Immergrün who do not share our faith. Do you think that you can bend her will?"

"There are true beliefs and false beliefs. She has chosen the false. It is our duty to save her from her bad choices." He spoke to the guards, who gave Andrew a prod.

"Wait!" Andrew shouted, trying to shrug off the strong hands that pushed them nearer and nearer the bishop's residence. "Martin!" He switched to Latin, so that the guards would not understand. "The bishop may kill me. You must take Cecilia away."

"Nonsense!" Martin answered in German, "Certainly he just wants to talk to you, to tell you of the consequences of your choices."

Andrew clung to the Latin: "I have seen those consequences. Have you? Do you know why I am no longer mute?"

Impatiently, Martin walked on. "No, and I can hardly see where—"

Andrew interrupted, switching back to German, but keeping his voice low. "I can speak today because on the way to Milan I witnessed the execution of two members of the group at Immergrün. They were burned at the stake, as my parents were."

"Martin, it's true," Cecilia begged. "Please help us to leave."

Martin shook his head. "I couldn't do that."

She jerked her chin upward and said, "Then I will die with Andrew!"

Suddenly, Andrew realized that she was taunting her cousin. *She doesn't even recognize how grave our danger is,* he thought.

But for some reason, her flippant remark got through to Martin.

Her cousin stopped dead in his tracks, and the guards had to halt again to avoid knocking him down.

"Die?" The one word sounded so final. He tried to convey confidence. "Aren't you exaggerating the severity of this?"

"Don't ever underestimate the cruelty with which the bishop will attempt to preserve his power," Andrew warned him. "Please take her to Immergrün and tell Josef Radl to keep her there."

Indecision rested on Martin's face as he said, "I'm not so sure . . ."

Andrew shoved the girl toward Martin, who instinctively wrapped his arms around her. "Martin, in heaven's name, do you think you could stand to watch her burn at the stake?" he cried. "Go! Now! Take her home, or you will be guilty of her death!"

Martin stood still, indecisively looking first at Andrew and then at the Hauptman. Finally, he said, "All right. I'll take her back to Immergrün, but you must see the bishop."

"No!" screamed Cecilia, pulling away from her cousin. She threw herself into Andrew's arms.

"Cecilia!" He clasped her to him and buried his face in her fragrant hair. Then grasping her shoulders, he held her away from him and said, "Cecilia, listen to me. You promised to trust me. Now you must do as I say. Go home and take care of our child. I do not want her to be an orphan." He could hardly bear the misery in her face, but he insisted, "Do you understand?"

She nodded, and tears filled her eyes but did not fall. "We will pray for you," she whispered.

He hugged her again and then lifted her chin to kiss her. "Go, now, so that I won't have to worry about you."

She relaxed and turned to Martin, who had been watching openmouthed. "I'm ready," she said, her voice calm. She embraced Andrew tightly and then released him without a struggle.

Andrew was so proud of his wife. Her courage touched him more than her grief. Martin spoke to the guard and then took Cecilia's arm and led her away from Andrew and out across Lärchenplatz. Just before one of the guards gave him a shove, Andrew saw her wrench her arm from Martin's grasp and continue her march alone across the square. With aching throat and heavy heart he turned to face the bishop's residence.

FORTY-TWO

ndrew's trial would be held the following day in Lärchenplatz. But the decisive hearing occurred the evening before, with no annoying impartiality or justice to interfere with the bishop's verdict. His hands bound, Andrew was shoved into the library, where Archdeacon Augustin and Bishop Gernot von Kärnten occupied the two chairs along the left-hand side of a long, shiny table. Behind them, the cream-colored parchments lay in the glass cabinets in silent support for the young man who believed every word written there. Andrew stood in the center of the room, the table between them. He was shocked to see how much weight the bishop had lost. The man was obviously dying.

The bishop dismissed all except one of the guards and murmured to Augustin, "It is worse than I thought." He looked at Andrew. "Where is your cassock? I hadn't expected that you would appear before me in this state. And your hair, your face! Do you need to shave? I hardly recognized you."

Andrew felt strengthened by the bishop's pretense of bewilderment. "I haven't worn a cassock for six months," Andrew answered cheerfully, "and my wife likes my hair the way it is."

The bishop choked and stammered, "Your wife?"

"Perhaps you remember Fräulein Cecilia?"

"That's enough!" Bishop Gernot snapped.

"I quite agree with you," said Andrew. "I did not come here to play games with you. Say what you have to say!"

"What we have—! It is you who are on trial!" cried the bishop.

"Not yet," retorted Andrew.

The archdeacon, realizing that the bishop was already out of control, glanced at his notes and asked solemnly, "Is it true that you live at Immergrün?"

"It is."

"And did you leave the bishop's residence without permission?"

"Not realizing I needed permission, I left without obtaining it, yes."

"Did you renounce the vows that you made to the church?"

"No. They were only valid because I chose to live by them."

"Have you been baptized into the sect of heretics who live at Immergrün?"

Andrew thought about his answer for a moment, but before he could formulate one, the bishop spoke up again. "You only need to answer 'ja' or 'nein.' We already know your answers."

Andrew pressed his lips together and remained silent.

"Well?" asked Augustin.

"If you already know my answers, then there is no need to ask the questions."

"We want to help you," said the bishop gently.

Andrew suppressed a laugh and said, "It would be much easier for us all if you would simply let me tell you what I believe—and how it is different from what I used to believe. You don't need to trick me into any answers to prove my heresy. I will testify freely, and you may judge me as you will. I don't care."

Bishop Gernot looked skeptical, but Augustin waved his hand in assent.

"I left this place—" He interrupted himself and began again. "I have been searching for God my whole life. I thought that serving the great bishop in Felsenburg would give me an opportunity to find God in service to others. As you well know, there is no satisfaction in servanthood when it is not accompanied by true faith and—"

"This is not working," the bishop broke in. "Are you married?"

Andrew sighed. "If I have a wife, I must be."

"You have broken vows made to the church."

"I have if they were ever valid." Andrew paused, and when they said nothing, he added, "But did you know that the Holy Scriptures teach that no church should forbid marriage, and that, in fact, a bishop should have one wife?"

Bishop Gernot looked at Augustin and said, "This is why we must keep the holy manuscripts away from the folk. If this foolish scribe cannot interpret them correctly, how can the illiterate masses?"

"Have you read them?" Andrew challenged.

"That is irrelevant. We know church doctrine, and those teachings are just as infallible as the Scriptures."

"And when they contradict?"

"Then the Holy Scriptures have been wrongly interpreted."

"How do you know if you haven't read them?"

The archdeacon referred to his notes and realized that his original question had still not been answered. He repeated it. "Have you been baptized into the sect of heretics who live at Immergrün?"

"I cannot—"

"Just answer 'ja' or 'nein.'"

"Either would be a lie," Andrew informed them.

"Very well," the canon said peevishly, "explain your excuses."

"I have been baptized to show that I repented of my sins."

"To whom did you confess them?"

"God." He let the one word drop into the quiet library, and although the two men exchanged knowing glances, they did not object. Andrew continued, "As for their being heretics, heretical teachings are those teachings that are in direct opposition to what one believes is the truth. To us—and I do consider myself a part of their group—you are the heretics who have twisted God's Word and misrepresented Him at every turn in history."

"Are you finished?" the bishop asked through clenched teeth.

"Only if you order me to be."

"You would do best to stop talking," Augustin advised him, "for the longer you talk, the more you condemn yourself."

"I am no longer condemned by God. There is nothing that you can do to me."

The bishop's hands were shaking, and he tried to stand but could not find the strength. "I can put you out of the church. Outside, you have no hope of eternal life!"

"You can't excommunicate someone who has already left of their own free will."

Bishop Gernot tried again. "Tomorrow you will stand before the city and be tried for heresy! The penalty for heresy is death."

Astounded by the feeling of peace that filled him, Andrew responded, "We all die, but I know I have eternal life. Do you?"

"No one can know that!" shouted the bishop. He suffered a coughing spell, which left him red in the face and trembling.

Augustin turned on the bishop and scolded, "Stop arguing with him! He is nobody, and tomorrow will prove that."

Andrew refused to be silenced, "You, too, will die, Canon Augustin, and what will you say to God when He asks you why you misled the folk?"

"Silence! Silence!" the bishop cried and then put his head on the table, gasping for air. "Make him be silent," he wheezed.

The guard drew his dagger and held it to Andrew's throat.

Andrew could feel the tip on his Adam's apple when he swallowed. His mouth was suddenly dry and his breathing very shallow. "You will lose everything if you kill me now," Andrew whispered.

"Get him out of here!" Bishop Gernot gasped. "I want to be alive tomorrow to see him condemned."

The guard sheathed his dagger and jerked Andrew roughly to the door. As he was thrust from the library, Andrew heard the bishop say, "Find his wife!"

Beneath the bishop's residence lay a labyrinth of windowless cellars, which had been dug over a period of half a century to accommodate the provisions for the cleric's household. The walls of each small cellar were reinforced with stone, and the year's supplies were then stored behind a solid door designed to discourage rodents. Above each door, a small window provided for ventilation, while iron bars would defeat the most determined thief. Because cold weather was merely a month away, most of the damp rooms were now full of cured meats, some vegetables, cheeses, and wine. However, since the residence was not feeding all of the canons, as it once had, there were several rooms that were kept empty to imprison enemies of the church.

Andrew's hands were freed, and he was shoved into one of these cellars to await his trial on the following day. He sat in the complete dark on some moldy, woven mats and tried to imagine where Cecilia was. His imagination conjured up many scenes to torment him. Perhaps guards had stopped her and Martin as they reached the gate. Perhaps she was already locked in another part of this dismal place to be used tomorrow as a puppet in the bishop's show of power. He imagined that she would stand before the city as a heretic, and Bishop Gernot von Kärnten would trade her life for Andrew's denial of his newfound faith. He knew that she would stand firm, but he was suffocated by the fear that he might, perhaps, be too weak. How could he remain strong when the price was so high?

He kept hearing the bishop's last threat ringing in his ears, but Cecilia's last words had been, "We will pray for you." He could do no less for her. Throwing himself face down onto the dirt floor, he poured out his grief and terror to the God he was just learning to trust. Gradually, his panic subsided in a way he did not understand, and although his mind continued inventing new fears, he no longer believed them.

He did not know how long he had lain there when he became aware of footsteps approaching very quietly. At first he thought that the guards were returning to take him to Lärchenplatz for the trial. How fast the night had gone! He sat up.

Through the window above the door, he could see the flickering shadows leaping across the uneven walls outside his cell. As the person drew nearer, Andrew heard someone whispering his name. Before his door, the candle was held high and the voice said quietly, "Brother Andrew? Are you there? It is I, Martin Steinmetz."

Andrew stood and answered, "Yes, I'm here." The window was too high, and there was nothing to stand upon, so he had to content himself with only hearing the young man. Then the light moved nearer as Martin placed a candle on the window ledge. "I had to come," he said softly.

"Cecilia?" Andrew asked at once. "Is she safe?"

"She's at Immergrün, and her people know that she is in danger."

Andrew leaned against the door in relief. "Thank you."

He heard movement on the other side of the door, and then another flame flared from another candle. Andrew stood beneath the barred window and waited.

Finally Martin spoke again. "I'm not supposed to be here."

"How late is it?"

"Very late. I don't know."

The silence grew awkward, and Andrew watched the dueling shadows quiver upon the walls.

Then very softly from the other side of the door came Martin's voice. "I'm so sorry."

Feeling sudden pity, Andrew murmured, "You did what you thought was right."

"Right? I did what was expected."

"Sometimes we do that, and we are wrong."

"I thought I was saving her by bringing her to the bishop. I never meant for the consequences to be so drastic."

"Trusting the bishop always has drastic consequences. Never forget that."

"I didn't come to listen to you rail against the bishop," Martin protested a little louder.

"I can say nothing against him, if you like," Andrew whispered calmly, "but that doesn't change him."

"He's not as bad as you say. He's God's representative here on earth."

"Fine. If you want that sort of God."

The sudden stillness beat upon their ears. The candles burned lower, and another one appeared at the top of the wall to replace the first one. "It's cold here," Martin remarked. "Are you cold?"

"Sometimes I miss my cassock," Andrew admitted.

"Why did you leave?"

"I found what I was looking for elsewhere. There was no reason to continue to believe something that does not solve mankind's most foundational problem."

"There's nothing wrong with the foundational beliefs."

"They lead the people away from trusting in God's grace, to trusting in their own goodness."

"Perhaps mankind is not as bad as you think," Martin offered hopefully.

"Perhaps we are worse than any of us can imagine."

After a pause, Martin said, "I cannot believe that."

"Your inability to believe doesn't make it not true. You are deceived, Martin. The core of God's message is grace, given freely to people who will never deserve it. It is a gift of eternal life, and you are so proud to presume that you can earn it!"

Martin sighed and pleaded, "Brother Andrew, give this up. Return to your faith—to your vocation. Don't you realize that the bishop has the power to end your life?"

"—Here on earth," he conceded, "but after that is eternal life, and the bishop can do nothing about it!"

"You can't know that!" he cried.

"Perhaps *you* can't, but I do," Andrew told him, wondering where the assurance was coming from.

Martin tried a different approach. "Think of Cecilia, then. Admit your foolishness and confess your sin in rejecting your vows. If you do this, you will not be condemned. And Cecilia will be cared for. Her family will see to that."

"Cecilia?"

"The bishop has promised—"

"The bishop!"

"He's not a monster," Martin's voice insisted earnestly. "The bishop can't be as bad as you say. How can he be? He is serving God and the people. He's a good man."

Andrew decided to tell him. "The bishop forced your cousin into his bed. That's how good he is."

Andrew could imagine the color draining from the young man's face. Andrew remembered how the revelation had devastated him, and he gave Martin time to recover. The first candle guttered out. A mouse scrabbled somewhere in another part of the cellar. He tried to picture what Martin was thinking. For himself, he longed to kill the bishop, but he had the feeling that God would do it for him. Although he could not understand it, he knew somehow that God would be very fair in the next life.

Finally Andrew spoke, "If you are truly seeking the truth, some of it will be almost unbearable. You will discover things that you did not want to know. But God waits there as well."

"I wish I had your assurance," was Martin's steady answer. "And I wish you'd change your mind."

Andrew had to admire Martin's granitelike self-control. He sensed that the interview was over. "Those two things are incompatible. I could never turn back now that God has given me peace on earth."

"I must go. You may keep the candle." There was another rustling and then a parchment scroll was pushed through the iron bars of the window. "You'll need it to read this. Josef and Cecilia sent it."

Andrew reached up and took the scroll with one hand and caught Martin's hand with the other. He squeezed it to give the young man comfort. "Thank you for coming. Do not let the search become your goal."

Reluctantly, Martin pulled away. "Lebe wohl, farewell, my friend."

"Lebe wohl."

Tears pricked Andrew's eyes, as he listened to the departing footsteps and watched the fluttering shadows recede. After Martin was gone, he fetched the candle into his cell and sat awhile, watching the candle flame dancing in the darkness. Then he opened the scroll.

Cecilia had sent him a portion of St. Paul's Letter to the Romans, which he had copied such a short time ago.

> Who shall separate us from the love of God? Shall tribulation or distress, or persecution or famine? . . . For I am convinced that neither death nor life nor angels nor principalities nor height nor depth nor any other created thing shall be able to separate us from the love of God which is in Christ Jesus. . . .

The candle sputtered and went out. Andrew rolled the parchment and tucked it into his tunic. Then he knelt in the dirt and prayed for those he knew and loved. He prayed that his faith would be strong enough for the next day, and he asked for protection for his wife and child. Finally, filled with an unexplainable calm, he lay down on the moldy mats and fell asleep.

That night, he dreamed of the fire again. It flared up and surrounded him, but he was no longer afraid. He opened his eyes, and through the flames, he could see his parents. And beyond them—his Savior, waiting with joy.

HAMMERING AT THE
DOORS OF HEAVEN

PROLOGUE

he golden forsythia glowed like sunshine in the shadows. Two bushes flanked the Madonna's black shrine. Above it hung her small picture—the Rosen Jungfrau—framed in gold filigree. Her lips, executed in deep red brush strokes upon the canvas, seemed to smile at the gaudy flowers, while her painted eyes were focused upon the cloudy sky beyond the opening in the buildings. Her ears were hidden beneath her deep blue veil, but the dozen candles flickering around her altar attested to her worshipers' hopes that she would hear their prayers.

Fifteen-year-old Raimund feared she might not hear his. He hesitated at the entrance to the shrine, surprised by the golden branches surrounding her dark altar with a heavenly glory. In his right hand, he clutched a bouquet of field flowers, soggy from the rain that had drenched him as he had climbed the hill to the city. In his other hand was his father's hammer, the tool of his sin.

She was looking at him. He dropped his gaze for a moment to study his bare, muddy toes and then peeked up again. If she had looked at him last week, none of this would have happened. He took a deep breath and descended into the shrine, where thousands of feet before his had worn a groove into the earth.

"I brought these for you," he murmured, standing before her. He pushed the meadow flowers into a pottery cup, thoughtfully provided for such offerings.

When he knelt on the stone step, his tunic just brushed the clean-swept granite. He made a sign of the cross and then clutched the mallet in his folded hands. He raised his head and spoke to the altar, which was bathed in the candle glow. "Dear Jungfrau Maria, I'm so sorry that we took coins from your offering box last week." He dared to look up at her, but she was once more staring out above his head. Had she even missed the coins?

The offering box had been mended, and the only evidence of the violence done it by three mischievous boys was the hammer scratches across the rusty tin.

Pushing the hammer through the protective gate, he laid it upon the altar, confessing, "We used this to break the lock. It's Papa's, and he'll be angry when he can't find it, but Father Augustin said that I'd made it a . . . I think he said a . . . an instrument of evil, so I had to bring it to you. Do you understand?"

The boy sighed. Somehow this was not going as he had planned. He knew, of course, that paintings in gold filigree picture frames do not talk. He had really hoped, however, that she would hear him from heaven and would have mercy on him. He wanted her to take away the hollow unhappiness which had followed him ever since he and his friends had spent her coins on honey at the church market.

Less certain of her interest now, he tried again: "The honey wasn't very good, and I don't know why Micki and Hannes don't feel like I feel." A tear slipped down his cheek. "Can you forgive sin? Will you forgive mine?"

The candle flames wavered through his tears, and he stood slowly, sketching another cross against his body. "Dear God, can't You hear me?" he begged. There had to be more he could do, but this was all Father Augustin had told him. It must be enough.

He turned and left the shrine. He did not look back. The rain had ceased. Turning eastward toward home, he inhaled the fresh, earthy air. As he reached the crest of the hill, he paused in wonder. Behind him to the west, the sun spread its rays beneath the dark clouds, and the whole countryside glowed in the late afternoon light. Before him across the valley, a double rainbow climbed into the sky. It was a sign, but it was not enough.

ONE

ou will follow me, Herren?" The servant-woman's question was more of an order than a request. She did not approve of them. She held her mouth in a tight, no-nonsense grimace, and her brown eyes examined them from cap to boots. Their clothing must somehow seem foreign to her, but she seemed too wise for her age.

Raimund, now the count of Immergrün, removed his cap and wiped his boots. The steward had admitted him and Conrad Winter into the stately manor with a strange combination of graciousness and suspicion. His explanation of who he was had been met with nods and blank expressions. After twenty years, how, indeed, could he convince them of his identity? He was no longer the fifteen-year-old boy who had run away to escape the suffocation of his elders' convictions. His life had changed him, his adventures had matured him, his sufferings had aged him. His sins had scratched irreparable damage onto his face and soul. Perhaps there would be nothing left for them to recognize.

Or perhaps they were merely protecting the deceased count's grieving widow who had agreed to receive him. Raimund left Conrad standing in the entryway (they had agreed upon this before they arrived) and followed the servant into the hall where he breathed in the familiar scent of stone and damp. The thought crept into his mind that this servant-woman must have still been a child when he left so long ago. Somehow he had thought that home would remain the same, regardless of how much he changed.

The floor was worn but clean-swept, and a new door swung on iron hinges. Well, it was new to him. He balanced on the threshold of the anteroom. Familiar pine smoke stung his eyes—or was it tears?

"Herr?" She turned to see why the well-dressed stranger was not following. "You will wait here."

Raimund stepped into the room, which he had always remembered as being larger, the hearth wider, the windows higher. What enchantment had transformed the entire manor into a miniature of his memories?

She left by another door, and he paced around the room, peering out of windows onto gardens that seemed to have overwhelmed the gigantic manor. The trees, clothed in their soft green, spring leaves, spread branches twenty years wider. Several gardeners labored over the brown flower beds and vegetable gardens; their arrangement was different than he remembered. But how accurate was his memory?

The door creaked open, and he turned to face the servant and an elderly woman, bent and tiny and dressed in black. He was surprised that she did not wear the headdress of an elderly widow, for he knew she must be his Tante Hilda. Before he could speak, the woman gasped, and one gnarled hand flew up to cover her mouth. With the other hand, she reached for the servant to steady herself. "Heinrich!" she cried and then rebuked the servant, "Susanna, you told me—"

"His name is Raimund, Herrin," the servant reminded her softly.

Relief loosened the tension at the back of Raimund's neck. "Dear Lady," he announced, trying to control his gladness. "I am Heinrich's son, Raimund von Immergrün."

The lady nodded and nodded and waved her hand as if asking him to wait. "I know. I know," she whispered. Leaning upon the arm of the servant, she shuffled to a chair near one of the windows. "Sit down, Bursch," she said.

It had been a long time since anyone had called him Bursch—young man, boy. A sob caught in his throat, but he swallowed it and sat in the indicated chair near hers.

"Susanna, something to drink, please." The woman heaved a shaky sigh and then reached out to capture Raimund's hand. "You are really

Raimund, come back after all these years?" It was not really a question; merely a statement of wonder.

Raimund held the small, bony hand, the skin soft like silk. "I am. And you are my Tante Hilda."

She smiled and nodded. "I prayed many times that you would come back; that the things that happened to you would lead you back to us." One solitary tear trickled down her wrinkled cheek. "You almost came too late," she whispered, "but God is never late."

God, the thought thundered through his mind, *is why I left in the first place*. Raimund held his tongue, however, and smiled.

Her smile had faded. "I thought I had lost you all. They're all gone, you know. Surely you expected it?"

He had, but the present reality struck harder than twenty years of possibility. "Mama, Papa, Onkel Robert," he murmured. And never a chance to say he was sorry. Would he have done it, if they had been here?

"And Berti and Rainer."

How could one absorb the deaths of so many at once? "I'm the only one left?" he whispered. He pulled from her grasp and leaned back in the chair as Susanna brought in refreshments. "What happened to my brothers?"

"While still a child, Berti died of an illness. Rainer was killed four years ago when he fell from his horse."

"Yes," he said after a while, "I expected it, but I never believed it. I refused to admit, so far from home, that I could not keep you as you were."

"You didn't like us as we were," she said sharply, as she waved Susanna to set the table, "else you wouldn't have run away."

The casual manner in which she delivered such a rebuke drove home the necessity of convincing her—them—that his self-inflicted exile had made home dearer. "You were in the middle of a religious conflict. Still," he insisted, folding his hands across his lap, "my one comfort in perilous times was to believe that at least in the Obersill Valley things remained constant."

Susanna poured a red currant wine into pewter cups and placed a small tray of pastries on a table between them. "Do you need anything else? Shall I stay, Herrin?"

Tante Hilda gave Susanna a sweet smile of reassurance. "He really is my nephew, Susanna. You may go about your duties."

Susanna curtseyed and left, but not before casting one worried glance in Raimund's direction.

He commended the servant. "She—and everyone else—cares for you very much. They're afraid I'm an impostor."

"They are. Your appearance upon our doorstep is very . . . timely, uncanny."

He agreed. "I can understand. They told me at the inn that Onkel Robert died only last month."

She nodded.

"You have my deepest sympathy, Tante Hilda. Is there anything I can do?"

She opened her mouth and then closed it; opened it again to say, "I am well cared for. Peter and Susanna are most devoted. And I have grandchildren, of course."

"Of course," he said calmly, as if the idea were not entirely new.

"Rainer's wife, Helen, still lives here, with her three children. Matti—Matthias—is ten. Until an hour ago, he was the heir to Immergrün. He's a fine boy. His two sisters, Anna and Irmi, are eleven and five."

They drank wine and nibbled on pastries, and then she said, "So, what perilous times kept you from us?"

"Tante Hilda, I think this is not the time. May I be so bold as to ask for shelter for myself and my servant, Conrad Winter?"

"You are very bold, Raimund. You must speak with Peter; he is our steward. Whatever decision he makes, I will abide by it."

Raimund did not like the sound of it. Judging from how suspicious the servants were acting, he had no chance of being welcomed back into his childhood home. "They think I'm an opportunist," he protested, "preying upon a helpless widow, which," he added with a charming smile, "you are not. Are you?"

Her eyebrows shot up and she chuckled. "I wouldn't want to deprive them of the joy they have in serving me."

"Joy?" he exclaimed.

She waved her hand and said, "Let's leave that for another time as well. I don't know whether you are an opportunist or not; that's up to Peter to decide. I do know that you are not an impostor."

"Do I really look so much like my father?"

She pressed her lips together into a grim line and rebuked him. "Exactly like he looked before his oldest son ran away and never came back!"

Raimund knew he deserved such a reprimand, although it was twenty years too late. It was also milder than any chastisement he had given himself. How foolish youth is to think that life will improve with distance from family! An image rose in his mind of him falling on his knees before this wizened old woman and begging her forgiveness. How would that end? What would she say? What would they think of him? He remained firmly seated upon his chair and tried to look contrite, while rebellion stormed through his heart—rebellion he had thought was vanquished years ago.

He suddenly became aware of Tante Hilda's silence, and that she had been studying him. He met her gaze and shook his head. "I want to come home," he said.

She turned both hands palms up and informed him, "This is your home; it always was. I'm sure that Peter and Susanna will see things my way, but we must have an understanding, and I'm not the one to make it." She paused and then said very carefully, "I only hope that what you've become will enrich our lives here. And I hope that you will allow us to enrich yours."

꽃ꝋ ꝋ

Convincing Peter was more difficult. He was not a young man, but he was younger than Raimund. His Norseman-like red beard and handsome features were only enhanced by blue, guileless eyes. It was obvious the steward had already talked with his wife, Susanna, and with the gatekeeper; the conversation with his mistress had been short. Raimund had the feeling, however, that Peter held more power than was suitable for a man in his position.

Obviously, Peter disagreed. "Gräfin Hildegund has assured me that you are, truly, her nephew, the son of Heinrich, and not coincidentally, the heir to Immergrün."

Raimund bowed his head in assent. He still sat beside the window, and the afternoon sun slanted onto his breeches.

Peter made things very clear. "My Herr, the late Graf Robert, made me promise at his deathbed that I'd care for the countess as if she were my own mother. The task's not difficult, for I love her as such, but I also acknowledge that she has her own ideas and can, at any time, choose to follow her own whims. Therefore, I must ask you first, as my master would have wished, if you don't have business elsewhere that will remove you once more from our lives?"

"You're . . . you're asking me to go away?" Raimund stammered in surprise.

"I am. There are other heirs—"

Raimund nodded. "Matti. The Gräfin told me."

"Yes, he's not yet of age, but shall be soon. Graf Robert never considered that you would ever return. The duke is prepared to pass Immergrün on to your nephew."

Raimund's determination tricked him into insisting too forcefully, "We'll just have to tell the duke things have changed. I tried to come back sooner! I wanted to, but I couldn't!"

Behind Peter's eyes were both compassion for Raimund's unhappiness and duty to serve the countess. Raimund knew that duty would win.

"So you will not leave," Peter stated the obvious. When Raimund, calm again, slowly shook his head, Peter continued, "Then I must ask you my second question: In what role do you wish to return to Immergrün?"

Raimund sighed. "I wish, simply, to come home."

"Are you returning home to collect your inheritance, then?"

Raimund crushed the indignation that rose in him and said honestly, "I returned home to make a pilgrimage, to fulfill a promise I made not too long ago. I didn't learn of my uncle's death until I inquired at the inn outside of Felsenburg. I . . . I only wanted to come home. I have been on my way for many years."

Peter cocked his head to the side as if a new thought had struck him. "Were you, perhaps, returning as the Prodigal Son in the Holy Scriptures?"

Raimund did not remember the story.

The steward enlightened him. "Sorry for the grief he had caused his family, and weary of the wicked life he had lived, the Prodigal

Son begged for forgiveness from his father, and renounced any claim to further inheritance."

Knowing that his future rested in this clever man's hands, Raimund chose his words carefully. "I . . . I must admit that I have not always lived a life that I am proud of. But if my sins were many, so were my sufferings. Surely, by now, my sufferings have atoned for my sins." He paused for Peter to agree with him.

"If that is what you believe," was all the steward said.

Raimund gathered his thoughts and pressed on. "I never had an inheritance, and just because I have not finally turned up dead should not mean that my inheritance should go to another."

Peter shrugged and said, "Then you are not casting yourself upon the mercy and goodness of your aunt?"

"You make me sound rather hard."

"I think you are. You broke many hearts when you left. I was very young, but I had grown to be a man before they were finally resigned to the fact that you would never return. No one ever worried so intensely about those who stayed."

"I was a child," Raimund explained, forgiving the selfishness of that child.

Abruptly, Peter stood and closed the lead and glass window. "The countess would like for you to stay. Except for three grandchildren, you are her only relation. I assume that you have some wealth acquired elsewhere, or you would not have come so far? Or be dressed so well?"

It was true, although Raimund could not comprehend the significance of the question.

"The countess would like for you to stay. That is all she has said. We will please her and let you and your servant stay. However," he continued, holding up his hand to stop any outburst of gratitude, "in order to obey my master, I must insist that you live here as our guest, but that you have no access to the inheritance for one year. At that time, perhaps the duke will decide to give you the land, if you have . . . have . . . ," here he stopped, groping for words that did not sting.

Raimund was suddenly touched by the kindness of the man and gallantly finished the awful sentence. " . . . proven myself worthy of being taken back into the family."

Peter nodded.

"Or until I have proven myself to be a scoundrel, at which time you can throw me out."

"I will personally throw you out." With a careful smile, Peter reached out and gripped Raimund's hand.

Relief surged through Raimund's heart, for at this moment, he knew that he was a good person, and that he would never harm these dear people. If any doubts lurked there, too, it was only because his sordid life was so recently behind him.